Darrion-Quieness

Book Three
of
The Abyss Walker Series

by

Shane Moore

Darrion-Quieness

© Shane Moore

All rights reserved.

A New Babel Books Release
381 High Point Drive

Holiday Shores, IL 62025

www.newbabelbooks.com

Genre: Fantasy / Series

ISBN: 978-1-63196-020-8

Revised Edition; First printing.

Printed in the United States of America.

Other Abyss Walker Works

White Wraith—Origins
White Wraith—The Lock of Requ *Coming soon!*
White Wraith—Maelstrom Serpents *Coming soon!*
The Wererat's Tale—Book One: Of Rat's and Men
The Wererat's Tale—Book Two: Ring of the Nonul
The Wererat's Tale—Book Three: Collar of Perdition

The Abyss Walker series
The Plea of Apollisian
The Trial of Innocence
Darrion-Quieness
Death of Kings
Tides of Winter
Return of the Father
Swords and Plowshares—Patrick Tomlison *Coming soon!*

Other Abyss Walker Works
Dwarven Cookbook *Coming soon!*

Other Works by Shane Moore
"I am Villain" I, Hero magazine #2
Apocalypse of Enoch I: Rapture
Apocalypse of Enoch II: Scourge

Table of Contents

I would like to dedicate this book to my best friend.

She is like the soft glow of a campfire ember.
She is seen best when surrounded by darkness.

This book is for you, Tracy Ross.

"…And behold, I witnessed a great king fall. He was destroyed by the fear of what he saw, and his mantle crushed by what he could not see. But in his death, a new king rose among the ashes of defeat. This new king commanded such profound fear that it gave him power over his enemies, though his wrath dwelt among them. He was born into a new name. He called himself hate. And hate smiled, knowing that fear was his servant…"

-Prophecy found on a brass plate in one of the great pyramids of Kahl near the eastern seaboard of Tyrine. Author is believed to be Emperor Kahl himself.

1

Irons of the Caged

The weight of the thick iron chains pulled and chafed into Jude's rough skin. The rusted manacles dangled and clanged as they bounced off his barrel chest when he walked. Large red patches of burn-like abrasions covered his arms, and deep gashes from the taskmaster's whip crisscrossed over his muscular back. Jude's corded muscles labored with each step, flexing then relaxing, making his powerful body seem to quiver as he walked. Sweat dripped down from his wind-scorched brow, only to freeze when it landed on his thin woolen jerkin. The mighty swordsman wore the bare minimum amount of clothing, which provided protection from the elements, but it offered little warmth. Soldiers wearing thick, brass-colored plate armor, on equally armored steeds, rode beside Jude as he was marched down the frigid trail. They held their heads high, while Jude's chin rested on his chest. The soldiers paraded down the dirt path like huntsmen returning with their catch, yet the mighty swordsman ignored them. As he marched down the frozen dirt path from the Minok Vale, Jude replayed the days that led up to this one.

After the attack by the undead monster, the fool elves charged him with some kind of typical elf nonsense and then released him to a large group of Beyklan high guards. At first, Jude struggled and argued; yet he received only heavy boots and sharp whips for his complaints. He had gathered that the elves had sold him, for reasons beyond his knowledge, and he had seen neither hide nor hair of the paladin. Jude had learned that an army of undead killed or scattering most of the elves, including the sorcerers and the mages, though the exact numbers lost was unknown to him. One thing he was sure of was that Central City officials wanted him for murder, though Jude could not think of anyone he or Lance could have murdered. Yet, that mattered little now. He had been marching on the cold autumn trail for weeks, and he figured winter was merely a few nights away. Jude hadn't decided which he longed for more, clear weather to make his journey easier or heavy snow to make the soldier's journey more difficult.

He had guessed part of his inability to decide came from the knowledge once he had, he would have little else to occupy his time. The Beyklan high guards had taken his boots, and his great sword, which was all that he had left. Once the elves pilfered his coin and his dwarven axe that he had commandeered when he killed the renegade dwarves in the sewers of Central City, they chained him and sent him away. Jude didn't even know if Lance was still with the elves, but he doubted it. Something in the back of his mind seemed to point out that if they had Lance, they either killed him or sold him off, too. The swordsman guessed that since Lance had some of their writings, and that robe, perhaps they treated him as a criminal.

Jude sighed as he plodded across the hard, frozen ground. Who understood Lance anyway? He just hoped that his friend was faring better than he. Why had he been arrested? Why the interest in Lance? They were two nobodies from Bureland. Yet they seemed to somehow have attracted the attention of the king of Beykla and the king of the elves, whatever his kingdom was called. Jude strained to recall the name of the Vale, but the streaming pain from the shackles, the cold, and the occasional crack from the whip, seemed to prevent him from too much thought. Jude knew those foolish papers with the elven writing on them were trouble. Anything elven was most likely trouble if you were human.

The lead man on horseback halted his steed. The large warhorse skirted underneath him for a moment, before finally pausing, though it pawed the ground and its ears flickered with anticipation. The leader's armor creaked as he held his metal plated hand up. The other soldiers halted their steeds as well, glancing about them nervously. Jude managed to raise his chin slightly as he gazed around with weary eyes. The cold forest seemed devoid of life, and the frigid wind howled as it whipped through the bare branches of the naked trees. The sun was hidden by a dark gray sky, and tiny snowflakes seemed to lightly float by every so and again. Some of the soldiers' horses pawed at the ground as well, aggravated that they were no longer moving, but no one seemed to notice. The men kept their eyes locked on the forest around them. There was little underbrush in the forest and Jude could easily see well into the distance. He could not guess what the men thought they saw, but the weight of the iron chains pulled Jude's weary head back down to his chin.

Jude sighed heavily and shifted his weight. The chains jingled as he moved, eliciting deep scowls from the solider next to him, though the men dared not speak. Jude ignored their threatening gaze as he stared weakly at the frozen earth. If only he were free with a sword, he would easily cut their numbers in half before he fell to their blades.

"What is it, Sir Oswald?" one of the soldiers asked, leaning from side to side in his saddle, to ease his lower back. The leather in the saddle creaked, as did the metal plate he wore. His red flowing cape whipped around him in the strong wind.

Sir Oswald Thorrin, captain of the royal guard, did not acknowledge the question, though his face creased and his eyes narrowed as he scanned the forest line. After a few long minutes, he lowered his arm and continued forward. His horse pranced the few first steps, and then leveled off. The taskmaster's whip cracked into Jude's back. Jude groaned under the hot stinging pain that tore in between his shoulders and he weakly stepped forward, carrying the heavy iron chains once again. Jude's legs quivered under him the first few steps, but he soon steadied himself under his powerful legs. Jude's bare feet were blistered and bloody, but under the strain from the irons and the whip, they seemed more of a nuisance then an injury.

Sir Oswald fell back into the crowd of soldiers. Two held Jude's chains, one in the front and one in the rear. The other four rode with two in the front and two in the rear. Oswald had four soldiers walking alongside of Jude, two on each side. They each carried a heavy crossbow with a thick leather quiver that was strung over their armored shoulders while a brilliantly polished short sword hung from their sides, which each bowman hoped to never have to use.

Oswald rode in the front but he occasionally dropped back and spoke to a crossbowman in the front ranks, but Jude could never hear his name. As Oswald had done many times before, he maneuvered his horse next to the lead bowman. "I believe I saw some signs of orcs, Walter."

The crossbowman rubbed his graying brown beard. "I did not notice, my lord."

Oswald nodded to himself slowly, watching the frozen dirt road with his hawk like eyes. "It was strange, though, for orcs," Oswald said, more to himself than to Walter.

The veteran crossbowman peered around the edge of forest assiduously, his brown eyes scanning the deep shadows for any hidden enemies. "More strange than the green-skinned beasts being this far south of the Serrin plains?" Walter asked nervously.

Oswald nodded and tightened the reins on his horse. The large steed flicked its ears timidly. It too seemed to sense something unnatural. The animal's nervousness was not lost on the captain of the guard. Oswald patted the beast's neck soothingly. "Keep an eye out men. There are things..."

Oswald was cut off by a deep guttural roar that erupted from within the forest. The crossbowmen immediately knelt raising their weapons and pointed them at the beasts that charged from both sides of the trail. The creatures were almost seven foot tall. They had thick fur that was light yellowish brown and covered their bodies from head to toe. Their green eyes were wild like hungry savage beasts. Their wedge-shaped ears were covered with long coarse hairs that jutted as much from the inside as the outside. These savage monsters wielded long metal staffs with a heavy solid iron ball on the end. The large metal sphere bore thick rusted spikes jutting out from it at all angles. The fiends gripped their wicked weapons with both of their dark, black, clawed hands and held them overhead as they charged. Their faces were shaped much like that of an orc except one of the lower tusks protruded, as did one of the upper. They wore thick hide armor, held onto their muscular bodies by heavy chains that jingled as they charged.

Large chunks of frozen dirt shot into the air behind the heavy marauding beasts as they attacked. Bolts flew from the well-oiled crossbows with many resounding clicks. The shafts cut through the air striking two of the three brown-skinned beasts. One shaft struck a beast in the chest while another wedged itself in a second one's thigh. Neither howled in pain, or slowed their charge.

On the other side of the trail, bolts were loosed in a murderous cloud. One struck a creature in the chest, yet it kept its deadly charge. Another bolt hit one brute between the eyes, but the monster's thick skull stopped the tip of the shaft from penetrating too deeply. The wounded creature stumbled and fell, dropping its giant mace as he pulled at the bloody wooden shaft, trying to wrench the bolt free.

"Greyshalks! Greyshalks! Greyshalks!" Oswald cried out as his mounted horsemen met the denizens charge while the bowman started reloading their crossbows. The yellow-and brown-skinned monsters met the mounted horsemen in a fury. Two of the horsemen fell under the crushing charge of the seven-foot beasts, as the other two slashed and cut into their spotted hides. Vast gouts of hot steamy blood flew through the air in great contrast with the small white snowflakes that floated down amid the bloody fight.

Oswald turned his stallion and charged into the battle. Great mounds of frozen earth kicked up from behind his powerful steed. Oswald swung an overhand slash down at one of the Greyshalk's that were on top of a nearby dying steed as it tried to get to the soldier that lay beneath. The captain's keen blade laid a deep bloody gash down the thing's back. The creature grunted in pain and whirled the heavy mace around, trying to hit the captain but he struck only air. Before the brute could right himself, a thick crossbow bolt struck him in the throat. The spotted beast fell to the ground, clutching the heavy shaft that protruded from its neck, and died in a multitude of thrashings and gurgling sounds.

One of the beasts on the north side of the trail swung his giant mace, striking a bowman in the chest. The weapon made a sickening pop as the bowman's ribs were snapped inwards, piercing the organs beneath and he was flung through the air. The wounded bowman landed in the light windblown snow on the side of the trail. His twisted, mangled body let out a final ragged breath as he died.

The Greyshalk that had taken the bolt to the forehead rolled around on the frozen ground howling and grasping at the shaft as it tried to stand. The thick wood that still protruded from his brow snapped off from the monster's thrashing. Bright red steamy blood dripped from the wound in his forehead and trickled down his fur-covered face and chest. It steamed like mini-puddles of lava in the snow.

Another of the brutes brought his thuggish weapon down onto the side of the neck of one of the mounted soldier's horses. The horse groaned in pain and fell dead from the power of the blow. Oswald spurred his steed forward and slashed a deep cut on the creature's shoulder. The powerful Greyshalk rolled with the gash and reached out and snatched the captain of the guard's horse by the right rear leg as he fell.

The huge beast's muscles flexed and it drug the captain's horse down. Oswald toppled forward over the animal's neck and landed hard onto the hard, snow-covered ground. The frozen earth caught under the captain's breastplate and catapulted him head over heels. Oswald rolled over weakly and glanced up to see the seven-foot tall hulking brown- and yellow-spotted beast lumbering toward him.

The ferocious Greyshalk had many crossbow bolts sticking out of its spotted hide and steamy, fresh, red blood dripped from its wicked spiked mace.

Jude maneuvered around in the center of the chaos. He had no weapon and was chained. He could not defend himself against the weakest of attacks, and he knew his only chance of survival came with his captors.

Had he been bound with ropes instead of ridiculously heavy iron chains, he could have cut himself free with one of the fallen soldier's swords. But it seemed as if his cap-

tors were going to win the fight. There was only one creature, Greyshalk he heard them called, left standing, though
it fought as furiously as all the others combined. It stood
among the remaining soldiers, swinging its heavy mace
from side to side, striking another guard and flinging his
body through the air like a limp child. Jude thought about
running into the woods. His chains were so heavy they kept
him from moving very fast, and if there were more of these
beasts roaming about, he would be easy prey. But there was
no guarantee that he would find someone to help him out
of his chains, and he was barely dressed warm enough to
survive if he was out in the weather very long. With a heavy
sigh, Jude plopped down on the cold ground and watched
the fight play out. He might as well try to rest his unbearably
weary muscles before his captors started the march again.

The mighty Greyshalk fought viciously, then turned and
ran. The soldiers didn't bother pursuing the fiend. They were
bloody and battered, and some were dead. Oswald limped
to his horse and inspected the beast. It had a profound limp
on its right rear leg where the monster had grabbed it. Two
of the mounted soldiers were dead as were three of their
horses, and one bowman. The others had small bruises or
cuts and were tending to themselves now that the battle was
over. It was not uncommon for a soldier to find a wound he
didn't feel until after the battle had ended.

Oswald adjusted his plate mail and dug the stiff frozen
dirt from it. He tightened the leather straps that held his
heavy shoulder plates in place. The straps were stretched
and the buckle was bent from the fall from his charging
steed. He removed his gauntlet hand and grunted from pain
that shot down his arm when he moved the tender shoulder.

"Secure the prisoner," he called out as he pulled roughly
on the leather strap.

The other soldiers staggered over and roughly pulled on
the thick iron chains that held Jude. The giant swordsman
tumbled over onto the cold ground, offering no resistance
to the tug. The guard kicked Jude in the legs with his thick
leather boot. "Get up, dog! This ain't the time to be lounging.
Three of our comrades died protecting your filthy ass," the

soldier said, kicking Jude again. "Get up!"

Jude muttered and groaned to himself and struggled to his feet. He did not feel too much anger toward the guard. Not that he didn't want to, but the weeks of hard marching carrying the heavy chains, coupled with the bitter cold, had sapped him of his strength. Jude struggled to his feet and groaned again as he stood erect. The iron chains clinked as they tumbled down from his shoulders and dangled around him. The guard glared up at him, but the swordsman seemed to gaze away distantly.

The bowmen were inspecting their crossbows and trying to gather up any spent bolts that could be used again. They were not far from Central City, but no one knew if they were going to be attacked a second time.

"Let's get moving. Secure the dead on the remaining horse. Use some ropes to tie them down. Do not try to stop their bleeding, or set them upright. Tie their hands to their feet and run the rope under the horse," Oswald commanded as he scanned the tree line for more of the seven-foot-tall beasts.

The men grumbled to themselves at the way their dead were to be arranged on the horse. They wanted more dignity for their fallen than to have them bleed out, strapped to a horse like a bounty that was being brought in for payment. Oswald heard the grumbling and shook his head.

"Do I hear grumbling?" the captain asked. " Perhaps you would like to make camp and brew some tea while that creature runs to his clan, tells of his defeat, and returns with twice as many as we just faced?" the captain asked sarcastically. The men did not respond. They started fetching the dead and doing as they were ordered. Satisfied, Oswald softened his tone. "I do not like the way they are to be transported either, but if it were me that was dead, I would hope you would have the common sense to get me home hastily, rather than risking dying yourselves and leaving all of our corpses to be cooked in some Greyshalk stew pot."

The men nodded to themselves and tossed the dead over the side of the horse. They tied thick cords of rope around their hands and ran the rope under the horse, tying the ends to the dead men's feet, securing them tightly to the horse's back.

In moments, the soldiers were marching again. Jude noticed that without mounted soldiers he was no longer whipped. He suffered an occasional kick or punch, but the dull thud of their blows was much more preferred than the sharp sting of the whip. He reflected back again on how he came about this predicament.

He was locked in his cell in the elven city. He had received plenty of food and water, and truth be told, his so-called cell was much better living conditions than his home in Bureland. He figured the elves led such a pampered lifestyle that these were most probably unbearable conditions for them. What Jude wondered about the most was that the jail seemed to be only a few cells. Had they been in a human city with the numbers that dwelled here, they would need thousands of cells. How the elves managed a city with such few criminals was beyond him; in fact, he didn't see any other elves imprisoned there. Perhaps they had a quite liberal death sentence. There seemed to be no one in the jail at all, save for Lance and him.

He had been locked up for what he thought was the third day, when he heard alarm bells and lots of screaming and yelling. Jude had no idea what might be causing the disturbance, but there was little he could do about it, nor could he see anything outside of his cell. The sounds of battle lasted for more than an hour, and then abruptly died off. There were many sounds that Jude could not make out, but some seemed to be construction, or clean up. He sat in his cell for two more days. He tried to ask what had happened when they brought his food, but the elves would not speak with him. In fact, they did not even speak around his cell in their own language, like they did the first couple days.

One morning the elves opened his cell door. The older elf, whom was wearing the multi-colored robe when he and Lance were captured, strode in and cast another spell that held him. Jude struggled against the invisible bonds that locked his arms at his side, but he could not budge them – he could have been cast in steel from head to toe. The elves placed him on horseback and rode him outside of the Vale for almost a day. That was where he met up with the Beyklan guards that had him today. He recognized Oswald Thorrin. He was the captain of the guard that he and Lance had encountered on their trip to Central City, though the other guards were different.

Oswald did not seem to recognize him and Jude was not about to bring up the encounter. Lance, being the arrogant mage he was who always seemed to hurl dweamors carelessly about, had cast some sort of spell that put the captain of the guard asleep. The other two men that were with Oswald seemed unsure what to do. So he and Lance managed to get by without blood being drawn, though the encounter would not have even occurred if Lance had not opened his arrogant mouth. King's guardsmen were known to be cocky. It was fact. Only fools allow them to chide you into a fight that they will win. Even a victory against them in battle is an overall loss. Better to lose some pride, than be labeled an outlaw of the crown. Jude was roused from his daydream by the shout of his captor's.

"Famen's Tree, Captain! We are almost home," Walter shouted, hoisting his heavy crossbow over his shoulder and stepping more lightly. Oswald nodded to himself and glanced around the edges of the forest more closely. "Step cautiously men. If these fur-brained monsters have any wits at all, they will try a second attack between now and the river."

The men quickly tensed and looked around the forest as if it were an angry bear that might try to swallow them. Oswald waved his hand forward and slowly urged his horse down the hard-packed frozen road. The soldiers followed timidly, glancing around. They seemed to forget about Jude and they marched the rest of the way to Central City.

The men gave a cry of relief when they rounded the corner and spied the great stone bridge that spanned the Dawson River. The bridge was over one hundred yards long and at least fifty feet wide. It was made of large stone bricks that seemed to be held together by mortar alone – a feat that would be impossible, given the stone's weight. Either the bridge was made with the aid of magic or superior architecture. There were two stone columns at each end of the bridge that were almost twenty feet tall. The columns were square and had recessed alcoves on the inside with a thick wooden ladder built into them. The ladder led to a small battlement atop the tower that contained two crossbowmen that kept watch and stopped brigands and other unsavory people from entering the city. There were two battlements at the center of the bridge, but they were larger at the beginning and end. These center towers were almost fifty feet wide and thirty feet tall. They had two crossbowman soldiers atop them like the others, but they also housed a large brass sconce that was lit at night to alert river bound ships that they were near the city docks. In the past, large merchant ships that were sailing the river would miss the small port and sail past without the aid of the large braziers.

Jude was barely aware of the horse's hooves clipping on the rough stone bridge as they crossed. His heavy chains dangled about him as the swordsman stumbled across the bridge. In the past, guards would have whipped him for that, but now they seemed happy to finally be home. Jude hung his head low from the weight of the thick iron chains, ignoring the shouts from the men atop the stone towers at the base of the bridge.

"Good day, Captain Thorrin," one of the men called out.

Waving his hand, Oswald dismissed the guards and continued on. The city seemed to be close to recovering from the dwarven attack several weeks earlier. Most of the buildings were repaired from the fires the bearded folk had set, and the buildings that were unable to be repaired had been completely torn down. The charred square areas that once held the foundations of the ruined buildings were completely flat and the black, soot-scarred dirt had been overturned and fresh brown earth mixed with that of the scorched made a grisly collage of black and browns.

The soldiers paid little heed to Jude other than calling out a few taunts or congratulations of being captured. The large swordsman paid little attention to them as he struggled under the strain of the iron chains through the cold cobblestone streets. Citizens tried to get close enough to throw a rock, or hurl some rotten vegetables at Jude, but the soldiers did their best at keeping the angry few at bay. The people were hesitant to throw something from so far away for fear they might hit one of the soldiers. The last commoner that hit a soldier with a potato was held in the stocks, a small wooden wall with three holes in it, one for your head and two for your arms. The poor man was there for three days before they decided to let him loose, of course not before many baskets of rotten fruit was placed on the ground by the city guards for commoners to throw at him. And of course, common citizens will not pass the chance to hurl putrid produce at anything, regardless if it was at a man that was one of their own.

The soldiers led Jude along the winding streets of Central City. Jude was pleased that the tall buildings stopped the wind from slicing into him, but some of the streets felt like a wind tunnel when they marched down them. The icy gale cut through him like he wasn't wearing any clothing at all. Jude held is head down as he forced himself to place one weary foot in front of the other. He walked with his head hung low, not out of embarrassment, he knew he had done nothing, but because the weighty chains put most of the burden on the back of his neck and shoulders.

There was a large pop as a head of lettuce landed at Jude's feet. Jude stepped over the vegetable as he plodded down the street. He could hear city guards shouting at the lettuce hurler and he could vaguely see their shapes run after him.

Jude was led down the street to a large stone building. He could not look up and see what it was, but he could tell by the shadow it cast that it was the largest building he had ever been next to. He was taken into a large stone archway that was at the end of a stone ramp that descended into the belly of this grand structure. It was made of dark brown rocks and decorated with hundreds of tiny tiles that created a mosaic across the ceiling. The archway extended down another gradual ramp into a large hallway that was sparingly lit. The top of the arch was about fifteen feet from the ground and the flickering torchlight danced across the ceiling tiles giving the picture of a well-muscled man fighting a lion of unnatural life. There were many heavy banners made of thick velvet that hung down along the recesses of the archway. Some had the Beyklan crest of a sword piercing a tilted crown on a background of red and white, while others seem to be crests of noble houses.

Oswald dismounted and pulled his thick leather gloves from his hands. He placed the gloves in his wide brown leather belt and approached the man that came from a wooden door under the archway. The man was middle-aged and balding. His thin gray wisps of greasy hair were combed over the bald area of his head. He had a very muscular frame that was overlapped with thick folds of fat that he kept bundled under dirty oily furs. He smiled a gap-toothed smile and he waddled up the soft slope.

Oswald watched Copel Nin shuffle up from the small door with a slight limp. The man had earned the limp as a gladiator slave in the fight that had earned his freedom. He could no longer fight in the arena so he took a job as the keeper. The keeper was in charge of handling the gladiator prisoners. He was paid a fair sum and the job suited him. "Good day, Captain," Copel called out.

"Is it?" Oswald responded as he grasped the man's cold sweaty hand. The fat man frowned and scratched his baldhead, then smoothed down the tuffs of thin greasy hair that he upturned with his scratching. "Why is it not a good day under the sun?" Copel asked nervously.

Oswald turned to his horse, pulling down a leather pouch that was tied near the rear of the saddle. "Had you not heard, Copel? Surely the drunken merchant tales reach even your old fat ears."

Copel stared at the dirt- and straw-covered floor of the archway and kicked at it lightly with his foot. He was embarrassed by his current state. He had once been a great fighter, a great champion, but now he was a fat old man with a limp. "No, Captain. I had only heard outrageous claims that there was an army of walking dead that attacked the elves. That tale was so absurd that I knew it to be a fake."

Oswald pulled out a brass key ring with several small steel keys from the leather pouch that was fastened to his saddlebag. He roughly handed them to Copel roughly, their bare hands slapping in the exchange. "I am happy that you still can discern fact from fiction."

Copel smiled at Oswald's compliment and motioned for the guards to lead Jude down into the dark corridor under the archway. Copel started to speak, but Oswald had already mounted and turned back down the cobblestone road. The plump keeper gazed down at the ring of keys and the parchment that Oswald had given him. He unrolled the thin paper and read its contents. Copel smiled and shook his head. *This one was going to die in the arena.* Copel's smile faded distantly as he tossed the keys into the air, only to catch them again in a tight fist. Sometimes he wished he had died under the roar of the crowd. *Not a bad way to go.*

Copel whistled as he limped down the stone ramp that led to the dark tunnel. The guardsmen were standing in front of the large wooden double doors. The doors were almost ten feet high and had two large iron bands that kept the long wooden planks in place. Jude followed slowly with small labored steps. He was beyond trying to escape at the moment. He was delirious with hypothermia and was desperately clinging to consciousness. Copel reached up and grabbed a bright brass ring that hung on the left door. It was polished from lots of use and fixed about head-high on the door. The keeper lifted the ring and pounded it back down on the iron plate several times. The loud metallic boom echoed down the cold stone hallway. Jude glanced back up the stone ramp. He could see the cold gray sky at the end of the archway and a few people as they strode by the opening. He strained to lift his head under the weight of the heavy chains, but he was too weak. He let out a defeated sigh and resigned to listen to the sounds of wagons bustling by and a few street merchants plying their trade. The large tapestries that hung down from inside of the stone archway flapped lightly in the cold wind, occasionally thumping against the stonewall.

Copel muttered some curse under his breath and rubbed his cold arms. It was just like his lazy men to not be in the booking room when he needed them. Finally, after a few moments in the cold, the lock clicked and shifted and the heavy door's hinges creaked. As the door slowly opened, Jude was hit with a blast of warm, stagnant air. He was led into a small room with an old worn bench and a thick table. A young man wearing leather armor walked by, paying him little attention. Jude could not see his face with his head held so low, but he smelled of sweat and ale. The man wore a thick wooden cudgel at his hip and his boots were bulky and well oiled.

"He's a big one," the guard in the leather armor said, tossing a roll of parchments down on the wooden desk and fetching a pen and ink from inside the drawer. He placed the small black bottle on the corner of the writing table and began unrolling the papers. Copel sat down at the desk and turned the papers to face him as the guard walked over to the far wall and pulled down a set of lightly rusted iron shackles. The fat keeper dabbed the quill into the ink and began scribing a few notes onto the parchments. He would rub his chin and scratch his baldhead. Frowning, he would then write down something else. Jude was led to the wall and his hands were lifted by the chains and fastened there. He felt the heavy chains being unlocked from his neck. The rough shackles slid from his shoulders and clanged to the floor. Instant hot searing pain shot into his muscles as blood seeped back into them. Jude struggled to stand upright. His muscles and back were beyond exhausted. Grimacing, he forced himself to do it anyway. Great bolts of pain shot down his spine and then back up his neck, but he found once he stood erect, the pain was gone.

"What's your name?" the guard asked as he stared up at the giant of a man.

Jude didn't respond. He was lost in thoughts of where Lance was, whether he was alive or dead. The shorter guard lightly slapped Jude's face.

Jude turned and looked down at the much smaller man with a glare of pure unadulterated hate. "If I had my sword, little man, I would cleave you into two," Jude said and was surprised as the fat man behind the desk laughed aloud as he picked up the papers and bounced them off of the table, straightening them. He placed the parchments back down flat, and dabbed the quill into the inkbottle again.

"I doubt you would, barbarian. Lyndall here is a veteran gladiator. He has almost earned his freedom. He has slain monsters and enemies you have yet to dream of," Copel said with a grin. "But do not fret. If you wish to leave this place in a pine box, I can set up the fight for you."

Jude glared at the fat man with murderous contempt. Copel merely smiled and scrolled down a few more lines. "I think you will work out well here, barbarian."

"Do not let him goad you into a box, friend," Lyndall whispered as he finished unlocking the heavy chains from Jude's body. "There are only two ways out of this place: in a coffin, or after you have earned your freedom. No one has ever escaped or ever will."

Jude frowned down at the short man wearing the leather armor. He bore no weapons and gave no outward appearance that he was a skilled warrior. He had no visible scars and was not even very old. Trusting his senses, Jude doubted Lyndall was much more than a parley boy with some measly tricks with a blade. "If you were this great swordsman as they claim, why do you not cut a path out of here?"

Lyndall chuckled. "Why would I want to? As soon as I leave, I have nothing. Sure I want freedom, but then again, all that a man needs is in here. I have money to spend from winnings. I have weapons and armor beyond anything I could afford outside. And the women, friend; I have more women than you could dream of."

"It's true, barbarian. I was once a great champion. I fought for almost ten years to earn my freedom, and when I did I was no longer able to provide for myself. I had to take this job as the keeper to sustain a living," Copel responded from his parchments without looking up. Jude gazed at the fat man with a limp. *If this fool was a champion, I will have no trouble getting out of this place,* he thought to himself. As if reading his thoughts Copel smiled. "Do you think I was always fat and lame?" Copel said, pointing to his leg. "I was once full of iron muscle as you are, well maybe not as much, but my fair share for sure. Age takes a toll on you, barbarian. I am sure you have good bloodlines, but the truth be told, you have to know when to accept your freedom. A wise man stays well beyond his freedom date, saving money so he can at least retire comfortably. I was not wise with my earnings. That is why I work here."

Jude studied the man for a moment. His dark eyes glared at the short fat man that stood before him, then swept over the guard in the leather armor. "I am a prisoner, you are my captors. I will kill you at first chance. Best remember that."

Copel's smile vanished and was replaced by a determined scowl. Lyndall merely smiled and nodded his head. "You will do well, I think, barbarian," Lyndall said, clapping Jude on the arm as he walked to the heavy door. As Lyndall squeezed through the narrow opening into a dark alley, Copel gave him an angry glare and then roughly grabbed the iron chains that held Jude to the wall. Jude grunted as he was dragged across the floor and through the small wooden door that Lyndall ducked through. He tried to resist being pulled, but he was weak from the march to Central City without food and little water. His muscles were cramped from the heavy chains and he felt weaker than a newborn babe. The passage smelled of urine and foul body odor mixed with old dusty straw. The corridor, about a hundred feet long, was lined with dozens of small cells with thick wooden doors. Each door had one small window about head high that was covered in rusted iron bars. The wooden doors were black from tar that was spread on them sparingly to keep out bugs that might infest the men and spread disease. Jude was led into a cell and chained to the wall. The thick shackles that held him were fastened above his head on a bulky iron eyelet. Jude hung his head low, trying to keep flecks of rust out of his eyes that flaked off and fell onto his head.

"Don't get too comfortable, barbarian," Copel said with a sneer. "The watcher of swords will be in to inspect and sanitize you."

Jude didn't look up. He hung his head low, trying to ignore the weak old rumble in his shriveling stomach. The door to his cell closed with a resounding boom that seemed to echo in his mind. *Caged again in irons. Animals were caged in irons,* Jude thought to himself and narrowed his weary eyes. Barbarians are animals. *If they intend to create an animal, Jude thought, then I will become an animal like they have never seen.*

"Luck. What is it? Can it be defined? Is it a tangible force, some kind of magic that is yet to bet tapped into to? I know many races that worship Lukerey, the god of luck and mischief. To me, it seems like the religion with the least merit, any event-good or bad, can be attributed to luck. I cannot deny these unseen forces exist, but is it something that can be harnessed? If you try to influence luck, are you? Or are you merely increasing the probability of fate?

To me, luck is when preparedness meets opportunity. If you are prepared to capitalize on an event, and you have the opportunity to do so, that would be luck. Yet despite my power and ability with the arcane arts, I cannot explain many things that are attributed to luck. They are, for lack of a better explanation, lucky!"

-Lancalion Levendis Lampara-

A Slave's Welcome

Lance was dragged from the alley by the scruff of his cloak. The hard rain poured down from the gray sky, bouncing off of the tall stonewalls of the buildings around him. The alleyway had a cobblestone floor and to Lance's surprise, contained no loose debris or garbage. There were no drunkards, no street urchins, nothing like any alley he had ever heard of. He was still held tight by the thick swirling arcane green rings that churned around him at amazing speed. He was sure the woman that led the trio that had captured him and killed the elf, Malwinar, was someone of importance, though he had no idea how. She wore a bright red robe that was made of thick velvet-like material. All of the women wore a similar robe, but hers was more ornate in a few subtle ways, with golden symbols near the collar and on the fringes of the cuffs. She wore a golden hairpin in her long flowing red hair. But what surprised Lance the most was the fact that the rain did not fall on any of the three women. The drops seemed to hit some kind of barrier and fall around them, as if a strange magical veil enshrouded the women, forcing the rain to part over them. Lance thought it a curious trick since he was soaked to the bone from the cold heavy downpour. What also struck him as odd was that it was soon to be winter in Beykla, so wherever in the world he was, he was not near there. He guessed he was someplace far to the south.

Lance strained to see the soft glow of the magical weaves that surrounded the women; a simple spell that created a rift in the air around them, causing the rain to fall away. As they walked, Lance memorized the flow and even thought about changing a few of the weaves to see about deflecting arrows, but he would not know if it was possible until some were shot at him. In the past Lance might have tried to escape, but it was obvious these women were powerful and escape might end in his death. They cared little for their prisoners after the way they had dispatched Malwinar, so Lance was in no hurry to anger his new captors. Perhaps he might charm them with his wit. He always seemed to be able to soften a girl's heart with a few smiles back home.

"So, where are we going?" Lance asked with a half chuckle, trying to wear the most alluring smile he could muster under the circumstance. The women at his side stopped and gave him murderous glares. Lance thought he had made a mistake until the one in front of him stopped and turned. She wore an evil scowl until her gaze rested on his disarming smile. Her scowl softened into a half smirk. Lance smiled wider, thinking he had achieved some minor victory until a sharp pain cracked into his nose. It felt like the biggest man in Bureland wearing metal gauntlets had punched him. His nose split from the invisible blow and blood immediately formed a steady drip down over his mouth and onto the front of his robe. Lance's head spun and had he been standing on his own his knees would have buckled. Stars erupted in his mind and he was vaguely aware of the giggling of the women around him. The worst part was that his hands were held and he was unable to grasp his bloody broken nose.

"You will not speak until spoken to, suda," the lead woman said with a wicked grin as she spoke over the other women's giggles. "I can direct a strike to other, more motivating areas of your anatomy," she said, glancing down between Lance's legs.

Lance swallowed hard as tears ran from his eyes. "As you will learn, suda, your pathetic magery is worthless next to power of an Aten woman. A wise thing to remember. We dispatched your elf friend with ease. You will be no more difficult if you give us reason."

Lance didn't respond. He had to rethink his whole charm idea. It obviously was not working. Perhaps these were women who liked other women instead of men. He had heard that things like that went on in the big cities and he certainly seemed to be in some giant city. It wasn't until they reached the roadway that Lance realized how majestic it was. The roads were paved with smooth stone bricks and had small grooves set at the sides of the road that allowed water to run off and drain away. The buildings were slender and unnaturally tall. They were crowned with great spires and colorful domes that were gilded with gold and other precious metals. There were hundreds of towers set among the typical rectangular buildings. The towers were thin and it appeared as if they were not formed of bricks, but carved out of stone. These towers spanned several hundred feet into the air. The streets were littered with women in amazing dress. They all wore the finest garments that Lance had ever seen. There were no beggars, no street urchins, and no cut-purses. There were horses that marched down the street hauling immaculate carriages carrying more women in the back. It seemed as if everyone was royalty in the streets. Lance spied several men sweeping the stone walkways on the side of the boulevard. They were dressed in fine clothing also, though nothing in comparison to the women he saw. There were a few men carrying fruits and vegetables down the streets, but they kept their heads down and did not look around themselves. The people of the city paid no attention to Lance being held and walked along the side of the street. He had hoped to call out for assistance or that perhaps the militia might recognize he was captured, but no one seemed to notice.

Strangely enough, the only armored people carrying weapons were women wearing glossy plate mail armor formed around their breasts. *Their breasts!* Lance almost blushed on their behalf. It was like they were topless in a way. What surprised Lance the most was the armor even had nipples crafted on them. Lance realized that every important person he saw was female. A sick, horrified feeling overtook him. He knew he had to be in Aten. The damned elf Garlibane must have sent him there. The sudden realization came crashing in on him. If the elf feared his magical ability, which Lance had no idea why; the best place to send him was Aten. He had occasionally overheard the elves arguing about what to do with him.

Apollisian was against his execution and was making quite a stir among the elves on his behalf. Lance would have felt a kinship or duty to the paladin, except he knew it had nothing to do with him personally. Apollisian was not trying to save Lance, but he was trying to save his own view of morality. Lance did not know why the elves feared him so much, other than they believed him to be some kind of monster that was in their prophecy. Boy, were they wrong, though Lance could not ignore the intense anger he was feeling toward the pointy-eared race at this moment. He was held against his will in a foreign land by a bunch of women who intended to make him a slave. Had he not seen the merciless dispatch of the elven mage Malwinar, or had not been punched in the nose by the invisible force of air, he might have looked at being a slave in a country of women as something favorable. But as he glanced around the busy streets that weaved around great looming towers and ornate buildings, Lance realized that he was most likely not going to find anything favorable about his capture until he was looking back at the borders of this country after his escape.

Lance was surprised to see that all the men on the streets were busy in their tasks and none of them raised their eyes above the multi-colored bricks of the paved streets. Lance glanced over at the beautiful, but venomous woman that led his trio of captors. She smiled a wicked grin that sent quivering shots of fear down Lance's limbs. Her bright green eyes that beamed with intelligence and mystery bored into his own reflective emerald orbs. He started to enjoy gazing into her luscious sea of green when a solid force smacked him in the ribs. He felt a sickening pop as one of his ribs shattered and a wave of nausea from the intense pain fell over him. His long black hair was roughly jerked to the side by one of the other women. She whispered into his ear with her hot breath. "Sudas are not allowed to raise their chins above the bricks. If I ever catch your disgusting eyes taking in the beauty of Mother Ramasiel again, I shall pluck them out," the woman said as she jerked Lance's head to the side and forced it lower to her mouth. "Do not even sicken us with your repulsive reply. Merely obey."

Lance muffled a painful moan and winced as the women jerked his head a bit lower and then shoved upright, letting go. Lance could not feel the sting of his scalp over the intense pain from his broken rib that was making his knees swoon. His long black hair remained ruffled where the woman's small fist had jerked his head down. Lance did not look down at the bricks as ordered. Instead he turned and gave the woman an angry glare. "You are nothing to me but my..." Before Lance could finish, he watched the woman create a green weave that muffled all sound. Yet another flow Lance watched in earnest, memorizing and seeing its possible potential. The woman's incredulous glare almost made him laugh. If it was so easy to taunt these women he knew his quick-witted mind was going to have a lot of fun with them, despite his injuries. It wouldn't take him long to break the dweamors that they placed on him and he would escape. He was close to identifying the links that held each ring together of the spell that currently bound him. It was much different from the elves' spell, but the pretense was the same.

The two women seemed horrified and furiously angry at him as they led him down the street. They shot glares and scowls that promised pain and torture but Lance imagined that this Ramasiel was in charge. If he was lucky, she would value him as a slave. Lance hoped she would not allow the other two wicked women near him, but as far as his luck went of late, he was better off not leaving things to chance. Yet, this Ramasiel seemed entertained by him. It did not matter really; he was much smarter than some fool woman. Lance knew no matter where he went, all women did was sit around and gossip. Just like the women's circle back home in Bureland. Oh, some of them were creative, he would give them that, but all in all they were too emotional to achieve anything really great. That was why men ran countries. Men had the necessary mind that thought with the required logic to govern a nation. He wasn't sure how this Queendom survived the ages, but he figured he would manage his escape in a few days. Not to mention pay revenge to the wicked woman who grabbed his hair and broke his rib. She surely needed to be brought to justice. Not just for his injuries, but for the murder of poor Malwinar. Yet as much as Lance believed that women where too emotional to be truly intelligent, he had learned their passion could dwarf a man's easily.

Lance had plainly seen it many times. A woman could love her husband so fiercely that she was loyal to her death, but many times he had seen married men frolicking with wenches in bars while their faithful wives where at home, probably sitting by the fire eagerly awaiting their husbands' return. Lance hoped that when, or if, he ever met his soul mate that he would never do to her what the men of Bureland so often did to their wives. He remembered his father always honoring his mother. He was a remarkable man and she was an amazing woman. If he could only live to have half of their potential he would consider himself successful. Lance kind of chuckled to himself. Here he was a prisoner in the country of Aten and he really didn't have much fear. It seemed that women were too motherly to strike much fear into him.

Lance was led down many of the elaborately crafted stone paved streets. The city was so expansive that he soon lost his bearing on direction. He was cold and soaked to the bone from the heavy downpour that reverberated off of the hard paved walkways. They took him to the base of the largest tower he had seen in the city yet. It reached high above the canopy of the buildings and disappeared into the thick dark gray blanket that covered the city. They paused at the base of the tower, made with large ornate rocks at the foundation that were twice as tall as Lance. The rocks had carvings of runes and small statuettes about them and seemed to meld into the sheer walls of the tower. The tower walls were made of stone that had a reddish brown hue to them that glistened in the heavy rain. No moss or plant life of any kind grew on the side of the unnaturally splendid tower. There was a single door made of bright polished brass depicting a winged horse and a unicorn standing alongside a large tree. At the top of the doorframe was a single stone that was about four feet long and three feet tall. The stone had an engraving of a crescent moon with two mountains below it and a rising sun that bridged between the crescent and the mountains. The lead woman paused before the door and sent a strand of energy into the door. The unicorn's eyes glowed red and the woman stepped to the side. The other two women sent a similar, but much weaker flow, by Lance's estimation, into the door causing the Pegasus' eyes to glow red. The door made a resounding click and slowly opened. The three women scooted inside and roughly pulled Lance with them.

The interior of the tower was splendid to behold. Every piece of furniture was made from enameled white ash and covered with red velvet where it was needed. The polished wooden floor was also made of white ash, displaying the dame huge bright red symbol of the moon, mountains, and sun that was located above the entrance. Lance watched as many man-servants scooted about their tasks. A few stared at the ground but most stared straight ahead. Lance assumed the significance of the direction the slaves looked was directly proportionate with their standing among the women.

Lance was led to a small brick building that was inside of the tower. It had no door, but a small archway that led down into darkness. The lead woman motioned the women to the stairs, but Lance could not hear with the shield of silence around him.

"Take the boy to the Takash. Teach him what happens when he defies a woman," Ramasiel said flatly. The other two women nodded eagerly as Ramasiel spoke. "After you are through with his lessons on defiance, brand him as the property of the red sept and find him some suitable clothing."

The other two women nodded, wringing their hands with anticipation. "What are we to do with his robe, Mother? It is quite nice and made of a fine quality," one woman asked.

Ramasiel rubbed her narrow chin with her delicate crimson fingernails. "See if the blacks want to purchase it. If they do not, then burn it."

The two women nodded hurriedly and as soon as Ramasiel turned, they grabbed Lance by the collar and rushed down the dark stairs. The women removed Lance's cloak and tossed it to onto the small bench that was at the bottom of the stairs. Lance saw several small iron-barred cells at the bottom of the strange room that housed a few men. The men were wearing dull brown rags and bore fresh wounds and old scars across their body. Some had what appeared to be deep wounds from a whip and some had dark purple scars from severe burns. The men did not lift their heads when the women brought Lance in, save for one. He not only raised his head, he stood up and grasped the bars with both hands.

He had been severely beaten and dark, dried blood matted his long sleek black hair. He was almost as tall as Jude and in fact, looked strangely like him. Jude had similar facial features, including the thick strong jaw and the deep powerful eyes. The man had the same dark tanned skin as Jude, though the man was not nearly as strong as him. The man shouted something at the women, but Lance could not hear it through the spell. One of the women turned and regarded the prisoner. The man suddenly clutched his midsection as he was hurled through the air, and slammed into the stonewall of his cell. He fell to the ground holding his muscled arms around his middle, trying to force his weak legs to stand, but instead his eyes rolled in the back of his head and he drifted into unconsciousness.

The women removed Lance's cloak and stripped him down to his bare skin. Lance fought the embarrassment of being naked before the women. Even though he despised them for capturing him, he could not hide the truth that he had never before been naked in front of anyone, let alone two women. The fact that he was helpless only added to his inescapable feeling of vulnerability that increased with each passing moment. The women looked him up and down, rubbing their chins as if appraising stock at the market. One of the women sent a small piece of energy into the shield that kept out sound, causing it to evaporate into nothingness. The wave of sounds swept over Lance like a sunrise in the black of night. He didn't realize how important that sound was to him and how much he relied on it. One of the women reached out and grabbed him between his legs. Lance flinched and tried to move, but the spell held him fast. She bounced him in her hands softly shaking her head from side to side. "This is much too small, I think. What say you, Reena?"

The other woman nodded her head and chewed on her

bottom lip in disappointment. "I would say, Second Sister. He has to be the smallest I have ever seen. Nothing like the Kai-Harkians," Reena said with a mocking chuckle. "I wonder how he even pleases himself with such meager equipment." Both women had a hardy laugh.

"I know what you are trying to do," Lance said.

Both women suddenly stopped laughing and turned on Lance in a fiery rage. They sent force after force into Lance's body, pounding him with hundreds of invisible fists, striking harder than any man could. They struck him in the ribs, the kidneys, the sides of his throat, and even the small of his back. The beating lasted many minutes until Lance lost consciousness.

Lance awoke slowly. His arms screamed in intense pain from holding his dead weight. He tried to stand up to relieve the pressure on his shoulders but his leg muscles had difficulty supporting him. He managed to stand erect after a few attempts. Looking down at himself, Lance gasped in horror. His legs were almost a solid bruise. There were large yellow pockets of fluid that floated above deep purple bruises so colorful one might take a second look to ensure they were not painted on. Every time he took a breath, the many broken ribs stabbed hot pain into his side, clouding his vision. The sides of his neck were so sore that it hurt to swallow and he had difficulty keeping his head upright.

It was then that Lance realized the enormity of his situation. Unrelenting dread poured into him. These women were not soft, delicate, and loving creatures. They were cold-hearted she-demons. The man in the cell directly across from Lance sat on his butt picking at the dirty straw that lined his tiny cell. He looked up at Lance nonchalantly and flipped some small piece of debris onto the floor. Lance winced as he swallowed and called out to the man. "How long have you been here?" Lance asked hoarsely.

The man with the dark skin and long black hair did not respond. He gave Lance a look of aggravation and stuck his thick finger into his nose. Lance frowned and tried to clear his throat before speaking again. "My name is Lance. I am from Beykla."

The man frowned again but stopped picking his nose, though his thick finger still remained embedded to his first knuckle. His dark eyes measured Lance for a moment, and then he withdrew the finger and flipped a piece of dark green debris onto the floor. "Your name is suda for the time-being, fool, at least until you are made into tuda," the man said as he stuck his finger back into his nose, this time moving it about rather vigorously.

Lance frowned. He had heard one of the women call him suda. She stated that he was not allowed to look above the ground. "What is a suda?" Lance asked as he shifted his weight under his weak, bruised legs.

The man pulled his finger out once more and held it the end of his face, looking at the glob of nasal matter that was stuck there. Lance tried to ignore his disgust at the man and waited for his reply. The man flipped his finger a couple of times and then resigned to wipe the glob onto the floor of his cell rather than trying without success to flip the green matter free.

"Look between your legs," the man said as he rubbed both sides of his finger on the cell floor and frowned at the persistent sticky substance that seemed to refuse to be dislodged.

Lance glanced down and saw nothing other than his normal anatomy. The dark-skinned man spoke up before Lance could ask again.

"When they cut that off, and I mean all of it, you will be a tuda. Until then, you're a suda. And when I say *when* they cut it off, I mean *when*. There is no *if*. It is only a matter of time before it goes. If you were meant for a bedroom slave you would not have been brought here. Those slaves are usually bought. They remain suda, but they slice off your fun bags, so-to-speak. It stops pregnancy. It is illegal for an Aten woman to be impregnated by anything but a Dall-kal-Mour."

Lance tested the strength of the chains that held his arms over his head. They rattled slightly, but were very taught. "What is a Dall-kal-Mour?"

The dark-skinned man yawned and stretched his large

arms behind his head. They popped and creaked as he stood up and walked to the edge of his cell. "Dall-kal-Mour are the sons of female Aten women. They are pure bloods, where you and I are from other countries. You might think the ruthless bitches could have at least some love for their own baby, but nope. Think again. Their babies are sold on the market to rich, noble houses. But more often than not, they are sold to the Carcarass until they are old enough to be used as breeding stock. As soon as they reach the old age of thirty-five, they are slain. No ifs, ands, or buts about it," the dark-skinned man said as he grabbed the thick iron bars that held him in his cell. He let his head hang down between his arms and chuckled. "And us sudas..." he trailed off. "We are doomed to be tudas. But, you see, there is much more than just being made a eunuch to make you a tuda. By the time they lop off your manhood, your will is broken and you are eager to please the vile she-bitches. Most tudas see themselves as better than sudas and will betray us, at any turn, so don't trust any of them. I have been suda longer than anyone ever has in the red sept. At least so they say. When they think I am unconscious I pick up on some things they say. I will die here, newcomer; I will die before I allow myself to be so disgraced," the dark-skinned man said without raising his head.

Lance frowned half out of pain from the beating he endured and half from frustration. "We should band together and feed off of each other's strength," Lance suggested.

The dark-skinned man laughed again, but to Lance, the laugh lacked cognitive sanity. "That seems to be something intelligent doesn't it?" the dark-skinned man replied as his head still hung low before the bars of his dark prison.

Lance nodded slowly.

"Well it isn't," the dark-skinned man said. "They have taken everything that I have here. They have nothing else to take from me; that is how I survive. Why would I create a friendship with you? That merely gives them one more thing to take away from me. I am not sure I could withstand to lose anything more. If I lost my manhood I know I would be defeated, but the irony of the situation is, they will not take it until I am broken," he said with a sick laugh. "If you are going to survive here, outlander, I suggest you quickly become wiser. They will return soon to begin your training. And I must say, it will not be fun. Try to remember the more you screw up the more you will be punished. You must learn to gain victory out of defeat, or you will lose everything."

Lance soaked up everything the dark-skinned man said like a sun-baked sponge that was tossed into a deep puddle. He was not sure he understood all of the man's twisted ramblings, but Lance figured it would make a little more sense later. He just hoped it would not be too late when it did.

Ramasiel walked into her chambers. The room was small, but quaint, with lavish furnishings and a single great mirror that was outlined with thick polished oak. There was a single window that gazed down into a vast sea of gray clouds that hung over the city, yet the bright rays of the sun shined into the room, warming it. Ramasiel was the Mother of the red sept. She was one three of such titles in all of Aten. The red sept differed little from any of the other septs, save that they were more battle-orientated than the others. Reds were known to argue the senate to make war with surrounding nations, but in the Queendom's history, they have never made war with any country. The senate maintains that men made war. Since Aten women were above men, it seemed foolish to lower themselves to such acts. Yet Ramasiel and her order saw things differently. That is why they went out of their way to capture men of high power from other cultures and make them slaves.

She felt that the entire continent of Terrigan should be ruled by her sept and all the men in the realms should be forced into bondage. Her country's history alone showed how men were a danger to the world. They were rash and reckless, often thinking with their donks rather than with their minds. *If the fool men would council with their women before they made decisions, many lives would be saved worldwide. Men were so weak and stupid.*

Ramasiel sat in her scarlet velvet-gilded chair with perfect posture and combed her long red hair with an ivory brush carved like a sea creature. Normally there were little clouds covering the city and she could gaze out over the ocean that was to the north and the vast mountain range that dwelled to the west. Today she could not see past the mountains due to the perpetual fog that blanketed the expansive bog. The swamp was home to the powerful black dragon named Androdius. The old woman, Hiramem, had mentioned a man in a black cloak would change the red sept forever, but the women could not say whether it was to be a good change or a bad change. All Hiramem ever spoke of was the importance of the black cloak. The red mother decided that she would order the cloak not to be sold after all. Ramasiel had almost forgotten about the foretelling until she saw the two men in the alley. The boy holding the black robe seemed confused while the elf obviously knew where he was and was trying futilely to get back through the portal. Ramasiel thought about creating a web to hold the portal open to investigate what was on the other side but she had learned long ago the price for underestimating elves.

They were a resourceful lot and she did not need the headaches at the moment.

A knock at her door roused Ramasiel from her daydream. She placed her ivory brush down on the polished wooden stand in front of the gilded mirror and slowly rose to place the golden pin in her hair. She took her time to make sure the pin was in correctly before slowly turning to face the door. "Do come in," she said in a honeyed voice that still sounded stern and unyielding.

A meek-looking man stepped in, wearing a bright red silk tunic and breeches with the sept symbol on the back in bright yellow thread. His brown hair was cut short, showing he had not been a tuda long, though he was eager to please. Yet he still stared at the ground out of habit for a brief moment, and then quickly raised his gaze, though he still did not look her in the eye.

Ramasiel took in the sight of the man. He had been a duke in Ladathon. He owned hundreds of acres of land and was lord to well over ten farms. Ramasiel liked taking men of station and reducing them to her servants. They already knew how a servant was supposed to act and after a little training they seemed to make the transition well. Strangely enough it was beggars and the homeless that clung to their dignity longer than the supposed men of station. Ramasiel could not remember his name. She thought it started with an "N" but she could not be sure. He was near the end of his usefulness and would be disposed of in the spring. Such a shame; he had been a good house servant. Though what would the other Mothers say if she clung to aging tudas? She dared not lose favor with the senate either. She was in prime position for political maneuvering. If she could get into the senate, she could possibly sway them into war.

What a grand world it would be under Aten rule. Ramasiel daydreamed briefly about every kingdom in the realms flying the Aten banner, and then turned to the slave before her. He stood completely motionless with his hands clasped behind his back. "What did you have to report, tuda?" Ramasiel asked, crossing her leg over the other, dangling her bare, slender but muscular calf out from under her robe in attempt to catch the man's eye.

The tuda glanced down ever-so-briefly and his eyes rocketed back up. His face flushed slightly then quickly subsided as he spoke. "Reena reports that they are to begin the new suda's training this afternoon. She asks if you have any special requests before she begins."

Ramasiel stood slowly and turned her back on the man. She was filled with fury. He was one of Reena's tudas, yet he gaped at her leg like some smitten schoolboy. Regardless of the fact he had obviously been recently moved up to tuda, he should not have been raised until he was properly trained. No man was to see her flesh other than her hands and her face. This foolish tuda's eyes practically feasted on the site of her with rampant lust. It was not unlike Reena to raise men to tuda's without removing their male parts. Reena was a lustful woman herself and often used the men in her own bedroom affairs. How a woman could ever demean themselves by allowing a man to place his donk into her and then pant and sweat like some animal was beyond the red mother. The mere thought of the act was so revolting she fought to keep her lunch down. Ramasiel gathered herself and turned to the tuda who was staring straight ahead in perfect posture and behavior. "How long have you been a tuda?" Ramasiel asked.

The tuda answered quickly, masking his fear well. "Three months, Mother," he said, rampant with terror. Had she seen him glance at her legs? He wasn't sure if he had or if he merely glanced close to them, allowing himself a better peripheral look. She could not have noticed. The look didn't last a half second, less than that even. The tuda felt thick beads of sweat welling up on the small of his back and the palms of his hands.

Ramasiel nodded with his response. She easily sent strong flows of energy whipping out from her hand that grabbed the tuda's silk breeches, ripping them from his body. The torn silk fell softly at the man's feet. Ramasiel smiled in satisfaction at the sight of his exceptionally long donk that hung down between his legs. He was clean shaven from his ankles to his groin, further supporting the fact that he was one of Reena's play things. The tuda didn't bother covering himself, though he shook visibly out of fear. His thin legs trembled and his face turned pale as if he were to vomit at any moment. Ramasiel smiled and walked up to the man, looking up into his eyes, though the man stared straight ahead. "You seem to have something the other tudas do not," Ramasiel said leaning closer to the man. He swallowed hard. He obviously was struggling with what to do. Ramasiel did not ask a question therefore he could not speak, but she had worded the statement in a form a question. The tuda did not speak. He guessed it was better to be beaten for not speaking than for disrespecting the Mother. Disrespect often ended with death. Ramasiel grinned slightly at the man's wisdom. Yet another shame that Reena had ruined him so. Men with wisdom were so hard to come by.

"Why are you so equipped?" Ramasiel asked, reaching down and grabbing the man by his donk. Ramasiel was disgusted at how warm and heavy it was. She pulled her knife and watched the man's eyes carefully. If he even so much as looked like he was thinking about enjoying what she was doing, she would plunge the weapon into his fool heart. But to her delight the only thing she saw in the man's eyes was stark-raving fear.

The tuda stuttered and swallowed hard. "Sh-she keeps me for special tasks and duties, Mother."

Ramasiel pictured the image of the tuda hunched over beautiful Reena, ramming and panting. The thought made her want to vomit. She released her hold on the man and walked across the small room, grabbed a small bell with her delicate fingers and rung it softly. A tuda walked in wearing thick velvety robes and had long brown hair that hung to the small of his back and was fastened into a pony-tail with a thin gold ring. The tuda glanced at the man with stark surprise and then at Ramasiel, though he did not look into her eyes. Ramasiel sat down and exposed her bare leg, just as she had done before, but the tuda that just walked in easily ignored her movements and stared straight ahead. Ramasiel smiled with satisfaction as she spoke. "Go to Reena. I want you to advise her that I intend to see the training of the newcomer myself. Tell her not to worry about my other functions, I have them taken care of and I do not want to be disturbed. Also, tell her I will be using her tuda for the afternoon for some special tasks."

The tuda nodded and departed from the room, showing a slight frown at the proclamation that the man standing nude from the waist down was a tuda. But the mention of Reena had cleared it up for him. She was known for doing such nonsense. The long haired tuda quietly departed from Ramasiel's chamber. The Mother of the red sept quickly turned to the tuda standing before her.

"I want you to do to me that in which you do to Reena," Ramasiel said, unfastening the golden pin that was clasped at the top of her robe. It fell open, slightly exposing cleavage of a deep tan bosom. The tuda was reluctant at first, then after further coaxing, he allowed his eyes to fall on the woman. Ramasiel was beautiful in her own right and her position of authority made her all the more attractive to the man. He hoped that she might take him for herself if he performed well. Ramasiel fought the nausea in her stomach as the man's donk began to grow fuller and rise. It became thicker and began to point upward. The thing was much larger than any she had ever seen, though she rarely appraised men so. The whole act was so disgusting and demeaning that she often wondered how women suffered it all. Ramasiel lowered herself to her bed that was covered in thick red silk sheets and spread her legs wide. She pulled down her bright crimson under garments and tossed them to the floor. The tuda climbed onto the bed and gently moved between her legs. Ramasiel quickly formed a weave on her bed sheets to protect them from fluid. She had devised this shield to protect her clothes from stains, now it would protect her sheets. She reached down and gently grabbed the tuda between his legs. The throbbing heat that came from him sickened and repulsed her. She pulled him close to her and just as the tip of him reached her, she moved the dagger she pulled from her belt and plunged it just above the man's donk. He screamed and tried to pull away but Ramasiel shot out several bright green weaves that encircled him, and held the tuda fast.

She sat up and smiled, wiping sweat from her brow that formed from the nausea of such a disgusting experience. It was worth the price to see the confused look of stark horror that was set upon the man's face. Ramasiel reached down, and like slicing up breakfast sausages, she severed him, held his bloody member before his face and shouted, "You dare to think you would bed a Mother of a Sept?" The man struggled for breath and convulsed in shock as he bled all over the floor.

Ramasiel smiled and gingerly sat back into her red velvet gilded chair. She crossed her legs and let the man's eyes feast on what had caused his agony. As she sat wide legged and naked in front of him and his lifeblood slowly drained from him, she took in the site with pure enjoyment. It took about five minutes for the tuda to die. Ramasiel laughed at the irony that collapsed before her. The man had lost his life because his lust prevented him from keeping his eyes where they belonged. Then, after it was obvious he was going to die, he hardly looked at a much greater prize she offered him. Men where such stupid creatures.

"Ignorance of youth. Is it not it grand? Can you recall one of the many moments as a child or a young adult when situations were much more grave than you could have imagined, but you lacked the wisdom that is only gained through years of life, to understand the seriousness of the turmoil you faced? The problem with youth is that it is wasted on the young. I had no idea at the time of my capture the depth of the allegations the elves leveled against me. I was confident that I had done nothing wrong and my foolish reliance in my supposed ability with magic. I had no idea that the elven mage, Garlibane, had most probably forgotten more about magic than I had ever learned. I could not grasp the seriousness of the charges that I faced, and had it not been for Apollisian who faced ridicule and discrimination at the hands of the elves on my behalf, I would have surely been executed by these self-proclaimed 'goodly' elves. Yet it was not until I met the cruel and wicked Ramasiel that I began to understand that world was nothing like my small hometown of Bureland. People were evil, malicious and often saw other people as property, pawns or merely stepping stones to achieve that in which they desired. I was almost executed and Jude was imprisoned for crimes we were thought we might commit, but these people – these kings, queens, and leaders of men, walked the earth unchecked everyday while people like Jude and I were made to suffer. Yes, I was taught a great many things during this period of my life. I learned the only one lesson that must be taught by another being. I learned the most abominable emotion, and it was deeply ingrained in my soul. Had I not learned this emotion, the purity of my youth would have gradually subsided and the wisdom I would have gained would have increased, giving me balance in my estimation of mankind. Yet, I was not allowed the luxury of time. I was taught a life's worth of this powerful emotion in a fraction of my existence. These women, these Mothers of Aten, they taught me to hate, and oh how they taught me well."

-Lancalion Levendis Lampara

3

Brohe-tah

The cold wind whipped through the thin bare trees like a cascading river over a rocky cliff. Amerix hugged his heavy blanket close around his old ageing body. The thick wool was a little itchy next to his arms and legs, but it was much better than the bitter cold. As the winter wind howled it enticed the flickering camp fire to perform a rapid cadence dance. The young orc seemed to not care for his thick winter blanket much either. He tossed and turned and finally sat up and scratched his oversized head. Amerix had been traveling with the orc whelp for a few weeks now and was beginning to see him as an individual identity, rather than a nuisance.

Not that he wasn't a nuisance. He was a damned orc for Durian's sake, but his bright blue eyes seemed to beam of intelligence and he was learning the dwarven tongue quite well. Amerix had never heard of an orc speaking dwarven, but it was not like he was going to defile his own tongue by learning to speak orc. Amerix despised orcs. They were evil, merciless raiders, but Vlargcar was different. He had to be taught many things. For instance, when they came upon the small farm where they got the blankets, Vlargcar immediately wanted to rush in and kill the farmers. Though Amerix didn't see too much of a problem with it, the humans had children. He remembered what it was like when the dark dwarves came in and invaded his home. So he restrained the young orc.

Amerix was surprised to learn of the power the little green-skinned monster possessed. It was all Amerix could do to restrain him and, had Vlargcar not elected to listen to him, Amerix did not think he would have been able to keep the little hellion at bay. The humans were frightened at first, but the male human was surprisingly receptive. Amerix could not speak much common, but he and the farmer had managed to work out a bargain. He had learned that the people in the south felt the humans in the north got their just deserve.

Amerix didn't bother telling them what role he played in the battles. He said he was too old for fighting. If they had learned who he was, it was no doubt this place would be crawling with soldiers. Not that Amerix was afraid of mere men, but he had Vlargcar to think about. Amerix chopped wood Vlargcar had hauled from the forest for the farmer. The orc was stronger than any dwarf he had ever seen. Amerix knew orcs were strong, but he was sure the whelp surpassed any orc in his clan. Amerix wondered how strong he would become. Vlargcar had a lot more growing to do.

After they were finished with the wood, the farmer gave them a hot meal and winter blankets to use as they slept in the barn. They were nice for humans. They didn't seem greedy or power hungry like the men of the Torrent Manor. Amerix figured there must be exceptions to every race. Just like young Vlargcar, though his orcish ways often shined through his thick-tusked smile. Watching him devour a live squirrel was certainly alarming, but the orc's innocent look when he was finished showed that it was just every day eating for him.

Amerix shuffled with his blanket to get his thick boot out from under the heavy cover and kicked one of the logs in the fire. The fire grew hotter and hundreds of sparks shot into the air and were quickly blown away by the cold wind. Vlargcar tossed off his blanket and grabbed another thick log that he and Amerix had gathered and tossed it onto the camp fire. He returned to his blanket and crawled under it. He turned to Amerix and spoke with his thick graveled voice. "Me thinks the wind is too fast. Makes the fire go small."

Amerix nodded and smiled. The orc had a fine deep voice that would make any dwarf proud. If only he had a beard and his skin wasn't so damned green. "Aye, Vlargcar. There is no wind in the mountains. Durian does not allow such cursed afflictions on his people," Amerix said while hugging his blanket tighter around his neck. Vlargcar nodded and looked off into the dark as if in thought. His blue eyes seemed to glow from the light from the flickering fire.

"Me thinks I would like to see under the mountains where Brohe-tah lives."

Amerix smiled. His old creased face had not done much of that in his life, but he seemed to do it a lot of late. Amerix found it much more to his liking than frowning. The old general had learned that Brohe-tah was the orc word for comrade, the closest thing to friend that was in the orc language. The orcs had well over thirty words for enemy that he had learned, yet they had no word for friend. No wonder they were such a savage race. Amerix turned back to his blue-eyed friend. Amerix liked his blue eyes. They were much like his when he was young. "Aye, my friend. There is nothing like the under mountain." Vlargcar smiled. His wicked visage probably looked murderous to most, but Amerix had become familiar with his snarls and smiles. The orc got up from under his blanket and shook it out. He walked over next to Amerix and sat down by him. He flipped out his blanket to straighten it and covered himself back up.

"Would you take me to under the mountain someday, Brohe-tah?" Vlargcar asked timidly, very similar to a young dwarf asking for a treat or a privilege.

Amerix turned and regarded the orc whelp. The boy had such a look of hope in his innocent blue eyes. He seemed on the edge of himself hoping to one day see the home of his only friend. Amerix did not have the heart to tell him if the orc ever set foot into a dwarven city, he would be slain on sight.

"One day, I suppose. But for now, dream of it. We have a hard march ahead of us in the morning," Amerix said turning over. It had taken him most of the long weeks since he met the orc to sleep with both eyes closed, but as of late he was becoming comfortable with the whelp. He didn't always see an orc when he looked at Vlargcar. He usually saw his friend. Amerix had to admit that in his long life, he had not had many friends.

Vlargcar laid back and rested his heavy head on the cold earth. He stared up at the brilliant stars in the sky. He didn't know much about this Durian that Amerix was always speaking about, and he surely cared nothing for Drunda, the orc god. His mother had tattooed him with magic wards, so she claimed, that protected Vlargcar from magic. He wasn't sure whether they worked or not. They were not important. His mother was dead, killed by his own people. Now he was traveling with a short bearded human that claimed to be called a dwarf. Vlargcar vaguely remembered his tribe teaching something about dwarves to him, but he couldn't remember it.

Amerix looked like a short, squat human that was all. The dwarf was old; Vlargcar could see that, but he still moved with great precision and balance. He must be a great warrior. Vlargcar hoped to one day be a great warrior and make his mother proud. He knew she was watching him from the stars. She had to be. The beautiful twinkling bulbs of light in the sky were the only things that could represent her beauty accurately, though his mother was much more beautiful than them. Vlargcar took a deep breath and closed his weary eyes. He dreamed of under the mountain and the fantastic cities that Amerix always told him about.

Vlargcar awoke in the morning just before dawn. He rolled over and saw Amerix was still asleep. The stocky old dwarf's chest rose and fell in deep growling breaths. Had Amerix been an orc he would surely have been a chief. He had all the traits that a great chief would have, except he was not wicked. Vlargcar smiled as he rose from under his blanket. He was glad Amerix was not an orc. Folding his blanket the way that Amerix had showed him so that it could be carried easy when they marched, Vlargcar set about looking for breakfast. He didn't have a fine blade like the sword Amerix carried, but he was proud of his axe. It was a mighty axe and quite durable. Orc axes were great weapons, superior to most any other kind. Though, Vlargcar was learning it was slow and predictable. Each of his attacks when he and Amerix were weapon training had to come in a wide arc, where the dwarf's attacks could lunge out, make wide or short arcs, and could even be held one-handed.

Vlargcar hoped to have a sword like it someday. Placing another thick log quietly on the fire so not to awake Amerix, Vlargcar set out to find some squirrels to hunt. They were remarkably easy to find and they never seemed to run far from their trees. Vlargcar had learned that the furry little morsels often lived on trees that made nuts, so those were the trees he usually looked into first. Vlargcar liked to learn new things and tried his best to memorize everything he could. He had quickly learned that knowledge was power.

After finding a tall thin tree with the shaggy bark, Vlargcar placed his heavy axe on the ground and started to climb it. He wrapped his thick muscular arms around the base of the tree and placed the flat of his feet on each side. He then lifted himself up a few feet and repeated the process until he was at the bottom branches of the tall thin tree. Vlargcar sat on the end of the branch and let is feet dangle off while he picked away at small pieces of bark that had been embedded in his skin. It was normal to get small cuts and scrapes when climbing a tree, but the juicy squirrels were more than worth the reward.

Vlargcar climbed higher until he got near a thick pile of leaves that was wedged between the fork of two small branches. He knew that was similar to the nests that squirrels made. He could see a fat juicy squirrel skitter around the thin trunk of the tree thinking it was on the wrong side and the orc couldn't see it. Vlargcar lashed out and around the tree with lightning speed and grabbed the squirrel in his powerful grip. The squirrel squirmed and bit his hand, drawing blood, but could not escape. Vlargcar ignored the stinging pain from the bite and squeezed until the squirrel went limp. He then placed the furry morsel in his belt pouch and climbed down, looking for more trees.

Vlargcar had gathered almost ten squirrels when he decided to stop. The eastern sky was orange from the glow of the rising sun and he figured Amerix was soon to be awaking. He hoped to surprise his bearded friend with fresh meat cooking on the fire. Taking quick deliberate strides, Vlargcar made his way back up the hill and towards camp.

They had been traveling miles off of the road for fear of discovery and had made camp atop a small hill. Amerix said he liked camping on hills – that it was like a mountain, only not as rocky and not as big. The dwarf was against building a fire at first but Vlargcar had coaxed him into making one since they had not encountered any problems since the dwarf had saved him.

Besides, Vlargcar was somewhat familiar with the area and he knew where his people made their patrols and they were much further south than his tribe's village. As Vlargcar returned from the base of the hill to his camp he heard strange voices. They were laughing and jovial. He guessed there was about ten of them and he could see the glow of the camp fire was raging higher than when he left it. Vlargcar could not make out what they were saying. It was a language he had never heard before, but he was sure all the voices were male. They seemed happy and gleeful. Amerix must have met some old friends and was having a good time.

Vlargcar hurried up the hill, eager to show his catch to his dwarf friend and the new visitors, but when Vlargcar reached the top of the hill, his smile faded and his heart dropped. He witnessed about ten humans that were armed with long swords and short swords dangling Amerix up by his feet. The dwarf was mumbling fiercely through the dirty brown rag they had stuffed in his mouth and his body was so bound by rope that he looked like a bug that had been caught by a spider and spun in web. His silver-streaked black beard hung to the side of his head and was matted with blood from a deep cut that was atop a deep purple lump on his lip.

Vlargcar didn't think about how many men stood around the fire. He didn't think about their swords of their thick chain shirts that dangled under their fur lined leather tunics. All he thought about was his mother. She had been captured and killed before his eyes by the other orcs of his tribe, because she had tried to protect him. Now his only friend he ever had in life, other than his mother, was hanging upside down by a rope. He had been beaten and he was being taunted. The men had clearly stoked the fire because they planned on eating the dwarf like the orcs had eaten his mother, but Vlargcar was not as scared as he had been. Amerix had taught him how to use his axe, taught him the basics of how to fight, and he was armed, unlike when the orcs came after his mother. No, the only thing these men were going to feast on was the cold hard air as they took their last breath.

Apollisian held his head in his hands. His fingers were twined in his long blond hair and he stared intently at the polished oaken floor of the elven throne room. The elves suffered great casualties at the hands of the wicked necromancer and the paladin struggled with why he did not detect any evil in the boy. Alexis sat across from him. She wore a beautiful form-hugging green leather suit of armor and her white ash bow lay beside her on the wooden bench that lined the walls of the great chamber. Her long blonde hair was gathered in a thick single braid that hung down in front of her and rested between her supple breasts. She felt the paladin's pain and placed a comforting hand on his shoulder. "I tried to tell you, but I knew that it would not matter. I knew that you must trust your ways for Justice," Alexis said soothingly.

Apollisian looked up from a tear-streaked face. His bright blue eyes shined fiercely under the strands of his golden hair in the pale light. "My ways?" he asked sarcastically. "They are not *my ways*, Alexis. They are the ways of Stephanis. The ways of Justice. He is not wrong; he is perfect in his knowledge. I must have erred, or your people have, but he did not. He is the epitome of Justice," he corrected with a voice dripping with venom.

Alexis pulled her hand back and donned an expression of hurt and anger. "I am not your enemy, Apollisian Bargoe of Westvon Keep, paladin of Stephanis and champion of justice," she said angrily.

Apollisian winced as she used his full title.

"But, I do disagree. How can it be that you are perfect? You must agree that you could have made a mistake."

Apollisian stood up, placed his hands behind his back and leaned backward, stretching sore muscles. "Of course I can make mistakes," he said impatiently. "I often do, but seeing inner evil is not my mistake to make. It comes from

Stephanis directly. The mighty hand of justice points to black hearts. I do not make such determinations with my mortal mind. That is why I am sure that your people are wrong."

Alexis shook her head and pointed out of the light green stain glassed window of the throne room. She gestured to the hundreds of elves cleaning up the bones of the nightmarish enemies they faced the previous week. The elves had been at the task ever since the end of the battle and there still was enough work for weeks to come. What disturbed the elves most was that there was not a single body from an elf that was slain in combat. The dead marched off with the armored knight of death. They marched west, away from Minok.

"Wrong? Tell me, paladin, how are my people wrong? Look at the death the boy has wrought," Alexis said, gesturing with an open hand at the ghastly scene that had taken place outside. "The prophecies are clear. He will wipe out an entire kingdom, crush an entire people's way of life with his wickedness. It is foretold. Perhaps he is shielded from your god with some kind of powerful magic, but trust me Apollisian of Bargoe, the world will be better place when he is no longer in it."

Apollisian did not acknowledge Alexis' claims, but he wrestled with them in his mind. She was right in a lot of ways, but she just did not understand how his god manifested his powers through him. There was no hiding your heart to Stephanis. There was no haven for the unjust when Stephanis laid his eyes upon them. Apollisian turned to Alexis with a new argument. "And what of the swordsman, Jude? Sure he was friends of Lance, but I could have been called such. Why am I not in chains?"

Alexis shrugged her shoulders. "Jude was wanted by Central City on a charge of murder. So he was given to them. It is up to you humans to decide your own justice amongst yourselves."

Fury welled up inside of Apollisian. His face flushed deep red and he stepped closer to Alexis, inches from her face. His bright blue eyes were ablaze with passion and anger at the excuse she so casually offered.

"That's orc shit and you know it, Overmoon!" Apollisian screamed shaking his finger in her face. "If the damned magistrate wanted him or Lance, they could have had them before we left. I know as well as you those are trumped up charges by either Central City or your father!"

Alexis was shocked at Apollisian's flagrant curse. She had rarely heard the man speak a harsh word, even in battle, yet he spewed forth obscenities in her father's sacred room.

"They are not charges of mine, I assure you, Apollisian," said a soft but aged voice from the behind them. Apollisian turned to see that the king had entered the chamber unsuspectingly. He was wearing a thick green robe that seemed as if it should be too heavy for the frail elf to carry, but it floated on the wind like a dandelion seed in a soft breeze. "And I ask for your apology for defiling my throne room with such obscenities."

Apollisian bowed his head and went to his knee. "I beg your humble forgiveness, your highness. As I beg yours," he added, looking up to Alexis. She smiled a heart-felt grin and stared lovingly in his deep blue eyes. If only he had been an elf, she thought, but she knew no elf would ever have his unbridled passion that made him who he was.

"Rise, my trusted companion," the king said, gesturing the paladin to his feet. Apollisian towered over the elf king, but the king's commanding presence seemed to bridge the gap effectively.

Apollisian rose slowly and held his head in embarrassment. "I am so sorry, King Overmoon. I know not what has come over me."

"Sure you do, Apollisian. That is what makes you special among your people. You have the intelligence to know when something is not right, the wisdom to understand how to uncover that which is hidden, and the unyielding passion to pursue righteousness despite the strength of the opposition you may face. In all of my years, and trust me young man, there have been more than you can begin to fathom, I have never witnessed nor read any recordings of a human doing what you have done over the past two weeks. You have stood up to the Minok Elders, a feat that few elves will even attempt, in pursuit of what you know in your heart as right. You have battled a nightmare alongside the finest elven warriors in defense of their home, and you have earned the undying trust of an elven king. Never has an elf, let alone a human, achieved such greatness. Your name will be sung in ballads by my people for millennia to come, Apollisian Bargoe."

Apollisian ran his hands through his sleek blonde hair. "With all due respect, your highness, I care nothing for praise of your people or my standings in ballads. All I want..."

Before Apollisian could finish the king placed his finger over his lips. "And that, my son, is what makes you great."

Alexis squeezed Apollisian's hand and smiled warmly at her father. "We should go, father. Apollisian and I have a hard road ahead of us to discover whether the boy summoned the undead and if he did not, then who."

Apollisian turned in shock at Alexis and then back to the king. The elderly elf wore a smile of admiration for his beloved daughter. "Enjoy your time, daughter; it will be ever so short. And may Leska cradle you in her bosom and keep you and yours safe. I have a lot of work to do here. It will be some time before Minok is settled and I am afraid it will be lifetimes before it will recover." The king patted the surprised paladin on his clean-shaven face. "Goodbye, Apollisian Bargoe. May Stephanis guide your sword as well as he has guided your heart," the king said as he turned and began to stride from the chamber.

Apollisian started to respond but Alexis held him fast, pulling his face toward hers. With both hands on his cheeks she pulled his strong jaw down to hers and kissed him lightly on the lips before softly whispering to him as her eyes danced across his handsome face. "My name is Alexis Alexandria Overmoon, and I expect you to call me as such."

Kalen rubbed his narrow chin as he tapped his thin fingers on the thick oak desk of his chamber. The news was startling to him. All this time he had thought the Ecnal was the Abyss Walker when it was his own creation, the monster,

Trinidy. Kalen chuckled to himself at the irony of prophecy. No matter how you tried to change it, events would still take place shaping it to become exactly what you sought to avoid. No matter. He would arrange for his departure before the Abyss Walker arrived in Nalir. The challenging part would be how to find the Ecnal.

If he had the Ecnal here in the castle, the dead knight would sense him and bring his army of undead here and crush Hector like the prophecy predicted. Once the Ecnal was dead, the magic that held Trinidy together would break apart, sending the tortured soul back to the abyss and once again leave a pile of ragged bones. The plan was simple to Kalen, but the elements were becoming more and more difficult to bring about. It was obvious that Hector suspected his plotting against him, but to what extent? Kalen had little spies among the keep, and it was not unlike the wicked king to have servants tortured until they revealed something he suspected. And if they were innocent of the charges that Hector brought against them, the wicked man would still have them killed. Kalen smiled to himself. It was hard not to like a man of such ambition.

Kellacun stood impatiently in front of the elf's desk. She was eager to get her money and be on her way. She was not about to get involved with the elves from the Minok Vale. The fact that there was an army of skeletons battling the elves was more than enough reason to give the wererat assassin pause. She knew when she was in over her head and anything with enough power to make the dead walk again was more power than she wanted to meddle with. She had gathered as much information she dared and even paid a group of Greyshalks to attack the soldiers that were escorting the swordsman that traveled with the Ecnal, but the damned fool goblinoids were cut down. She knew that the Ecnal had not left the Vale, so he was still there, but whether he was alive or dead was beyond her. She had reported all of her findings, careful not to mix her surmises with the facts she had gathered but was sure to share both.

Kalen turned his gaze to the wererat assassin that stood before him. Kellacun was tall and wore her sleek burnished black leather outfit that hugged her form perfectly. She had two large thigh high boots with a red spider just under the cuff of the knee on the outside of each leg. She wore her long sleek black hair in a single pony tail, clasped with a silver pin that was a small dagger. She was the only wererat that Kalen had ever heard of that actually carried a silver weapon. Almost all lycanthropes did not wield weapons that could harm them in case the blade was lost in battle, but Kalen figured this dangerous little vixen had often crossed swords with her brethren and the hair pin came in handy on many occasions. Her long black cloak hung down over her, hiding the form of her breasts. That upset Kalen a bit. He liked gawking at her breasts. But he dared not get intimate with such a fiend. She had many tricks and getting close to her was too dangerous. Not that she ever offered to be intimate with him, but that was never an issue with Kalen. He took what he wanted, and there were few that were powerful enough to deny him.

Instead Kalen enjoyed mulling over the news she had brought and he enjoyed watching Kellacun squirm impatiently awaiting her money before she could flee his chamber.

The elf considered killing her right then and there. He surely didn't want the wrong people tracing her back to him. But then again, if the right people found out who he was looking for, they would seek him out in Kalen's favor, but what to happen above all else was that the boy should survive. If he died, Trinidy would cease to exist. Without the knight of death, how was he going to overthrow Hector?

Kellacun shifted her weight impatiently. The tight black leather that clung to her body creaked and popped. She fingered the bright red spider that was embroidered on the back of her gloves and eyed the dangerous elf cautiously. "I have done what you asked, Kalen. Now about my payment..," she said.

The elf looked up from his contemplation under his long silver hair. He slowly opened a drawer in his desk and withdrew a small brown leather pouch. He roughly set it on the top of the desk and then scooted it toward Kellacun. She quickly snatched up the pouch and stuffed it into her cloak. "Are there any other tasks you might need done?" Kellacun asked.

Kalen smiled a devious grin. "I do recall a certain task you performed quite well in the dungeons of Central City," the elf said with a sadistic chuckle.

Kellacun turned and entered the portal without another word. Kalen called out after her, but the portal quickly closed and in moments the small orange dot popped into nothingness.

Kalen rose from his chair and gracefully walked over to his large oaken bookshelf. He thumbed his chin a few seconds then pulled down an ancient tome. The old book seemed like it might crumble if he handled it too roughly. Kalen gently placed the ancient tome onto his reading podium and traced his fingers across the gilded platinum cover. He was close to having the ancient elven prophecies completely translated. Then he would have a better idea who the Abyss Walker really was, and more important, he would have a clear path his to rise of power.

Vlargcar erupted from the blackness of the campfire's edge. The humans could not see as well as he could in the dark and the orc used it to his full advantage. Vlargcar did not hear the men's startled shouts as he burst from the dark veil that surrounded them, nor did he hear the cry of pain as his heavy axe came crashing down into the shoulder of the first man. The crude orc weapon sliced deep into his enemy's shoulder, becoming wedged as if he had chopped into soft wet wood.

The men that were standing next to the orc whelp placed their hands on their swords and started to draw them. The others scanned the horizon looking for the other green-skinned beasts. They believed there had to be more; no single orc whelp would dare attack five men.

Vlargcar released his useless weapon as the dying human clutched at it and fell to his knees wide-eyed. Blood trickled out from around the thick blade and soaked into his armor. The orc reached down and grasped the dying man's long sword, placing his foot on the small of the human's back. With a metallic ring Vlargcar pushed the human with his foot and pulled the much lighter weapon free. Slicing the rope that held the dangling Amerix, Vlargcar spun and faced the four other men that circled him cautiously.

The dwarf tucked his head just in time as the hard frozen earth rushed up to meet him. He landed hard on the back of his shoulders and grunted under the force of the blow. He had difficulty seeing out of his left eye from the swelling. He struggled against the thick ropes that held him but quickly stopped, realizing he would need assistance in getting loose. He worked his chin and neck until he forced the dirty gag from around his mouth. "Cut me loose, whelp!" Amerix shouted and tried to sit up.

Vlargcar was too engrossed in battle to hear the dwarf. The long sword felt good in his large hands. It was light and he remembered how the dwarf had so many options in which to launch an attack. One of the men came in at Vlargcar with a low slash of his short sword. Vlargcar deflected the strike into the ground with his newfound blade. He smiled a wicked yellow-tusked smile at the speed of the sword. It was faster than his axe, much faster. Vlargcar stomped his foot down at the hilt of the blade he parried, forcing it from the man's hands. The short sword thudded into the frozen earth as the orc lashed out and kicked the soldier between the legs. The man grabbed himself and toppled over, moaning pitifully.

Another soldier lunged in to stab the orc in the exposed belly. Vlargcar was unaccustomed to the quickness of the long sword and nearly missed his parry. Steel rang against steel as he barely caught the end of the sword, sending the deadly thrust wide. The soldier quickly pulled his blade back from the thrust only to catch a bone-crunching punch square in the nose. Blood rocketed out from the soldier's face and he staggered and collapsed onto the cold ground. Vlargcar hooked his left foot under the short sword he had pinned to the ground and flipped it up into his hand as he ducked low under another strike. He brought the shorter, fast blade around behind his back and thrust it into the soft belly of the fourth guard. Releasing the short sword that fell with the dead solider, Vlargcar deflected an overhand slash from the final guard. Steel rang against steel as the weapons became locked. In an instant, Vlargcar reached up and grabbed the man by the throat. His dark green muscular fingers squeezed like an iron vise. The guard's eyes went wide as he struggled to escape, but in mere moments his throat was crushed and he collapsed.

Amerix struggled to his feet. If the fool orc was not going to cut him free, that was fine and dandy. But he was not going to let the whelp have all the fun. He stepped on both sides of the head of the man that Vlargcar had kicked in the groin. Placing his thick boots tight against the man's cheeks, he quickly shifted his hips and in a quick motion he snapped the man's neck. The other men had fled into the darkness while Vlargcar fought like a wild beast.

After watching the man's chest cease to rise and fall, Amerix went to the man who the orc had knocked unconscious. The man's nose was grotesquely broken and twisted to the right side of his face. Bright red blood poured from his nostrils and a small stream dripped from the man's ear. Amerix doubted the human would survive the horrible blow, but using the same method as before, Amerix snapped his neck just in case.

Vlargcar roughly pulled the short sword from the stomach of the human. The man was still alive and cried out in pain as the orc ripped the weapon free. Vlargcar stood over the bloody scene with both swords in hand, the thin narrow blades dripping hot sticky blood. Large gouts of steam poured from the orc's nose as he exhaled his hot breath in the cold air. He scanned the area for more enemies and when he was satisfied there were none, he turned to the old dwarf that stood grinning from ear to ear.

"Yer an orc after me own heart, Vlargcar," Amerix said taking in the full extent of the carnage. The orc was still but a boy, yet he was as vicious of a fighter as any orc. Amerix's smile suddenly faded at the thought of the dead men having families of their own. He was sad for the men. Surely they deserved to die, but he felt bad for the men's wives or sons and daughters. He was suddenly sad for them. Shaking off his sudden wave of empathy, Amerix motioned his head down at the thick corded rope that held him. "How 'bout cuttin' me loose, whelp?"

Vlargcar looked over at the dwarf and finally a bright smile crossed his face and his blue eyes shined with youthful happiness once again. Amerix marveled at how the whelp went from vicious killer to innocent child in mere moments. He would have doubted it was possible for those cobalt orbs to show such a fluctuation of emotions if he had not seen it for his own eyes.

Vlargcar took the keen short sword and easily sliced through the thick rope, letting the heavy bonds fall at the dwarf's feet. Amerix rubbed his wrists and arms, trying to get circulation back and picked up his gear.

"I don't suppose ye speak their foul tongue?" Amerix asked as he motioned to the wounded human that was lying on his back holding a horrible stomach wound made from Vlargcar's sword. Vlargcar looked down at the man and then turned back to Amerix shaking his head from side to side. Amerix shrugged his shoulders, pulling the heavy orc axe from the dead man's shoulder. He walked over to the wounded man and stared down. The man's eyes went wide and darted around, looking for some of his friends that would not come. Amerix decided to use the orc axe to finish off the man. He wasn't sure why he didn't want to use the magnificent long sword he had gotten from the human champion at the Torrent Manor. The act just seemed dirty to him, yet it had to be done. With a heavy slice, Amerix brought the crude orc weapon down and cleaved the man's head from his body. The severed head scooted a few feet across the cold earth and came to rest against a tree.

Amerix gave the axe back to Vlargcar. The whelp took it and smiled as he tossed the blades to the earth. The old dwarf looked down at the thin swords and then back to the orc. "Ye know what, whelp?" Amerix asked as he chewed on his bottom lip and stroked his blood-matted beard. "I think ye is better suited with the two swords than that ugly old axe."

Vlargcar frowned and pondered the idea for a moment.

Surely there were advantages to using a sword. He had noticed the many different attacks that could be used, but there was something about the raw power that he could summon using the axe to cut a vicious blow in his enemies. "I think you right, Brohe-tah, but I keep axe too, just in case."

Amerix nodded. The orc was smart also. Another trait that was unusual. Sure he was not a great sage, but he was more intelligent than any orc he had ever met. Though in truth he had never met one he hadn't killed. Amerix rifled through the men's pockets. He found seven silver crowns and fifteen coppers. Not a great sum, but the fact the men carried silver crowns meant they were not peasants or mere mercenaries. They usually carried non-minted coins. Amerix pondered the significance of the money for a moment and turned to Vlargcar. "What do ye suppose..?" Amerix trailed off. He stood in disbelief as Vlargcar held the man's severed head on a long sword and dangled it over the fire.

The orc turned and smiled his yellow-tusked smile. "I cook breakfast, Brohe-tah."

Amerix jumped up waving his hands. "No, no, no! We don't eat people, ye damned dirty orc!" Amerix screamed as he jerked the sword from Vlargcar's hands. He reared back and swung the sword sending the burning head flying into the night. The sound of charred skull bouncing off of the hard ground resounded through the forest.

Vlargcar frowned and stood up, placing his hands on his hips. Amerix turned to him. He was sure the orc had grown a full inch since he met him. "Ye don't eat people. Ye might of in the past, but not no more!" the old dwarf said with a grim glare that turned into a soft chuckle when he saw the confused look on the orc's face.

"Why? You never eat human?" Vlargcar asked with his hands on his hips.

Amerix chuckled again, but a disgusted look crept on his face from the mere mention of the idea. "No. I kill them, but I don't eat them."

Vlargcar frowned and shrugged his shoulders. "If you no eat them, how you know they no good?" Vlargcar asked.

Amerix was struck speechless with the orc's reasoning.

He tried to respond but merely stuttered.

"Human is..." the orc frowned trying to remember the word the dwarf used when he described the good tasting mountain nuts he was always talking about. He smiled when it came to him. "...Delicious."

Amerix shook his head and clapped the orc on the shoulder. "Me boy, humans are many things, delicious is not one of them."

Vlargcar frowned. He didn't understand why the dwarf didn't want to eat the humans. The meat was going to waste. To Vlargcar, waste was almost as bad as cowardice, maybe worse, but he knew he was different than Amerix in many ways. Perhaps this was yet another difference he had discovered. He was sure that if the dwarf thought something was wrong he wouldn't do it. So that is what Vlargcar would do, regardless of how ridiculous it was. "Ok. If Brohe-tah says they no good, then from now on, they no good," Vlargcar said with his wicked smile. "Anyway, I have many squirrels," he added as he pulled them out form his pouch. "I don't think the coward humans will be back for a while, let's eat."

Amerix nodded, though he wanted to be on his way. He did not like being discovered by humans. He figured since the battles, any dwarf was better off keeping to the shadows. Especially one that was friends with a dirty orc. "Speaking of squirrels," Amerix said with an accusing tone. "I like to know how those humans managed to sneak up on me and tie me up," Amerix said sarcastically, angry because Vlargcar left camp unattended and worse of all, left him asleep.

Vlargcar shrugged his shoulders. Amerix was usually so smart. "They club you in head while you sleep, and then tied you up. Don't you think?"

Amerix's jaw dropped. "Ye flamin orc-brained oaf! I *know* they did. Why in the name of Durion do ye think I was still asleep?"

"I think you tired, and didn't wake in time," Vlargcar responded confused at the question.

Amerix frowned and tightened his fists at his side. "I was still asleep, ye green-skinned monster, because ye...,"

Amerix said as he poked Vlargcar roughly in the chest. "did not wake me! Whenever one of us leaves camp, we have to wake the other, so no one can sneak up on us. Humans hate ye as much as they do me. Understand?"

Vlargcar smiled and lifted his head in realization. "Ohhhhh."

Amerix couldn't help but smile. The whelp may indeed be as stupid as all the other orcs. Vlargcar began pulling the fur off of the squirrels and cooking them over the fire. He pulled the guts out of five of them and left the guts in the other five. Vlargcar didn't like the squirrels cooked as much as he did raw, but he refused to take the guts out like Amerix wanted. If the silly dwarf wanted to eat dry juiceless food, he could, but that is where Vlargcar drew the line.

Amerix gathered up the swords in a pile. He checked to make sure they were not all the same, and was relieved when he found each one was different. Uniformity meant organization, and organization meant trouble. The old dwarf gathered up as much chain armor as possible and placed it in his pack. The pack was heavy, but he was strong enough, and he and the orc would need some armor sooner or later. He would fashion some as the nights went on, if he could find the right tools. He thought about maybe going into one of these southern towns the farmer talked about where they didn't hate the dwarves as much as the north. He might be able to buy something there. In the meantime, he cut two leather straps and made a shoulder and waist harness for the orc. He figured the orc could keep the short sword over his back and the long sword at his side and he could carry his great axe in his hand. Amerix couldn't wait to make some armor for the whelp. Once he was armored he would be quite a sight to behold.

Amerix glanced at the thin parchment he had found on one of the bodies. It had a drawing of what looked like a dwarf and a bunch of writing that he couldn't read. He thought when he bought his blacksmith's tools in town, he might ask someone what it meant. He hoped he didn't kill any men that were friends to a dwarf.

Stuffing the thin, dry parchment into his pack, just above

the thick pile of chain mail, Amerix pulled the five squirrels from the fire. The meat was hot and a little charred, but the warmth was welcome in the cold frigid air of the early morning. Amerix picked around the small bones as he ate, while Vlargcar crunched through them, eating the squirrel in its entirety. The old dwarf shook his head as he watched the young orc eat. Had he not gotten to know Vlargcar, he would have been disgusted by him as he would any foul orc.

After they were finished eating, Amerix quickly hurried them along to get further down the trail. The humans undoubtedly would return with more soldiers once it was told they were cut down by a dwarf and an orc. Amerix figured by human's usual cowardice they would stretch the story to ten or more orcs and dwarves. The thought made him chuckle as he made his way through the thick underbrush of the forest.

The day turned out to be a mild one. The temperature rose well above freezing and the once frozen ground turned soft and muddy on the surface. The sun rose high into the cloudless sky making Amerix sweat profusely from carrying the heavy weight of the chain armor in his pack. He frequently stopped, allowing the heavy straps to slide from his old shoulder. The leather pack hit the soft muddy ground and the rings of the chain mail made a resounding cling as it hit the earth. Vlargcar didn't miss stride as he scooped up the heavy pack and tossed it over his well-muscled shoulder. Amerix started to complain, but he was silenced by a wave of Vlargcar's hand.

For the next few weeks they traveled day and night, taking little rest and living off of what the orc managed to catch. Amerix taught Vlargcar everything he knew about fighting with a sword at night and they frequently practiced before going to sleep. The orc seemed to soak up everything the dwarf taught him and was eager to learn more, often having to be ordered to sleep. Amerix had found a road that ran north and south. Occasionally they saw a human merchant wagon hauling goods. The wagons were well armed with at least three armed men on each one and some even had large war dogs. Amerix feared the dogs more than he did the guards. He had faced humans before. They were weak and poor fighters. Yet they stayed well off of the road during the day to avoid any encounters with the merchants. If the merchant's guards attacked them they would have to kill them. Dead merchants and guards would surely attract attention.

The following night, after nearly being detected by a group of men in leather armor, Amerix and Vlargcar came across their first town. They stood at the top of a wooded hill. The farther south they had traveled, the warmer the days and nights became. Though it was still obviously winter, the trees had no leaves, and it was much warmer than when he was outside of Central City. He and Vlargcar sat down next to a large oak tree. He let the heavy pack down and leaned against it. Wiping his sweaty brow with the sleeve of his tunic, he pulled his waterskin and took a drink. Water ran from the corners of his mouth and ran into his silver-streaked beard. He passed the waterskin to Vlargcar. The orc took a long drink and gazed at the town. He had never seen a human village before. They didn't live in caves like he had thought. They lived in strange wooden structures that they had obviously built. He looked at Amerix who ran his thick stubby fingers through his long greasy hair.

The town was larger than he expected. It seemed there were well over three thousand humans living there, almost as large as Central City, but it seemed much poorer. There were no grand buildings of stone or marble statues. Their soldiers didn't wear plate armor like the soldiers in Central City did, and their weapons were not as fine of quality either. The town was inside a small valley with high hills on all sides. What was strange was that every building had a large stone foundation and had stairs that rose to the first level. Amerix looked closer and noticed that there were many water stains on the stone foundations, which led Amerix to believe the town must flood frequently. He scanned around the buildings looking for something that might resemble a blacksmith when he spied a small stone building. It had a dark black wooden staircase on the north side of it that led to the roof. On the roof was a man wearing bright brass colored plate armor with a red silk cape. There were two men on the ground just outside the door wearing the same armor. Amerix recognized the armor and capes from the battle at the Torrent Manor and at the battle of Central City. He didn't know what the significance of the uniform was, but he remembered that the men that wore those colored uniforms were much better fighters than any other human he fought, save for the champion that he fought at the Manor and at Central City.

Amerix gazed at the magnificent long sword that he got from that champion and then he wondered what the human was doing. Had he met the man on different circumstances he figured he may have liked him. But the persecution of his clan had superseded anything but the destruction of the keep and the city, though both battles seemed so long ago to him. Amerix drew the beautiful sword from its scabbard and gazed at its polished chrome finish. The bright blade shone in the pale moonlight of the cool winter night. The sword needed a name. Something so beautiful that he gained in such a memorable way surely needed a name. Amerix rubbed his heavily bearded chin and pondered what he could call the sword. Many names ran through his head, but all were names you might name an axe, or a hammer – names for large dwarven weapons, not a thin sleek long sword. Then out of nowhere it came to him, like someone had whispered the thought into his mind. *Songsinger.* Amerix smiled as he gazed down at the amazing weapon. Yes, Songsinger was a fitting name.

"Change. A person goes through changes as surely as the sun rises and sets, yet what causes these changes? Some argue change is set about by a traumatic event. It can happen that way, but as soon as the normalcy of life sets in, I am sure the person will return to the same character flaws, or strengths, that they possessed before the traumatic event occurred. For a person to truly change, the process is long and requires a lengthy support, or cause, if you will, by some event or influence. It wasn't until much later in my life that I learned of the transformation of the evil Amerix Stormhammer. I had only encountered the little beast once in my life, and that was early at the battle of Central City. I was merely trying to escape with my life and was caught up in the whole affair that really meant nothing to me whatsoever, save that I was in the wrong place at the wrong time. Though, had the dwarf not attacked the city, I would have surely found another way to translate those parchments instead of going to the Vale. It was the Vale that truly started me on the path of the prophecy, even though I had no idea it even existed. It took years for me to be changed by my horrible captors in Aten. It took Amerix about half a year for his change, though the need to guide young Vlargcar to a path of righteousness instead of the ways of an orc surely helped him look inside of himself. Amerix did quite a job on the giant orc. He was surely a sight to behold, the blue-eyed monster. I envy the orc's iron resolve. I doubt the cataclysmic end of life as we know it could tempt the orc to evil. If only Amerix and I had a lower level of intelligence, maybe we could have hung onto how we were before our own personal tragedies. Or perhaps the orc's simple view of morality was what protected him from wickedness. Regardless, the green-skinned forsaker saved more than just my life. He demonstrated the raw foundation of character that I still hope to one day achieve."

-Lancalion Levendis Lampara-

4
The Guise of Friendship

King Theobold reached with his ring-encrusted hand, ripped a leg from the roasted goose and dropped it on his clay ceramic plate. The plate was not overly ornate but had the engraved symbol of Beykla in the center. He wiped his greasy fingers on the white cotton towel that was next to him and picked up his heavy wooden soup bowl with both of his hands. Holding the bowl to his lips, he gingerly tipped it until the hot soup barely reached his mouth so as not to burn his lips. He sucked in a small mouthful of the spicy broth and made a crude sipping sound. Theobold then lowered the bowl and wiped his mouth with his towel. He took a deep breath and addressed the twenty or so other visitors that were supping with him in his grand hall.

The hall was longer than it was wide and housed a long narrow table that was made of polished cherry. The dark wood was stark in contrast with the long gleaming white linen that lined the table under the hundreds of foodstuffs and vegetable dishes that were placed in genteel silver trays. There were five different menorahs that held thick red candles that were aflame, giving the room a well-lit, but majestic quality.

Theobold wore his finest red velvet robe and his heavy golden crown. His son Darious sat to his right, garbed in equally fine robes, though the impatient boy scratched at the robe at the table. He was going to have to instruct the nannies to train the boy better. He would not want to be embarrassed at his functions. Theobold pondered for a brief moment, which would be worse – an uncouth son or an absent one. Both would show a sign of weakness to his nobles. And now at one of the most tumultuous times of his rule, weakness was the last thing he wished to show.

Every southern noble was present to hear about his proclamation with the dwarves of the Pyberian Mountains.

Theobold grasped his platinum-gilded chalice that was thickly covered in precious rubies. He stood up slowly and raised the chalice into the air. All of the other nobles rose also and held their goblets, though they were not nearly as ornate as the king's. Theobold motioned everyone to sit and cast an angry eye at his son, whom he doubted had risen at all. Yes, he was going to give those nannies a choice, either they be more stern with the boy in his lessons, or they would find themselves selling their bodies at the local taverns, because they would not be working at the palace.

Theobold turned to the nobles again. "Greetings, my nobles from far and away. I welcome you tonight in my home, the home of our fathers, and the home of our father's fathers. I would like to announce that the war with the dwarves is well at hand and has all but been quelled. We suffered a minor loss at the Torrent Manor by the honorless fiends, but we were much more prepared at Central City. We routed their attack and dispersed them. I made it clear to their king, that if they did not flee back to the mountains we would crush their entire way of life. I plan to sign a treaty with the bearded folk soon and I am willing to answer any questions you might have in regards to that treaty," Theobold said with a smile. He tried to list the dwarves as despicable enemies, but kept the condescending tones as light as possible since it was rumored the southern nobles were sympathetic to their plight.

A noble who sat on the far end of the table cleared his throat as he stood up to speak. Doogan Raymer always wore all dark-colored tunics and kept his trend tonight with a deep blue silk outfit. "What about the mines, my lord? The little folk have refused to trade any precious gems or metals and the price has shot through the roof. It is becoming harder every day for a man such as me to properly clothe and decorate my house with such ridiculous costs."

Theobold lowered his hands to quiet the soft murmurs in the crowd as they silently agreed with the Nobleman Raymer's query. "Fear not, Nobleman Raymer. I have addressed that item in the treaty and demand that the dwarves trade with us at a fifty percent decrease in price to offset the toll we have paid in battle." Another Nobleman rose. He wore an angry scowl that seemed spawned out of the abyss. The king recognized him well. He was Kareeg Hutt. His brother had been a captain at the Torrent Manor. He demanded the blood of every dwarf in the Pyberian Mountains.

Nobleman Hut was not a rich man by normal means of wealth, but he owned expansive tracks of land and had a strong following of the people that lived on his estates. He led his life simply and never wore silk clothing or baubles save for when he attended meetings with the king and even then he wore the less than any other noble might wear on an everyday occasion. He was the largest supporter of open war with the dwarves in the north. "My Liege...," Nobleman Hut began. "Surely you do not intend to make peace with the filthy dogs. Let me remind you my brother was mercilessly slain at the hands of wicked bastard dwarves. His blood cries out to me from the bellies of the vultures that he was left to. We had peace with them before they attacked. How can peace again actually keep our people safe?"

Theobold smiled in attempt to disarm him. But it was clear after a few moments that the Nobleman was stark-raving mad. Only war would sate his hunger for revenge. The king replied, "Nobleman Hut, my deepest sympathies for your lost brother, but many lost brothers in the battle of the Torrent Manor. They lost husbands, children, wives, and many lost the same at Central City. The wisest thing we can do is to decrease the cost of their wares and control the flow of goods in and out with the presence of our powerful army."

Nobleman Hut sat back down slowly and held his head up with his hand. "I recall the tariffs we had in place before the bearded demons mercilessly killed our brethren. We had taxes and embargos in place then that were controlled by our military. I recall that very military being overrun and killed to the man in a matter of hours. How will this be different, my Liege?"

The king smiled inside. He always liked Hutt, and in truth he agreed with him in more ways than one. He had every intention of killing the dwarves, only he had to do so with support of the south, or they might try to sabotage his rule. He was not going down as the only king that did not expand the lands of Beykla. He was going to be remembered as the greatest king Beykla had ever had. After the treaty, he would make it impossible for the dwarves to live with the insanely high taxes. They would attack the army again and then he would have all the backing in the south to wipe the dirty little folk from the face of his country. By then he hoped to have more than half of the southern nobles slain and replaced with men that were loyal to him. Surely a tricky endeavor, but he had plenty of time to set it up. Theobold took a deep breath and smiled a knowing grin at the frustrated nobleman.

"Nobleman Hutt, I am glad you asked. It will be different this time for a couple of reasons. One, the entire western army is going to sit on their doorstep and oversee everything. And as you know, the western army is five times the size of the population that was at the Torrent Manor. Secondly, for the lives lost, half of the dwarves' clan will be relocated to the south at the Lalin Plateau. They will mine the north side of the Plateau just south of Terrace Folly. The central army will camp outside of Terrace Folly, boosting the economy of the small town, and overseeing the daily operations of the dwarves there. With their numbers split and an army sitting on each of them, the dwarves will not dare defy us a second time."

The nobles all muttered amongst themselves. Nobleman Hut grinned slightly, but it was obvious he was not completely satisfied. One of the nobles from the south stood up. "My Liege, surely you do not intend to enslave these people?" the nobleman asked. Nobleman Hut wanted to argue, but he knew it was not allowed to break in on another noble. It was surely bad form that often lost the respect and support from the other noblemen.

The king smiled and gestured his hands in a disarming way. "Of course not, Nobleman Gersian." The king had learned that Nobleman Jordan Gersian, one of the biggest supporters of the dwarves, was secretly planning to pull away from the north when he wiped out the bearded folk in open war. It was obvious he was upset that he lost the fuel to his treasonous fire. "I intend to indenture them for a time, so to speak. It may seem a long time to us humans, but it will be no more than a fifth of their lives."

All the nobles in the room murmured amongst themselves. Some drank large portions of their wine, while others shook their heads, but what pleased Theobold was that none argued any disconcertion. He cleared his throat and addressed the nobles again. "It would seem the war party took place without the consent of the dwarven king," he let the men speak amongst themselves before he continued. "There was a rogue leader, a general named Amerix Stormhammer. I have already taken the liberty of dispatching warrants for his arrest to the four corners of our kingdom and even petitioned the aid from the kingdom of Tyrine to the south, and the Kai-Harkians to the northwest. I doubt he would try to flee through Aten, and if he did, the foul wenches would surely kill him regardless of any warrant of mine. I anticipate the rogue general's capture within the year. Once he is captured, he will be executed in Central City after a grand celebration. I have already informed King Tharxton that my men will make regular inspections of their cities and land to ensure they are not hiding the rogue general."

Nobleman Gersian rose to his feet angrily. "My king, surely the dwarves did not approve of our men intruding in their sacred homeland."

Theobold smiled as he looked directly at Nobleman Raymer. It was important for Theobold to convey his support to the northern leader. "They approve as equally as our citizens at the Torrent Manor and our citizens at Central City approved when they intruded on our homeland. Just as our citizens had little choice, they have little choice. If they did not accept my terms I would have been forced to conquer them," Theobold said, turning to Nobleman Gersian and looking the aging man sternly in the eye. "That was the only way I could preserve their culture without needlessly endangering the lives of our citizens further."

Nobleman Gersian did not protest. Though he did not look satisfied it would have to do for now. Theobold had to meet with the dwarven king next month and he needed the nobles' blessing before he left the country to govern itself while he was preoccupied. "I asked for a vote of contention with the treaty from my nobles. Not out of necessity, but out of courtesy that I, and the kings before me, have extended to the noblemen of our country since the recording of history," Theobold asked. Though it was just as he said, there had been many king's that went against the nobles when they did not vote in contention with him, though he found they reported less taxes and opposed him for years to come after. Theobold wanted to avoid going against them if he could, but regardless he had to keep the south from tearing the country in two.

The nobles voted by a show of hands. Both sides were reluctant but by the end, Nobleman Gersian and Nobleman Raymer raised their hands in agreement, however a precarious agreement it may have been. Theobold smiled. He had achieved what he set out to do. He had placated the north with harsher treatment and the promise of death for the rogue general, Amerix, and he had avoided war to appease the south, though in truth he wasn't sure how long he could keep both sides happy. All he needed to do was meet with the dwarven king Tharxton and get the treaty signed. He hoped some of his hired mercenary groups could find a dwarf that looked similar to Amerix.

Theobold needed some kind of victory to hold the country together. The civil war would be over soon with Andoria and Adoria. There would much land to grab. The nobles finished their meal and discussed other topics such as the price of grain and upcoming festivals. The nobles of the south didn't linger and left as soon as it was proper. The northerners huddled amongst each other filling their own heads with their self-proclaimed greatness. Yes, Theobold was going to be known in history as Theobold the conqueror. It was all just a matter of time.

The sun was high in the eastern sky sparsely covered

by dark flat purple clouds that seemed more like a blanket than bulbous masses. The thin billows floated ever so slowly, taunting the cold earth with brief glimpses of the warming sun. Amerix sat by the small fire trying to absorb as much of its heat, though the small flame made little. He had kept the fire at little more than embers to try to avoid attention in the night. They had camped close to the town and he did not want any roaming militia to stumble across their camp. The old dwarf used a sturdy stick and picked at the matted dry blood that was in his beard from the fight with the humans a few weeks back. He didn't bother cleaning himself because of the cold, but he decided to try to make himself less conspicuous since he was going into the town today. He dumped a small handful of frigid water from his waterskin and used his dirty hand to try to soften up his hard, crusted beard. He had worked at the task most of the morning and used his reflection from the polished blade of Songsinger to monitor his progress. It was slow going, yet he had nothing but time. Vlargcar had stayed up late hunting in the night and the longer he took cleaning himself, the longer the boy could sleep.

Amerix set down his stick and checked the meat that was slowly cooking on the weak fire. Amerix never thought he would grow tired of one kind of food, but Vlargcar proved a terrible hunter unless he was hunting squirrels, which he provided with abundance. Amerix felt useless most of the time, but he had never hunted outside of the under mountain, where the game was less dangerous and more docile, but flightier and harder for a man with short stubby little legs to run down. The meaty little morsels were cooking fine and the old dwarf set back to his task.

He had already prepared his rusted chain armor the best he could and cleaned his tunics and breaches. They hung from a low branch drying next to the warm fire while Amerix wrapped himself snuggly in the itchy winter blanket. The old dwarf looked over at the sleeping orc. With a face as ugly as the whelp's, he figured the little monster would snore loud enough to make a dragon whine, but never had he heard the little blue-eyed whelp so much as snort when he was sleeping. Amerix figured it probably had something to do with the way his people lived. Though he remembered several times waking up to a blue-eyed, green-skinned face glaring down with bright yellow tusks asking him to sleep quieter because the woods were making sounds back.

Amerix took small steps over to his hanging clothes to keep his blanket from falling down from around him. He reached out from under the wool cover and felt his breeches and tunic. They were dry for the most part, but under the arms and around the groin were still cold and a little damp. He figured it would be summer before those areas dried fully with this fire, so he pulled the clothes from the branch. His old teeth chattered as he placed on the tunic. The belly was warm but the cold damp armpits gave him more than a chill. As he placed on the breeches he had to take a deep breath and hold it in when the damp area came in contact with his groin. He quickly placed on his boots and ran to the small fire, straddling it. He smiled in relief as the crouch of his pants warmed. While standing over the small glowing embers, he reached down and laced his boot with his cold, stubby fingers. His boots had held up considering the terrible strain he had placed on them, but even they were beginning to show signs of irreparable wear and would need to be replaced soon. He glanced over at the orc's bare green feet that stuck out from under his blanket. The orc must have grown another inch in the last two weeks or so. He was a bit taller than Amerix now and he was obviously becoming thicker around the chest. Amerix shook his head from side to side as he straddled the embers with his hands on his hips. It was going to be difficult to clothe the whelp if he kept growing like that.

Amerix reluctantly stepped from the fire and heaved his heavy chain over his head and slid into it. The weight of the armor felt good, but the links were very cold and he hopped back over the fire again. He rubbed his calloused hands and lowered them, shaking his head and chuckling to himself. Here he was, Amerix the Great, Amerix the Mighty, a horrible foe and one of the best dwarven warriors of all time, and he was huddled over the fire like a young dwarven soldier who was wet behind the ears. His old bones just seemed to not function in the cold like they used to. His smile quickly faded when he thought of the old dwarven warrior's creed:

'Twas a grand day I came into the world,
always shitting and pissing meself.
But woe the day I dropped me sword,
and become pampered with riches and wealth.
I promise to grow old from victories in battle,
not from the naggings of me wife.
Rather me enemy's sword find me heart
than be lame and diapered at the end of me life.

Amerix recited the ancient dwarven soldier's creed a few times and forced himself to step away from the warm fire. He was surprised at how difficult it was to make himself move. It really felt silly to make himself suffer just to show how much of soldier he was. But looking back, he used to run around in the snow naked to train to fight when he couldn't feel his fingers. It made sense to him still, kind of, but now he almost would rather sit by a fire rather than be filled with it.

The old dwarf strapped his scabbard on with a sad face. Old age was surely well set within him. He was older than any dwarf that was a soldier, and older still than any of the elders, who had a hard time keeping their bowel movements from soiling their pants, yet he still lived and fought.

Amerix figured the fire in him had burned longer and hotter than any other dwarf, but now, now his fire was like the warm glow of the flame that stood before him. It provided just enough heat to function and soon would be nothing more than cool ashes. Amerix never wanted to die old in a bed, but what recourse did he have? He could not simply allow himself to be killed by an enemy. Was it his fault that there was no warrior alive that could match steel with him? Yes, he had became too good, taught himself too much, now there was no one to defeat him. He shook his head and kicked the orc lightly in the foot. Vlargcar opened his bright blue eyes instantly but did not move his body at all. With

the quick precision in which the orc's eyes took in everything, he saw in an instant and gauged whether he needed
to erupt in a bloody fury or smile at his dwarf friend. It was
the blue-eyed orc's smile that made Amerix sad and happy
at the same time. He was glad the orc had honed his skills to
fight, but he was sad that his own had faded with the passing of time. "I be going to town today. If I do not return by
the height of the sun, leave me for dead, or ye will soon be."

The orc nodded reluctantly. They had discussed that
possibility. Though Vlargcar wanted to rush down and slay
the entire village for harming him, it took Amerix some time
to convince the orc to carry on. The orc was as ferocious as
he was fearless – a trait that Amerix kept honed as sharp as
the blade of his axe.

The dwarf started down the steep hill with both of his
hands snugly tucked under the straps of his backpack. He
didn't carry the chain armor with him, but added a few of
the supplies from camp. He planned on giving the guise of
being an adventurer. He also didn't want anyone from the
town recognizing the chain armor, if some of the men were
indeed from this village. Amerix doubted they were, but he
had learned he knew little of human culture.

The dwarf made his way to the base of the hill and
walked toward the house he suspected was a smithy. He
saw children playing outside of a village home with sticks
shaped like swords and a dog barked and nipped at their
heels as they jumped about. There was a steady stream of
black smoke that came from the chimney of the second
smaller building that was behind the home and Amerix saw
a large pile of scrap iron that had not been melted down.
There were a lot of old bent or bits of horseshoes overflow-
ing from a decrepit wooden barrel that was stacked next to
the bars of scrap iron. The kids stopped playing as soon as
they saw Amerix and ran into the smaller house. The dog
ran toward him barking, though Amerix could tell the dog
did not think of him as an intruder. Its long shaggy tail was
wagging from side to side and it tossed its head back in long
bellowing barks instead of usual menacing growls of an animal trying to intimidate. Amerix paused about thirty feet

from the smaller house and kneeled in front of the dog. He pulled a piece of meat from his pack and extended it out in front of him. The weary dog had mud encrusted in its long brown fur and a few burs in its ears but seemed to well fed and cared for.

The animal sniffed the air and took a few steps toward Amerix. He snatched the meat from his hand timidly and backed away, gulping the meat down quickly as if the dwarf might change his mind and try to take it back. The dog finished the treat and wagged his tail as he approached the dwarf again. Amerix took off his pack, set it on the ground and fished out another piece to hand to the dog. This time the shaggy brown mutt let Amerix pat his head as he eagerly ate the meat.

"Shags, come here," a man called out from the open door of the small building. He was average height for a human and to Amerix's delight, he wore a heavy leather smelter's apron that was covered with scorch marks and soot, the sign of a smithy. The dog turned back to the shed and tucked his tail as he slowly trotted back to the man. Amerix didn't know what the man had said and quickly realized it was going to be difficult communicating with him. The old dwarf placed his hands up in a defensive manner and approached the smithy. He wasn't imposing by any means, but Amerix detected a slight gleam in his eye that told of battles of old and sights that he would have just as soon forgotten. Amerix knew how the man may have felt. He had too many memories in his long life that he had learned were better off forgotten. "What do you want, dwarf?" the man asked in almost perfect dwarven tongue.

Amerix was almost staggered as if struck with a mighty blow. Never would he imagine in a thousand years that a human in some backwoods hamlet would be able to speak his language. Amerix immediately became suspicious and a wave of hate poured over him. How dare this human scum defile his sacred language by letting it roll from his tainted mouth. How dare he...Amerix paused. No, that was not right. This man had nothing to do with his family's death. Amerix composed himself and ran his thick hand down his silver-streaked beard, smoothing it. "I have traveled many miles from the south, adventuring and the like. I was hoping to purchase some blacksmithing tools from ye. Nothing grand, maybe an apprentice set, if ye have one to spare," Amerix asked, trying to be humble.

The man nodded slowly and measured the dwarf. "I have much work to do, can you smith?"

Amerix smiled a wide grin. "Sir, I can smith better than most dwarves can drink," Amerix boasted.

The man smiled out of the corner of his mouth. "Let's make a deal, then. You smith for me a couple of days and I will give you the set for free."

Amerix mulled the thought over in his head. He didn't want to stay near the town but if he pushed on, the man might be suspicious. It would be fun to smith for a while. It had been a long time once he worked a forge. Plus, it would easier to construct chain mail for him and the orc if he had a few nights to work, rather than being on the trail. "I accept, smithy, but I will sleep at me camp south of town. You know how me kin have a bad effect on folks."

The man nodded slowly. "Aye, I do. Come back tomorrow morning and I will have work for you."

Amerix smiled. This was working out better than he had ever imagined. "Aye, I will. My name's Am...," Amerix choked. He almost said his name. That might be recognized. "Am Neeison."

"Well met, Am," the man said as he extended his hand and grasped Amerix's. "My names Thomas. Thomas Smith."

"Well met, indeed," Amerix said as he released the man's hand and turned to pick up his pack. As Amerix walked back up the hill, he couldn't believe how good his luck was today. Durian must be smiling down on him.

The man turned and went back into his small building. The heat from the forge assailed him as he closed the door and exhaled deeply. He grabbed his cloak from a brass peg that was fastened to the back of the door and darted out of his shop. "Tend the forges for me, boys. I have some unexpected business in town."

The boys smiled eagerly and rushed into the small building, trying to push each other down to get in the door first, all the while, Shags the dog barked playfully at their heels. Thomas hurried across town, holding his heavy cloak close to his body to keep out the chilling wind. He made his way through town, ignoring calls of morning and greeting until he stopped in front of a small brick building on the north side. He walked to the front of the small stone structure and opened the heavy wooden door. The inside of the building was well heated. There was a large fireplace on the right hand wall and on the left side of the room was a large desk. Directly in front of him was a narrow archway that was filled with two men dressed in splint mail armor that gleamed like polished brass and they wore bright red silk tunic and breeches. The man behind the desk wore plate mail armor of the same colors and he rubbed his new grown beard. "What can I do for you this glorious morning under our king, citizen?" the man asked.

Thomas wavered slightly, and then gathered himself. "I was approached by a dwarf this morning wanting to buy smithy tools."

The royal guardsman leaned back in his chair and gulped down some wine directly from the bottle. He set the bottle back down on the desk roughly. "Dwarves tend to need those kind of things, smithy. Fear not, though, their army was turned back by us brave soldiers, by the blessing of the king may his light shine on us all."

Thomas sighed. The hell with the king. Had the man not been so unyielding with the bearded folk, they would have never attacked. But that did not excuse the murder that went on there. "This dwarf was over five foot tall and had a long black and silver-streaked beard that was not braided..."

The royal guardsman sat up in his desk and suddenly took interest in what the man was saying.

Thomas continued. "He claimed to be coming from the south, but his clothing was wintry, suggesting he came from the north, since the farther south you go the warmer it gets. He wore a long sword, an unusual weapon for a dwarf. The sword was polished and new, where his armor and clothing was old and worn out. He claimed to be an adventurer that was hard on the road, yet he fed my dog fresh meat that suggested he has been camping nearby. Had he been traveling by, like he said, he would have had salted meat. And lastly, the dwarf is old, very old, much too old to be adventuring. He started to give me his name, he paused, and said it was Am Neeison. I believe he started to say Amerix. Amerix Alistair Stormhammer."

The guard eyed the blacksmith curiously. "And how did you speak with this dwarf? I suppose he just walked right up to and said hello in perfect common?" the guard asked sarcastically.

Thomas narrowed his eyes in impatience. "I understand there is a large reward for the capture of Amerix. I want it noted that I mentioned that he was in the area. When he is caught, I want some of the reward. Stephanis knows my family needs it."

"Now see here, Thomas. I know you think you saw..."

Thomas cut the guard off. "Secondly! Tell your captain that Thomas Arwar of Central City is employing the dwarf at his leisure and I would appreciate his immediate response to this matter," Thomas said as he turned and started out of the small royal guardhouse.

"Jenkins!" the man called out to one of the guards that were standing in the doorway.

"Yes, Sergeant?" the guard asked.

"Find me anything you can on this Thomas Arwar as soon as possible."

"Yes sir," the guard said as he turned to go up the stairs to the second floor of the small guard house.

"Oh, and Jenkins," the sergeant called back.

The guard paused halfway up the stairs and turned back down. "Sir?"

"Notify Captain Oswald Thorrin that someone claiming the name Thomas Arwar says he is employing the Amerix Alistair Stormhammer and requests his immediate audience. The Captain is in Central City. Send a message pigeon. I don't know who this Thomas is, but I am not going to take any chances with the name Amerix floating around," the sergeant said with a sneer.

"Consider it done, Sir," the guard said as he hurried up the stone stairs of the small guardhouse. The sergeant sat back and pondered the events that took place that day. Perhaps he should have the man watched. If the man could be proven to be helping the dwarf, perhaps he could show Thomas was a traitor and keep all of the reward himself. Yes, this could prove to be a good week after all.

King Theobold sat on his heavy warhorse outside of the remains of the Torrent Manor. The once proud keep was merely a battered shell of its former self. The large stone-walls that once were strong and straight were now battered and beaten, sagging in on themselves. The two great stone battlements that overlooked the damaged portcullis were black from fire. The north battlement had partially collapsed and the chain rigging that hoisted the great portcullis sagged low and was now covered in bright orange rust. Brown grass almost as tall as a man now littered the inner courtyard that was once covered with a bright green field of lush vegetation. The portcullis had been boarded up by his order and the place was declared a national tomb, to never be entered under penalty of death. Many thousand men, women and children lost their lives under the ruthless cunning of the dwarves from the Pyberian Mountains. King Theobold thought it fitting to remind himself of the lives lost before he traveled the remaining hundred or so miles to make a treaty with the villainous bearded people.

A bright winter sun shone down from twilight and glinted off of his polished golden plate mail as his bright crimson silk cape fluttered in the cold north wind. He removed his great helm and rested the ornate headset on the horn of his saddle. Taking in the view of the entire western army was a sight to behold. Some thirty thousand soldiers littered the country side. Only the commanding officers allowed to camp in the outer courtyard of the Torrent Manor were within ear shot and the remaining soldiers were camped throughout the dense forest. Theobold's horse impatiently pawed at the hard frozen ground with its front hoof and snorted. A cloud of steam erupted from the heavy warhorse's nose and floated up past its golden barded head. Theobold patted the animal's neck to calm it and then motioned to Edgar Sorenson. Edgar was the king's closest friend, advisor, and a powerful cleric of Surshy, the Water Goddess.

Edgar trotted his horse over to the king. Edgar was dressed in a cobalt colored plate mail bearing crossed tridents over a multitude of waves and a flowing silk azure cape dangled over his back. He had a heavy war mace strapped to his saddle and a wooden staff with a fist-sized sapphire gem resting across his lap. He strode over to Theobold confidently, yet he showed deep obsequiousness to his king. When his horse stopped alongside of Theobold's, Edgar bowed his head low in salute. "Yes, My King?"

Theobold regarded the cleric with a warm creased smile that had a commanding air about it. "I wish to regard my men. Will you amplify my voice so that many may hear?"

Edgar nodded his head again. He grasped the small wooden holy symbol that hung from his neck. He chanted a few unintelligible words then turned back to the king. "By the grace of Surshy it shall be so."

Theobold nodded slightly and turned to his men. The leather cracked and popped from his saddle and his metal armor grated under the shift of his weight. "Good morning mighty soldiers of the western army and faithful warriors of the crown."

Theobold said, pausing as the men raised their weapons high in the air and let out a deafening cheer. The resounding roar echoed across the forest shaking the trees and like a thunder clap. When they died down he spoke again. "We are here before the blessed tomb of the men, women, and children that were viciously cut down under the vindictive blades of the Pyberian dwarves," Theobold was forced to give pause again as the men roared angry shouting curses and promise of death and destruction to the bearded folk. He lightly patted the empty air to quiet the men. "It will do us well to remember we are not here to make war with them in a conventional fashion." This time the men muttered amongst themselves. They had been told they were not going to attack the dwarves but many hoped they would anyway. "We are going to camp outside of their home for a long time. We are going into their homes when we wish, to inspect what we wish. We are going to take half of their numbers and escort them to the Lalin Plateau where they will mine for our glorious country for free. We will impose our laws of justice on them, and they will submit."

"What if they do not, great king?" a man called out from the crowd. Others echoed the man's question with similar shouts.

Theobold waited for the crowd to quiet. He smiled a devious grin. "If they do not submit, they will be crushed."

The men erupted in cries of battle and promises of death again. Theobold smiled at his men's enthusiasm. It would be needed in a few years when he decided to make war with them. He patted the air again softly and the men quieted down. "I wanted to stop here to remind us that our enemies, regardless of how superior our numbers are, regardless of how timid they may appear, are cunning ruthless killers. It will do us well to remember that and keep a diligent watch so that if they think to catch us sleeping like they did our brethren of the Torrent Manor, we will rise up and slaughter them in the Torrent's name. We will move out in the morning. Drink well tonight and eat heartily. It will be a time before we stop again."

The men raised another cheer chanting the king's name. "Theobold! Theobold! Theobold!"

The king nodded to Edgar and he waved his hand dismissing the dweomor that amplified his voice. The cleric moved his horse closer to Theobold. The animal protested at first with a toss of its head, before stepping reluctantly near the king's sable stallion. "An inspiring speech, My Lord."

Theobold eyed the cleric for a moment and a wry smile cracked his face. "Thank you, Edgar. But we will see how much inspiration holds after the long march into Pyberia."

Edgar nodded and gazed out distantly at the mighty western army. The army was larger than the army of most kingdoms, yet Theobold commanded three others like it. "I am to leave this night to head east, My King. There are wild reports of an undead army sweeping into Minok. The rumors are too similar and widespread for them to be entirely false. And by the age of the rumors, if there is an army, it should be hitting the Vale by now. Where this army came from, My Lord, I know not, but surely it needs investigated in case, if it does exist, it turns west or east into one of our cities."

The king nodded. He was aware of the wild reports of the undead army and it did strike him as odd. Regardless of whether the reports were true or not, he would make claims that the evil dwarven mages summoned the nightmarish creatures. It might even work to his favor if the army sacked a town or two. Theobold was not worried about the undead regardless. He commanded the greatest kingdom in the world. No one had ever conquered an inch of Beyklan soil. And no one ever would as long as he was king. Theobold turned to Edgar and rubbed his chin with his cold gauntleted hand. "I agree it needs looked in to. Go to Dawson and command the mage tower to support a campaign of mages into the Vale. Then send word for Central City to defend the eastern bridge in case of attack."

Edgar nodded thoughtfully and bowed from the top of his horse. "As you command, My King. Shall I depart tonight, or in the morrow?"

Theobold grinned. "Why, tomorrow, of course."

Edgar removed his gloved hand and took the king's in a powerful handshake. The two men stared at each other in the eye. One was the king, the other an advisor, but at that moment the two men were equals – longtime friends that shared the same ambitions for their country. After a moment they released their grasps. Edgar turned his horse and trotted back to the lavish tents that were set as a makeshift church for the officers. His acolytes had dispersed among the men setting up single tents and small shrines so that they might worship before they go to bed. Many of the men followed Stephanis, the god of Justice, but praying to the elemental gods was not a violation of their devotion.

Theobold turned his horse and rode to his personal

quarters. The tent was constructed of heavy crimson fabric that hung down from the tent supports like thin walls. The tent itself had four walls set up in a large square. Its top was cone shaped that concaved within itself, having a singular golden pike that was fastened at the tip of a central pole. There were many golden-fringed tassels that hung down from the corners of the lavish tent. Many great banners depicting symbols of heroism and conquest of past campaigns hung from banner poles that were stood up outside of the tent's entrance. Four large honor guards dressed in full plate mail armor stood with their arms resting on the hilt of their great broad swords that were shoved into the ground directly in front of them. They stood motionless and did not speak as the king walked by and into his grand tent. Scents of spiced soup wafted from the inside. Small candles flickered on iron sconces as a plump man stirred a large black cooking pot that hung over a fire at the far end of the tent. The man wore red silk clothing with a dull brown apron that protected the expensive garments from the soup splashes. The rest of the room was furnished with heavy oaken furniture and the floor was lined with great fringed rugs that bore a mosaic of colors and designs.

Theobold tossed his helm onto the felt-padded cot that he slept on and started removing his armor. He tossed his gauntlets onto the table and unfastened the thick leather straps that held his breast plate in place.

The cook poured a thick ladle full of soup into a polished silver bowl and placed it on the table next to the king's gantlets. He then opened a small chest and withdrew a red velvet towel. The cook opened the cloth and removed the silverware that was rolled inside and placed both next to the bowl of soup. The cook bowed deeply. "Does My Lord require anything else?"

Theobold continued to remove his armor, sliding his heavy chain mail over his head, tossing it onto the floor next to his breast-plate. "No, that will be all."

The cook kept his bow and backed away from Theobold, then stood up. "Shall I retire then, Sire?"

Theobold waved his hand in dismissal. "Yes, good day."

The cook turned and walked from the tent. A blast of cold air ripped through the loose structure briefly as the cook refastened the thick flaps that acted as the king's door. Theobold sat down on the cot wearing his small clothes and removed his leggings. Tomorrow he and his men would march into the Pyberian Mountains. The mountains were dangerous and not patrolled by his men. He doubted a force this size would meet any opposition, but he was sure he would lose more than a few scouting parties. Lazing back on the soft cart, he ran the imagined encounter with the dwarf king through his head over and over. After eating half of the soup, he placed the polished silver bowl on the wooden chest next to his cot and drifted off to sleep.

Dark, billowing clouds with hints of bright sulfurous yellow cores danced and shifted along the sky of the deep Abyss. Great winged beasts and half-men soared across the sky, occasionally coming into violent contact with each other. Sometimes these confrontations ended in the death of one or the other, but most frequently one escaped and the other gloated. The same confrontations occurred throughout the Abyss from the smallest gweits to the largest arch demon. Every demon of every type was vying for power – to move up in station and command those who were once under them. There were no friendships here, only temporary alliances that teetered on equivocal power. Once one demon was able, or it was advantageous to kill the other demon it was allied with, there was no hesitation. One less demon was one step closer to more power. A few demons sought power in the Abyss by making alliances with much more powerful demons and, riding their rise to power, were able to command those that were conquered.

Kornicus was one such demon. He was small, about three feet high. He had large oversized bat wings with a single long black talon at the tips. His bald, knotted head was covered with thin green skin that clung to his bony frame. His large hands had long slender fingers that bore long sharp talons, as did his tiny feet. His legs were small and probably would function only to hold his weight for brief periods of time.

Kornicus hovered above the expansive room that was carved out of raw stone. The room was shaped like a half sphere with a large, undecorated dome at the top. The room, however, was adorned with bright colors of clothing and a myriad of dwarven, elven, and human symbols. There was no door to the structure. No way in, and no way out. Kornicus had served here for over three thousand years. Before that, he had served the powerful Archdemon Dadramedion. Dadramedion had sought to kill Kornicus when the little demon failed a menial task. It was then that he met Delania. At first he suspected she was an agent of Dadramedion but he quickly noticed she was nothing like any other succubus he had ever been in contact with. She was just as all other succubae – disgusting in appearance, looking like a horrid human female, but she actually was nice to the little demon. Even after being with the succubus for over a thousand years, he still suspected she would turn on him and betray him at any moment; it was just the way of the Abyss. Yet day after day she did not. He knew she was especially sly to keep the facade going so long. Only the most wicked demons could keep it up, but he was not about to show her his trust, for fear that she'd step in and stab him in the back. He knew she could kill him at any time, but she wanted to wait until he trusted her, until he saw her as more than a master, then she would crush him. He knew she wanted to see the devastation in his eyes as she choked the life from him. That is why Kornicus served her. She was quite possibly the most cunning wicked demon on the entire Abyss. Kornicus grew impatient often, wishing she would conquer at least a few lesser demons, but he knew if he waited long enough, he would be rewarded. He just had no idea when.

Kornicus' keen eyes caught movement from the base of the wall and the floor, near Delania's bed. The small imp flew across the room at rocket speed, sweeping down and scooping up the gweit that had burrowed through the stone wall. He quickly devoured the tiny little demon, licking his lips and patting his morbidly thin belly in delight. It had been a long time since he had enjoyed a gweit. The small imp pondered why one would burrow in here in the first place. Gweits would be able to detect the change in the air here. It still was sulfuric and acrid, but it was incredibly mild compared to the surface, and besides, this little haven was several miles beneath the surface. *Why would a gweit burrow this deep?* Any food they might consume was on the surface from the flesh of the damned, not down here in Delania's Haven. Then suddenly it occurred to the imp why a gweit would burrow. Dadramedion could use the little demons as spies, seeing from their eyes. Kornicus immediately tried to find some place to hide, but as he started to flee the chamber, a large powerful red-clawed hand grabbed him by the throat from behind. Kornicus could feel the intense cold wafting from the creature's skin as bright red flames danced across him. Terror coursed through his veins like ice. Dadramedion had found him at last.

The claw hand turned him around and a wave of intense relief washed over him. This wasn't Dadramedion. This was some other arch demon. The monster was as tall as Dadramedion, but he was more muscular and his skin was red, afire with red flames, not bright blue. The archdemon had the same great bat wings, but his eyes had a long horizontal glow that extended past his face. The arch demon's eyes narrowed as he studied the tiny imp in his vise-like grip.

"You are not who I expected to find here, imp," the arch demon said. His booming voice rattled the walls and shook the furniture that Delania had created from stone.

Kornicus tried to swallow, but the monster's grip prevented him from even taking a breath, if he had needed one. "Great demon I am but a servant. My master is away. How may I serve you?" the imp rasped.

The archdemon bellowed. He tilted his head back and his massive muscled chest shook as he laughed. "Your master is here, fool. If you do not serve me well, I will make you wish Dadramedion had found you instead of me."

The imp nearly lost consciousness at the mention of his former master. "Yes, I will obey. Please command me great demon."

The archdemon smiled and released his grasp on the imp. Kornicus thought about trying to escape into the small tunnels Delania had crafted for him. He was sure he would be able to escape before he was caught, but did he want to escape? This demon was surely more powerful than Delania. The thought of no longer serving her pained him. Then suddenly unexpected anger erupted from within. That bitch. She had managed to trick him without his knowing. He had served her for two thousand years and she had managed to make him like her. Him, like her!

Demons do not like other demons. She was a crafty one. Kornicus knew he needed a change and fast. She was probably planning his betrayal at any moment. The thought of her doing that made him sick. He had grown to feel safe near her, believing she would keep him from Dadramedion, when she was probably planning on giving him up any time now. This new archdemon knew Dadramedion wanted him and he did not offer to give him away. Kornicus was finally realizing the depth of Delania's trickeries. She was a powerful demon. It was a shame he was too weak to serve her when she ascended.

The archdemon chuckled. His fanged maw moved with each bellow like an iron trap awaiting soft flesh to catch. "It is simple, imp. You are to place this necklace around her neck. Tell her you made it for her and you knew she would like it."

Kornicus frowned and beat his oversized wings in anticipation. "She won't fall for that, great demon. She is wise and powerful."

The great demon arched his head back and laughed again, this time stomping his foot and grabbing his midsection. "Delania is many things, but wise and powerful are not either of them. You are such a refreshing fool. I see why she kept your pathetic carcass around." The demon turned angry and deadly serious in an instant. "Obey me imp, or I will take you to Dadramedion myself. She will trust you because you have been with her so long. She thinks you like her."

There it was. This great demon knew first-hand that she was trying to trick him into liking her. He had exposed her plan. "When should I find you and tell of my service?" Kornicus asked.

The great demon stood. His giant body barely fit under the middle of the rocky dome. "Merely call out my name."

Kornicus nodded and examined the necklace in his slender green fingers. His deft claws fingered each opaque stone with great care. The necklace was made of many shimmering perfectly round spheres that seemed to be white, but as he turned them, they changed color to a form of off-white, then back to white again. He quickly looked up when he realized he did not know the demon's name. "How shall I call you, great demon?"

The large demon stepped his thick-muscled body through the bright orange portal gate that he had opened. He turned and faced the imp as it was closing. His deep growling voice echoed in the small stone room. "You can call me… Bykalicus."

"*Perception. It is a powerful tool. Sometimes it is the core of all magic itself. A wizard or sorcerer that is skilled in the power of perception can create images that someone might believe to be real. As the mage become more skilled he can actually trick people into believing they have been injured, and sometimes killed, by nothing more than a few illusions. It was not the illusion that killed them, but perception. If I perceive someone is my friend then, in my mind, they are. Whether that person really is, remains unimportant because of my perception. It is the way all people can deceive others that gives perception its power. A cheating husband who is believed by his wife to be faithful is faithful, regardless of how many times he cheats. This is because of her perception of him. It is not until she discovers his unfaithfulness, that he becomes an adulterer in her eyes. A thief that steals something that no one knows they have, is not theft by perception. If that person never realizes that they are missing what the thief stole, by their perceptions no one stole from them. It is amazing at the power of deceit. It is a grand tool used best by politicians and illusionists. A true master, however, will allow a person to deceive themselves. Allowing them to believe in what they wish. This removes all accountability from them and places it on the person that has deceived himself. A fine example of this is a thief that thinks everyone is trying to steal from him, when no one really is. In his mind he knows that he would steal what he owns if he were someone else, so he naturally assumes others will act accordingly. Or the thief that steals the obscure property that someone doesn't know is stolen, and then convinces that person that they gave it way some time ago. I was once tricked into thinking someone was something they were not. That person knew the truth of it, so their view of themselves was different than my perception of them. But they did not count on the perception that I had formed of them was as equally powerful as the one they had of themselves. So powerful in fact that I believed that the assessment they had of themselves was the false one and I set out to show them my perception was true. I knew what that person was, but I knew what I wanted that person to be. I simply used the same illusion they used on me. But once they believed the acuity I had shown them, it became reality. Ah, the similarities of perception and reality, something to learn another time.*"

-Lancalion Levendis Lampara-

5

The Tides of War

Amerix woke the next morning with a smile on his face. The old dwarf couldn't remember the last time he felt like smiling, but the thought of working a forge again brought the grin to his face with little effort. He rose from his itchy winter blanket that he got from the farmers on the journey and folded it neatly. He slid the heavy, rusted chain armor over his head and strapped on Songsinger. He felt a kinship to the sword that confused him. It seemed as if the blade had been in his possession since his birth, instead of only a few months. The old dwarf guessed it was because the weapon came from a defeated enemy. There was always satisfaction in claiming a weapon that had drawn your blood.

Amerix ran his stubby fingers through his greasy hair and stood by the small fire they had built the night before. Vlargcar was uneasy about the dwarf going into the town again and voiced his displeasure more than once, but his complaints fell on deaf ears. The orc paced around the fire tossing his short sword into the air, flipping it once and catching it again. He had been practicing the trick for some time and was becoming quite good at it. Amerix had frequently lectured him on how it was a useless trick, but Vlargcar, in his youth, liked it just the same. Amerix hefted his backpack that contained his personal belongings and some camping gear over his shoulder. The old dwarf watched the orc pace around the fire in the early morning. Great wisps of steam poured out of his nose and mouth in the cold winter air.

"Want a lesson before I go?" Amerix asked as he slipped his other shoulder into the second strap of the backpack.

Vlargcar stopped pacing and regarded the dwarf, catching his short sword by the handle. "I thinking," the orc said, frowning and tapping his lower lip with the tip of the thin-bladed short sword. "I like axe better than sword, but sword has more moves. What if you made me axe like sword?"

Amerix frowned. "What in the name of Durian would something like that look like?" Amerix asked with a puzzled look on his old creased face.

Vlargcar stared off into the dark forest for a moment deep in thought, and then turned with a thin smile, his bright yellow tusks protruding far from his lower lip out past his wide upturned nose. "I thinking you might make axe with axe head on each side with long spike on end to make it balance like sword. Then I could slash and stab just like sword, but it heavy like axe to cut through small armor."

Amerix frowned as he imagined what such a weapon would look like. "It will take a bit for me to draw that up, but I think I can do it."

Vlargcar smiled and began tossing the short sword into the air again, making it flip once, and then catching it by the handle as he had been doing before. "No lesson," the orc said without looking at the dwarf as he paced around the small fire again. "I think about axe."

Amerix smiled. "I will return at dark. Be careful and watch out for hunters. If they see ye we will have to leave. Once they lay eyes on ye they will not rest until yer head is on a pike."

"I be careful, but it is dwarfs they hate more, I think," Vlargcar said with a wry smile as he tossed the sword into the air, making it flip twice before catching it by the handle.

"Ye gonna keep doing that stupid short sword trick all day?" Amerix asked as he turned and started down the rough frozen grass hill.

"No, I do it until I get it right, then I learn stupid long sword trick," the orc said smiling, looking at the dwarf out of the corner of his eye.

Amerix shook his head and started walking down the hill. He tucked his hands into the straps of the backpack muttering as he vanished over the ridge. "Stupid orcs..."

Amerix walked down the hill, jumping from shadow to shadow, eager to get to the smithy, but wanting to avoid undue notice. He arrived and petted the shaggy dog, giving the animal a piece of meat. The animal wagged its tail, but did not bark. The dwarf went to the front of the smelting shack and pushed the door open. To his surprise Thomas was already dressed and stacking wood and coal near the fire pit. He looked up from his labors and saw the old dwarf.

"Good day," he called out. "Surprised to see you so soon. I just got out here."

Amerix forced down the bile that rose from his stomach when he heard a human speaking his language. Thomas spoke it well and if Amerix closed his eyes he was sure he would envision a dwarf speaking instead of a filthy human. The old dwarf had to frequently remind himself that Thomas had nothing to do with the current predicament of his people. With the dwarven army defeated at Central City, Amerix doubted there was anything left of Clan Stoneheart. The humans would have surely wiped them out. Clanless once again, Amerix knew he had to forge out on his own. This brief friendship with this Thomas was necessary.

Amerix removed his backpack and set it next to the wall. He placed on a pair of oversized leather gloves and apron. "Ye said ye had a lot of work. The best way to do a lot of work is to work a lot."

Thomas smiled briefly then pointed to a small metal box that was sitting on the edge of the large wooden table at the far end of the room. "There are some basic tools on the table, but first I need one hundred needles made for Terrace Folly. Apparently the small town has had a cat burglar running around stealing things, and they want to make some nasty needle traps for him. It is a strange request for such a small town, but I don't ask, I just fill the orders. There are some iron casts next to the fire pit. Smelt some ore and fill the casts. Hopefully you will be done by lunch. I have some more work that I am behind on."

Amerix nodded, grabbed the tool set from the table and made his way to the casts. He stoked the fire with the iron poker and set the large keg into it. He placed a few bars of ore inside and closed the heavy metal door. The door had bricks lining the inside to help prevent the intense heat from damaging the smelting chamber. Amerix was not used to metal furnaces. In dwarven communities they had great stone furnaces, not tiny metal ones with bricks to act as insulators. Humans were so strange. "This tiny thing gonna get hot enough to melt the ore?" Amerix asked with a doubting tone.

Thomas chuckled. "We use much softer ore than you dwarves. It does not require heat from the bowels of hell."

Amerix muttered under his breath as he prepared the molds. "That is why yer workings don't last more than twenty years."

"What?" Thomas asked.

Amerix shook his head from side to side. "Nothing, I was just saying how I prefer the dwarven way, that's all."

Thomas smiled as he placed about one hundred iron half-moons onto a long hook and slid it into the second furnace. "It will take a little getting used to, but you will see it is effective for what we need."

Amerix doubted that. This inferior way of smithing could never be effective. But he would do whatever was needed to get the basic smithy tools so he could splice the chain mail for him and Vlargcar.

Amerix checked the thick iron cask that held the ore he had placed in the furnace. To his surprise the ore was completely melted. Bright orange liquid ore swirled around in the heavy cask like thick syrup. He grabbed the thick wire cask handle and grunted as he hefted it out of the furnace. His old corded muscles strained under the weight. He waddled over to the molds he had laid out. The old dwarf grabbed the bottom of the cask with one hand and the other held the wire handle. He grunted and poured the liquid metal into the molds. Smoke rose from the leather gloves against the bottom of the searing hot cask. Amerix ignored the tingling pain in his hand as he held the bottom hot iron bowl. "What are you doing?!" Thomas yelled as Amerix pouring the liquid metal.

The old dwarf finished his job and easily hoisted the much lighter cask with one arm and calmly walked over to the furnace and re-hung it. He glanced at Thomas with a confused look on his face. "What?"

Thomas rushed over to the dwarf's work bench. "You filled all of the molds at once! You should have told me the ore was ready, I would have helped you with the cask," the smithy said, bewildered at the dwarf's strength. "I couldn't have moved that cask by myself, let alone full of ore."

Amerix shrugged his shoulders as he flipped the tops of the molds closed and hammered a cotter pin into them, securing the two halves together. "Ye humans do things so strange. Why would ye make a tool that ye couldn't use by yerself?"

Thomas shook his head in disbelief. He had worked with the dwarves in Clan Stoneheart for many years. He had heard tales of Amerix's great strength, along with his wickedness in battle, but to witness the dwarf's power first-hand was more than alarming. "You see, we make larger casks so we can smelt more ore. It takes less time to dip the ore out than it does to smelt it, so we do it in mass quantities."

Amerix shook his head. His long sliver-streaked beard bounced across his chest. "Humans are always in such a rush. Orcs don't live as long as humans and I think even they are more patient."

Thomas laughed uneasily. "You ever know an orc?" the smithy asked doubtfully.

Amerix frowned and chewed on his lower lip. The long hairs of his thick bushy eyebrows protruded in all directions from his creased brow. "I knew one. Pretty smart for a dumb orc, but I guess you will find a smart one every now and then."

Thomas laughed until Amerix gave him a questioning look. The smithy's smile faded rapidly when he realized the dwarf was being serious about knowing an orc once.

"Whatever made you befriend a wicked orc?" Thomas asked.

Amerix gave him a glance with an expression of warning. "He had blue eyes," Amerix answered truthfully. "Ye never know when something is going to strike yer fancy."

Thomas nodded nervously. He hoped the message to the captain of the guard arrived soon. He wondered how long he could employ this vicious creature before the old dwarf turned on him. Thomas started grasping the molds with heavy metal tongs and began to set them outside. Amerix grabbed Thomas by his arm. The smithy felt the dwarf's powerful vice like grip seize him. He knew instantly that the dwarf could break the bones in his arm on a whim if he so desired.

"What are ye doing?" Amerix asked.

Thomas looked down at the molds then back at the dwarf. "What do you mean? I'm setting the molds outside to cool. They will harden faster outside than inside."

Amerix growled and grabbed the searing hot cask with his leathered glove. "Silly smithy, they may harden quicker, but if they cool off too soon, tiny hairline cracks will form in the metal. If that happens, the metal won't hold longer than thirty years or so."

Thomas scratched his head as the dwarf placed the mold back on the cooling bricks. "Am, thirty years is ten years longer than most metal works last. They will not need these that long, and if they did, I would be out of work in no time. No one would need any more of my products before I died."

Amerix frowned. He hadn't considered the short lifespan humans had. It made sense to him after he thought about it. Dwarves made metal works that lasted about four hundred years, about as long as a dwarf's lifespan. The old dwarf nodded to himself and grabbed the molds from the cooling bricks and began to place them outside next to the building.

"What are you doing?" Thomas asked.

"Keeping ye in business," Amerix replied.

Thomas smiled as he picked up a mold with his heavy tongs and placed it alongside the molds Amerix had set outside. As they finished placing all of the molds out alongside the exterior of the smelting shack, they rested and ate fresh butter cakes that Thomas' wife had made. Amerix wiped his dirty greasy hands on his apron before stuffing each butter cake into his mouth. The warm rolls were delicious and rivaled anything any of the dwarven bakers had ever made. "Vis if delifus," Amerix said with a mouthful of cake.

Thomas nodded in agreement, but waited until he chewed and swallowed before he spoke. "So Am, I don't mean to pry, but I have worked around dwarves most of my life and your sword is not a typical dwarven weapon."

Amerix glanced at Songsinger. The brilliant sword gleamed in the faint light of the smelting shack. The blade remained hidden by the finely crafted metal scabbard, but the polished hilt shone and glimmered like a bride's ring on her wedding day. Amerix cursed himself for bringing the blade, but he just could not bring himself to leave it at the camp. "Aye, I got Songsinger from a great battle from a...," Amerix paused. "...from the champion of an enemy of mine. He was a worthy opponent."

Thomas eyed the sword, and then regarded the dwarf again. He had been a soldier but he had not faced many enemies. He was skilled with a blade, but he considered himself far below the skill of the old dwarf that sat before him.

Amerix stuffed three of the butter cakes into his backpack. "I hope to one day have a final showdown with the champion," Amerix said off-handedly.

Thomas paused a minute before he realized what Amerix was talking about. "So you can kill him once and for all?" the smithy asked with disgust.

Amerix shook his head from side to side. "No," the old dwarf said with a sigh. "So he can give me release. I am way past old age fer a dwarf. No enemy has ever been able to best me in battle, but with each waning day, I grow closer to the time I will die in me bed. Not a fitting death for a warrior like me. I need to die in battle with the respect of me enemy. He is the only one that I have battled so far in me life that deserves the honor, yet I have faced him twice and bested him each time. Only by the grace of his god did he survive each encounter." A surprised look came across Amerix's creased visage. "Ye do not think he was hoping for the same from me, do ye?" the old dwarf asked worriedly.

Thomas shrugged his shoulders. "How old was this champion?"

Amerix then shrugged his. "Not very old I think. I would feel terrible if he was hoping for release by me hand, and I failed him twice. Not only did he not get release, but he had to face defeat twice. I owe the champion much. I pray to Durian that I might face him again before I pass."

Thomas regarded the dwarf with a new understanding. He wasn't a vicious cold-blooded killer. Fierce killer yes, but he saw rules to the fighting that Thomas was sure his enemies did not. There was a sense of a strange honor about the dwarf. If this was indeed Amerix Alistair Stormhammer he surely had committed unspeakable crimes against the Beyklans, but perhaps there was more to these charges than was understood.

The pair finished eating and rose from the hard wooden bench outside the shack. Amerix began to pick up the molds and carry them back inside and Thomas began to remove the glowing half-moon shaped metal rings from the fire by the heavy tongs that hung from a peg in his workshop. He pounded on them with a small sledge until the shapes took on the appearance of a horse shoe. When Thomas finished hammering one out, he tossed it into a large bucket of water. The water hissed from the intense heat of the newly forged horseshoe, and Thomas grabbed another from the ring to repeat the process.

Amerix pounded the cotter pins from the molds and then hammered the bottom of them, forcing the thin needles out onto a large leather strip that was placed on the floor. Once Amerix had all of the needles onto the leather square he stacked all of the molds back up next to the wall where he had gotten them. Then he locked down three needles at a time in the small vise that was anchored to a heavy anvil on the far wall. The old dwarf delicately ran a thin file across the sides of the needles smoothing out any blemishes that may have formed from the molding. After he was satisfied the needles were of passable quality he placed them gently onto a second leather square on the work table. The dwarf worked meticulously as the smithy's hammer rang out with each pounding of the horse shoes. He shaved the ridges off each thin needle with short fast strokes of the small file. His sliver-streaked beard bounced back and forth as he worked each small silver colored needle. Occasionally Amerix glanced over at Thomas and wiped his brow with his soot-covered sleeve. The smithy was hard at work pounding out the horseshoes. The old dwarf watched him for a while. Thomas

had a nice stroke with the mallet but his strikes were not precise and he often had to hit the same spot several times when
he should have needed only one. Then he had to reheat the
rapidly cooling metal before starting again. Amerix returned
to his needles and sighed. Thomas was probably one of the
best humans at his trade, but a dwarf had hundreds of years
to perfect what this human had learned in a fraction of that
time. Amerix was glad he had lived a long, full life. He had
a few regrets, but for the most part he had little complaints.

Sliding the final needle into the sash on the felt-lined
leather, Amerix walked over and grabbed a second metal
mallet form the wall. The mallet was well made and its head
was filed flat to remove and burs that might make flaws in
the metal he pounded. He grabbed a red hot shoe from the
fire and began shaping it with quick fast strokes. In moments he had shaped the hot metal into a perfectly balanced
and shaped horseshoe. He tossed the metal into the cooling
barrel and grabbed another from the fire. The red hot shoe
hissed as it sunk to the bottom of the barrel. Amerix picked
up the mallet and began pounding again. In moments he
had finished shaping the shoe. He tossed it into the cooling
barrel just like the last one and grabbed a third piece of red
hot metal from the furnace and picked up his mallet. Out of
the corner of his eye he saw Thomas gaping at him with his
mallet in hand. He had stopped pounding his shoe and the
metal was already cooled to the point that it needed tossed
back into the fire.

Amerix smiled a deep grin under his thick silver-
streaked beard, pounding the third shoe into form with a
few precise strokes and tossed it into the cooling barrel as
well. He turned, placing his stout hairy fists on his hips. "Do
not make a big deal of it, Thomas. I have spent more time on
the smithy shitter, than ye have being a smith. The skill I got,
comes from two of yer lifetimes," Amerix said as he turned,
grabbing another shoe and began pounding it out in a few
short precise strokes as well. "Yer shoe is cold, better toss it
back into the furnace."

Thomas glanced down at the rapidly cooling piece of
metal that was held by his tongs and tossed the object back

into the furnace. He shook his head as he retrieved another red hot shoe and began shaping it.

The pair worked for the rest of the afternoon. Thomas was amazed at how much work the dwarf did. Not that he was a harder worker, no Thomas matched him in effort. But, the dwarf seemed to quadruple his results. In all of Thomas' life and years working with the dwarves, he had never seen someone as skilled and quick as Amerix. Thomas wanted to ask him how he learned so much skill as a smithy when he was general of an army, but he knew that would tell the dwarf he knew his identity. Fighting a rabid animal like Amerix was not on his wish list, so the smithy swallowed his curiosity for the moment.

When the sun started its zenith, Thomas threw some large pieces of wood onto the fire to keep them stoked for the night for the next day's work. He bid Amerix a good night and slipped into his small house. The old dwarf slid his pack over his shoulder that was lying next to the smelting shack door and marched back up the hill.

The smithy returned with a single key on a small brass ring. He locked up the shack and went back inside his warm house. Pouring a hot bath from the heated water his wife had warmed on the stove, Thomas cleaned himself up. He gingerly took the dark colored washing rag and dipped it into the hot water and ran it across a bar of milky white lye. The air was cold in the house even though it was well heated so Thomas bathed quickly. As he washed, his thoughts were of Amerix. The dwarf surprised him on every facet of character. On first meeting, Thomas assumed he was the ruthless killer everyone had made him out to be, but the grizzled old dwarf seemed to have a great deal of underlying temperament. But Thomas was no fool. He knew if the dwarf suspected he even had an inkling of his true identity, the dwarf would not hesitate to slay him and his family to make his escape. The old general did not survive all the impossible trials he had by not being ruthless.

Thomas climbed from the bath and placed on his night robe. He slid under the warm covers and snuggled with his wife. He wondered what Amerix was doing under the cold night sky and what new revelations the dwarf would show tomorrow. Thomas hoped he would hear from the royal guard soon. He might grow to like the deadly renegade.

Amerix climbed the hill that led to his and Vlargcar's camp. His old legs ached and his feet hurt something fierce. He finally reached the camp and found Vlargcar practicing the fighting forms he had shown him with some kind of long stick. The orc had lashed some heavy flat bark on both ends like the head of a great axe, both heads sporting a double blade. The orc had removed his tunic and his deeply tattooed green skin shone with perspiration in the cold winter night. His breath rocketed out from his upturned nose and his yellow-tusked mouth as

he swung the makeshift double axe into the night. The orc was strong, looking more like a young warrior than a whelp with every passing day.

Vlargcar's eyes slid across the dwarf as the tired Amerix plodded into camp. Amerix saw the orc's blue eyes reflecting the hint of crimson that showed the orc was using his night vision. Amerix sighed. Even though the orc had blue eyes, they were still eyes of a ruthless orc.

"I glad to see, Amerix," Vlargcar said as he panted from the exertion of the long day at training. "How goes your work day?"

Amerix smiled as he plopped down on a large piece of wood they had drug over to act as a bench in front of the fire. He removed his boots and wiggled his aching toes as he dangled them in front of the fire to get warm. "'Twas a fulfilling day," Amerix said with a smile. "I got the tools I needed so I can start on making that chain mail fit us."

Vlargcar smiled eagerly and held out the strange looking double-headed training axe. The thing wasn't made well and if the orc ever hit anything with it, the blasted thing would surely break. Vlargcar, reading the dwarf's thoughts, smiled. "I know, it not sturdy, but good for training. I already make changes to form so I work with weapon better. I hoped that one day, you might make me a real double axe."

Amerix smiled as he pressed his thick hands behind the small of his back, arching forward until he heard many resounding pops. He then relaxed, pulling the small wooden box from his pack. "One day, me green-skinned friend, but fer now, I am going to make us some presentable chain mail to wear."

Vlargcar nodded and gently laid the wooden practice weapon by the side of the log and slid his arms into his tunic. He then wrapped himself up in his blanket and warmed himself by the small fire that produced little heat in the cold night. Amerix pulled the chain mail out and laid it in his lap. He opened the small wooden box and began clipping the tiny links and then twisting them back together with the metal tools. "Here," the dwarf said, tossing Vlargcar a cloth bundle that was tied neatly with a small twine. The orc popped the twine and unwrapped the cloth, revealing three large butter cakes from the smithy's wife. Vlargcar sniffed the cakes reluctantly and scrunched up his nose.

"They are called butter cakes," Amerix said as he clipped the links to the chain mail. "The smithy's wife made them. They are really good and ye need to eat them."

Vlargcar looked down at the light brown toasted pastry with a degree of disgust. "I try them for you, but I no think I like them."

Amerix smiled as the orc eagerly devoured every one. What surprised the old general was the orc said they were not bad. The orc never seemed to cease in amazing him. Amerix worked for a about an hour, eventually falling over on his soft bedroll, succumbing to sleep. Vlargcar shook out the dwarf's blanket and laid it over his curled up form.

The dwarf had worked hard all day. Vlargcar hoped Amerix didn't bring any more of the horrid butter cakes. How he managed to choke down a one of them, let alone all three, was a surprise. They were the most horrid things he had ever eaten. Vlargcar knew the dwarf was thinking of him when he brought them back and it was probably important to his bearded friend that he eat them. Vlargcar shook his head as he snuggled up in his bed roll next to the fire.

No eating humans, no eating squirrels with fur, not with the guts inside, and eating butter cakes. Vlargcar guessed it was a dwarf's way to strengthen himself by keeping such a horrid diet. It surely was giving Vlargcar a stronger stomach. After the butter cake ordeal, Vlargcar figured next he could eat a pound of sugar and not vomit, but the thought made him queasy. Orc's hated sugar, it burned their throats.

Vlargcar nestled into his sleeping roll and the warm blanket he got from the farmer's wife. No one besides Amerix had ever given him anything other than what was his from battle. The orc clung to that itchy wool blanket like he often did his mother. He closed his eyes and soon, the orc whelp drifted off into sleep.

"They are here, Sire!" came a gruff voice from the unlit doorway of the large expansive stone chamber. The floor of the chamber was a myriad of multi-colored polished granite and marble slates. The inner portion of the room was lined with a thin tan colored polished brick. On the inside of that line, the bricks were a checker board of bright blue and gold. There were large dark colored wooden shelves and benches that held violet and crimson mushrooms that decorated the room like small eruptions of color. The center of the chamber was lit by a multi-paned blue stained glass that was a hundred feet above the spacious room. Directly below the glass dome was the large thick wooden bed of Tharxton Stoneheart, King of Clan Stoneheart and the ruler of Mountain Heart.

Tharxton rubbed the sleep from his eyes and propped himself up on his elbows. The room was cool, but not cold. Mountain Heart was both warmed and cooled by being deep into the heart of the mountain and seldom got warmer or cooler than sixty degrees, regardless of the time of year.

Tossing the heavy silk and satin sheets from his bed, Tharxton kicked his thick powerful legs out and plopped down onto the cold marbled floor. He stretched his bulky muscular arms and yawned while his foot probed under the bed for his slippers. Upon finding the furry shoes, he slipped his bare feet inside and scooted across the floor to one of the large wooden tables that held the crimson mushroom. He reached behind the red fungus's pot and retrieved a heavy porcelain pitcher. The dwarf king poured some of the water into the pots of the mushrooms, and then took a long draw himself. Placing the heavy porcelain pitcher back behind the potted fungus, he turned to the dwarf that stood at his door.

"How far are they?" Tharxton asked with a deep raspy voice as he thumped his chest and cleared his throat.

The dwarf shifted in his heavy golden gilded ring mail. He wore a long blue tunic that hung down to the back of his heels. His legs and arms were covered in thick metal plates that bore thousands of engravings and runes. He had two large golden moons that were gilded into the thick metal collar that hung from the front of his chest and circled his neck rising about six inches off of his shoulder, protecting him in battle. His short black beard was trimmed flat and held by a single silver band that was fastened just under the dwarf's strong square chin. "They are at least a day off, sire. But, they are moving swiftly...," the dwarf said, trailing off.

Tharxton frowned. He had many duties to see to as king. Although the king of Beykla coming to talk about a treaty was the most important thing to happen to Clan Stoneheart in five hundred years, there were more pressing matters, like addressing the council on why they were unable to open the chamber of Leska. Tharxton noticed Targavian wanted to say more. He was a powerful warrior in Clan Stoneheart and seemed a fitting replacement for the renegade outlaw, Amerix. The men liked him, and he was as wise as he was fair. He would have made an excellent king. "What is it, General?" Tharxton asked as he removed his heavy sleeping robe and slid his arms into the thick pleated suit of his under armor.

The general paused for a moment, clearly troubled with the news he was about to tell. "Sire, you say King Theobold was coming personally to make a peace treaty with us and their country?" Targavian said in more of a questioning tone that a statement.

Tharxton stopped sliding his arms through his pleated

shirt and stared out of the neck hole of the garment. "Yes, that is correct. Why?"

Targavian cleared his throat and shifted his weight, staring at the glossy marble floor momentarily before looking up at his king. "Because sire, scouts report that the entire western army comes with him. Over thirty thousand strong."

Thirty thousand strong. The words seemed to come in slow motion from the dwarf's mouth and echoed in Tharxton's head. The young dwarf king felt the weight of his crown come crashing down as if the great Mount Steeple fell onto his shoulders. If he did not hold the weight, his clan would be crushed. "The entire western army!" Tharxton said as he stared in disbelief at his general. "Why would he bring his entire western army? We are only four thousand strong. He outnumbers us close to ten to one!" Tharxton shouted.

Targavian wore a grave expression. "Why did Amerix take the entire army against Torrent, Sire?" Targavian asked in a quiet somber tone.

The reality soaked into Tharxton like a flood rushing through a narrow valley. "You think he means to conquer us?" Tharxton asked rhetorically. "Have someone fetch my armor and weapons. Get the clan started into fleeing into Mountain Heart. Never have we faced such a force, but the city fortress has defended armies of half that number..."

"Sire, shouldn't we meet...?" Targavian interrupted.

"Do not interrupt me, General!" Tharxton shouted, spittle spraying from his mouth as he barked. "The future of the clan may ride on you following my orders without question, without hesitation. Let's get used to that now, before we find ourselves at war. Now do as I say. Start getting the clan to defensive positions in Mountain Heart. You will stay behind while I meet with Theobold. Send notice to my advisors so I may hold an emergency meeting with them before I go and face the bastard king. I will meet you in the Valley of Mist with one hundred men. I will take the men to meet the Beyklan king. Be sure that hundred consists of only volunteers, in case he intends to make dishonorable war. After we depart, you are to return to Mountain Heart and defend it to the last. When the Stormghast falls, retreat with the remaining members of the clan into the deep under mountain. We will live in the dark recess of the earth before Clan Stoneheart will be conquered by the likes of the human dogs!" Tharxton growled as he quickly placed on his boots, nearly falling. "Let's get moving! We have more to do today than can be done in ten days!" Tharxton said as he started running for the door. General Targavian ran from the king's chambers and started heading toward the servant's quarters. He had to make sure they inspected and brought his armor down to the valley.

Tharxton's mind whirled. *Why was the king bringing the entire army?* Sure the Torrent Manor must have been a ghastly scene, but his people reported that the southern nobles were sympathetic to their plight and they were threatening to pull away from the north if the king made war with them. Tharxton had worked hard drafting letters and correspondence with the king, yet he came, marching his army of war on the dwarve's doorsteps. Tharxton doubted he could stand against half of the western army. True, the clan had stood against that many in past history, but the clan was twice as strong as it is now, and even then it could hardly have been called a victory. The clan had been decimated to mere hundreds. Men, women and children had died with weapons in hand. It had taken over a thousand years to rebuild the clan's numbers to where they are today, now history threatened to repeat itself. Well, Tharxton wouldn't make the same mistakes as past kings. He would have the clan flee into the under mountain. True there were endless creatures and untold horrors in the under mountain, but at least the clan had a fighting chance. The humans would not be interested in claiming Mountain Heart, and when they left, the clan would retake the ancient underground city. It would take a few hundred years to rebuild, but in that time two Beyklan kings would have come and gone, paving the way for new relations.

Tharxton rounded the corner, ignoring the many salutes and salutations he received as he made his way down the hall. When he reached the door he was searching for, the dwarf king forced it open with more of his shoulder than by turning the handle. The room was made of stone and was colored bright blue. The floor was covered in many thick rugs that had frilly tassels on each end.

A dwarven woman with striking features pulled the thick satin blankets up to cover her chest. She was garbed in loose silk sleeping clothes yet her well-muscled frame was obvious from under the flowing fitting garb. She wore a frown of a mixture between disgust and incredulousness. "Tharxton Stoneheart!" she shouted. "Just because you are courting me, is no excuse to barge into my room, uninvited, and don't think that the old 'I'm the king' excuse will work this time!" she said, shooing him away with her left hand that bore a single thick gold ring.

Tharxton ignored her commands and rushed to the tall wooden chiffonier. He flung the wooden doors open and pulled down a few outfits and tossed them onto the bed.

"Usually a man tries his best to pull the clothes off of his women, not pull them out of her closet," she said with half amusement and half annoyance.

"Mylaneia, I have no time to explain. Just trust me. We may have to flee into the under mountain..," Tharxton tried to explain.

"What? Under mountain? Why...?" Mylaneia said as her expression changed from annoyed amusement to worried and scared.

"Let me finish!" Tharxton growled, angrier than he meant. He paused and moved to the bed, softening his tone. "The Beyklans have moved the entire western army against us. I do not know if they mean for war, or for show of force, but I'll not let our clan be wiped out because of pride. Take what you can carry and prepare for a long stay in the under mountain."

Mylaneia's deep brown eyes darted back and forth across Tharxton's flushed face. Fear welled up inside of her. It was not fear of the under mountain, though she did fear it. What she feared was spending her time there without him. She silently scolded herself for allowing the young king to court her. She knew that his duties to the clan outweighed his duties to her, but he was so handsome and dashing; she could not help herself. Now she was paying for her lack of restraint. Her father had warned her, but she chose not to listen. She stroked his soft hair that covered his chin nervously and suddenly hugged him. She pulled him tight in her powerful arms and felt his embrace was equally strong.

Tharxton pulled away and kissed her gently on the lips. He moved his face in front of hers and stared deep into her big brown eyes. He took a long moment and memorized her beautiful face from her large round eyes to her soft supple smile. He inhaled and savored her sweet perfumed smell. "I will not be longer than necessary, and then I will join you. There may be fighting, and there may not be, but you must understand that I have to put the clan above what I want... What we want."

Mylaneia nodded and kissed him back, but more passionately. "If I never see you again Tharxton, I want your head clear. No regrets, no doubts on the battlefield."

Tharxton frowned as she got up quickly from her bed and dashed to the door. She gently closed it, placed her back to the door, and turned to the dwarf king. She stood facing him in her silk night clothes that clung to her large thick breasts. The state of her arousal crowned through her silk lacy top in the cool room. Tharxton sat on the edge of the bed with a confused look on his face. He had never seen Mylaneia so brazen as to stand in daylight in her sleeping clothes. He was even more amazed when she rushed back to the bed and roughly shoved him onto his back, kissing his mouth with hot heated pants.

"Before you rush off to do your duty to the clan..," Mylaneia said as her hands slid under his pleated tunic skirt. "You will do your duty to me."

Tharxton's eyes went wild and he tried to protest, but her quick hot kisses, soft silky tongue, and her caressing hand, quickly convinced the dwarf king that he had a few moments before he was needed at the valley. His muffled cries of protest quickly turned to moans of pleasure. He had well thought out plans how their first interlude would develop and this was not it. The dwarf king had lost his first battle that day, and he enjoyed the defeat quite well. He hoped it would be his last defeat of his lifetime.

King Theobold rode into the valley after the long march into the Pyberian Mountains. His men were tired and fatigued, yet eager to face their dwarven foes and deal them swift defeat if needed.

The high mountain valley was narrow and the cold windy air was thin. Theobold's hair whipped across his face from the frigid breeze, yet to his surprise the valley was not snow covered. There was short green grass littered with dark gray boulders that had fallen from their high lofty peaks throughout the gorge. The ceiling of the dale was not more than a hundred feet and was covered with a dense fog that acted like a blanket that kept in the mild temperature.

There was an old dirt trail that spilt the lush grass down the center of the valley and extended along the eastern wall, traveling north, until it rose on a ledge and disappeared into the murky haze. Theobold had brought a legion of pikemen, archers, and horsemen into the valley and ordered the remaining soldiers to march around the mountain to try to find the entrance to the other side. The king had also dispatched ten riders to travel north into the valley to see if there was indeed another exit. Though his force was divided, Theobold was still over twenty thousand strong. Sounds of hammers ringing on steel tent spikes and the low murmur of his soldier's voices echoed around him. His tent was almost erected and he would take refuge there until the dwarf king came to him. Theobold planned on camping for three days. If Tharxton did not come by then, he would assume the dwarves had hostile intent and march his army either up the narrow trail, or deep into the valley, depending on what his scouts had told him.

Theobold walked around the camp with the general of the western army, Bodrell Marx. Bodrell had moved up to his station as a general quickly – quicker than most in fact, but he was seasoned. Despite his youthful appearance, he lacked vigor. He was not lazy by any means, but he was

known as more of a politician than a warrior. General Bodrell was as skilled with his blade as his men, but he lacked
the inner fire that drove most soldiers. The general seldom
wore armor unless battle was imminent, and often was criti-
cized for letting the men have too much time off, which in
turn made the men love him. As true to form, Bodrell wore a
long red trench coat with frills on the collar and around the
cuffs. He reeked of perfumes and soaps and his clean tidy
hair was cut short and held aloft by oils and jellies that he
kept himself in ready supply of. The coat he wore bore the
symbol of Beykla on its chest and the double breasted gold
buttons glistened in the sparse light that managed to per-
meate the fog haze. He rested his gloved right hand on the
hilt of his sheathed sword, keeping the thin platinum-hilted
rapier in place. The general's boots were high walking boots,
well-oiled and fastened by bright golden buckles with thick
leather laces. Had the men not known who was king, Bodrell
could have easily been mistaken for royalty standing next
to the armored Theobold. Though Theobold's armor was
grand and immaculately maintained, Bodrell just seemed to
keep a kingly air about him.

The pair surveyed the camp, talking and laughing about
bringing the dwarves to heel, while giving words of en-
couragement to the men. They were eager to cross swords
with dwarves, though the rumor of the bearded folk's battle
prowess had most on edge.

"So I suppose the march was not too rough on the men?"
the king asked.

Bodrell arched his thin eyebrow as he glanced at the
king. He knew where Theobold was going. Bodrell always
asked for the men to be able to break into the valley with ale
and wine in celebration of a long march. Bodrell believed
to let the men unwind and relax before battle. He knew the
king was opposed of such practices and often took it upon
himself to see that their needs were met. "The march was not
overwhelming, your majesty, but it was tiring. The men are
exhausted and could surely use a night of festivities."

Theobold sighed. He knew Bodrell would want such
things. The general was weak when it came to military bear-

ing. Theobold believed that it was important to be like steel in the field – hard and sharp. Whereas, General Bodrell treated his men like boots –constant maintenance. "Do as you feel you must, General. But I expect a full report from the scouts in the morning. If they have not returned, then you will lead the expedition to discover what happened to them."

General Bodrell's eyes widened briefly before the king interjected. "You will remain at the rear of the expedition of course and you are to retreat the men at first sign of battle. It is foolish to engage an enemy with a fraction of our force."

The general bowed deeply and spread his arms out wide. "By your command, Your Highness."

Theobold shook his head in disgust as he turned and started back toward his tent. It was probably up by now and he wanted to have some lunch before he signed the orders for the smithies and other workers to begin setting up their tents. Theobold paid them daily for traveling with the army, but he had to pay them more if they worked. Of course he tried to avoid as many costs as possible.

The general watched Theobold walk away toward the royal tent with sincere revulsion masked behind a loyal smile. When the king was out of sight, he dusted his arms and legs off, as if they had become soiled by standing so close to the king. After straightening his petticoat, Bodrell made his way to his personal tent. It was of fine quality and afforded him room to stand, but it was nothing like the outrageous structure that Theobold carried with him. True, the king had proven himself in battle on more than one occasion, but it just didn't seem proper to surround himself in such luxuries when the soldiers were sleeping two men to a single tent, keeping their weapons and what few personal items they carried outside in the weather.

As Bodrell ducked under the heavy flap that acted as the tent door, he was greeted by grave faces. Two men in the room were his assistants. They cooked for him and performed other menial tasks. Some argued that if he scorned other officers for extreme privileges in the field,

then he was being hypercritical with his cooks, but Bodrell pointed out that every night he drew from a lottery, allowing one of the men to dine with him, enjoy the warmth of his tent and tell stories of old, to keep morale high. His assistants wore grave faces at the intrusion, no doubt, but the other scowl was worn by Edward Thigpen, an old grizzled horsemen that had been promoted to the rank of captain since he refused to retire. Bodrell feared for his health, so he promoted him and gave him an easier job. Edward had a younger brother, named Walter, a bowman who worked for Captain Oswald. So sad. Bodrell doubted either had a life outside of the army. "What is there to report, Captain Thigpen?"

The old captain's expression didn't shift but Bodrell could clearly tell he was disturbed. He removed his leather coif that sat on his head and held it in his hands. "General, the scouts did not return."

Bodrell dismissed his assistants with a wave of his hand and bid the old captain to sit. The two well-dressed men departed with a shallow bow and exited the small tent.

"I'd prefer to stand, Sir," Edward said as he held his thin leather coif nervously.

General Bodrell sat back in his soft folding canvas chair and sipped wine from a wooden goblet. The goblet was plain, but more of a luxury than any of the men had.

"Sir, as I had said, the scouts did not return," the captain said again.

Bodrell waved his hand, dismissing the captain's report. "No problem, Edward. We will send another group of considerable strength to investigate; a group that cannot be felled by any force completely. We will return with our findings and report them directly to the king and let him decide what course of action to take."

Edward stared at the ground and shifted his feet from side to side. "Sir, we sent a second patrol. I led it. We traveled deep into the valley and followed the scouts' tracks up a narrow shelf that appeared it might lead out the back side of the gorge."

Bodrell sat up and placed his wooden goblet on the small chest that sat next to his canvas folding chair. "Dwarves?" Bodrell asked. "Did the dwarves find and kill them?"

"I don't think so, Sir. It was a horrid scene. I have never seen anything like it in all of my days as a soldier. It was even more gruesome than the last days of the orc war," Edward said as his voice cracked.

Bodrell leaned forward and poured another goblet of wine eagerly, splashing a bit over the side. "Explain, Captain."

The captain wiped beads of sweat from his brow with the sleeve of his shirt. "Sir, the men, they were...frozen solid, some in blocks of ice, like they had been submerged in frigid water, then hauled out. And the others...," the captain trailed off staring at horrors his eyes had seen on the mountain.

"What of the others?" Bodrell asked, standing up and offering the bottle of wine to the grizzled old captain. Edward took the bottle without hesitation and gulped down the remaining fluid. He finished, wiped his mouth with his sleeve and set the bottle down on the chest. "Thank you, Sir. Some of the bodies, well, were not bodies at all. All that was left were a few arms or a leg, but no bodies. And every one of the horses were missing. The ground was red from blood, but no horses. There were a few hooves and a part of hind leg, I think. Whatever it was that killed them, I think it ate them," Edward said. His face was pale and wet with perspiration.

Bodrell took it all in. Clearly it was disturbing news. There were ogres and other giants that lived in the mountains; that was no surprise. But they rarely, if ever, had enough in a band that could have killed and eaten the entire scouting party. And if for some reason they did band together, why? Were they working for the dwarves? Surely there was easier prey than a heavily armed group of well-trained soldiers. And where were the dead giants? They never carried off their own dead and what about the men that were frozen solid? It was not cold enough in this valley to have snow, let alone men frozen in ice. Bodrell decided he was going to have to lead an expedition to investigate for himself. He would take a few clerics and head out in the afternoon. The king did not know of the second expedition and he ordered one sent anyway. "Captain Thigpen, have my assistants send for my horse and gather your best men. We are going to see what we can. I plan to take some clerics; perhaps magic can reveal what our senses cannot."

The captain smiled nervously and bowed, backing out of the tent. "As you command, General."

Bodrell sat there for a moment, contemplating what they might encounter. He planned on taking about one hundred horsemen. That would be more than sufficient to allow someone to escape – mainly himself – if they encountered some incredible dwarven assault force. Besides, dwarves were not known to have mounts and their short little legs prevented from running any great speeds.

The general poured himself another drink and finished it before slipping into his hard leather armor. He placed his bright red petticoat over the top of the leather and stepped out into the cold mountain air. One of his assistants stood with his mount fully barded with two saddle bags of supplies. Bodrell removed his gloves and checked through the packs, ensuring he had a spyglass, flint and steel, some iron rations, and of course, a good goblet with a bottle of fine elven wine. Satisfied, he placed his gloves back onto his well-manicured hand, and mounted his horse. The steed was not a large war horse by any means, but it was well groomed and well fed. Its sleek gray coat shone like a silk sheet under the heavy brass-colored plate armor. The barding rested on thin, padded red cushions that kept the heavy armor from chafing the horse. His reins were made of light brass-colored chain and the bridle was fastened into the barding that protected the horse's head. Bodrell gently patted the neck of his horse and climbed atop it, fitting his boots snugly into the stirrups. The general then turned and rode the horse with a slow trot to the north end of the camp, where the men would be waiting.

Just as he expected, there were about one hundred horsemen mounted on heavy war horses. Their bright barding glinted in the feint light of the valley. The visibility was mediocre at best with the thick haze of the valley ceiling lowered and wisps of fog floating by in small clouds that made it difficult to see through. The men were eager to be along on the journey as were their horses. They pranced around and pawed at the ground, snorting at the displeasure of standing about.

"Are we to be off, Sir? There is a lot of scuttlebutt about them men being eaten and frozen by some beast that the dwarves sent," one of the men called out.

"Yes, we are off, and yes, the rumors are true, save for the fact the dwarves sent the beast. That is what we are to find out, that and if there was a beast, or some dwarven trick to scare us off," Bodrell said.

"We won't scare!" one of the men shouted.

"Yea! The bearded bastards will pay for spilling Beyklan blood!" another yelled.

"Calm down," Bodrell commanded with an angry scowl. "I'll decide after I see first-hand what happened."

The men quieted down as Bodrell pushed his horse to the front and started the ride north into the misty vale. As much as Bodrell wanted to crush the dwarves, he knew there was a dangerous mystery that needed to be solved. He didn't rise to the rank of general by being a fool.

"A wise man must create his facts before he creates his theories. If he creates theories before the facts, he will bend the facts to fit the theory. You will hear me speak of this truth from time to time. It is a wisdom that covers a broad spectrum of events in life. King Theobold didn't use any wisdom when he was in the mountains, and even though he was thirsty for power and would step on anyone that got in his way, he was in fact quite wise. But when he was enthralled with the sight of his victory, he should have realized that if the dwarves had control of any powerful monsters they would have used them in the battle for the Torrent Manor and/or in the battle of Central City. But let's say the dwarves found their monstrous alley later. The king would have been wise to discover the monster's identity. True, he had his entire western army with him, but armies have been defeated. It was his impatient arrogance that cost him. It cost him much."

-Lancalion Levendis Lampara-

6

A Mershul's Rage

"You mean there is no such spell that will catch some-one's soul in a gem?" Stieny asked eagerly, his bushy brown eyebrows arched up with surprise.

The old sage's long white hair bounced as he shook his head from side to side. "Not that I am aware of, little one, but why the interest in dragons and soul spells?"

Stieny shifted nervously from side to side in front of the sage's tall wooden counter. He shuffled his feet and fingered the bright lustrous gold and ruby pin that he happened across a few nights ago. People were always leaving things out for him to stumble across. If they really didn't want him to have things, they wouldn't have left them in such obvious places for him to find them.

Stieny eyed the floor for a moment and then looked up into the sage's deep gray eyes. Stieny was a superb thief. There were few as skilled as he in opening locks and picking pockets. He could hide in a sapling's shadow at noon and he was quieter than a gentle breeze blowing across a smooth pond, but the little halfling was absolutely terrible at lying. No, terrible was not a bad enough word to describe his in-ability to deceive others. Deplorable was more accurate. So he stood before the old sage, shifting his furry feet, fiddling with his brown curly locks with his little finger and picking at his ruby pin. No, lying was not the halfling's strong point.

"No reason, just wondering. Not that I have encoun-tered any dragons or anything like that. I just like to know about soul spells and dragons and stuff," the little thief said, stuttering and tripping over his words as he went along.

The sage arched an eyebrow and looked down at the little thief from behind his hawk-like nose. Stieny felt the sage's silence and became more nervous. The old man's lack of speech made the little halfling feel like he needed to ex-plain more.

"You see, I have a friend. His name is... Fred. Fred met a dragon that said he could put his soul into a gem if he didn't do what the dragon wanted," Stieny said with his squeaky little voice.

The sage smiled worriedly. "And what did this 'Fred' do?"

Stieny stared at the ceiling for a moment, twirled his hair around his little finger, and then looked back at the sage. "He drew his sword, 'cause ya know Fred was a great warrior, and he cut the dragon's head off," Stieny said as he made a swinging motion in the air as if he were acting in a local play.

The sage dismissed any real threat of a dragon being nearby by the halfling's outrageous tale. "Ooooo. This Fred must be mighty indeed!" the sage said with mock admiration.

Stieny smiled all the wider. He was such a good story-teller. His momma was right. He should have been a bard. Too bad being a bard didn't pay as well as being a treasure hunter. All halfling thieves called themselves treasure hunt-ers. Thief was such a roguish term. "Oh, Fred is! He also said that if anyone ever messes with me he will chop their heads off, too!"

The sage tossed his hands up in front of him, feigning a defensive posture. "Well, I hope I have helped Master Git-tledorf to his liking," the sage said as he took the leather purse containing a few gold coins and sliding it under the table. In truth, he knew as little about magic as most sages. Sages knew about history, prophecy and any other kind of teachings, but they knew little of the actual workings of spells. Only mages and sorcerers knew exactly how they worked, but the sage did not feel bad about leading the little halfling astray. He was sure the brown leather purse with the cut string that he pulled from the counter had been taken by the greedy little thief. Sometimes the right justice for a thief was a little theft. "Is there anything else I can do for Master Gittledorf today?"

Stieny shook his head from side to side, satisfied with the sage's explanations of spells and even more satisfied at his own storytelling. He had tricked a supposed genius that he had a friend named Fred who could cut off a dragon's head. It wasn't until the little thief walked out into the cold morning air of the street that it occurred to him, that if he could trick a genius so easily, what if whoever taught him that there was no spell about trapping someone's soul had tricked him just as easily. Stieny silently cursed himself for ruining his otherwise good mood with such negative thoughts as he made his way down the street. It really didn't matter anyway. He stole the gold coins from a guardsman. After close inspection of the coins, Stieny noticed they were dirty, or marked. It was common for Beyklan officials to place small nicks or imprints on certain coins that they allow thieves to steal. When the thief tries to spend the coins at any city owned establishment, the city official looks for the mark and then arrests whoever tried to spend it. Stieny covered his mouth as he giggled uncontrollably at the thought of the sage trying to spend the coins and getting arrested. It was then that it dawned on him, that the sage would tell the guards that he got the coins from a halfling named Stieny Gittledorf. Stieny cursed himself again for ruining an otherwise perfect day, but it was painfully clear that he could not stay in town – not with the sage flapping his tongue about him. Perhaps he should go see a gladiator fight before he left. The arena was Central City's largest pull and people came from thousands of miles to see the gladiator fights. He might as well, too, since he was close by.

Stieny made his way through the thick crowd that was gathered in the streets on the cold winter day. He had to consciously make himself place his hands in his pockets to keep from snatching coin purses as he made his way through the herd of people. The halfling really wanted to take a few of the coin purses, but he felt if he got caught, it would ruin his chances to see the fight for the rest of his life. Stieny guessed he could refrain from stealing for a bit longer.

The halfling made his way across the city, deftly maneuvering among the crowd of people that infested the city streets. There were many wagons and horse-drawn carriages that rode down the center of the roads, and twice as many men and women on foot at the edges. Central City was surely more bustling than the thief had ever imagined. Dipping and ducking, he managed to move west toward the expansive round stone structure that he kept in his vision. The structure was an amazing feat of architecture. The halfling was dumbfounded at how tall and wide it was, each brick detailed with immaculate carvings and designs – like some kind of gigantic mosaic. The building seemed out of place among the other human buildings. They were all large and seemed to stretch to the sky, but most of them were drab in comparison, lacking the divine detail that the arena possessed. The other buildings seemed infinitely newer also. Not that the arena looked old, or crumbled – it merely it looked older. It almost seemed to Stieny as if the other buildings were built around the spherical monument.

As the halfling made his way to the base of the arena, he had to place his hand over his mouth in admiration. The little halfling didn't normally appreciate such things, but he found himself breathless. How the humans could move about such a grand work of art so nonchalantly was beyond him. They were a reckless culture that lacked any real ability or appreciation in art and the other finer things in life. Though few halflings were great artisans and craftsman, it did not mean they could not appreciate them.

Stieny ducked and weaved his way to the base of the thick marble steps that led up into the stone structure. People came and went from the stairs that led into the middle of the stands. He could hear trumpets and drums sounding from inside and the yell of fruit and bread vendors plying their trade. Stieny climbed his way up the large staircase, moving around people that gave him angry stares and mutters for getting in their way. Humans were so rude. Stieny figured it was because they rarely gave to charity, the little halfling thought to himself as he slid a fat coin purse into the deep pockets of his breeches. At least he was able to ease that one's suffering. By the feel of the leather coin pouch, that man had been suffering a great deal.

Stieny reached the top of the stairs and was taken aback by the sight. The arena was the largest structure he had ever been in. It could easily fit daisy valley, Stieny's home town, within its walls. Tens of thousands sat on the stone benches that surrounded the center area like steep hills. There was about a fifteen foot sheer stone wall that divided the staging area from the seating area. Every thirty feet or so was a stone battlement that was flush with the top of the wall that housed three guards with crossbows that surely shot anyone that might try to escape from the fight. The whole gruesome scene excited the little halfling. He had never been exposed to such a sport in his entire life. He liked thieving because it gave him a rush. He could only imagine the rush the gladiators must feel, though Stieny never once thought of trying it himself. Thieving was much easier and safer too.

The center of the arena was flat and had a dark brown dirt floor that was littered with weapons and bodies. There were men coming out of four small iron portcullis gates at the base of the walls at the north, south, east and west. Stieny couldn't see far into the gates, but it appeared that there was stone ramp that led down no doubt into the dungeons where the prisoners were kept. The men in the arena stacked the bodies onto a thick wooden cart while others gathered up the swords and shields, placing them on a separate cart. There was a third cart that was brought over to the pile of bodies and any armor they were wearing was striped and tossed into it. The men didn't bother wiping the bloodied metal plates down and soon the blood that dripped off of them made a small crimson-dotted trail in the dirt as it was pulled from the arena. The crowd was up and moving, buying buttered bread, fruits and meats on sticks. Stieny noticed that some of the patrons were still sitting so he figured that there was another show. He wandered his way to the front bleacher area, directly over a portcullis. The marbled bench that ringed the arena was not comfortable at all, but he noticed that many people brought their own soft padding to sit on. He stood for a while until someone left their padded cushion unattended. He quickly snatched it up and made his way along the rail at the bottom of the seating area. After moving to the other side of the arena, Stieny placed the cushion down on the cold stone seat. It was quite a fancy seat made of red silk and golden lacey frills that dangled down from each side. The halfling smiled as he snuggled his little behind into the cushion, curling his legs up as he fished for the money purse he had stolen earlier. He retrieved a few coppers and when a vending man walked by, he waved his arm. The vendor came over with a smile. He was about twenty years old, Stieny guessed, though he never could tell with humans.

"Three copper, little one," the vendor said as he held out a nice thick slice of buttery bread.

Stieny frowned. Three coppers! That was outrageous. He could buy an entire meal at an inn for one cooper, let alone three. "That is outrageous! I could buy..."

The vendor turned and started walking away.

"Where are you going?" Stieny asked.

The vendor stopped and turned around. "There are thousands of other people that will pay for the bread without griping about it. If you want some, dish out the coin. If not, then shut up."

Stieny was taken aback by the vendor's rudeness and stuck out his tongue in response. The vendor huffed and started walking away, immediately assailed by requests to buy his bread. Stieny quickly picked up his seat and made his way higher into the crowd, away from the vendor. When he reached the top of the lower level, on the opposite side, he pulled a second money purse from his pockets. The coin purse was fat with coppers and a few silver. *The vendor didn't deserve it,* he thought to himself. He could tell by his rudeness that his money was obviously going to his head. Stieny was glad he was able to help the man rid himself of his rudeness.

The halfling quickly called a second bread vendor and gladly paid for the hot buttered bread. He didn't mind so much since the first vendor bought it for him, but the prices were outrageously high. Before the little thief could ponder it more, he spied a small balcony near the top of the lower level that held men and women with bright instruments. Some held steel drumsticks before a large set of drums, while others held bright brass-colored instruments. They scrambled about to get into place as one of them stood up and blew a long single trumpet sound. The high pitched honk echoed throughout the arena.

Men and women of the crowd quieted themselves as the

portcullis at the north end opened up. The iron gate creaked and squeaked as it was hoisted and the band played a deep drum base with occasional symbol clangs. Fifteen men marched out of the chamber wearing various types of armor, though none seemed to be matched well. Some wore pieces of plate armor over skin, where others wore bits of chain and leather. The armor was stained and rusted from blood and often bore deep gashes and dents from previous battles. Most of the men were short and thin, obviously underfed. They had long greasy hair and held their weapons as awkwardly as they wore the mismatched armor. One of the men stood out, though. He was about six and a half feet tall, much taller than the other men, and he wore a chain shirt that he had fastened into his belt to keep it from dangling about. He held a large two-handed sword in his hands and seemed to stalk out of the north portcullis rather than walk. He had long greasy brown hair that hung down to his shoulders in thick dirty strands. His skin was darker than theirs and he was twice as muscular. The other men glanced around the arena nervously, while he ignored the crowd and watched the closed iron gates as if he expected a monster to come out of them at any moment. The little halfling nestled himself deep into the red cushion and feasted on his buttery bread. *Not a bad day at all*, he thought to himself. He had double-crossed a dragon, earned some coin, and managed to get into the greatest arena in Terrigan for free. *Not a bad day at all.*

That morning, when Jude awoke in his dirty cell, there was fresh straw that had been tossed in through the narrow bars and some kind of soupy brown mush in an iron bowl had been slid under the small rectangular hole in the bottom of his door. He had been in the cell for over a week and had regained some of his lost strength by eating the slop. He wasn't sure what was in it, but it tasted like some kind of meat, mashed with potatoes and bread. It was always cold and often had small dead beetles in it, but he knew he had to eat if he was to keep his strength. Jude rubbed the sleep from his eyes and stretched his sore muscles. He still felt the effects from the long walk to Central City, but the stiff wooden bed he slept on seemed to have more of an effect on him now.

Grabbing the cold iron bowl, Jude picked out the straw and the bugs from the surface of the soupy concoction. He sighed as they insects broke apart when he tried to remove them, leaving many of their little black legs behind. Jude quickly grew tired of picking at the food and poured a large swallow into his mouth. He didn't chew the substance, it really didn't need to be chewed. He merely mashed the large chunks with the roof of his mouth and swallowed. He had eaten worse when Lance tried to cook a supposed elven dish a few years back. Jude shook his head sorrowful at the thought of his lost friend. What had happened to him? Was he still with the elves or had they killed him? Had he been tried by the local magistrate and then killed because they knew he could not fight in the arena? He wanted to ask about him, but was worried that the city officials did not know Lance had been with him, and they might go after him if they hadn't already.

Jude recalled the commotion in Lance's cell the day the fighting occurred outside the small hill-like prison of the elves. The swordsman suspected that the elves either still had Lance or they killed him. They were obdurate about some deed he was about to do or with him directly for some reason. Jude thought of the elf that was with the paladin. Overmoon was her name. What he wouldn't do for thirty seconds with her alone with his sword. She would scream for her betrayal of them. The wicked bitch probably pocketed the money that they did have when they were arrested. How she duped the paladin was beyond him, but Jude didn't doubt he was a holy sword of Justice. Jude had seen him work some of his god's power and imposters or conmen couldn't do the things he did.

Jude finished swallowing the lumpy paste when the door to his cell opened. Three guards stood in front of him, one with manacles and the other two had swords. Jude thought about making his break right then and there, but he had seen little of the inside of the arena and wasn't sure where to run once he had killed the three men that stood before him. He was sure if he failed to escape, they would kill him. It was foolish to waste his only chance when he hadn't educated himself on the ins and outs of the place.

"Put these on," said the guard as he tossed the manacles to the floor in front of Jude. The heavy iron bindings clanged on the stone floor. Jude stared at the iron cuffs for a moment before bending down slowly and sliding them over his wrists. The guard then stepped forward and clicked them in place, locking them securely.

"This way, oaf," the man said as he grabbed the center of the chain that held the manacles together.

"No need to hurt my feelings," Jude said with sarcasm as he was led down a small corridor.

"Don't worry, oaf. In a few minutes, hurt feelings will be the least of your problems," the guard said as he led Jude into a large room with a high ceiling. The room was made of stone, as was the rest of the arena, but there was a large wooden bench that surrounded the room with fourteen other men sitting on it. They were mostly haggard and small, with the look of stark horror on their faces. The guard motioned for Jude to sit. Jude sat down and the guard fed his shackles through an iron pole connected to the wooden bench. The guards turned and walked from the room as another man wearing a dirty tunic and breeches and was not armed, walked into the room with an arrogant stride. When he stepped into the light, Jude recognized him as Lyndall, the gladiator champion who was close to buying his freedom. He wore no shackles but he claimed he was as much as a slave as Jude was, though Jude imagined given an open door or his cell, and the gladiator would choose his cell every time. Jude figured the man had been fighting so long, he knew little else.

Lyndall looked over the group of haggard men and shook his head with disappointment. "My name is Lyndall. If you have not heard of me, I am the reigning champion of the arena. Today you go through your first fight as gladiators. Most of you will die. In fact, it is unfortunate for you since you are picked to represent the battle of the Torrent Manor. You are to face many dwarves that were captured after the attack on Central City. They will be well armed, as the dwarves were, and you will not be, as the soldiers were not. As you all know the outcome of the battle, you know the odds are against you. I am not here to belittle you for your crimes, or call you evil vermin. I am here to embrace you as brothers and send you into battle."

Jude growled under his breath and jerked against the manacles that held him to the heavy wooden bench. "Brothers! Pah!" Jude spit at Lyndall's feet. "You are no brother of mine. A real brother would face the vermin with us, not cower behind his name. Who have you fought, champion? Thieves? Beggars? Come face the dwarves with us, like the real men of the Torrent Manor. They had no titles to hide behind."

The other men looked at Jude and then back at Lyndall. They couldn't figure out if Jude was brave or stupid. Lyndall glared at Jude. His ice cold murderous stare silenced the room. "It is too bad you will die today, oaf, or I would teach you some humility," Lyndall said as he turned and closed the door to the cell. The heavy iron door banged into place and the click of the lock resounded like the pounding of a judge's gavel. Jude growled again as the short gladiator marched down the corridor.

"I will return after this fight with the dwarves, you so-called champion. I am eager for this lesson in humility. I am sure I will learn it well when I humiliate you," Jude yelled after Lyndall.

Lyndall turned and stood at the end of the corridor and fixed his cold stare on Jude as the heavy wooden door was closed by one of the other guards. As soon as the wooden door closed at the end of the corridor, a wooden plank set into the wall was raised, revealing a small room containing many pieces of mismatched armor and poor quality weapons. The iron bar that was fed through each man's manacles slid back through a hole in the wall releasing the men. Jude stood and rubbed his wrists while the other men made their way into the room.

"You have two minutes to get ready," a voice called out from behind a small opening in the wall in the room with the weapons and armor. The other prisoners rushed into the room and started trying to piece together the plate armor. Some fought over the heavy, bulky plates. Most had broken leather straps and deep dents and gashes in them from previous battles. Jude located a thick chain shirt that had been tossed onto the corner by the men as they hurried to get the bulkier armor. Jude slid his head and arms through the rusted mail and tucked the lower part of it through his belt to keep it from bouncing around. He tossed most of the weapons aside until he located a large two-handed sword, much like the one he carried when he was captured by the elves. He held the sword over his head and swung it about, careful not to hit one of the other men in the small room. The sword was not created by a master, but it had a decent edge on it. The blade was too large for most men to wield so it didn't get used often.

"Time's up. You have thirty seconds to make your way to the end of the corridor. If you are not in the arena when the portcullis goes down, you will be trapped in the corridor with a pair of lions," the guard called out from the narrow hole in the wall.

The men rushed down the corridor until it turned right and went up a steep cobblestone ramp, leading into bright sunlight. The men slowed when they reached the top of the ramp and entered the arena. The crowd cheered and whooped as the men walked out like scared mice. Jude was the last to walk from the corridor. As soon as he stepped into the arena, the portcullis behind him was lowered. He began to wonder if they had any lions at all. Jude ignored the deafening roar of the crowd and scanned the arena. Its level floor was made of fine dirt. The three other portcullises were closed. There was one directly across from them, and one to each side. The arena was huge, probably one hundred yards across, and Jude imagined they could stage just about any kind of fight they wanted in here. One of the men dropped his sword and grabbed his stomach as he doubled over and vomited. The crowd began laughing and booing, sensing that the prisoners were not skilled fighters.

The group of men stood in the arena for a few minutes when the iron portcullis from the other side started to open slowly. The crowd roared, drowning out the sound of the heavy iron gate being cranked open. When the gate opened fully, dozens of dwarves poured from the open corridor. Some of the men that came out with Jude screamed and ran, while others dropped to their knees and prayed to their gods. Jude shook his head and put his back to the wall next to the iron portcullis he came out of.

The dwarves were wearing poor-fitting chain shirts and wielded oversized axes. Jude figured he could use the poor balanced weapons to his advantage. The dwarves split up and began cutting down the stragglers with relative ease, but they were soon winded. Jude noticed the dwarves were thin and malnourished. The dwarves were easily killing the poor thieves and beggars. The crowd booed realizing there was not going to be much of a fight. Even though the dwarves were weak and underfed, it was obvious they were trained soldiers.

One dwarf cut the man next to him down and Jude sprang into action. With a swift motion he brought the hefty blade down in an angled slice. The strike hit the dwarf with such force that it severed the arm at the shoulder. The dwarf grabbed at his bloody nub and screamed as a fountain of crimson fluid rocketed from the horrid wound. The dwarf turned in shock as Jude laid a wicked gash down his chest. The dwarf fell to the soft dirt with a heavy thud. This seemed to inspire the remaining men and they lifted their weapons to fight, rather than defend.

The crowd sensed the change in the prisoners and roared to life with a deafening cheer.

Jude ducked and dodged attacks, suffering minor hits here and there. Some laying thin slices on his arms and legs, and some were repelled by his chin shirt. His skin glistened with red blood and sweat as he tore into the bearded enemies with savage fury. The realization that he was most probably going to die evoked a primal surge from deep within him. Jude suddenly felt stronger, faster, and braver. He lunged forward into the thick of the dwarves, chopping and slicing, cutting down enemy after enemy. The crowd cheered, rising to their feet. They clapped and roared as the fight raged on. Jude ducked an awkward overhand strike and stabbed his heavy sword forward, impaling it in the chest of the bearded attacker. The weapon made a sucking sound as he tried to free it. Realizing the heavy two-handed sword was lodged in the dwarf, he released it and turned. Another dwarf's axe came slicing down at Jude's head. The large swordsman fell backward, lessening the force of the strike and caught the axe by the shaft, just below the blade. To Jude's surprise, the axes the dwarves used were not dwarven at all. They were of poor quality showing many nicks and scratches of countless battles. Jude hit his back on the hard dirt floor of the arena. Though the dwarf was malnourished, Jude could feel that he was still extremely strong. The swordsman kicked out, striking the dwarf in the legs, knocking them out from under him.

The dwarf fell as Jude rose in time to deflect another axe from a second foe. The dwarves were all around Jude, recognizing him as a skilled enemy, rather than some beggar or thief wearing armor. The battle ensued for minutes longer. Jude noticed when he was pulling his sword free from the body of the dead dwarf that the other men that came out with him were not in any condition to fight for long periods of time and quickly fell to the dwarven axes. The bearded folk pushed Jude and the two remaining men back into a corner of the arena. Jude wished it was a real corner instead of the curve of an oval. The corner would be better defended given the long axes the dwarves were using.

The crowd was on their feet cheering and yelling. There were twelve dwarves remaining from the original forty or so, more than half slain by Jude. The large swordsman towered over everyone in the arena. He gripped his two-handed sword and growled as sweat and blood ran down his arms and legs. The dwarves stood back, just out of range of the deadly reach of Jude's wicked blade. The swordsman could feel the pounding in him, like his heart was pumping twice as much blood as before. His fingers tingled and his nose was numb from rage. His vision was focused on the enemies in front of him. He could not hear nor even see the crowd. There was no one else in the arena save for him and his enemies. There was no arena. It was if he and the dwarves were in some other time. Alone. Nothing else existed.

Jude rushed forward and brought his heavy two-handed sword around in a great sweeping motion. The first dwarf tried to deflect the powerful strike with his axe, but the thick blade cut through the shaft and cleaved the dwarf's head from his shoulder. The blade made a sharp ring as it sliced through the neck of the dwarf, and the bearded man's heavy head made a sickening sound as it bounced off of the arena floor. The crowd made an "ooo" sound, and then roared even louder at the bloody carnage that was unfolding before them.

Jude sliced again and again. He felt the sting of their axes in his flesh, but it seemed distant to him, like it was someone else's pain. He cut again and again until he turned to find there were no dwarves left. All around him lay bodies horribly hacked and cut. The only thing that moved was a man wearing heavy plate armor that had become twisted, more of a hindrance than a help. He was lying on his back with his hands in the air shaking back and forth. He was saying something, Jude thought, as he could see his mouth moving but he couldn't hear anything except for his own breathing. Then in a few seconds all of his other senses came rushing back to him. He could hear the man begging him not to end his life. He could hear the deafening roar of the crowd as they applauded him, and then came the pain. Oh, the terrible pain. It assailed his senses like he had never felt before. His entire body ached and stung and he felt dizzy and woozy from loss of blood. His vision shifted from great focus to white and fuzzy. The sounds that were so loud just moments ago, once again seemed distant. He barely felt the hard dirt floor of the arena as it rushed up and greeted him. Then there was blackness.

"*Determination. It can allow men to achieve things they cannot. It can give someone the strength to overcome trials and tribulations that they would not normally overcome. I once stood at the foot of despair and stared long seep into its great chasm. Yet, my determination allowed me soar above it on the wisps of the wind, when I should not have been able to do so.*

This is why Amerix has not died. There is no magic that is keeping him alive, other than his own determination to not surrender. It is his own wicked stubbornness to not fail that keeps his old stocky legs moving. I often wish I possessed his determination in all the times of my life, rather than during small periods of brief emotional turmoil. Just imagine the great things I would have been able to accomplish had I not been led by emotion rather than blind stubbornness."

-Lancalion Levendis Lampara-

7

The Price of Betrayal

Delania stepped through her bright orange portal into her small, but quaint, underground room. She smiled. She wasn't sure what it was about her little cove that made her make such a strange face, but it always made her heart warm whenever she did it. Nothing else in the Abyss made her feel that way. Usually it was the opposite. She had no qualms about tossing the new spawn into the lake of the damned or severing their heads and tossing them into some deep crevice so the gweits could feast on them for eternity. New spawn were not really anything important. They always appeared and had no power whatsoever, but she couldn't explain her inner need for something more. Delania was powerful, she had a fine grasp of magic and occasionally would match herself against some of the new spawn that thought themselves skilled in the magical arts, but the battles were always brief at best. The truly powerful new spawn were dealt with by the archdemons or sometimes Rha-Cordan himself, but that had not happened in over six hundred years.

The arrogant spawn sometimes thought they could rival the strength of the gods. Such fools. Delania had been studying the necromancies for thousands of years and she could not even begin to wield the power that the archdemons could. The only thing that kept her from Bykalicus' clutches was that she could blink in and out. It was not a magical talent, but more of an innate ability. She could use the ability to cease to exist in some place, at the same time she began to exist in another. It was as easy as thinking for her. As powerful as the archdemon was, he could not keep her from blinking. There were spells that could hold portals that were created by others, keeping the gateway open, but she did not travel through portals. She was not sure exactly how it worked per se; rather that it was simply part of her that she never really questioned.

But today when she appeared in her dwelling, something was different. She was not sure, but something was amiss. She rubbed her pale naked arms and walked over to her wooden bed. Wood was as rare in the Abyss as was a ray of sunshine, but there were demons that had escaped into the real world. They usually didn't last long before they were banished back, but some managed to bring back artifacts. They were traded and kept to confuse and torture the newly spawned in order to break their spirits. Archdemons especially loved to break the will of men.

She found the task loathsome though, and instead relished the chase. She enjoyed chasing the weak and wicked that found themselves in the Abyss. She always could tell the noble from the wicked. The nobles usually seemed confused as to where they were, when the wicked always seemed to realize exactly where they found themselves. She could always smell the disgusting fear that wafted from them.

"Kornicus, are you here?" she called out as she strode across the stone room. She always knew the imp was in the room. He had not the ability to leave, though she had offered him the chance time and time again. But the imp always seemed to want to stay. She had difficulty understanding the imp at times. He had been an agent of the wicked arch demon, Dadramedion, but she offered him a place of retreat, away from the archdemon who threatened him with an eternity of pain and suffering. Eternal suffering was something that there was an abundance of in the Abyss.

Kornicus flew across the room. His wide mouth grinned, deviously exposing hundreds of needlelike teeth. As he came up behind Delania he took in her shapely form. Her long elegant legs rose from her feet and met her perfectly shaped pale white buttocks. The curve of her back was well-muscled and the tail of her long straight black hair was stark contrast against the pale white skin. Her large bright red and black bat wings were neatly folded behind her as she straightened the doily on the stone night stand. What a fool she was, Kornicus thought to himself. She had been planning his demise for thousands of years and just when she thought she had broken him, and she almost had, he would betray her and show her his strength. If Bykalicus did not kill her, she would be so proud of him. He had proven that he could resist her charms for eternity and maybe then she would let him in on her plans. Kornicus was so proud of himself for seeing through her test. He wanted to please Delania.

His clawed imp hands flashed out and stretched the necklace around her neck, securing it there. Delania didn't turn quickly or try to fight she merely turned and stared at him with a look of confusion.

"What are you about, Kornicus?" she asked as she looked down and fingered the pearl necklace that was around her neck.

"You will be so proud of me, Mistress," Kornicus said as he floated in the air in front of her and rubbed his clawed hands together.

Delania froze. The imp had not called her mistress since the beginning when she first allowed him to stay. That was when he thought she had some kind of sinister plan like the other demons. That was when he did not trust her. That was when they were not friends. "What do you mean, *Mistress?*" Delania asked. She could feel the rise of a thick bulge in her throat.

"Just as I said it, Mistress. You will be so proud of me. I almost fell for your devious plot, Mistress, but at the last minute I discovered what you had been trying to teach me."

Delania tried to pull the necklace free from her neck, but it would not budge. She started to pull frantically. She could feel the necklace starting to cut the delicate skin on her neck as she pulled violently, trying to break the pearl collar. "Kornicus, you fool. What have you done?" Delania asked as her voice started to crack with fear.

The imp looked confused. "I figured out your test, Mistress. Aren't you proud of me?"

Delania tugged at the tight pearl necklace in horror. She realized what was different about her humble abode. It had the stink of the sulfuric air from the surface. Only one demon would actively seek her out, or have the ability to penetrate her subterranean lair. Bykalicus.

"Kornicus. Get this thing off of me. You have been

tricked!" she shouted.

The imp frowned, bearing his sharp needlelike teeth. "I have not been tricked, Mistress," he said in a mocking tone. "I figured out what you were..." Delania rushed across the room and grabbed the imp by his ears. Her beautiful face was twisted in fear. "Kornicus, you fool!" she shouted as the imp winced in pain. "I have never, nor will I ever, trick you! Who put you up to this?" she asked, fearing the answer.

Kornicus winced and tried to pry her fingers away from his ears, but she was too strong. "Ow! Let go! You are hurting my ears!" Kornicus pleaded.

Delania let go and hysterically scanned her room. There didn't seem to be any demons around, but they had the ability to disguise themselves as rocks, or anything they wished. "I am sorry for hurting you, Kornicus, but you have placed me in great danger. You must help me get this necklace off," Delania said as she fumbled her delicate fingers around the necklace looking for a clasp. "Why did you do this to me?"

Kornicus frowned. His face wore a look of worried concern. "Bykalicus said I needed to do this to pass your test."

Bykalicus. The name was like murder to her ears. The archdemon was one of the most wicked, ruthless and vile demons she had ever known, and she had known many in her long existence.

"Kornicus," Delania said as she dropped to her knees. "He has tricked you. I have never been anything but true to you. I did not hide you from Dadramedion in order to deceive you. You have nothing to offer me that I cannot attain," Delania pleaded.

Kornicus' mouth hung open in confusion. He realized what she said was true. She was a succubus, one of the more powerful demons of the abyss. Why would she need him for anything? Why, to spy, of course. That was what Dadramedion used him for, spying. "For spying on other demons so you can increase your army."

Delania quickly searched her room for something with which to try to cut the foul collar.

"Kornicus, I have no army. I never have had one. I do not plot or scheme, even if I was like the other of my kind, they do not build armies. Use your head, you fool imp!"

Kornicus felt the insult stab him deep into his chest. He was overcome with an emotion that he had never felt before. It was almost like he felt responsible or an obligation to help Delania. The imp had never felt anything like that before. You do not help anyone but yourself in the Abyss.

A small orange ball of magical energy appeared in the air in front of Delania and Kornicus. The succubus immediately recognized the spell, teleportation. The small orange dot would stretch into a long line and then vertical until a small door that linked two places in the same plane of existence appeared. There were few demons in the Abyss that had the ability to teleport. Of the demons that could teleport, the archdemons were the most predominate. The only archdemons who would have any desire to invade her lair were Dadramedion and Bykalicus. Neither of whom she wished to engage in verbal, or any other kind of, contact. "Kornicus, we can discuss this later. Come, grab a hold of me. We have to escape."

The imp flew out of Delania's reach. His tiny bat wings moved swiftly. "No, why would I flee?"

Delania looked at the portal that was beginning to enlarge vertically, allowing the fetid stench of the surface waft into the room. "Kornicus, whatever he has promised you, he will not fulfill it. Please, Kornicus. You must trust me," Delania pleaded. She understood how demons worked in the Abyss. There were no partnerships, only brief alliances that hinged on a balance of power. As soon as it was advantageous for one demon to betray the other, they did so without hesitation. Delania had searched the Abyss since her creation to find another demon that might not think the same way the others did. She had finally stumbled across Kornicus when she saved him from Dadramedion's clutches. She had kept the imp from harm since, and she had hoped she had managed to show him that betrayal was not the only way. Now it appeared she may be the one to be betrayed.

The imp flew high into the chamber. "He has told me of your test, Mistress. I will show you that I am powerful enough to resist your mind traps. Then you will see my use, and if you don't, Bykalicus will."

Delania shook her head from side to side as the large muscular red leg stepped from the portal. Its foot had long back claws that extended from scaled reptilian toes. Small flames flickered across the demon's skin like long fur in a breeze.

The large powerful form of Bykalicus stepped through the portal. His bright yellow eyes quickly scanned the room and he smiled in victory as he stared at the pearl necklace that was around the succubus' neck. Delania stood against the twelve foot arch demon defiantly, her fists tight against her side. "You come uninvited, Bykalicus."

The archdemon growled deeply at the use of his name. "I have warned you against using my name, wench," he said, his reptilian eyes never wavering from the pearl necklace that was snug against Delania's neck.

Delania ignored the archdemon and turned her attention to Kornicus. "Last chance, Kornicus. Come with me or suffer the consequences."

The imp crossed his arms and shook his bony head defiantly. "I'll not come this far, to be tricked now," the imp said boldly.

Bykalicus laughed suddenly. "Go ahead and blink from here, Delania. You will find yourself in a much worse place than here, or I could remove the pesky thing from your neck after you have given me a bit of your time."

Delania glowered at him. "I will not be trapped by you, Bykalicus. You are pathetic and weak. You have been chasing me for thousands of years and for the first time you manage to get this string of rocks on my neck. As for a bit of my time, I would rather cease to exist!"

The archdemon's smile slowly faded from his face. He drew his sword with impossible speed and brought it down toward Delania's head. The wicked blade rocketed toward her, but just as the sinister weapon would have sliced into her delicate skin, she was gone. The archdemon bent over and roared where the succubus had been standing. The flames that danced across his body flared in a bright flash. The archdemon brought his sword down into Delania's wooden furniture, shattering it into hundreds of pieces. He kicked the stone fixtures, breaking them. After the raging archdemon had destroyed everything in the dwelling, he turned his attention to Kornicus. The little green-skinned imp was hovering at the top of the chamber with a half-smile on his impish little face. "Why have you not ever left Kornicus?" Bykalicus asked as his massive chest heaved in his fury.

The imp fiddled with his fingers nervously. "I cannot, great master. I would have never come here, since I cannot see in the darkness at this depth."

Bykalicus nodded to himself and created another portal. The thin orange light of the magical door illuminated the room in a pale ginger hue. "That is what we thought," Bykalicus said as he stepped halfway into the portal and ducked his great horned head under. The archdemon turned and looked back into the stone structure from the other side of the magical gateway. "That's good, even better that you cannot see in the dark at this depth. Dadramedion hopes you enjoy your stay. If you become lonely you can embrace the darkness, it will never leave you."

Kornicus' eyes went wide with fear at the archdemon's name. "M-my stay? What do you mean, great master?" the imp asked as the orange portal Bykalicus had stepped through grew smaller and smaller, until it was a small dot hovering in the air. Kornicus flew over to the spec of magical energy that grew paler every second. The imp glanced around the room as it slowly grew darker and darker. "Bykalicus wait! You can't leave me here forever!" the imp said as he clawed at the spot in vain. "Bykalicus!" the imp shrieked in a long drawn-out piercing scream.

The small magical light vanished with a brief flash, then all was black. Kornicus stared around at his pitch black stone prison. He suddenly felt foolish. Then he wished for a death that would never come.

Amerix pounded the red-hot iron with the heavy smithy hammer. The metal cried out with shrill rings that resounded off of the wooden walls of the small building. Thomas wiped his sweaty brow with the dirty, oily sleeve of his tunic as he also shaped the hot metal. It was the fifteenth day since the dwarf arrived and started working in his shop and he had already cleared his orders for the next six months. He had been backlogged for years and he never guessed in his wildest dreams he would be caught up. Yet, he and the dwarf pounded out horseshoes, door claps, wagon axels, wheel housings, and a myriad of other metal items that the locals had ordered.

Thomas was known as an accomplished smith and people would wait for his product rather than go with another. Since he had been working with the dwarf he had learned a great deal about smithing that he had never known. He often paused to watch the skill of Amerix as he pounded out in a few quick strikes what would have taken him more than an hour. The old grizzled dwarf was surely a master in his own right. Thomas shook his head as he finished pounding out the long round haft of a heavy door lock. The dwarf, Amerix, was supposed to be this vicious killer, and Thomas knew he was. The smith knew of firsthand accounts of what Amerix had left for the others to find at the Torrent, yet the old dwarf with the ratty silver-streaked beard and leathery face, was friendly and considerate as a smith partner. Thomas was going to hate when the royal guards arrived and took him. It hadn't taken long for a response back from Central City and they had dispatched two units of thirty seasoned men as soon as they received his account. That was about a week ago. At a hard ride they would be at Portia anytime.

The smithy felt a pang of guilt every time he thought of the men coming to take his dwarf partner so he always began a conversation to ease his mind whenever he thought about it. "So uh,... Am," Thomas began, tossing the long slender hasp into the cooling bucket as he leaned against the thick scarred wooden bench that rested against the wall. "What is your grand plan for life?"

Amerix finished hammering the hot iron and tossed it into the cooling barrel. It made a hissing splash as Amerix wiped his dirty soot-covered hands on his apron. He turned and stared up at the smithy and cocked his head as he squinted. The smithy always seemed to pose the strangest off-the-wall questions sometimes.

"What do ye mean?" Amerix asked as he hung the heavy steel mallet on the wall, placing the head between two wooden pegs.

Thomas shrugged his shoulders as he too wiped his hands on his apron. "I don't know. I mean, do you plan to make a life here in Portia? You said you were just passing through, but you have stayed for fifteen days so far. You plan on leaving soon, or are you going to stick around for a while?"

Amerix's mind raced. *What did the human mean? Why had he counted the days since he arrived? Had the smithy recognized him?* Amerix cursed himself for a flea-bitten orc. Of course he had recognized him. The man spoke fluent dwarven. That meant he had most probably worked up in the Pyberian Mountains. Humans didn't live as long as dwarves, so he must have been there recently, before Tharxton had ordered all the humans from Mountain Heart. Amerix cursed himself again. *How could he have been so stupid?* He was a five foot tall dwarf with a long, unbraided beard that was streaked with silver. There were few of those. In fact, he guessed he was the tallest dwarf in history. Amerix figured that the smithy had assumed that he was Amerix and if he wasn't, what did the smithy have to lose? There probably was a large bounty on his head put out by the wicked King Theobold.

Amerix glanced at the hammer that hung from the wall. He was sure he could reach and crush the smith's head in before he could make it to the door. But Amerix thought of the smith's kids. He had grown to like them over the last two weeks and his wife made the most succulent butter cakes. She was always so nice and patted his cheeks with her soft hands. As a dwarf, Amerix didn't like soft hands, but they seemed appropriate on her. Amerix shook his head. He was surely getting weak. In his youth he wouldn't have even given second thought about killing the smith and moving on. After all, he was nothing more than a disgusting, loathsome human. *No,* Amerix thought to himself. *No, Thomas was more than a human. He was a husband, a father and the closest thing to a friend I have had in over a hundred years, other than Vlargcar that is.* Vlargcar. Amerix needed to leave soon. The humans were probably due at Portia anytime. Thomas wouldn't have even mentioned such a ridiculous question if they were not.

Amerix had fashioned the chain armor for himself and Vlargcar, and was now working out of enjoyment. It had been a long time since he had worked a forge and the butter cakes.... "No, Thomas, I was thinking of staying in the area. I really like helping ye with yer forge, even if it is primitive and backwards," Amerix said with a half-smile.

Thomas' smile faded. *If the dwarf planned on staying longer, why did he keep glancing at the door? Had he given away too much by asking the dwarf if he planned on staying around a while?* Thomas cursed himself. The general didn't live as long as he had by being blind. He might as well have told the dwarf that the men were coming and would be here any minute, by his stupid comments. Then strangely, the thought of the dwarf getting away didn't seem to bother him. He wasn't sure why. The men of the Torrent Manor had been mercilessly slaughtered, but surely this Amerix had nothing to do with it. Perhaps the reports were exaggerated, or it was some propaganda plot by the king. Thomas was sure the slaughter took place, but perhaps the reports he heard were inflated to great horrors to aid the king in swaying the south to his views on controlling the gold and silver rich mountains. Thomas didn't even need the reward money now. Sure the money would allow his family, for generations to come, to never have to work again, but he wasn't hurting for money. All the work the dwarf did would bring in about five months of wages in a single month, not counting all the new business it would bring in. He would be able to hire that second person he had been thinking about. Too bad he couldn't hire Amerix. He knew the dwarf was worth his weight in gold.

Amerix studied the smith for a few more moments. The smith had to be smarter than to let something like that slip. He was sure the smith planted the conversation in order to warn him without actually warning him. Thomas was his friend, after all. How the humans of the village figured out who he was, he wasn't sure, because as far as he was concerned, very few, if any, had ever seen him. He came before the sun came up, and went home after it had set. Considering how poor human's eyes were in nighttime, they probably just took him for a short man. It didn't matter now, though. He and Vlargcar had to flee today.

"Thank ye," Amerix said as he grabbed the surprised smithy's hand and shook it firmly.

"For what?" the smithy asked in a confused tone. Amerix was undaunted by the smithy's claim of ignorance. "Ye know for what. And if ye don't, then I thank yer foolishness just the same. Ye are truly a good friend, and I hope to pound the forges with ye again tomorrow," Amerix said as he grabbed his leather pack and opened the door.

Thomas frowned as the dwarf shook his hand. *How did he know?* He hadn't said much at all. If he did, he didn't mean too, did he? The smile on the old dwarf's face warmed him somehow and the sight of the so-called bearded demon leaving his shack brought a smile to his face. He did mean to ask such a thought provoking question. He just didn't realize it at the time. "You are welcome, Am," Thomas said, fearing that if actually said what he suspected the dwarf's name really was, the dwarf's unseen sinister side might shine and cut him down.

Amerix ducked out of the smithy shop and hurried up the hill to the camp sight. It was in the middle of the day, but he could not afford to wait until nightfall for the guards to come. He and the orc needed as much time between them as possible.

Thomas felt a profound sense of loss as he watched the dwarf run up the hill. The old smithy went inside and hugged his wife. She looked at him puzzled for moment then she smiled back at him. "You are a good man, Thomas Arwar," she said as she gently stroked his arm. "We don't need the money that bad. I'm sure the reports from the north were an exaggeration in order to sway our stand on the war with the bearded folk. You would kill too, if someone was trying to hurt me or the boys."

Thomas nodded and smiled. His wife was so wise and

supportive of him. He was a lucky man. It was the knock at the door that roused him of his doldrums with his wife. Thomas calmly walked over and opened it, surprised to be staring down the tip of a heavy crossbow. There were about ten men outside. They were heavily armed and armored, though they bore no semblance to a military unit. They appeared as a disheveled rowdy looking lot. Thomas tried to look past the crossbow bolt as he regarded the only man that was atop of a horse. The smithy figured he was the leader of the band. "Is there something I might help you with?" he asked.

The man atop the horse spit at the ground and didn't wipe his mouth, leaving the spit to drip from his unshaven chin. "Word is, you gotsa dwarf living with you that is wanted by Beyklan law."

Thomas almost chuckled. A mercenary group. The man on the horse was probably a bounty hunter and he hired the other men to hunt the dwarf with him. Bounties were illegal by common citizens and this lot didn't look to be in the army. "No dwarves here, I assure you, but you don't look to be from the army."

The man chuckled and spat again. "I ain't from no army, fool. And I don't care 'bout no laws either. I am working for bounty up north and I ain't afraid of yer pathetic guards round here. Now move aside so I can look through yer house and see for myself that there ain't no dwarves in here."

Thomas felt his anger rage. "You are not coming in my house, pig. If you wish to look in it, go and fetch the watch. I'll not..."

The pang of the crossbow's string was the last thing the smithy heard as the heavy bolt rocketed into his forehead. Thomas's body fell limp to the floor.

"Search the house. If ya find more traitors to the crown in there, kill them too. If the watch tries to give ya a hard time, kill them. We will cut down any who stand in the way of the king. I'll be with the rest of the men, circling the village and seeing if the dwarf is camping outside of town," the dirty leader said as he reined his horse away.

One of the men chuckled as he stepped over the still

body of Thomas. "That's the price of betrayal, traitor."

"What do we do after we search the house, Meirgan?" another of the men asked.

Meirgan didn't look back as he calmly rode his horse to the north. "Burn it."

"One who kills expects to be killed. One who steals expects to be stolen from. It is a strange fact of human nature. It is a fact that people see others as they see themselves. Just as a thief imagines others are thinking of stealing his property like he thinks of stealing theirs, a cheating spouse often imagines or convinces himself that his spouse is cheating also. One who enslaves imagines others seek to enslave, and so on and so forth.

Kornicus was a victim to his own character flaws. He imagined that Delania, the only being in his long existence that offered him a true companionship, had betrayed him. Their's was certainly not a friendship; she was unable to comprehend the meaning of friendship at that time in her existence. There was no such emotion as friendship in the Abyss. She knew only death and dying, though she longed for something more. She created a haven or a retreat if you will from the everyday horrors of life in the Abyss. Ultimately Kornicus betrayed her, thinking that she was trying to betray him. The sad fact is he acted as he did to impress the succubus. He hoped by betraying her she would see how intelligent he was. The poor creature spent thousands of years with Delania with the thought of his every waking hour that she was plotting against him. He imagined that with each passing second he existed was a narrow escape from her ruthlessness. What a sad existence for those creatures created to rule in the Abyss. Yet, there is some mercy in their tortured existence. They knew nothing of a better place, or if they had experience, their black and incorrigible hearts had no desire for something better. They enjoyed the endless torment and the hate that they perpetuated by their own actions. But what of Delania? She had longed for something better. Can you imagine the pain and strife of a being that had known nothing since her creation but pain and endless torment and one day she discovered the beauty of the world? She was enabled to experience companionship, friendship, love, only to have these powerful emotions ripped away from her.

Delania was sent to walk the earth for a short time then forced to return to the deep Abyss from which she was created. She had never known anything better than the endless screams and torments of those in the Abyss. She had never heard laughter of a child. Some argue that she was blessed to learn such emotions, even if it was for a short time, but I say she was cursed. She was cursed to know what love is, only to be sent back into the horrible pit of despair for eternity to forever long and cry for what she would never have again. Sometimes the truest form of evil is knowledge. I should know. Knowledge put a black scar on my heart that stretched space and time. The bliss of ignorance. How I often long for it."

-Lancalion Levendis Lampara-

8

Darrion-Quieness

General Bodrell trotted his horse through the misty vale. It was strange that the valley had a grassy floor and was much warmer than anywhere else in Beykla during wintertime. The grassy valley was littered with dark gray boulders that had fallen from the rocky slopes surrounding it on both sides. There were occasionally bright yellow lichens and other tundra plant life. Though the valley was warmer than anywhere else, it was still a mountain valley and was too cool year round to grow any deciduous trees or other warmer climate-based vegetation.

The general and his men had rode most of the day through the mist. His clothes were damp from the fog, making him feel chilled. It was near dark when they discovered the first sign of the initial scouting party.

Bodrell dismounted from his horse and walked to the front of the animal, pulling down twice on the reins, and then leaving them hanging in front of it. The horse was well trained and knew he was not to go anywhere that he was to stand as if tied. The general knelt down and felt the valley floor. There was a three inch thick sheen of ice that covered the grass, extending as far as he could see in the thick fog. The ice had been melting and was very slick, with steam rising off of it. The general guessed that the melting ice was what was causing the unusual fog that cascaded down the valley toward the army. The ice was too slippery to march the horses on, and he didn't dare take only the men much further.

Bodrell removed his gloves and gingerly stepped onto the icy valley floor. The ice didn't break, or crack, but it was slippery under his thick-soled riding boots. He walked until he could no longer see his men. The horseman wanted to complain, or issue a voice of warning, but the general had warned them of speaking when they arrived near the location of the battle. He said that whatever it was that had slain the soldiers, they surely didn't want to give it any idea of their presence if they didn't have to.

As Bodrell moved through the fog, he noticed a large thick shape in the distance. He paused and knelt, hoping the shape, if it was a monster of some kind, would think him a rock if it looked in his direction. Bodrell watched the shape for some minutes but the silhouette never stirred. He took a deep breath and stepped closer. What he saw horrified him. There, frozen in block of ice, was one of their scouts and his horse. The animal was frozen from the base of its neck to its hind quarters. The rider atop it was frozen from the waist down. Not just frozen, but encased in a thick block of murky ice. The horse was missing its head, as if something had cut it off leaving jagged pieces of frozen flesh hanging down. The front of horse was covered in dark red frozen blood that had spilled out from the animal. The rider had his head slumped forward with his arms hanging limp at his side.

Bodrell inched forward, glancing around himself, searching for whatever beast or wizard could do such a thing. The general had heard of monsters that could breathe a breath of ice so cold that it could freeze creatures instantly. But he knew of powerful wizards that could do such things, too. Though what confused him was that there were very few dwarven clerics, let alone dwarven wizards. He didn't think he had ever heard of a dwarven wizard, at least none of any real power. Surely not powerful enough to do something like this.

As Bodrell examined the frozen corpse of the rider, he noticed that the rider's sword was lying on the ice at the base of the ghastly scene. The rider was undoubtedly dead, but the ice around his waist had thick groves in it, suggesting the rider was not killed instantly and tried to chip his way out from the frozen tomb. The thought of the pain and terror the rider must have endured made Bodrell shudder.

The general made his way to the front of the frozen mass

and examined the neck area of the horse. The ice around the horse's missing head was jagged and cut, like it had been sheared off. There were no pieces of meat from the horse lying on the ground and the frozen blood was not disturbed. Had the head been cut off of the animal, there would undoubtedly be footprints of the creature that did it, or at least the arterial spray would be imperfect, yet there were no footprints and the spray of blood was congruent as if it spurted out without any obstructions.

Bodrell went back and examined the rider closer. He had no injuries that Bodrell could see and there were tiny frozen droplets of blood on the rider's clothes, further suggesting the animal lost its head after it had been frozen. If the dwarves were behind the attack, they went out of their way to make it appear like a beast. Bodrell left the ghastly scene and scanned the frozen ground, looking for any signs of footprints, weapons or dwarven bodies, but he found none. Even outside of the icy floor, there were no disruptions in the grass. Bodrell doubted the dwarves were behind the attack. The general quickly scanned the murky fog ceiling of the valley. There was something in these mountains that killed these men. Something besides dwarves. Something big.

Bodrell quickly made his way back to his horse. He could see his men's desire to speak, to ask him what he found, to ask whether the dwarves were behind the attack, but they were a well-disciplined unit. They didn't speak, even when the general gave the unexpected order to return to camp. Their duties would lead them to war against the cursed dwarven people of the mountains. The people who killed their friends and comrades at the Torrent Manor, the ones who had slain their children at the battle of Central City. No, the horsemen knew they would have their revenge. It was only a matter of time. The king would not have brought the entire western army if he planned on making treaties.

Bodrell dismounted his horse when he arrived at camp. The valley was dark, save for a few fires that the smithies had blazing. The valley was especially dark at night with the thick blanket of fog that covered them. Bodrell handed the steed to one of his two assistants and entered his tent.

The warm blast of air hit him like a maiden's kiss and he removed his armor, his heavy wet tunic and breeches. He tossed the soggy clothing onto his cot and opened the thick wooden chest that sat at the foot of it. The chest creaked open and he removed another fine red velvety garment that had delicate white frill at the cuffs and amazing golden embroidery about the chest and the pockets. Bodrell quickly placed the garment on and pulled down at the bottom of it, straightening the lavish tunic. He slid his cold legs into the breeches and sat on the cot as he placed on a dry pair of stockings that had been hanging by the fire. He smiled as his cold toes slid into the warm socks and then he put on his walking boots. They were dry also and warm, since they had been resting near the fire. He didn't normally keep a fire hearth in his tent, but he felt unusually cold here in the damp air of the mountain valley. He guessed he was just getting old, though he couldn't recall ever fighting any campaigns in any mountains. The general didn't wait for his assistant to tend to his thick leather armor. He grabbed a bulky towel from the rack that also hung his fine dining jacket, and wiped the moisture from the inside of his armor. When he had soaked up most of the moisture, he slid the heavy leather armor over his tunic and secured the thick leather straps at the side and under the arms.

He checked himself in the mirror and smiled. He was certainly a handsome man. He should have been playboy, not a soldier. His father was unquestionably wealthy enough to have tended to his material needs, but he discovered that life around the mansion was boring and he longed for something more. He ended up in the army and quickly rose among the lower ranking officers with his quick wit and battle sense.

Bodrell stepped from the tent and started toward the king's chambers. He frowned at the cold damp air, but it was nothing compared to the sticky wet air that was high up the valley. He hoped the king would hear his report and recommendations and leave the valley if the dwarves didn't make an arrival. He knew his western army could easily guard the mountain's base until his scouts managed to find their exact location in the spring.

The general stepped into the king's tent. It was warm and dry with the fresh smell of cinnamon that hung in the air like a baker's pantry. The king was lounging in an easy chair and his red silk-covered feet dangled by the fire on a velvety foot cushion. He held aloft a fine crystal goblet of red liquid that he swirled and stared at for some time. The sight of the king angered Bodrell. Though his anger quickly subsided when he saw the thick battle-scarred suit of brass colored plate mail armor hanging on the wooden armor stand. The king may enjoy his comforts on the battlefield, but when the battle arrived, he was the first into the fray, the fact that kept Bodrell for harboring contempt against him.

"My King, I bring word from the scouting party," Bodrell announced as he removed his gloves and tucked them under his belt.

The king swished the red wine around in the goblet again before swallowing it in a deep gulp. "And what have you to report, General Bodrell? Were the dwarves behind the missing scouts?"

General Bodrell shifted his weight and cleared his throat. "No, My King. I do not believe they were."

Theobold sat up in his easy chair and set the goblet on the wooden stand next to him. He gave the general an odd look and gestured to a wooden chair that was resting by the fire. "Please sit, General. Tell me of your findings."

General Bodrell pressed the bottom of his long tunic that hung down past his rump under his armor and sat down on the chair. "My King...," he began.

Theobold waved his hand and frowned. "Do end the charade, Bodrell. We are here in my tent. Let us speak as men."

The general nodded and leaned back in the chair, accepting a goblet of wine that one of the king's attendants handed to him. He took a sip of the fine red liquid and held it in his mouth, savoring the full-bodied drink. The general swallowed after a few moments and cleared his throat, setting the crystal goblet down on the wooden stand next to his chair. "Theobold, I found the most peculiar scene. First, the entire valley floor was covered in a three inch icy sheen that was melting and slippery, explaining the thick fog that has wafted from up the valley. I didn't want to risk any of the horses breaking a leg, so I dismounted and continued into the thick fog on foot."

The king took a deep breath, showing his displeasure at his general risking himself so. Bodrell sensed the king's annoyance, but continued anyway. "Remember, I am but a soldier, despite all the stars and titles," he said, gesturing to his collar. "Anyway, as I was saying, I noticed a large shape in the fog. I couldn't make it out, but it was big, so I knelt down and watched it. It didn't move so I cautiously advanced. Theobold, I saw the most ghastly scene. There was one of our horsemen, frozen on his horse. The animal was encased in solid ice up to its head, which was missing from what I believe to be some kind of bite. The rider..."

Theobold cut in. "A bite? What on earth could bite off a horse's head and encase it in solid ice, other than a white dragon, and there hasn't been one of those in Beykla in over two hundred years?"

Bodrell cleared his throat. "Well, if it wasn't a white dragon, there is some other kind of beast roaming the valley that walks on ice and doesn't leave any claw marks in the surface, that can bite off the head of a horse in a single bite, and has the ability to freeze horseman solid in mid-stride. I can think of nothing else that fits the description. We should move the army from the mountains and deal with the dwarves in the spring. We shouldn't risk the men over..."

The king hammered his fist onto the wooden stand, spilling the goblet that held the red wine. "I will not flee from a dragon that has not even been confirmed to exist other than by the fearful ramblings of my timid general. I will have the dwarves in chains by the end of the week. If there was a dragon in these mountains, we would have received reports of it. I will not be frightened by the obvious attempts of the dwarven army to scare us off. And if there is one of the white beasts making a home of these mountains, we shall place his head at the front of our lances as we ride home victorious. Not only will I not stand for the dwarves thinking they can live under my banner, in my mountains, and not adhere to my will, neither will I stand for one of the loathsome winged lizards thinking he can make a meal of my men."

"My king, surely we mustn't act in haste. If this is a dragon it must be of enormous size. Let us tell the wizard's guild and let their kind come back with a force and deal with it," Bodrell pleaded.

"What? Retreat? My entire western army... Retreat? Are you mad, General? The mere idea that we might retreat would inspire the damned bearded bastards with the idea they can stand against me. I remember well what happens when the back-stabbing dwarves believe they can stand against me. Do you know why the little cowards haven't come to greet us? Because they are holed up in their stone fortress, or city, or whatever the hell it is, gnawing their fingers to the bone out of dread," Theobold said as he pounded his fist against his chest.

Bodrell sat forward in his chair. "But sire, why risk the defeat when we are assured victory if we show patience?"

The king ground his teeth together and narrowed his cold, dark eyes. "General, I am king of the most powerful kingdom in all of Terrigan, and quite possibly the world. I am assured victory at every endeavor. Nothing can stand against my armies. No Beyklan army has ever been defeated, and even in total annihilation, General Laricin West was victorious," Theobold said as he rose from his chair and poured himself another goblet of red wine. The liquid sloshed around the inside of the glass as he poured it. "No, General, we will not retreat. We will push forward and defeat our enemies at our discretion, not theirs. If you do not wish to command them, tell me in the morning. I will find a suitable replacement for you. You could be home in a few weeks sitting by the fire. Or you can stand with me, as a man, and defeat the evil that threatens our nation. You are excused, General."

General Bodrell stood and bowed slightly as he exited the tent. Even the cold night air could not cool the rage that was welled up inside of him. The king was a fool, letting his arrogance and conniving schemes outweigh his common sense. Bodrell actually contemplated the idea of resigning his commission and returning home. He surely could enjoy the relaxing duties of being a pampered rich man. But he knew he not only had duties to the men he led, but he had a duty to Beykla as a nation. If Theobold was slain tonight by an assassin, he would claim fealty to the king's son, the heir to the throne. Bodrell was a loyal man, despite how foolish the leaders were that he was loyal to.

The general arrived at his tent and slipped inside. The fire was dying down, but the tent was warm and cozy compared to the cold damp outside air. Bodrell removed his armor and tossed it on the floor next to the cot. He plopped down on the stiff bed and removed his walking boots and breeches. He then slipped the heavy red tunic over his head and picked his fluffy sleeping jacket from the wooden rack and put it on. Slipping under his heavy blankets, he snuggled up for the last good night of sleep. He knew battles of this scale were seldom finished in a month, let alone a week. When he was in battle, Bodrell slept with his men, as a soldier. Yes, in the morning he would don his battle armor and prepare for death, just as he had done every battle he fought. If there was a dragon in the mountains and it was as large as he thought, he would mostly likely perish. In fact, he figured if any of the army survived it should be considered a victory.

Leska, the Goddess of Earth, knelt under the great tree of wisdom that grew at the center of her garden in Merioulus. She was ready for the battle for her existence against the God of Gods, Dicermadon, as was her sister and other two brothers. Flunt, the God of Fire, stood in his fiery cape of molten lava, distorted by the volcanic heat that wafted from him. His fiery hair flickered nervously like a small flame in a strong wind and his narrowed eyes glowed like the furnace at the center of the earth. Whisten, the God of Air, stood with his gleaming silver cloak rippling about him as if he stood in a gale force wind storm, and Surshy, the Goddess of Water, stood next to them both, her sleek blue skin and long azure hair glistened in perpetual wetness as her form was tense in preparedness for what was to come.

The four had stood like this for some time. To the mortals, it could have been years, or days, but to the gods, they just stood. There was no real time. A year could be as a day. Time simply went as they wished. They could perform a thousand tasks in a single second if they wished it, by simply freezing time. Or they could do nothing and will a hundred years to go by. Each god could control time, or lack thereof, in this way without affecting each other. There was no such thing as time in Merioulus; therefore they all could act in different time periods in essence, without changing anything. The one thing the gods could not do was stop time or reverse it. Not even Dicermadon could do such things. It was above all gods. There was legend among the gods that there was an original god of creation, that he created time and created the gods to reign over it, but if it were true, the god had long since passed on and his truths were lost in his passing. It was this fact that caused the much dissention among the pantheon.

Often the workings of one god overlapped the workings of another, like when the god's clerics battled each other. The old ritual called for the gods to meet each other, calling for the return of the creator, as they watched their pupils battled it out. None of the gods really knew the exact meaning of the ritual, though they performed it each time as they had since they had been in existence. Now, instead of preparing for their mortal followers to battle, the elemental gods stood poised to battle themselves, but their foe had yet to show himself.

"Do you think he is coming?" Surshy asked aloud, never taking her bright blue eyes from the entrance to the magnificent garden.

Whisten shrugged his shoulders as the wind that seemed to blow his cloak around him lessened. "I think he will not show himself against us."

Flunt and Leska nodded their heads in agreement and relaxed. "We must take steps to discover his plots and why he is consorting with demons," Flunt said as his cloak of molten rock turned from a bright orange to a cooler red.

"He mentioned to the demon, Bykalicus, that he was interested in the location of Panoleen's mortal son. I am not sure why he would be interested in such knowledge, unless he wished the offspring to be destroyed. It would not be difficult to kill the boy on the prime plane," Whisten said.

Surshy nodded, but kept her eye on the garden entrance. They were not sure the God King had abandoned the battle. "Perhaps we should go and speak with the demon ourselves, though I doubt he would tell us much. The talk of a necklace that transforms a she-demon into a mortal is clear proof he has plots of his own."

The other gods looked at the goddess incredulously. "Surshy, the Abyss is Rha-Cordan's domain. His link to the mortals prevents us from going there, just as your link prevents any of us going to the plane of water and so on," Leska said.

Flunt nodded his head as he understood what Surshy was suggesting. "We must sever the link," the God of Fire said in a low, grave tone.

Whisten was shocked, as was Leska. The Earth Mother shook her head in wide-eyed disbelief. "You cannot be serious. Do you not remember what happened the last time the link was destroyed? Rha-Cordan fled Merioulus and created the Abyss to re-establish his connection. If we severed it...," Leska trailed off in thought of the ramifications.

"If we severed it, we would sever the link to all mortals, keeping Dicermadon from plotting for the boy's death, if that is what he seeks. Remember the meeting he held, Leska, when he held you in high favor?" Whisten asked, causing the Earth Mother to blush in embarrassment. She had solicited the God King's bedroom many times after Panoleen was disposed of. "He called the boy an abomination, stating that he should no longer be shielded from the evils of the realms. Then, I catch him consorting with the very evil he hoped to expose the boy to. I believe he surely wants the boy killed."

"But could we recreate the link once we severed it?" Leska asked.

"Worse than that, what happens if the boy is killed? He has a soul. What will Rha-Cordan do with him? What kind of deals has Dicermadon made with him?" Surshy asked.

"I do not think Rha-Cordan would make any deals with Dicermadon since the God King was the one behind blocking the link that caused the God of Death to flee Merioulus. If he was making deals with him, I do not think he would be speaking with an archdemon. There are a few things that are much more powerful in the Abyss. The fact that he was speaking to the archdemon tells me he is going behind Rha-Cordan's back, since the demons do not pledge themselves to the God of Death. Only the god's avatars did that. The demons pledged themselves to chaos and power only. Besides, what would happen with the boy in the Abyss? He surely must be powerful in his magic, since he is Panoleen's offspring. Secondly he has a soul, which can never be destroyed. They can be captured, held, imprisoned, but never destroyed. Can you imagine the power of a god that would never cease to exist?" Whisten said.

The others nodded with concern. "If we severed the link, and I mean sever, not block, Dicermadon would not have a platform to try to reestablish with his mortals," Leska said.

Surshy agreed. "We could easily recreate the link, I believe, from our home realm."

Flunt shook his head, too. "But if we sever the link, we will make Merioulus weak. What of Yahna?"

Leska took a deep breath. "I cannot recreate a link to the world, since it is my home realm. I will stay behind and watch over the souls in Yahna until the gods can create their own home plane. But you must look after my children as often as possible. I will be able to hear their pleas, but I will not be able to answer," Leska said with a shudder. She feared what would happen with Panoleen's offspring after his mortal body died. He could simply be powerless like other mortals or he could be.... The thought made her shudder again.

"So it is agreed that we will sever the link to all mortal beings on all planes?" Flunt asked.

All of the other gods nodded their heads solemnly. They were the elemental gods. They had the most power of all the gods when they acted collectively. Was that about to change? Who was this child of Panoleen? Why was Dicermadon so interested in him?

The four elemental gods walked through the immaculate streets of Merioulus. They glanced around, half searching for Dicermadon, half enjoying the fabled city of the gods for the last time. They knew as soon as they severed the link, the gods would flee it by the scores. They neared the small marbled structure at the edge of the city. The building was round with a small ornate archway. The four entered and stood around a well. It extended deep into the ground like a hollow duct into existence. There was a small crystal on the ceiling of the room that shone with soft amber light. There was a thin strand of magical energy that extended from the end of the crystal and down into the deep shaft. Many gods tried to peer in from the outside of the chamber, knowing what the chamber was for, and knowing that the four elemental gods were the only ones that could affect it. The four each channeled a small flow of their magic into the thread. They each felt the energy pulses through them. They could feel the feed of each god in Merioulus as they used the thread to channel their power to their disciples. Then as simple as blowing out a candle, like snapping a twig, the link was severed. The thin thread vanished, leaving no trace suggesting it was ever there.

"It is done," Flunt said. He opened a portal and returned to his home realm, stepping through into the endless lakes of molten rock and fiery skies.

Surshy placed a reassuring hand on Leska's shoulder as she opened a portal to her home. "We will discover the madness behind Dicermadon's plots," she said as she stepped through into a world of endless water in all directions with no beginning and no end.

Whisten said nothing as he opened the portal to the elemental realm of air. He just nodded briefly to the Earth Mother as he flew into a world of endless skies and great castles built on clouds. Leska knew what he meant, though. It was a nod of approval at her decision to stay back with the mortals in Yahna. The plots of Dicermadon were not their fault. They were helpless and she would look after them. She would not lose a single soul until each god came for them.

Leska just hoped that the other gods would look after hers as she was looking after theirs.

The Earth Mother walked through the small archway of the tiny stone chamber that had held the link. She stared at the confused and angry faces of Merioulus. The Earth Mother took a deep breath and began the explanation. The other gods would not be happy.

The cold artic air of the high mountain howled by, sending a steady cloud of blown snow about the glistening scales of the great white dragon. Even in his wicked splendor, the beast was a sight to behold. Darrion-Quieness tucked his arms and legs close to his body and enfolded himself with his pallid, leathery wings. He kept his sail-crested head tucked close to his chest, often stretching out to take another bite of the fine horse flesh the group of humans were nice enough to send to him. He wasn't sure why the armed riders ventured so close to his peak, but surprisingly there were no mountain ogres around and he had been getting dreadfully hungry.

With the lack of the gray-skinned giant kin, he suspected that there was some kind of dwarven outpost nearby. That worried him. They were a sturdy lot and had given him scars more times than he cared to remember. But the human riders confounded him. Why were they here? After he had a nice leisurely nap, he was going to investigate the area. Perhaps the halfling betrayed him. It wouldn't be the first time. No matter, he had would eat the little spec the next time he saw him. Until then, he would deal with matters at hand. The dragon drifted off to sleep with visions of the boy that the king of Nalir was looking for.

Darrion-Quieness opened his bright emerald eyes, trying to catch a glimpse of the voices that had awakened him. He raised his beak crusted head slowly, toppling the faint mound of snow that had built up as he slept. He was fairly annoyed at being awakened from his wonderful nap, but he was more intrigued as the voices sounded like the common tongue being spoken by humans. Using cat-like grace that was near majestic for a beast of his size, Darrion-Quieness made his way to the edge of the rocky platform he was perched on. To his surprise, a much larger group of humans had gathered at the base of his roost. He keened his head sideways to hear them better. It appeared as if they were two groups that had converged together. He saw separate tracks coming from opposite directions and the thousand or so horsemen were mingling together.

They were dressed the same, but Darrion-Quieness had learned that meant nothing among humans. Perhaps they might fight each other. The dragon enjoyed watching battles, but it seemed they were holding friendly conversations with one another, therefore he decided to listen. But to his dismay he couldn't understand what they were saying. It occurred to him that the humans might be trying to avenge their lost comrades he had eaten and that they had somehow discovered where he was hiding. That damned halfling was turning out to have been more trouble than he was worth.

Darrion-Quieness studied the men. They were all on horseback so they were most likely lightly armored. There were about a thousand, a fair number to defeat, he thought to himself. After all, if he let them live they would surely pursue him to the ends of the world for his transgressions against whoever the halfling was. He must have been some kind of prince. The dragon shook his head slowly. Why did he always get mixed up with princes? The dragon had been a young adult when he got mixed up with a dark dwarven prince. One thing led to another, and he found himself attacking a great and powerful dwarven city.

He had suffered grievous wounds and how was he repaid? The dammed gray-skinned bastards turned on him when he was wounded from the battle so they wouldn't have to pay him the promised diamonds. Well, one less dark dwarven prince later, he managed to escape with the little gray skinned monsters on his heels. He didn't mind too much, he guessed. The little gray-skinned spec tasted better than he would have thought. From that day, Darrion-Quieness had vowed to avoid princes. Now he was fully grown, smarter and wiser, yet he somehow managed to get mixed up with some damned prince again. Nevertheless, he was going to have to kill the prince's men. A thousand wasn't that many. He might suffer a few scratches but in the long run, it was better than facing an entire army.

Darrion-Quieness closed his eyes and concentrated a moment. He reached out to the snow, to the ice. He could feel the textures, the coldness of them. Though he couldn't explain how he could do such things, he had always been able to feel them. It wasn't until a few hundred years ago that he was able to actually summon them to his bidding. Darrion-Quieness pictured the image of a great fog in his mind. He imagined it rising from the east and the west, from where the riders had come from. He pictured the fog building and growing, until he felt it doing so. Opening his bright green eyes, he waited. He waited until it began to roll in, a great fog that was a hundred feet high and extended as far north as he could see.

"Let's see how well the humans fare in the fog," he thought to himself.

The great beast launched high into the air. His powerful muscles flapped his vast wings, forcing the air under him, making him rise. When he was just over the thick of the fog, he tucked his mighty wings under himself and dove. His brilliant ashen scaled hide formed a two hundred ton projectile that rocketed toward the earth at blinding speed.

"I vaguely recall the rumors I heard about the battle of the Torrent Manor. And my experience with the attack on Central City was one sided at best, but both battles were won and loss by arrogance and confidence.

The battle for the Torrent Manor was lost by the Beyklans because of their arrogance. They believed that the walls of their keep were impenetrable from the outside. And in truth they were, but they were also impenetrable from the inside. The Beyklans did not consider all possible forms or methods of attacks and in their arrogance, ignored the few warnings of danger when they received them.

The dwarves, through confidence and superior tactics, knew of their strengths and weaknesses and exploited each prospectively. They did not have the force, or ability to siege the castle, so they struck in the dark from inside. Therefore their confidence in their ability to see at night allowed the victory over the humans' arrogant belief that they were invincible.

In the fight for Central City however, the dwarves' arrogance at not containing their foe as they had done in the battle for the Torrent Manor, allowed for a second force to charge across the bridge. Had the dwarves been more aware of their weaknesses, they might have sealed the bridge, or destroyed it outright, thus eliminating and outside surge of re-enforcements. Alas arrogance and confidence is applied to more than just battles, it can be applied within one's life. I was fortunate enough within my adventures to have never been so arrogant that it overshadowed my confidence, yet being aware of the implications of such a claim is what keeps each in check."

-Lancalion Levendis Lampara-

9
Cold Wind of War

The cold wind whipped around the air, blowing sting-ing debris and snow into the faces of the Beyklan horsemen. They had broken into two small groups and rode all the way around the small mountain searching for a back side to the valley in which the entire western Beyklan army was camped, but they located no such pass. The thousand or so horseman sat atop their steeds at the foot of a great cliff. Its gray, snow-blasted walls rose straight up about three or four hundred feet above them. The cliff face was to their south as a vast range of mountains stretched out to their north. The great rocky wall reflected the icy wind off of it and into the faces of the horsemen that gathered below.

"What are you to report, Sergeant?" Lieutenant Harmon yelled, as he gripped the reins to his horse in one hand and held his heavy winter cloak closed with the other in an at-tempt to keep out the howling wind.

The man, dressed in a heavy winter blanket tied to his arms and waist with thin leather straps, sat on the horse across from the lieutenant. He was seemingly unfazed by the frigid wind, despite the large pieces of ice hanging from his long brown hair. His rank was indistinguishable from under the thick wool blanket that he wore like a coat. "My men and I have ridden hard around the western pass. I sent run-ners into each cove we came across. They all returned and reported nothing. Unless you have found some pass or trail into the valley from the east side, it does not exist."

The lieutenant nodded as he tried to pull his cloak tight-er. The cold wind was not something he was accustomed too, and neither were the men, though they were more than accustomed to the outdoors more than he. He had been sta-tioned at the warm confines of the Torrent Manor for most of the last three years, but was away at the Dawson Stronghold in northern Beykla when the dwarves attacked. He was more than eager to pay the bearded bastards back for the loss of his posh duty station. He cared little for the men lost, and cared less of the men from the western army. They were a proud, arrogant lot that drank and fought too much. He was used to well-refined men that were habituated to duty at a keep or city.

Lieutenant Harmon regarded the sergeant again as he contemplated which pass to take back. The man was a rude, uncouth savage that probably got his promotion due to the death of the previous sergeant. He would be glad to rid himself of this ridiculous assignment. "We will take the men back together, down the east pass," Lieutenant Harmon said as he pointed his gloved hand back the way he came. "The mountain walls will act as buffer from this damnable wind, not to mention this cursed fog..." The lieutenant trailed off as his eye caught a glimpse of a dense fog that was rolling in from the north.

"Fog?" the sergeant asked as he turned around to see what the uppity officer was staring at. He squinted his hawk-like eyes and watched a three hundred yard long wall of dense fog roll toward them at blinding speed from between the vast mountain range to their north.

"What do you make of that, Sergeant?" Lieutenant Harmon asked nervously.

"Gather together!" the sergeant screamed, ignoring the lieutenant's question. "Try to stay as a group, do not split up and do not allow the man next to you to get out of your sight," the sergeant yelled as he kicked his horse into action toward the fog while his men moved their horses together. His horse dug into the hard snow, throwing great clods of dirt and ice into the air as it ran.

The lieutenant watched in confusion as the sergeant rode off to the north, drawing his sword and dropping the thick winter blanket that he had tied around himself. What was the madman attacking? And why would he take off his only protection from the arctic air? He undoubtedly expected some foe in the fog, but no enemy would dare attack a thousand heavily armored Beyklan horseman. No foe had defeated more than two hundred horseman, even in the orc wars, let alone a thousand.

The wall of fog overtook the horsemen like a blast of a storm. Stinging snow hit the men's faces, forcing them to turn their heads down and raise the hoods of their cloaks to shield their eyes from the horrid arctic blast. The horses put their heads down and also tried to look away from the frigid storm. Visibility went from a few miles to a few feet instantly, causing a milky white blur all around the lieutenant and the men. A thin layer of ice immediately formed on the men's outer clothing, their hair, and in the horse's manes and tails. The lieutenant tried to draw his sword, but he found his blade was locked tight in his scabbard from the cold air and the rapidly growing layer of ice that surrounded it. He tried to call out to the men to remove their swords from the scabbards if they could, but the screaming howl of the wind drowned out all sound. It was the thunderous rumble in the earth that made him pause. It was as if the very earth had shaken. He thought he heard a large boom from the north where the rumble came from, but he wasn't sure. Lieutenant Harmon looked around. The men around him, those who he could see, seemed to have felt the thunderous boom also. They strained their eyes to the north, but had to take brief glances due to the stinging ice.

One of the men made his way over to the lieutenant, moving his horse as close to the lieutenant's as possible, before leaning over and yelling as loud as he could. "Did you feel that?!" the man screamed.

Lieutenant Harmon nodded. "I think it was thunder from this winter storm! I have heard of winter storms having thunder before!" he yelled back in the howling wind.

The man nodded his head reluctantly. "When should we head back? Do you think the sergeant will return soon?"

The man was interrupted by a second rumble. This one was larger than before. It made the horses flinch as the animals turned their heads to the north, ignoring the stinging snow. Their ears flickered nervously toward the rumble and had they not been battle trained animals, they surely would have fled the other way. The men around the Lieutenant sensed their horses' uneasiness and tightened their hold on their reins.

"There it goes again, sir!" the man said as large chunks of snow and ice rained down on them. "What is that?" the man yelled, ducking under his cloak to shield himself from the rock-like debris. The lieutenant started to answer when a piece of rubble the size of a man landed about ten feet away.

"Great Leska!" the man shouted as he pointed to the debris that was laying flat in the snow. "What was that?"

The lieutenant didn't bother answering in the howling wind. He motioned for the man to follow and he slowly moved his horse over to the large piece of debris. As they neared the dark-colored mound, it became obvious it was no piece of snow. It was horse! The animal's back was broken and lay hideously twisted in the snow. Ice covered its brown hide and snow was packed into the saddle that was still strapped to its back.

"Did that just fall?!" the man asked.

Lieutenant Harmon gazed in wonder at the dead horse, wondering where the rider ended up. *What could have hurled an entire horse in the air? Was the wind that strong?* As if answered by the gods, the lieutenant quickly glanced north, ignoring the stinging ice and the frigid wind. He stared in horror as the silhouette of a great serpentine beast rose a hundred or so feet before him. Its throat swelled, filling with air as its head reared back like a snake about to strike. Fear ripped through the young officer. He could not yell, he could not run, he could not even give warning to the man who was standing next to him.

"Sir, I asked if you...," the soldier started to respond.

The beast extended his neck down and exhaled with such force it sounded like a roar. A blast of air hit the man that was so bitter cold, they were frozen instantly. The wet air of the fog, coupled with the top snow that was being blown through the air, created their icy tombs. After the reptilian juggernaut finished with his assault, his powerful legs the size of tree trunks flexed and rocketed out, launching the beast into the air with the aid of its powerful leathery wings. The dragon's stark white scaled hide made it near invisible in the icy fog as it prepared for yet another deadly plunge. Had the wicked beast been a man, he would have worn such a sinister grin that would make the hackles of the evilest demon rise. It had been a long time since he laid waste to an army of men. He was doing such a complete job; he even surprised himself with his power.

"He was murdered!" Jordan Gersian screamed as he pounded his fist against the polished oak table of the city hall in Motivas. Jordan was one of the most predominant and powerful nobles in the south. He was in full support of the south pulling away from the north after the debacle with the dwarves. Not only did he and his supporters strongly dislike the king and his policies, they feared if they stayed with the north, the little folk might turn on them. He also felt that the way King Theobold treated the bearded folk was morally wrong.

"Now, now, Nobleman Gersian," Nobleman Herwain said with his hands out, palms down, patting the air, trying to calm Jordan down. "We haven't checked out all the facts yet."

The Herwain house had been noble for centuries, unlike House Gersian. Nobleman Gregory Herwain was rich with titles and estates. He disagreed with the king also, and felt sympathy for the dwarves' plot, but his house had not retained its power by becoming passionate about a great deal of things. Passion, as Nobleman Herwain saw it, was like a paper fire – it may burn bright, but it never burns long. Self-preservation was more important than any great accomplishment. It was better to survive to engage in many future arguments and debates, than to die fighting one battle.

"All the facts?" Jordan said as he raised his hands in the air and stood from his seat. "All the facts?" he repeated skeptically.

The other nobles in the meeting moved out of the hotheaded man's way as he rose from his chair and began to step around the long polished oak table. His fine lace-gilded silk tunic and breeches shone in the bright torchlight of the meeting room. "Witnesses saw two groups of ten men, both being led by the well-known bounty hunter, enter Thomas Arwar's home. While inside, they killed..."

"You are out of order, Gersian!" Noble Herwain growled as he hammered his gavel on the thick polished oak desk that sat before the long table at which the other nobles sat. Gersian continued undaunted by Noble Herwain's proclamation. "...his wife and two sons. They butchered their dogs..."

"You will sit down, Gersian, or I..."

"I will NOT sit down! I will do nothing, except speak out against the atrocities that our king willfully inflicts on us as a nation. A family has been slain. A family that was good and just. They were cut down and burned in our backyard and we do nothing! We sit around and debate about having a debate on whether we will act!" I will debate no longer! The time for action is now! I am going to fund a party of militiamen, or adventurers, or damned orcs for all I care! It matters little to me who, but I will hunt down these ruthless killers and bring them to justice. If our so-called king disagrees with my actions, then let him come to my estates and take me from them by force!" Gersian said as he kicked over his chair and stormed out of the room.

The nobles gasped. Never before had anyone spoke out against the king openly before. Disagreement against his policies had been meekly whispered at best. Yet to come out and scream it in such a fashion was unheard of. A loud murmur immediately broke out among the others. The sound of their surprised voices vanished as Gersian slammed the door shut and stormed to his carriage. His fists were tight against his side. The cool night air was refreshing, yet warm. Gersian liked the warm southern air near Motivas, the southernmost city in Beykla. It rested a few miles north of the Tyrine border.

The driver of the carriage jumped down quickly as Gersian barged out of the door. The driver rushed over, opened the glossy black carriage door and extended his hand to help Gersian up into the small covered cart. Gersian batted the driver's hand away with a sneer and hopped into the carriage, sitting down on the dark blue padded bench seat. The driver shut the door, ignoring Jordan's rudeness, and hopped atop the carriage. As the driver flipped the reins to the two sleek back horses, the animals sprang to life and pulled the coach along the stone roadways of Motivas.

What made Motivas different from any other Beyklan city was not its size. No, the city was average size, almost the size of Central City. What made it unique was the fact it was built on a mysterious flat bricked area. The bricks were thirty feet by thirty feet and were made of mostly granite, though there were some clay ones on the northern side. The bricks were flush with the earth, and were as tall as they were wide. Some years ago, the mayor of Motivas ordered the land next to the outlaying bricks dug up, until it could be determined how far into the ground they went. They discovered the bricks were thirty feet tall as well. Scholars and sages were contacted across the realms to discover who or what would have placed the bricks in the ground, but no one ever gave any definitive answers, though a wide range of speculation was offered. The most common theory was hundreds of thousands of years ago there was an ancient emperor known simply as Kahl. Not much is recorded of his civilization other than he created great pyramids. Why they were created is unknown, but it is believed that the stone bricks at Motivas were the foundation for one of those pyramids.

"Shall we go home, Sir?" the driver called back from the front of the carriage.

Jordan stared out of a small opening in the side of the carriage that acted like a window. "Yes, driver. I hope to not have to look at this despicable countryside until next month's meeting."

The driver nodded and turned his attention back to the task at hand. He had often seen the normally friendly Jordan turn into piggish noble after these meetings. He figured he would act the same way, had he been forced to sit among such loathsome men. Swatting a few mosquitoes as he drove the carriage home, the driver was happy he had such a simple life.

Amerix rushed up the hill, carrying his pack over his shoulder. The other arm swung violently as he ran. When he reached the top he placed his hands on his knees, dropping the heavy leather pack, and panted hard. In his youth, he could have ran that hill a hundred times and would not have even been winded. Amerix pushed the thought from his mind and forced his old body to pick up the pack and make his way into camp. Vlargcar had been practicing with the long sword and short sword again, wearing the heavy chain armor Amerix had made for him. The armor fit him well. The orc wore the chain shirt tucked under his thick leather belt and the lower ends hung down in a protective shroud to his knees. Amerix left the shroud wide, as to not limit the orc's movement. He fashioned Vlargcar a chain coif that was hooked to a bishop's collar, or a thick chain ring that extended around the neck and shoulders overlapping any area where the chain mail did not cover.

Vlargcar came up from the trees with his swords drawn and smiled a yellow-tusked grin. His bright cobalt eyes blazing from under the dull gray coif in contrast with his green skin gave him a clown-like appearance. Amerix chuckled and dropped the pack, holding his belly.

"What is funny?" Vlargcar asked as his smile faded thinking the dwarf was laughing at his expense. Amerix tended to do that often.

"Nothing, whelp," Amerix said as he regained his composure. "Here," he said, tossing the heavy pack at the orc's feet. "Get what ye need outta there. We have to get moving and *fast*. I think the friends of the human scum we cut down back on the trail have got wind of us. We need to make tracks!"

Vlargcar frowned as he stabbed his two swords in the ground and picked up the heavy pack, fumbling through it, taking this and that and putting it in his bundle. Amerix quickly tossed his soot-covered clothing into the fire and slipped into the chain armor he had fashioned for himself. The armor was exactly like Vlargcar's, but on a much smaller scale. He slipped Songsinger over his shoulder and stuffed two small daggers into his belt. He grabbed the pack after Vlargcar was done with it and hefted it over his muscular shoulder. The old grizzled dwarf kicked dirt into the small fire until it was extinguished and started to head south east. Vlargcar sheathed his swords and stuck his thick green thumbs under the straps of his pack and skipped along behind the old dwarf.

Amerix glanced over his shoulder and rolled his eyes. "How are ye gonna strike fear into the hearts of our enemies if ye go about skipping like a schoolgirl?"

Vlargcar stopped and felt his face go hot. Had his skin not been green his cheeks would surely been red. The orc paused for a moment, then hunched his shoulders and leaned forward clenching his hands into tight, rock hard fists and started growling as he took oversized steps and looked around with a squinted eye.

Amerix shook his head as he started back to the south east. "Everything's a blasted game to ye, isn't it?"

Vlargcar didn't answer. He just smiled and stuck out his green tongue at the back of the dwarf's head as they walked.

The pair traveled for several days, taking few rest stops and eating as they went. They took no time for hunting, relying on the supply of dried squirrel that Vlargcar had hunted down for them. Amerix was amazed that something as savage as Vlargcar could successfully hunt nothing but squirrels. By looking at the green-skinned monster, he figured the orc could at least bring down a full grown deer. Yet day after day, he suffered through the stringy squirrel meat. But, meat was meat.

It was in the middle of the day when they came across a clearing in the trees. Amerix raised his hand to lips and motioned for Vlargcar to keep quiet. The orc froze and his bright blue orbs immediately scanned the horizon for enemies. He watched Amerix as the dwarf drew the chrome-bladed sword and stalked forward. Vlargcar reached back and with his right hand, drew the long sword that was strapped to his back, and with his left hand he drew the short sword that he kept on his hip. Staying a good twenty paces behind Amerix, the orc walked cautiously forward.

The old dwarf reached the base of a large oak tree and relaxed. He puffed out a heavy sigh that ruffled his long shaggy silver-streaked beard and turned to the orc who was stalking behind him. "'Tis nothing, whelp. Just some blasted road."

Vlargcar relaxed a bit, but did not put his weapons away. The dwarf had terrified the orc with his tales of ruthless evil humans that frequently patrolled the roads and killed dwarves and orcs that they found alone.

Amerix walked out into the open road, sliding Songsinger back into its scabbard and scratched his beard. The road extended as far as the eye could see to the north and as far as the eye could see south until it appeared to run directly into the great Lalin Plateau that loomed over the southern horizon. The road was well traveled with only small patches of green grass that grew in the middle. There were deep wagon grooves from days when heavy wagons traveled in the rain. Amerix checked the ground tracks for any other kinds of creatures, but found nothing more than what he believed to be dog tracks. Though in truth, he was a poor tracker. Amerix had spent a great deal of his life in the under mountain and had little experience on the surface. He turned to the orc. "It's clear. Let's get on the other side and head a bit more east before we cut south."

Vlargcar nodded slowly, but kept a firm grip on his swords. The pair made their way across the road and continued through the thick forest. The leaves were thicker here, as was the underbrush. Vlargcar frequently saw broad vines and a variety of animals that he had not seen before. The air was cold here, but was much warmer than where the old dwarf had found him, and warmer still from the small town they had camped outside of. Vlargcar wasn't sure where they were headed, but he realized that either spring was coming faster than it ever had, or they were going to a warmer land. He had heard of such lands from his mother. She had told him fantastic stories of great lands where it never snows. He had believed it to be just nothing more than stories but as the air slowly became warmer, he began to wonder about her stories. If the stories of the warmer lands were true, what about the stories of great winged lizards that breathed fire? He hoped those were just stories. They couldn't all be true.

"Hey, Amerix," Vlargcar called out as he stepped over a small stream that trickled between two hills.

The dwarf didn't turn around as he ducked under a thick vine that was wrapped around the base of tree trunk and stuck out, making a small hole for him to squeeze through. "What do ye want, whelp? I'm busy trying to make way through this cursed forest."

Vlargcar made his way around the thick vine instead of ducking under it. "My mother always told me about land where it never snows. Do you think there are such places?" Amerix smiled as he hopped a downed log that was covered in thick green moss. He didn't smile at the orc's question, but at how well the orc had increased his grasp of the dwarven language. For a stupid green-skinned buffoon, he was kind of smart. Of course it was his superior teaching ability that bridged the gap, some credit had to go to the whelp. "Sure, there is. The farther we head south, the closer to those lands we come."

Vlargcar gulped. "If there are lands where it does not snow, are there such things as giant winged lizards that breathe fire?" the orc asked reluctantly.

Amerix shook his head up and down as he crested the top of yet another hill. "Of course, you pea brained orc. They are called dragons, but there are many different kinds. There are some that breathe fire, some that breathe cold and some that breathe gas. Even some that breathe a bolt of lightning."

"Lightning?" Vlargcar gasped. "If they are so powerful, why don't they take over the world?"

"They try. But there are good dragons just like there are evil dragons. The good ones battle them, as do the wizards and great warriors of the realms," Amerix said starting back down the other side of the hill.

Vlargcar frowned as he followed. "How could a warrior battle such a monster?"

Amerix paused and turned around to face the orc. "Do not ever stop to think how ye would battle an enemy. Ye can think about the terrain, or what tactics to use, but when it comes time to fight them, ye take those swords of yer scabbards and ram them into their belly. Whether it's a dragon or a human, it will die. If it does not, then run, because it can't be killed."

Vlargcar nodded as if he was just blessed by some great wisdom. The dwarf turned and started back on the arduous trek. The pair walked at a hurried pace for three more days. Amerix frequently took short breaks to rub his tired old feet and legs while Vlargcar took the opportunity to hunt for more squirrels. It was on the third day that they arrived at the base of the Lalin Plateau. The Plateau was as unique of a land formation as any found in the realms. It was a large forty mile rock oval that was raised over six hundred feet in the air. Its jagged walls were mostly dark brown granite, but some sedimentary lines were noticeable as you reached the higher levels. There were some smooth spots where the wind and rain had worn the walls smooth, but just as the walls wore down, the smooth areas would break away and fall to the base. The base of the plateau was raised to a steep slope for about one hundred feet that was littered with large boulders that had fallen and become wedged between the large deciduous trees that grew on the rocky slopes. There was little ground foliage on the slopes, but the forest canopy was still thick and did a good job blocking out the sun.

Amerix found a suitable area between two large boulders, which must have weighed two or three tons each and had fallen and wedged themselves next to a large oak tree. The tree leaned to the north under the tremendous weight it supported from the oblong shaped boulders and the bark was scarred, but it appeared the tree was managing to hold the rocky weight. The old dwarf plopped down and didn't bother to remove his pack from his shoulders. He leaned back, using the heavy leather pack as a prop and stuck his legs out in front of him in a wide "v" while his arms rested limp at his sides.

Vlargcar leaned against the cold dark brown boulder, resting his head on the cool rock. He inhaled the moldy smell of the bright green moss that grew on its side and turned to face the exhausted dwarf. "Where do we go now?" Vlargcar asked, wiping a small amount of sweat that was beading up on his forehead with the sleeve of his shirt.

Amerix studied the orc. Vlargcar seemed to have grown yet another inch taller and was almost six foot tall. That was a little taller than most orcs, yet it was obvious the orc still had much more growing to do. He sighed knowing that he would soon have to adjust his armor again, to make sure it fit the sprout properly. As the orc spoke, Amerix still and often found himself resenting the green-skinned beast for using his sacred language, but after looking at the innocent blue-eyed orc, his resentment quickly changed into a strange sense of pride that he could not explain. Amerix felt a profound sense of guilt from not telling Vlargcar why they fled to the south. Sure, he mentioned the humans were after them, but in truth, the humans were after him, not the orc. "Vlargcar," Amerix started as he sat up and slipped his arms from under the heavy pack. "I haven't been totally honest with ye."

Vlargcar frowned and slipped his pack from his shoulders also. The heavy leather satchel fell with a resounding thud on the hard rocky ground of the plateau slope. "How so?"

Amerix moved his stare to the dirt in front of him and shook his head slowly as he spoke. "The humans that chase us don't chase both of us. They chase me," Amerix admitted.

Vlargcar frowned and scratched his head with his thick index finger. "I don't think they like me much either."

Amerix chuckled as he placed his old hand on his knee and grunted. He forced his tired old bones to stand and he rose to his feet. "No, me green-skinned friend. No they do not, but they are after me. Ye see, I was once a predominant general in Clan Stoneheart of the Pyberian Mountains."

Vlargcar nodded and smiled. "Yes, you told me of the great under mountain city. I hope to see it one day. I bet it is grand."

Amerix lost his smile and a pained look blossomed on the old dwarf's creased features. "There are many things ye will learn about the world me boy. I wish I had the time to teach ye, but the truth is I am long overdue for my death."

Vlargcar frowned and snapped a twig off of a branch nervously and flipped it through his thick green fingers. "How is that?"

Amerix sighed and dropped his arms to his side. "Vlargcar, I am well over four hundred fifty years old – fifty years older than any dwarf is supposed to live, let alone be able to fight competently and gallivant across the countryside."

Vlargcar chuckled nervously as he tried to lighten the mood. "So, when will you die old dwarf?"

Amerix smiled. "I used to think never. I always imagined that if I was mean and nasty enough, I could deny death, but with every passing moment I feel me old friend seeping into me bones. I used to think he called for me, tried to take me. That made me fight harder in each battle. I used to rush to the front of every fight, so I could emerge victorious and taunt death with me life. I wanted to laugh as he tried to claim me. But it was not until recently, that in me old wisdom I realized that I spent my life thinking wrong."

"Wrong? About what?" Vlargcar asked, moving closer to his only friend.

Amerix looked up into the orc's blazing sapphire orbs. Oh how they shone with innocence and youth. "Ye see, Vlargcar, as I thought it was death that sought me out, it was in fact I, who sought him. Death doesn't come for us. He will have us. No one lives forever. Death is in no rush for any of us. It was every battle that I ever fought when I rushed to the front, rushed to the thick to kill or be killed, when in truth, I really rushed to meet him."

Vlargcar frowned. He didn't understand really what Amerix was saying, but he did understand it was profound and important so he listened intently and tried to memorize all that he could. If he could memorize it, he could think of it later and understand it. He never thought of death as a person. Death was just death. But it dawned on the orc that no one could tell what death was like because after you died, you were dead. How could anyone tell what it was like when you were dead? He wondered how the dwarf knew what death was like, but he didn't dare interrupt his Brohe-tah for fear he might not hear something important.

"Even with me enemies at me heels, I longed to embrace them, to cut them into pieces. I long to feel my blade as it slices into their soft bodies and the shrill cry of their final breath as it flees them forever. Yet, I know I long to find death. I cannot find it with a blade in my hand. I am too skilled of a fighter. There is no one alive in the realms that can best me. I can only find death at the ancient temple of Durian. I can only find peace at the temple of the rock."

Vlargcar put his arm around the old dwarf. He was surprised at the rock-hard muscles that were under the dwarf's chain armor. Vlargcar knew the old dwarf was strong, but his body felt like wrought iron. "You cannot die now," the orc said, worriedly. "You are all I have."

Amerix gently pushed the orc's arm from his shoulder and faced him. He grabbed Vlargcar by the shoulders and stared directly into those innocent blue eyes. "I must go, my friend. Years ago, before your grandfather's birth, I lost me wife and son to an illness that could have been prevented had the humans of Beykla not been the greedy lot they were. I held them responsible for me loneliness and when the first opportunity arose, I marched an army under the Torrent Manor, a keep that regulated my clan, and killed every man woman and child inside. I then marched to the closest town named Central City. I attacked that city and burned close to half of it and killed hundreds if not thousands of civilians and soldiers. Me army was defeated and was left for dead when I fell from a great stone bridge that spanned the Dawson River. The humans hunt me because I am responsible for the death of thousands of their kin."

Vlargcar glowered. That was no surprise. His clan hunted and killed humans all the time. Women and children were usually the easiest to kill. The way Amerix said it, it seemed like killing the women and children was a bad thing. It was just easiest, that was all. He didn't fault him for that. He would do it too had he been there. "Do not feel bad. I would have killed the women and children, too, had it been me."

Amerix's vise-like grip grabbed the orc's arms. He was

amazed at the muscles the whelp possessed at such a young age. He knew orcs aged faster than humans, but the whelp still should not have half the strength he had. "Ye must never kill women or children, unless they are armed in battle. Ye must promise me that. And if the children are armed in battle, ye must not kill them unless ye need to protect yer life or someone else's."

Vlargcar nodded his head slowly. The dwarf was always full of surprises that Vlargcar didn't like. Just like the damned butter cakes. He would try not to kill women or children for his old friend's sake, but if they so much as made him bleed, sorry for them, but he would squash their heads. No one ever gave his mother a chance, and they were going to kill him until Amerix stopped them, so why should he give anyone else's a chance?

"Vlargcar, I am going to climb the summit here and search out the Temple of the Rock. Ye do not have to go with me if ye do not want to. I really hope ye do not. There is a great green dragon named Yohr-Acht that lives atop the plateau, not to mention the hunters that chase us will undoubtedly follow," Amerix said as he gripped the orc's arms.

Vlargcar shook his arms loose from the painful grip and tried rub feeling back into them. "What do you plan to do when you reach this Temple of the Rock?" the orc asked.

Amerix smiled and gazed off into the sky like he was thinking of a great fantasy that had eluded him his entire life. "I plan to kill the men that chase us, then pray to me god to take me. Whether he sends me to Yahna or to the Abyss, only he knows, but I hope he will forgive me fer all the wrongs I have done."

Vlargcar nodded. "Well, since you plan to kill the men that chase us, I will go with you. You can't have all the fun. Anyway, after you die, someone has to eat your body to get your strength."

Amerix choked on his own spit. "Eat me body!? What in the blazes of the dark Abyss are ye talking about, ye green-skinned freak!"

Vlargcar stepped back. Clearly he had offended his friend, but he didn't know why. "When a respected orc dies, his closest Brohe-tah, or Kar, eats his body to keep his strength so that future warriors will be able to prosper in battle," the orc said matter-of-factly. "Why do you think us orcs are so strong?"

Amerix shook his head from side to side violently. "No, no, no. Ye are not going to eat any more bodies of friends or enemies. That is not what gives you strength."

"Sure it is, Drunda teaches..," Vlargcar began.

"No more Drunda, okay? I need ye for... uh ... me forge. Yea, forge," Amerix said as he tried to come up with something quickly to divert the orc. *Eat his body?* The whelp had too much orc in him and not enough dwarf.

"Forge?" Vlargcar asked.

"Yea, forge. Ye see, Durion says in order for my soul to get to Yahna, it must be burned or buried. Preferably buried, and I must have a forge to carry on my traditions and beliefs," Amerix lied.

"But I don't know much about dwarven beliefs. Not to mention you dwarves eat the most rotten of things," Vlargcar said as he stuck out his tongue in disgust.

"I will teach ye all that ye need to know. As far as eating, ye can eat whatever ye want as long as ye cannot be able to talk to it. Like ye cannot eat, say, a halfling because ye can talk to them. But a deer, ye can't talk to them so they are fair game," Amerix said. Vlargcar nodded worriedly. He wanted to help his friend get to this Yahna, but he didn't really want to give up eating things. Vlargcar loved to eat things. He guessed he could give up eating things he could talk to, that wasn't very many things. After all, he couldn't speak a lick of elven.

"Ok, Amerix. I will do it," the orc agreed.

The old dwarf smiled and clapped the orc on the shoulder. "Good, me boy, now let's get camp made. I want to ascend the cliff in the morning. We need to keep a diligent eye out. I do not think the dogs that are chasing us will be able to find where we are as long as we do not make a fire, but we still need to keep watch. I'll take the first watch, you the second."

Vlargcar nodded as he loosened the wrappings that

held his bed roll and flipped the soft cloth out on the rocky ground. He neatly unbuckled his blanket the old farm woman had given to him and hugged it briefly before laying it atop the bedroll. He was sad Amerix was going to die, but everything died. Vlargcar was an orc. And if there was ever a society that could deal with death, it was the orc society.

"*Faith. No word is so intangible and yet so strong. Few men truly possess it, yet most men claim to have it. It is the single, most misunderstood word used by men. Faith is not the belief that someone will perform some task. You can never have faith in another person unless he or she is omnipotent and omnipresent. Mortals fail, even though they may intend not to. Even gods fail sometimes. Faith is more than a belief that some event will occur as you thought. If I leapt from a cliff top, you could claim faith that I would fall, but could I not fly? Or could not a blast of wind hurl me back to the top? Perhaps I could make myself light as a feather and float to the bottom rather than fall. All of these are spells and dweamors that I have learned over the years. No faith is more than a certainty in someone or something. Faith is not even a belief. Faith is knowing that without fail, without pause or uncertainty, that an event will occur. The only way to make sure this occurs is to do it yourself. People are imperfect; therefore they will fail you. There is no true faith that can be placed in them due to that fact. Faith has to be placed on oneself. I have faith that if I need to, I can perform any feat. I developed this faith when I lost someone more important to me than existence itself. I did what was impossible, what was unheard of, what others said I could not, and I did so without pause. That is faith. I had faith in myself. I didn't care what men said I could not do. I cared little for the laws the gods created to govern me. They had helped me little since my birth. It was not until later how I learned they were behind the very trials of my life. I learned they were behind the loss of my love. Once more I was hated and persecuted for what I was to become, not what I was. This persecution set me on the path to be what I would have never been had they left me alone. I would have never realized my potential. I would have lived and died as man. It was not until everything that I had ever had was stripped away from me. I was denied the very thing that I sought since my birth that was torn from my grasp. I had been a victim long enough. I would simply not allow it. There was no indecision on my part. No confusion in how I would complete the task. I simply did it. No there is no true faith, save for the faith that one places in themselves. Sometimes it may be a resolve rather than a known action. A paladin has faith in the honoring of his god. In the times of the severance it became clear to men that the gods could fail. But a paladin could take his faith in his honor to his grave and beyond. Even Trinidy, my father, was true to his honor while in his conscious soul. The hideous undead apparition he became was not my father, but a manifestation of evil. It was like a mold that consumed an apple, soon there was no apple left, but a budding mass of fungus. True faith is something that no one can take from you, and no one can give you. It must be found within. I often ponder how the world would have fared had I not discovered my faith."*

-Lancalion Levendis Lampara-

10
Power of the Dragon

Delania opened her eyes and immediately shut them again to block out the blinding light all around her. She could hear strange sounds and squeaks from around the corner, and the surface of the Abyss had the strangest smell. The normal overwhelming stench of sulfur and toxic gases was replaced by a strange mixture of other unknown scents. They were equally repulsive to her, but they were surely different. *And the heat!* Nowhere, in the entire Abyss, had she felt such heat before. It was overwhelming. She felt her body convulse involuntarily from the sensation of it. Delania rubbed her bare arms with her soft delicate hands and was surprised to feel hundreds of strange tiny bumps that rose up. She forced open her eyes and prepared to rein a barrage of spells if some fool gweits thought they could burrow into her skin, but to her surprise she saw only small little raised areas where her white arm hair came from her arm. Delania squinted in the bright light, opening her eyes for only brief periods of time to get her bearings.

She was in some kind of stone trench between two rock walls that were bricked. She had only seen bricks once and that was when she had been near the great palace of Rha-Cordan himself. She figured she must have ended up there again, but she had never heard that the area around his palace was so strange.

Delania folded her slender pale arms under her bare voluptuous breasts and walked down the narrow trench. To her surprise, she didn't see any sign of any gweits and she didn't see heads of new spawned that usually littered the floor of every trench in the Abyss. What Delania saw when she rounded the corner of the strange bricked trench shocked her to her core. The source of the damnable bright light was a glowing orb that hung in the sky. She couldn't bring her eyes to even look in its direction. But most astonishing of all were the number of new spawned that littered the streets. They moved about wearing clothes and some wore weapons and armor! She even saw a strange hairy beast with a long neck and tail that was pulling a wooden cart with wheels on it. A wooden cart! What an amazing artifact! The only place wood came from was the prime realm. She had only heard stories of that strange place. How a demon managed to get one of the wooden carts down into the Abyss was beyond her, but she had to figure out a way to steal it. She backed into the corner and peered out from around the side. She didn't see any demons around – none in the air and none hunting. With all the new spawn walking around, how could they resist the urge to chase and taunt them? She wasn't much interested in doing those things, but sometimes a new spawn would think they were powerful enough to command or destroy her. She enjoyed sucking their power with her lustful kiss.

Delania struggled a moment with where she was. She had used her ability to blink to the surface directly above her dorm, but it was readily apparent that she was not there. She fumbled with the necklace that was still tight around her neck. She was sure Bykalicus had concocted some kind of dweamor around it, but where did she go? She surely wasn't in the Abyss. At least she thought she wasn't. It wasn't until another wooden cart went by being drawn by one of the four-legged hairy beasts that she understood. She was in the material realm. But why would he send her here? Demons longed to get here to torture and kill the helpless mortals. She was surely not like the other demons of the Abyss, but if the demon had the power to get here, she figured he would have come himself.

Delania decided to fly atop one of these bricked formations to get a better view of her surroundings, but she did not move. She tried to flex her wings but did not feel them. She glanced over her shoulder and to her shock they were gone. Her beautiful black and red leathery wings were gone! She ran her smooth fingers over her soft back where her bat-like wings should have been, but she felt nothing but her bare skin. She quickly felt the top of her head for her small black horns, but felt nothing. She bit her lip to see if her fangs were there, and they too were gone. A terror greater than she had never imagined tore through her. Bykalicus had changed her into a mortal. He had always planned on bedding her. She had resisted and taunted him for thousands of years. Now she would grow old and die. Her soul would return to the Abyss and he would have control of it. She would be as helpless as a new spawn, she *would* be a new spawn.

Delania fell to her knees, placed her beautiful face into her delicate hands, and cried. She didn't know what crying was and the wet tears that streamed down her face surprised her, but the overwhelming totality of the events that were unfolding before her made the sensation seem of little importance. She was doomed.

Lance limped down the paved street of Aquabar. He had been beaten every day for the last four weeks. That bitch Ramasiel had prodded him between his legs with some kind of stick that produced a horrid electric shock and punched him into unconsciousness more times than he could count.

She was an evil, vile woman, that Ramasiel, and she seemed to concentrate on his groin when she "taught" him. That was what they called it, teaching. The wicked red haired wench thought that she was close to breaking him, he let her believe that, but what he was close to doing was learning how to break the shield that Reena had woven around him. It was almost as thick as the shield that Garlibane had put over him, keeping him from reaching his inner magic ability, but it was not as strong. He had pushed against it a couple of times, only to be beat horrendously when he tried. Apparently the witch could feel when he pushed against it. So Lance used his mage ability to examine the outside of the so-called shield. It was much similar to the one the elves used with a few variances that would pose little trouble. He hadn't figured out how to escape once he had broken the shield, but being able to break it was the first step. Once he was sure he could do that, he would start planning phase two. Part of that phase involved killing the bitch Ramasiel and turning her whole damned tower to rubble.

Lance was afraid, though. He started noticing little changes in himself, like he didn't need to think consciously about looking down now and he was starting to appreciate praise from the other women when he went on errands. That disgusted him, but the fact was true: if he did not escape, he was sure he would find himself a hairless eunuch like the other men before him. But Lance was sure the other men did not possess the ability to cast both types of arcane magic. This was his way out. The women had grown tired of trying to break the dark-haired, dark-skinned man that spoke with Lance when he first arrived, so they killed the man in front of him. After of course they cut his manhood away while he kicked and screamed. Lance watched all of their eyes as the three wenches did the disgustingly horrible task. Reena seemed disappointed for some reason, but the other wench, whose name Lance did not know, seemed excited and eager. Ramasiel seemed repulsed at having to touch the man, but satisfied at her work when she was finished. Lance made a promise that if he was this Abyss Whisperer the elves spoke of, then when he destroyed the world, he was going to start here. Then at least he would be doing some kind of good.

Today, the bitch, Ramasiel, had him going to the market to buy her a new dress and he was on his way back to the tower with the cursed thing. Everything the bitch wore was red. The other women wore different colors. Lance had learned it had something to do with a political affiliation among the women, but he had learned little more. They were as secret in their societal dealings as they were about keeping men as slaves.

Lance had his lacy little shopping smock on, not the elven robe his mother had left him. The smock had no back to it, so his bare bottom hung out for all to see, further humiliating him. That was just one more reason he dreamed of strangulating the life from Ramasiel. Reena liked to slap his bare bottom and sometimes cup it with her bare hand, giving Lance a disgusted feeling of shame. He figured if that was what tavern wenches felt like when drunken thugs did it, he was going to throttle every drunken thug he saw that fondled a tavern wench until he died.

Lance walked slowly back to the tower. He knew he was going to be beaten if he wasted time, but he figured he was going to be beaten for something anyway, so a little fresh air was worth whatever imaginary crime he committed. It was the sound of a woman crying that caught his attention. He hadn't heard that sound since his arrival in this hellish country. It was almost refreshing to hear a woman crying. It was touch of normalcy in this cursed county. Lance knew better than to stick his nose into another woman's affairs, but if it ticked off a Mother somewhere, he was up to the task.

Lance strolled along the side walking area next to The Reagle, a fancy clothing store that Ramasiel usually sent him to, but today she had sent all the way to the southern part of town to get the dress from an old woman. Lance figured she was trying to get him lost or something. The truth was he wasn't sure what she was up to, only that she was up to something.

Lance paused at the edge of the dark alleyway before ducking inside. If any tudas were walking around, they would surely come and cause him trouble. What Lance saw when he entered the alley shocked him. On the alley floor was a nude woman with pale skin holding her face in her hands and crying. Her long black hair cascaded over her head like a brilliant ebony waterfall. The beauty of her perfect form took Lance by complete surprise. Never had he seen the female form in such splendor. It was not a lustful way, but more of awe at her statuesque form, as if someone had chiseled her from granite. The woman sensed Lance's presence and looked up from red, puffy, tear-streaked eyes. Lance did not have to look away. Out of habit, he stared at the floor of the alley, taking in the woman by his peripheral vision.

"What do you want, spawn?" the woman asked.

Lance was speechless. Spawn? What was a spawn? He had heard tuda and suda, but spawn was a new one to him. He figured he would play along until he figured out what a spawn was. "Have you been accosted, Mother?" Lance asked without looking at her.

The woman stood up and wiped her tear-streaked face with the back of her hand. She was nearly six foot tall, almost as tall as Lance. What was more shocking was that she displayed her nakedness without the slightest hesitation or bashfulness. The woman stood with confidence and strength that should not have been present after huddling and crying like she had. Lance guessed he had been accurate in calling her Mother, they were the only women in Aten that could act so haughty. But Lance had never heard of a Mother going about stark naked, or being accosted. If anything, a Mother's sorcery would keep her safe if some thug did try to hurt her.

The woman frowned and stepped closer to Lance, staring at him with her bright red eyes. Red eyes! Lance nearly jumped out of his skin. "Who would accost me, spawn? I am Delania, Queen of the Barbetin," she said. She thought about it for a moment, there was no way this mortal would know what the Barbetin was. And as she considered her predicament, it was better that no one learn of her existence just yet. She was going to have to kill this one.

"I am sorry, your majesty," Lance said with a deep bow. "It is just that I noticed...," Lance gulped. He was going to have to be tactful with this observation. "It is just that I noticed your highness was not dressed as other queens I have met."

Delania paused. Dressed? Of course. Mortals all wore clothing. They only disrobed to bath and reproduce. She looked Lance from head to toe. The man was handsome and seemed well built, though a little on the scrawny side. She had wanted to bed a spawn since her creation yet that cursed Bykalicus always seemed to get in the way. He would do nicely if he would look at her. Never had a spawn been able to resist her charms once she looked him in the eye. But this one refused to do so much as look at her foot. It didn't matter. She would have him one way or the other. "Where are you now, Bykalicus?"

Lance looked around nervously. Bykalicus? Was he her tuda? Or perhaps some bodyguard? "Your highness, I know of no Bykalicus, but my name is... or was Lance." Delania chuckled. The poor spawn had no idea about anything. He was conversing with one of the most feared demons in all the realms like he was speaking to some mortal woman with a pitiful title. "What do you mean was?"

Lance felt sweat bead up on his forehead. Perhaps coming into this alley was not one of his more intelligent ideas. Where was Jude when he needed him? "I am called suda now."

Delania frowned as she took her finger and placed her shimmering hair behind her ear. "Suda? That is a foolish name. Lance suits you much better. I suggest you use that," Delania said, frustrated still by the fact the mortal wouldn't look at her. He must have the will of an archdemon himself.

Lance wanted to run with fright. Who was this queen? Maybe she was the queen of Aten and this Barbetin was another name for Aten. The truth was Lance had no idea what she was, other than the most beautiful woman he had ever seen. "Perhaps your highness would like to have this dress. It may be a little small, but it should suit you until you find better accommodations," Lance said as he held out the bright red dress of Ramasiel's.

He knew he was going to be severely beaten for giving the dress away but he figured he was going to be beaten anyway, so what did it really matter? All he knew was that this woman was different than any he had met in Aten so far, he might be able to use her to escape.

Delania smiled and giggled. The sound surprised her as much as it surprised Lance, but she took the red silk dress and held it up. The colors were so vibrant and alive. Never in her existence had she owned such a wonderful thing. The idea of wearing the artifact seemed foolish, but she did need to blend in. The moment overtook her and she leaned forward and kissed Lance on the cheek before she thought about what she was doing.

When she realized what she had done, she grabbed him by both cheeks and nearly broke into sobs again. "I don't know what came over me, I am so sorry."

But to Delania's surprise, Lance stood unharmed. He was surely shocked and seemed to be frozen with fear, but he was unharmed. Unharmed? How could that be? Her kiss drained the life force of mortals. She had used it countless times. Why did it fail now? Delania focused on her inner magical force and sent hundreds of tiny weaves out from her body. The mortal must have some kind of protection. Delania was surprised at how difficult it was to control the simple weaves. It was as if they had a mind of their own and she had to concentrate to make each individual one go where it was supposed to go. She strained until the thin gray weaves probed and engulfed Lance. She felt a shield that had been placed around him. It was a weak shield, at least weak by her standards, but it was powerful for a mortal. Though with the peculiar way her flows were acting, she might find it a more difficult task than it should be.

Lance stood in fear as the woman kissed his cheek with her voluptuous lips. They were warm and she smelled of honeysuckle blossoms. She was very alluring and he found himself intrigued by her. Even stranger was that she quickly grasped his face with her soft hands and apologized for the kiss, as if it would hurt him. He started to reply when the strange woman sent out more magical flows than he had ever seen sent out at one time, and had even kept control of them. The flows were grayish black, like necromancy, but they were something different. He stood frozen as her weaves enveloped him and encircled for a few moments and then as quickly as she sent them out, they vanished.

Delania stared at Lance for a few moments. The kiss must not have hurt him because she was in a human body. It felt like hers, but she guessed it was not. The shield that surrounded him would have no effect on her kiss. "You must be powerful to be shielded so."

Lance shrugged nervously. "They seem to think I am. All I wanted to do was find why my parents were murdered. I ended up mixed up with a bunch of elves, which led me here."

Delania nodded as she hastily placed on the silk red dress. It did not fit her in the chest, making her large breasts seem larger than they were and the length was too short, giving it a skirt like appearance, but she looked presentable at least. She hated the feel of the thing. It was so constricting and confining. Why mortals wore them at all was beyond her. "Where is here?" Delania asked after she finished lacing up the strings in the back of the dress.

Lance nearly choked. The woman didn't know where she was? That would explain a lot. "We are in Aquabar. The capital of the Queendom of Aten."

Aten. The named sounded like music in her ears. She had heard of such a place when she was in the Abyss. The female spawns from there were fun to break, thinking they had more power than they possessed. But most of the female spawns from Aten were snatched up by the archdemons. Bykalicus sometimes would take them and show the foolish women how weak they really were, but the wicked Dadramedion made them the mainstay of his entertainment. "If we are in Aten, that means you are a slave."

Lance nodded sadly, though he still did not look at Delania.

Delania examined the dress that she wore, smoothing it with the palm of her hands. "If you are a slave, then this dress belongs to your master and is not for you to give away."

Lance felt the lump in his throat double in size. "Yes, but..."

"And what will happen to you when your master finds that you have given her dress away to a stranger?" Delania asked eagerly.

Lance exhaled and tried to calm himself. He knew this would happen regardless. "I will be violently beaten until I lose consciousness, if I am lucky. If I am unlucky I will remain awake through the whole affair."

Delania bit her bottom lip in thought, before she spoke. "If you will suffer so, then why did you give me the dress?" she was interested in why the human acted so. No demon would do such a thing unless he could profit from it.

Lance felt a fool. The woman had been playing him all along. She was probably one of Ramasiel's lackeys and the whole thing had been set up by the despicable bitch. Lance felt his anger rising to the point of hate. He wanted to shatter the shield, march into Ramasiel's chamber and strike her dead. He fought the hate. The man with the dark hair and bronze skin that the witches had killed told him to hold onto the hate, but to not to let it go, and he might survive intact until they killed him. He had said that was the best thing that would happen to him, to die with his manhood. Lance accepted his fate and forced the white-hot fire that dwelled inside of him to simmer and cool. He took a deep breath and answered. "Because I felt bad for you. There, I said it. Do your worst!" Lance said stretching out his arms and sticking out his chest. But to his surprise, Delania grabbed him by his coal black hair and forced his lips into hers. The beautiful dark-haired woman kissed him violently. She exhaled deeply and moaned, biting his lip hard, but not enough to make him bleed. When she finished, she released his hair and smiled in such an innocent, but commanding way that Lance nearly fainted.

"Thank you, Mister Lance. I will be in touch with your mistress to discuss your gift," Delania said as she rounded the corner and pulled down on the bottom of the dress in attempt to make it a better fit. She was amazed at how much fun kissing was, even though she didn't drain the other person's life-force. It was almost more fun since it lacked any real purpose other than the sheer pleasure she got from doing it. If she never discovered how to thwart Bykalicus' plan, she was determined to enjoy her brief stay here on the prime material plane.

Lance merely stood in dumfounded shock. Had he a net he could have caught the torrential cloud of butterflies that fluttered around in his stomach. How was he going to explain this one to Ramasiel? He figured he would be as vague as possible in case the dark-haired woman's story was different than his own. Lance walked back to the tower as quickly as possible. No doubt the wicked woman had memorized the exact steps and time it would have taken him to go there and back. *Goddess of Mercy, hear my plea,* Lance thought to himself. If only he knew the goddess's name, perhaps she might have heard him long ago.

Trinidy marched through the thick forest in the dead of

night. There were no clouds in the night sky, only a wintry, blissful darkness. He liked the dark and the cold. It had always seemed to depress him before, but now, now he enjoyed it. It was as if he found some serene solace in the quiet night. It was the day that depressed him. Things were alive, chirping and running around. There was the damned sun that seemed to mock his very existence. The trees were so green, the flowers so bright it was as if life itself mocked him. The dead knight paused under a large oak tree and leaned against it. Hundreds of glossy black beetles scurried out from his balefully corroded armor and infested the great tree. Some burrowed into its wood; others scampered around, ducking under the dark recess of its thick bark.

Trinidy was not tired, nor hungry. He had not been either since awakening in that strange castle. Ever since he had been forced along a relentless trek across the land, covering great distances that even a horse could not traverse without great fatigue or death. Trinidy had learned he could resist the insatiable draw that pulled him north for short periods of time, but it was as if it were an itch he needed to scratch. If he ignored the call too long, he found himself marching involuntarily on. He had followed the call north until he came across a large city of evil elves.

They had to have been evil because they had attacked him. He didn't blame them, though; he had led an army of rotten corpses and skeletons toward them, but he knew they would attack him to begin with. He could feel their hate inside of him. He didn't know why they hated him, but the skeletons surely served their purpose. Trinidy surely wasn't comfortable commanding an army of undead. That was usually reserved for evil clerics and mages, but he knew in order to fulfill his god's needs, he would have to use whatever tools he could manage.

Trinidy wasn't sure how he knew the elves would receive him so sourly, but it seemed as if he expected it, like he somehow felt their feelings. Most of the elves he faced turned and ran with fear. Trinidy didn't blame them. Most evil ran when it was faced with the shining righteousness of their enemy's goodness.

The death knight pondered his wife and son. His memories of them were vague at best, leaving him with only brief feelings and thoughts – nothing tangible he could put his finger on, but he knew she was beautiful, and he knew his son was strong and intelligent. He couldn't recall if they were alive still. He thought them dead. It seemed as if they should be dead. There was an unknown pain there for him when he thought of them that made him think they must have died somehow. Trinidy was alone in the world. That was okay with him, really. He enjoyed the darkness and the solitude that he had made his home recently. He was sure he would have liked to see them again, if he could just remember what they looked like. *A name at least,* he thought to himself, *If I could only remember a name.* Then just as a flash of an image, it came to him. Panoleen. The death knight's face cracked as he smiled. The rotten skin of his mouth split, causing a dark black ooze to drip from the corner of his mouth and down his chin. Trinidy didn't feel the drip, nor did he feel any pain from the cracked skin. He was a dead knight, a form of undead, but with more inherent malevolence and wickedness than the most vile living being. He was the essence of death, a death knight, and it followed him wherever he walked.

Panoleen. That was her name. Why couldn't he remember it before? It seemed since the pull had changed from close to leagues away again, things had changed. It was shortly after the source of the magical pull changed, that it went away completely. Now he was lost, wandering the forest that was to the south and west of the wicked elven vale. He contemplated returning to the wicked elves and killing them to the last, but instead he sought something else. Trinidy wasn't sure what he was looking for, but the horrible elves could wait. He had killed a great number of them anyway with his undead army. The undead army; that was one of the things he needed to contemplate. How could he use the righteous power of his god, Dicermadon, the God of Magic, to summon an army of undead? In his life he had battled hundreds of undead creatures, and never once had they been anything of goodness.

In his life... Trinidy froze. He didn't move a single inch.

In his life... The thought beckoned him from the recesses of his mind. It was on the tip of his tongue, he could almost taste the thought, yet it eluded him. Like a sneeze that he just couldn't sneeze. It was there, he could feel it, but he could no more understand it, than he could have flew. Trinidy shrugged his shoulders and dismissed the thought. It would come to him sooner or later. Now he needed to wait for his servant to return. The hill giant he had resurrected in the open plains had somehow been killed and was now a walking dead, like the skeletons that he had commanded against the elves. Trinidy was glad that the powers that his god had bestowed on him had taken away his need to eat, sleep, and drink, also took his sense of smell, because he was sure the rotting hill giant had a disgusting stench. The poor thing. He almost felt pity for the dead giant. Almost.

Trinidy could feel the giant's evil when he first came across it on the open plains. It thumped at him, like a heartbeat. Thump-thump. Thump-thump. Now, there was only silence that sounded from the thing's massive chest. No loud pounding sense of evil like before. Strange how he enjoyed the presence of the hill giant more dead, than he did alive. *Alive*...the thought came to him again. It hovered on the edge of his consciousness, just out of his reach. Then as quickly as he sensed it, it was gone.

Well with the insatiable pull that urged him onward gone, Trinidy now searched for a place to live. He needed servants and henchmen to find this wrong that his god, Dicermadon, wanted him to right. Now all he had to do was wait, which was difficult when you didn't need to sleep. Trinidy sat down under the great oak tree. He noticed a small black scorpion that crawled across his hand. He flinched, drawing his hand back quickly and rubbed it. How was a scorpion surviving in the cold winter? Trinidy jumped up and searched the ground for the wicked little stinging monster, but he could not find it. After a few minutes of diligent searching that produced no scorpion, he resumed his rest under the tree. Trinidy rubbed the side of his temples. It didn't soothe him, but he felt like it should have. His head didn't hurt, but he figured he had been seeing things. Scorpions couldn't survive in the harsh Beyklan winters.

Surviving...there it was again. That damned thought that was just on the edge of his consciousness, lingering, taunting. It was annoying, this hidden thought, it was almost as if he sensed something, then as he tried to understand it, to pinpoint it, it was gone. He hoped that cursed hill giant returned soon. This forest was not as empty as it needed to be and it was giving him the creeps.

"What is evil? I mean can it really be defined in a concrete term? Is it a way of life, a thought process, or merely a title given by those who lack the majority view? Is thievery evil? And if so, what defines it? Is not a salesman that deceives the masses about the quality of his product stealing? Are not the lords of the land, stealing when they demand taxes?

Is hanging a horse thief not evil? Why not, because it is law? What if the law said that if you do not worship this god, we will burn you at the stake? Who is the evil one? Too many times evil is nothing more than a word used by the powers that be to manipulate the masses. The Beyklans had committed evil acts when they tried to oppress Clan Stoneheart, yet their own people viewed the dwarves as a wicked lot. But were they attacking, or merely defending?

Evil is not as clear as one would like to convince others it is. Evil is little more than a blanket term used to cover the truth."

-Lancalion Levendis Lampara-

The Proudarrow's Trail

Quadry and Silas Proudarrow each sat hidden under a thick grass-like rug that looked like a small mound of grass-covered dirt. They had been tailing the death knight for over a week in the undead monster's exhausting pace to the east. They had almost given up on following him when the death knight paused under this cusp of trees and ordered his undead hill giant off to search for something. The medallions that Garlibane had given them, made them invisible to the undead. The high mage explained that undead did not see like the living did. He told them that undead sensed life instead of seeing it. The undead often heard the heartbeat of the living or felt their life. Garlibane taught them that undead hated all life because life mocked them in their undeath. The high mage was not certain the death knight was like most undead, but he suspected he was. Fortunately for Quadry and Silas, the high mage's theory proved true.

The pair had worried that the death knight could sense them, it seemed as if he would turn their way and stare as if he sensed them, but as quick as he looked in their direction, he looked away and focused on something else. The elves dared not get within thirty feet of the death knight. Silas had made that mistake a few days earlier and was overcome with unquenchable fear. Silas darted out from under his mowaka, or camouflaged rug, and ran as fast as his nimble elven legs would carry him. The elf didn't return for some minutes. Luckily, the death knight didn't see him as he fled. But now, after following the death knight over the last three days, the pair doubted the beast could see them if they stood right in front of him, yet they stayed hidden under their mowaka just in case.

The pair of legionnaires had seen many sights in their long tenure with the Darayal Legion, but they had never witnessed the unbridled evil that sat under the large oak tree. The walking corpse wore what was once magnificent mail of the finest elven make. It bore thousands of tiny runes that could not be seen during the battle at the vale, though the corpse was unmistakably human. It had long stringy black hair that was thin and falling out of its rotting scalp. It wielded a wicked sword that was covered with small skulls that made up the hilt and the pommel that occasionally glowed blue when the undead monster was angry. When the death knight's rage flared, the eyes on the head of the large beast skull on the outside of his shield glowed. Wherever the corpse walked, hundreds of stinging and biting venomous insects erupted from under its boots and crawled away into the grass. Most died in seconds from the cold winter air, but some burrowed under rocks and in the bark of trees. It seemed as if the death knight was oblivious to the hundreds of tiny black beetles and spiders that crawled from his hallow eye sockets into his ears, nose and mouth. The whole sight was disturbing and sickening, but the elves were managing better after a couple days of exposure to the walking, rotting hell.

What confounded the two legionnaires the most was that wherever the undead apparition walked, every living thing died that could not get away. Plants wilted and died, leaves turned brown and tree's bark turned black and flaked off. It wasn't until tonight that the elves were able to witness what would happen to prolonged exposure to the death knight's evil. The large oak tree that he had sat under since the previous day as he awaited the return of his lifeless hill giant, had turned black, died, and it's limbs seemed to grow and twist in the most unnatural and hideous way. The trunk stayed dark black, but it thickened and twisted, turning the once winterized oak tree into some kind of dark, twisted plant that seemed to sprout dark red leaves overnight. It was almost purple in color with what looked like bright red blood veins instead of the normal green veins that are found in leaves. The pair dared not intervene, and they were beginning to wonder if they should head back to the vale to report what they had learned.

Trinidy waited next to the tree for the rest of the night. He was certain he saw more strange black beetles out of the corner of his eye, but whenever he turned to look directly at the insect, it was always gone, not to be found. The little hiding insects annoyed him about as much as that lingering thought that seemed to come then go before he could put his finger on it. He felt as if the thought would enrage him if he ever could remember it, but since he couldn't remember it, he wasn't sure. It was near dawn when the hill giant crashed through the trees from its search. The large beast was almost beautiful in its undead splendor. Trinidy paused for a moment. *Beautiful? Where did that thought come from? The undead hill giant was interesting at best, but beautiful, no.*

Trinidy thought about what was beautiful for a moment. His mind quickly passed up images of flowers and women, symbols of his god and sunrise, until it came to rest on the dark of night. Nighttime was beautiful. It was quiet and tranquil, beautiful in every way.

The undead hill giant stood motionless in the dark night. It's pale white, bloated body was free of insects due to the cold winter, but it's rotting flesh clung to it sparingly, with an occasional piece of yellow puss-filled flesh falling to splat to the ground as it walked. The giant still bore the grievous leg wound that led to its death and its gray and black leg bone peeked out from under the rotting flesh with every step. The hill giant didn't say anything as it stood motionless in the night. Trinidy wasn't sure if it could speak, but speech was not necessary. He had commanded it not to return until it found a suitable lair. The fact that it returned told the death knight it had found anything from an old keep to an abandoned cave. Well, whether or not the cave was abandoned meant little, it would empty soon after he arrived, one way or another.

The hill giant turned and lifelessly plodded away, back the way it came. Trinidy rose from his feet and started following. He half expected his feet to begin to ache, or his back to hurt, but as usual, he felt nothing.

The giant led throughout the day over hills and around small ponds, making most of the journey in a southerly direction. It was close to twilight when they emerged into what appeared to be endless grassland. Trinidy recalled the grassland when he headed north to find the wrong that he had to right. That was where he had met the first of the evil elves and the hill giant. It was ironic how the thing led him back to where it had been killed.

They walked a few hours after dark until they crested an abnormally large hill for the grasslands. What Trinidy saw on the other side was a small stone fortress. It had been damaged in a siege some years ago, but for the most part seemed intact. The moss-covered brick walls were about fifteen feet tall with small wooden battlements at the corners. The fortress was like two small squares that had been joined in overlapping corners with a large square-shaped tower that rose from the overlapping corner area. The tower had black scorch marks from siege fire and was severely damaged at the top, with its canopy caved in, probably from a catapult boulder. The outer walls of the fortress were in decent shape. There was a section of the south wall that was caved in, but Trinidy figured that it shouldn't take too long to repair. He was going to need some minions to perform his work.

Trinidy flipped his tattered cloak over his shoulder and raised his corroded mail-covered arms into the air in an outstretched fashion. He sent flows of black energy out from his hands that crossed each other in a rapid succession until they entered the earth. He felt the flows weaving and probing into the frozen ground that surrounded the old fortress. The flows eventually found what they sought and the death knight released the flows. In moments, the ground around the fortress came alive as clawed hands forced themselves free from the dirt, pulling out their skeletal bodies and standing atop the upturned earth. Trinidy watched in satisfaction as the skeletons stood before him, their eyeless sockets ablaze with a soft blue glow. There was probably two or three hundred of the bone soldiers. The death knight smiled again. His face cracked as before and the dark black fluid dripped out of the corners of his mouth and down his chin. He gave the idea of beautiful a second thought. There was something majestic about creating an instant army of death.

He wasn't so sure it was beautiful as it was invigorating, but it was enjoyable just the same.

Quadry and Silas watched in horror as the death knight raised about three hundred skeletal soldiers with little difficulty. There was no mistaking what the apparition planned to do. He had sent the undead hill giant out to find a lair. The undead beast had discovered the old orc place from the orc wars. The death knight undoubtedly planned to restore the old fortress and build another army. Fortunately, the surrounding land was filled with orcs and hill giants, but by the look of the death knight's hill giant henchmen, he would have no problem dealing with his neighbors. The two legionnaires retreated back slowly and removed their mowakas. They had a long journey back to the Vale, and they needed to get there as quickly as possible. They had just watched an enemy that their greatest wizards and sorcerers could not defeat set his roots deep into the Serrin Plains. If the prophecies were right like Garlibane had said, it would matter little. This walking apparition would be victorious as long as the Ecnal lived. They hoped the high mage would discover his location soon, for who could stand against such pure evil?

Apollisian and Alexis rode across the large stone bridge that spanned the Dawson River at the east gate of Central City. The amazing work of craftsmanship had stood for centuries and had seen many battles in its lifetime. Bright green moss hung down from the sides and bottom of the bridge like dirty stringy hair that dangled over the raging waters of the great Dawson River. The cliff face on each side of the river was home to many species of birds and other cliff-dwelling animals. The river had a strong current and was at its narrowest here and had never frozen in its recorded history. It started in the Pyberian Mountains, where powerful snow storms and perpetual melting runoffs fueled the great river. As it traveled south, other tributaries fed it, making it a powerful wave of rapids and waterfalls as it made its way through Beykla. Once the river arrived at the southern reaches of the powerful kingdom, it slowed and widened, becoming more of a lumbering giant that the raging torrent it was here.

The pair's warhorse's hooves clipped and clopped as they made their way across the magnificent bridge. When they reached the city side of the bridge, Apollisian pointed to where he and Amerix dueled and where the wicked dwarf was thrown over the bridge to his death. Alexis smiled as she watched the blonde-haired paladin rehash the tale with enthusiasm and regret when he came to the part where Victor fell. Apollisian bowed his head and said a prayer to Stephanis to look after the young squire's soul and see that he is well cared for in Yahna. It was a city guard that roused the paladin from his saddened doldrums after his brief prayer.

"Excuse me, Sir," the militiaman said.

Apollisian turned his attention to the man. He was maybe sixteen years old at most with a smooth baby face and short brown hair. He carried his bec-de-corbin nervously, but held his chin proudly. He wore light studded leather armor and a bright red silk scarf with a golden crown embroider just under his neck. The scarf wrapped round his neck several times and was fastened at the ends to his leather armor with a bright silver chain. Apollisian nodded his head to the young man. "Yes, Sir. What can I do for you?"

The guard glanced at Alexis and then back to Apollisian. He was clearly shaken by speaking with a man armored such as the paladin was, and the fact he was traveling with an elf surely meant he was someone important or was royalty of some kind. The fact Apollisian called him sir, and then asked what he could do for him, shook him visibly. "Uh, Sir, you can do nothing for me. That is, you could, but I mean that you shouldn't..," the guard said nervously, trying not to offend the obviously important man.

"What Apollisian means, boy, is to tell him why you spoke in the first place," Alexis said. She was frustrated with the way people acted when they first met the pair. If they met commoners, they acted like this lout and they met nobles, the nobles either kissed their feet, or tried to make it known to them that they were their superior. She just wished that people would just treat them as equals for once.

Apollisian glared at Alexis, and then turned his attention to the militiaman that stood before his Vendaigehn steed. She was so rude sometimes. "Pay no heed to my elf. What is it you want?"

This time it was Alexis who gave him a dirty look. *His elf, indeed!* She immediately began planning how to make Apollisian pay for that insult at a later time. Perhaps when they were alone. She fought to suppress a giggle as she imagined the event.

The guard stammered and kicked at the dirt as he spoke. "Well, I just overheard you talking about when Amerix fell to his death, Sir. Not that I was eaves dropping on My Lord's conversation, I just accidentally overheard, that's all."

"What about Amerix?" Apollisian asked, feeling bile rise to his throat, hoping against hope that the dwarf's body was found and Songsinger was with it. "Was his body found?"

The guard stammered a bit more and then continued. "Well, it was found. Found by a smithy in Portia that hired him to work his forges for a bit."

Apollisian jumped down from his horse. His heavy plate armor squeaked against itself as he grabbed the man's leather chest covering. *"He is alive?"*

Alexis hopped down from her horse as well and pulled on the paladin's metal-plated arm, trying to tear him away from the terrified guard. She was amazed at how strong he was sometimes. He didn't look much stronger than an average man. She guessed it was the human in him; they were typically stronger than elves. "You are scaring the poor guard, Apollisian."

Apollisian was oblivious to her. He focused on each syllable of each word as the militiaman spoke nervously. "Yes, he was found by Thomas Arwar. Thomas used to work as a liaison to the dwarves in the mountains, or so the story goes. He was working at his forge in Portia when a large dwarf with a long black stringy beard that was streaked with gray came to his forge and asked for some tools. Thomas recognized him and offered the dwarf a job, immediately sending word to Captain Oswald. The captain dispatched the bounty hunter, Meirgan, to fetch him. Supposedly Thomas didn't think much of the dwarf, except he carried a fancy sword that was too big for him. That spiked some old memories of his."

Songsinger! *It had to be Songsinger,* Apollisian thought. How the dwarf endured the swords shrill wine it made when it was around evil, he wasn't sure, but at least the dwarf and his sword were found. Apollisian doubted that Meirgan would be able to bring the dwarf in. Amerix was as crafty as he was ruthless. Meirgan was a skilled tracker and warrior but he played on fear and intimidation to catch most of his prey – the two things the old dwarven general did not have an abundance of. And besides, Apollisian despised the bounty hunter. Anyone who tries to pass off monetary gain as justice was a fool. Though the bounty hunter had yet to fail in a mark, Apollisian was sure he would fail at this one. "Thank you, good Sir. That is all," Apollisian said.

The relieved militiaman quickly darted off, cursing himself for opening his mouth in the first place.

The paladin immediately turned to Alexis. The wry elf raised her hand to silence the paladin. "No."

Apollisian dropped his arms and lowered his head in defeat. "But you have no idea what I was going to say."

"You were about to try to justify abandoning the search for the Ecnal to run off to Portia looking for your cursed dwarf and your sword, Songsinger. Reclaiming the fabled blade is surely a worthy adventure, but we are already up to our elbows in adventure looking for the boy."

Apollisian shook his head sadly and slowly mounted his horse. "Perhaps after we find the boy who is supposed to end the world...," the paladin said as he raised his hands in a mocking display, "we can hunt down the scourge of Beykla and reclaim what was stolen from me and finally achieve justice."

Alexis smiled as she tightened her grip on the reins to her horse. "Perhaps," she said as she spurred her horse ahead and down the dirt road of Central City.

Apollisian shook his head. That Alexis. She may be an elf, but most of the time she was one hundred percent a controlling and annoying woman.

They rode into town and stopped a few buildings in. Dismounting and handing their reins to the stable boy, Alexis and Apollisian entered the Blue Dragon Inn. The building had been almost fully repaired from the dwarven battle. The once scorched common room had been repainted and refurnished. There were many patrons inside and the place was ablaze with low mumbled talking and occasional laughing. Apollisian had a hard time picturing the grotesque scene he had witnessed just outside these very doors in the street. He could almost still hear the screams of men, women and children as the dwarven horde cut them down and set their homes on fire. He could still hear the twang of Alexis' bow as she fired arrow after arrow from the top of this roof into the dwarven invaders. He remembered the cries of battle that erupted from the normally docile Victor. Victor. The named haunted him. Victor's memory was a horrible reminder to Apollisian that no matter how skilled he became with his blade, he could not save everyone or win every battle – a fact he would as just soon forget.

As he and Alexis strolled across the room, all eyes fell on them. They were an unlikely pair in the city, a man with an elf, but none of the men gave more than a long stare before returning to whatever activity they were pursuing.

The paladin walked up to the bar with the elf. He ordered a goblet of cider and she ordered wine. The innkeeper, a fat middle-aged man with brown hair, studied them a bit as if trying to remember them, then he shook his head and fetched the drinks. He tilted the silver goblet to the side as he poured Alexis' wine and roughly filled the wooden mug with cider. He didn't spill any of the contents, but made it clear he disliked dispensing the inexpensive drink.

Apollisian turned his back to the bar and scanned the crowd, a rough-looking lot made up of mostly drunkards and gamblers. In the corner were a couple of adventurers. Adventurers were easy to spot. They were always loaded down with gear stuffed into heavy backpacks and enough weapons to arm a small city. They always wore dirty clothes and often smelled like a cross between a swamp rat and a guttersnipe. The group sat at a far table. There was the usual fighter sort. He carried an oversized sword and wore scarred-up chain armor and was kind of big. There was a man of the cloth, a cleric of some kind, but Apollisian couldn't make out the holy symbol from here. He figured it to be one of the elemental gods. Their clerics were the most likely to don armor and weapons to go adventuring. There was the cloak-clad mage, who sat with a perpetual wrinkled nose at the stench of his comrades, but they seemed to be missing a thief. Most adventures had a thief with them. The thief was important for linking with the locals and finding out what monsters or bandits there were to hunt down. Perhaps their thief had died in some remote dungeon. Apollisian smiled. Adventuring sounded like a fun life, though it wasn't the life for him. He had more important matters to attempt to than his own entertainment.

"We need to find out where they took him," Alexis said softly as she sipped her wine.

Apollisian nodded. He would check with the local magistrate first, since he was turned over as some kind of prisoner. "I figure we will start at the local magistrate's office."

Alexis nodded and finished her wine, setting it down gently and signaling to the innkeeper that she would like it refilled. He smiled as he wiped his hands off on a towel. He quickly popped the cork on a new bottle and filled the silver goblet. Alexis fished in her pockets and slid a five mark of silver on the table toward him. The innkeeper's eyes went wide and he set the bottle down next to her, picked up the five mark and gave her a wink. She nodded arrogantly and turned to face the crowd with Apollisian. "Should we secure a room now?"

Apollisian pondered the thought for a moment. Did she say secure *a* room, or secure *our* rooms? The thought of sleeping in the same room as Alexis excited and confounded him at the same time. He longed to hold her in the night, to smell her hair as he slept, to feel her slender body pressed against his... "No, I think we should get our rooms later. I want to be in contact with the magistrate before the sun sets."

Alexis nodded and finished her second goblet of wine,

sliding the near full bottle into her pack. Apollisian downed his cider and the pair walked from the inn across the street to the large marble building with the great pillars known as city hall.

"Is he awake?" Lyndall asked as he deftly strolled into the room, his short sword dangling from his belt. The weapon was of immaculate quality. It glimmered and shone in the flickering torchlight of the dark stone room.

Copel glared at the champion with contemptuous fury. "Are you so afraid of him, Lyndall?"

Lyndall ignored the fat keeper's comment and strode up to the cell door. Lyndall tugged on the thick iron bars of the cell door that held a sleeping Jude. "Think this will hold the Mershul?"

Copel limped over to the gladiator champion. "There is no proof he is a Mershul."

"No proof?" Lyndall scoffed as he turned and faced the keeper. "I figured you of all people would recognize one of their kind," Lyndall said as he motioned to the fat keeper's lame leg. "Did you not see the fight? He was pit against about forty dwarves. The men he fought with were untrained fodder. They had poor weapons and poor-fitting armor that was pieced together at best. It was supposed to be a reenactment of the battle of the Torrent Manor. Even if there were the same number of trained soldiers, they could not have survived that fight, let alone a bunch of beggars and thieves. He has to be a Mershul," Lyndall said as he turned back and regarded the sleeping warrior.

Copel glared at the champion. Lyndall wasn't really a champion as far as he was concerned. The little gladiator had never fought any beasts, only men. Copel did not doubt the man's prowess with a sword; he was certainly masterful with it. But it took more than skill at swordplay to become a champion in the arena. "He didn't kill any of the men round him."

Lyndall turned his head and regarded the fat keeper of

slaves. "What?"

Copel smiled victoriously. "He didn't kill any of the slaves that were round him. He only killed dwarves. A Mershul would not have stopped until all around him were dead."

Lyndall pushed himself from the bars forcefully and glared at the fat keeper. As I recall there was only one man left and he collapsed after he raised his sword victoriously. He probably didn't see the man, but we shall see, old man. Better hope these bars are strong enough," Lyndall said as he patted his hand on the thick iron bars. "We both know what can happen when a Mershul rages, how their strength doubles."

Copel looked to the ground. He had battled a Mershul in his last gladiator fight. Copel had cut the man's head from his shoulders and the Mershul still brought his axe down, severing the tendons in Copel's leg and crippling him for life.

"I understand the duke wants him for the battle of the Quigen. Seems he thinks the man looks like General Laricin West. Better fetch the slave some food. He will be ravenously hungry when he comes to. We both know how Mershuls eat after a rage," Lyndall said triumphantly as Copel stared at the ground quietly. Satisfied when Copel would not argue further, he marched from the room.

Copel sneered at Lyndall as he glided like a proud cock down the corridor. After the short swordsman had departed, the keeper softened his gaze and turned back to regard Jude. He had seen the mindless rage in Jude's eyes during the fight. Jude didn't raise his sword in victory as he cut down the final dwarf like all others had thought. Copel had seen the fury in a Mershul's eyes firsthand. He knew the look of unbridled ferocity when he saw it. Jude had raised his sword to kill the slave that was next to him. It was his countless wounds that had taken its toll on him, not any amount of self-control. It was clear to Copel that this was Jude's first time in his rage, or he would have killed the man without thought. Jude's next rage would be uncontrollable. A Mershul's rage only worsened as they aged, each rage ever-so-slowly becoming worse than the previous one. Copel shook his head sadly. This Jude had expressed his hope to earn his freedom, but he would not live that long. Mershuls were always pitted against beings and beasts that were far beyond their ability to defeat. It was the rage that kept them alive. But eventually, the rage would not be enough, and he would die. Copel limped from the small lonely room toward the nearby kitchen. He hated Mershuls almost as much as they hated themselves, but perhaps this one would dethrone the pig-headed Lyndall. The short gladiator was no Champion. The thought of the short champion dying in the arena urged the portly keeper to the kitchen with an abnormal pep to his step. Yes, this Jude was the prayer he had asked for many times. Finally, the imposter champion, Lyndall, would be exposed for the weak one-sided warrior he was.

Jude opened his eyes and squinted, trying to focus his blurry vision. His head was pounding like orcish war drums and his ears were ringing like the belfry of a church on the day of a king's wedding. Jude rubbed his eyes with his fists and strained to see his surroundings again. The dark stone cell slowly took form. He was lying on his back atop a dry canvas cot. The walls of the cell were made of gray stone and the door was made of thick iron bars with several horizontal crossbars that doubled the door's strength. Jude sat up and ran his hands through his hair, trying to recall how he got in this cell. He remembered the battle in the arena. He remembered it until all that was left was he and another man whose poor fitting armor acted more like a net on top of him, than a form of protection. He remembered expecting to die. He had expected to die before, but he had never actually believed it would occur without some sort of a chance for survival. He remembered actually believing death was inescapable. He was wounded severely and there were more than ten of the bearded demons left. Jude had lost count of the number he had killed before that moment, but he knew that in his condition, death was inevitable. It was then he felt a surge of anger so great his skin tingled and his nose went numb. He couldn't feel his wounds, and the first seconds seemed like he was in someone else's body, like he was watching himself from somewhere else. The roar of the crowd was drowned out by the beating of his heart and his vision focused on one thing: the enemy in front of him. After that, his memory was blank.

Jude ran his fingers across his skin and was surprised to see that not only had his wounds been healed, he had no scarring other than what he had before the fight. Divine healing. His captor must have taken him to some cleric. Jude spat on the floor. He despised magic. Magic was what had gotten him into this damned cell in the first place. Had Lance not been some sort of mage, he would have never attracted the attention that he had. Jude tightened his fists as he imagined punching his only friend in the nose. That was the first time he sensed it. It was there, lingering at the edge of consciousness, something clawing to get out, like a hunger, or an itch. Jude took a few deep breaths and pushed the strange sensation back down. He wasn't sure what it was, but he didn't like how he could feel the need to surrender to it.

Jude kicked his feet over the edge of the cot and stood. His legs were still weak and shaky, but he managed to make his way to the iron-barred door. The room outside of his cell was small and there was a long hallway to his right that extended as far as he could see. There were no furnishings in the room, save for a small desk with a chair and a large flat wooden bed-like contraption. There was dried blood on the wooden bed's surface and many empty wooden shelves. Jude suspected that it was the surgery table and the battle surgeons probably worked on the wounded there. Jude craned his head and peered down the corridor. There were many other cells with wooden doors and small barred windows that extended as far as he could see. To his right, all he could see was the bare stone wall. He soon detected a faint aroma of cooked meat and baked potatoes. The smells awakened a hunger in Jude that he fought to control. He wanted nothing more than to tear down the door, charge toward the wonderful smell and kill anyone who was between him and the savory meat. He was equally surprised when the keeper emerged from the hallway with a small wooden cart that had enough food on it for several people.

Copel slowed the heavy cart in front of Jude's cell. The

squeaky wooden wheels slowed and then stopped as Copel grabbed a thick plate that was loaded with steaming roast beef and potatoes. The plump keeper sniffed as he slid the wooden plate under a feeding slot in the bottom of Jude's door. Jude stared at the meat and looked back up at the fat man. He had met many kinds of men since his arrival here at the arena and all were backstabbing weasels. His stomach almost jumped from his chest and ate the food on the spot, but the large swordsman ignored the loud rumblings and stared at Copel. The fat keeper looked confused as he started to pick up a second thick wooden plate of beef. "Aren't you going to eat? You got to be hungry, Mershul."

Jude glanced down at the food. He was so hungry he felt as if he hadn't eaten in days, when in truth he had eaten just before the match. How long had he been asleep? "How long have I been out, fat man?" Jude asked, struggling to keep his eyes from the steaming food whose invigorating odor wafted up to his nose.

Copel glanced down at the food, then back up to Jude. He could see the restraint in the large swordsman's eyes. Copel found it amazing he could ignore the recovery hunger with such food in front of him. "You have been down about eight hours," Copel answered nonchalantly, sliding the second plate under the bars.

Jude glanced down at the plate of food. He could feel the insatiable hunger gnawing at him, but he ignored it. Small beads of sweat formed on his forehead. "Pah! I have been down longer than eight hours, old man."

Copel smiled and lifted the third plate from the cart. "Why? Because you are so hungry? Mershuls are always ravenously hungry after their rage."

After their rage? Mershul? That was the second time the fat man had called him that. "I don't know what presumes you to think I am half starved..," Jude began, staring at the plates.

Jude was interrupted by Copel's thick-bellied laughter as he slid the third plate of heaping roast beef smothered in soft white potatoes. "You don't understand, swordsman. You are a Mershul. Do you not know what that is?"

Jude shook his head slowly from side to side and wiped the small beads of sweat from his forehead with his hand. He stared at his wet palm in confusion and found his eyes creeping toward the three plates of food. One bite, he told himself. If there was poison, one bite probably wouldn't kill him. The food had to be poisoned, why else would they give him anything but the gruel he had been eating for weeks?

Copel lowered his shoulders and pulled up a wooden chair from the small desk that was sitting at the far wall in the tiny room. He placed the chair in front of Jude's cell and sat in it, leaning forward with his elbows on his knees. He folded his fingers together and took a deep breath. "Mershuls are vicious warriors. So vicious that when in battle, a Mershul gives in to a primal rage that few men possess. This rage gives the Mershul incredible strength, incredible constitution, and an insatiable will. For all intents and purposes, he is unstoppable. What makes Mershuls feared is that when in their rage, they cannot distinguish friend from foe. They will kill any living thing that is in their vision. Mershuls have been known to kill the horse they are riding on when they have no enemies left to slay."

Jude broke in. "That is all well and good, old man. But what does that have to do with me? I have been in countless battles since my youth, and I assure you, I have never killed my horse."

Copel ignored Jude and continued as if he had never been interrupted. "When a Mershul goes into his rage, he loses the feeling in his arms and legs. They are there, but pain is far away, like he is in his own body, but watching it from far away while someone else controls it..." Jude started shaking his head and stumbled backward, landing on his cot.

"His nose tingles from the animalistic power that is surging through him. While in his rage, a Mershul cannot hear the people around him. He can hear that they are speaking, but he cannot distinguish if the words are threatening or friendly, in fact he cares little because he will kill them regardless. The only thing that he hears that a Mershul can distinguish is the pounding of his own heart as it hammers twice as much blood as it did before. And vision, a Mershul's vision is reduced to the immediate few feet in front of him."

Jude placed his hands on his head. His father had been a soldier in the Beyklan army. He said there were a few men that fought like that. He said in the old times, these men were considered great warriors and they were sent into the front lines, while the men behind them kept their distance. His father had explained how they could not get to close to the man, even if he was being killed, for fear he would turn on them. Jude couldn't believe he was one of those men. A Mershul, as Copel called it. The keeper described everything that he had felt in the arena. Jude looked up from his hands. "You think I am one of these... these Mershuls?"

Copel nodded grimly. "I do."

Jude shook his head from side to side and rose from his cot. His legs were weaker than before and now he felt dizzy. "I have been in many battles and I have never experienced what you describe."

Copel nodded his head grimly. "Never experienced it until yesterday."

"Yes... no," Jude said frustrated. "I don't know. It all happened so fast. If I was a Mershul, wouldn't I have gone into this transformation before?"

Copel shrugged his shoulders. "After a Mershul comes out of his rage, he must eat about three times what he normally would or he will collapse. After he falls unconscious, he will seldom wake."

Jude glanced back at the plate of food, then back at the keeper. "How many have awakened after you have ever seen them collapse?" Jude asked.

Copel shrugged and stood up from his chair. "Truth be told, I have never seen one ignore the food as long as you have. You undoubtedly suspect that the food is poisoned, but I tell you this. You are in the arena for a purpose. That purpose is to die at the hands of a gladiator champion or that of some wicked beast that they have managed to capture. The city makes money from wages placed before the fights. They always charge when they send a man to be slaughtered by some monster or a bunch of lions because no one will bet on the man. But when they discover that they have a Mershul, there is a chance he will be able to defeat the creatures they send him against. The longer the Mershul lives, the more money the city makes. That means you are worth ten times as much today as you were yesterday. That also means you will most likely die in the arena under the roar of the crowd."

Jude stared at the thick slabs of luscious beef. "How many Mershuls have ever earned their freedom in the arena?" Jude asked.

Copel silently slid the chair back under the desk and started down the long corridor, pushing the empty food cart. "You want to know how many Mershuls have earned their freedom?" Copel repeated as he pushed the squeaky cart down the hall. "None."

The words barely reached Jude's ears. All he could hear was his own frantic chewing as he devoured each of the wooden plates of roast beef.

"Do the gods really exist? My mother often spoke to me about the goddess of mercy. She had been a loving goddess that forgave all and understood why some men were driven to great evil by being victims of it themselves. She had explained to me that evil only begot more evil, that it was a long chain that sometimes never ended. She explained to me that when someone wronged us, it was better to find why they wronged us. What had they suffered to cause them to act so?

My father loved my mother so, but he argued it mattered little. Their wickedness was a chosen action and by the own decision they brought the hammer of jusctie down on their own heads. I used to listen to them rgue for hours about it. My mother always seemed to win, much to my father's dismay, but he loved her for it. He used to brag he had never met a man with her wisdom, let alone another woman. I miss my mother. I will do as she says and pity the men that took her from me, but as my father taught; I will pity them to the dark recesses of the Abyss!"

-Lancalion Levendis Lampara-

12
A Serpent's Siege

The fog cleared slowly, blown south by the north easterly winds, revealing a grisly scene. The thick snow took on a pinkish hue from the loft where Darrion-Quieness sat perched, occasionally taking a bite of the many frozen horse carcasses that he had stored in the snow bank. Down below, about one thousand human bodies lay dead. Some were unrecognizable as men, others frozen solid in an icy tomb, and others simply bitten in half. The dragon had made easy work of the small army and surprised himself at his own prowess. He chuckled in a low growl. That fool halfling prince had sent his army at him, and he had killed them without so much as suffering a scratch.

Darrion-Quieness knew he was strong, but he had no idea that he was that strong. *I bet I could rival Renagargus,* he thought to himself. He quickly dismissed the thought as foolishness. Renagargus was the most feared dragon in all of the realms. He was almost twice the size of Darrion-Quieness and he was a red. The reds were the fiercest, most wicked, of all the dragons. They breathed fire so hot that it could melt rocks and evaporate lakes. Darrion-Quieness hated anything warm let alone hot. Even if he could defeat the great red, why would he want to? It would surely be a horrible battle and the great white made it a point to steer clear of injury when it could be avoided.

Darrion-Quieness scanned the grisly battle field a final time before he took flight. He had done well. It was too bad the backstabbing halfling wasn't among them. He would have liked to eat his tiny body. After all, revenge was a dish best eaten when cold.

The dragon extended his wings and launched himself into the air with his powerful legs. Large chunks of snow and ice fell from the peak as his massive form slowly climbed into the mountain sky. He would return to Nalir and his frozen lair. Hopefully something had moved in so he could kill it. After all, he was powerful. He need not fear anything or anyone.

As he glided just below the clouds, Darrion-Quieness spotted what appeared to be a large gathering of men. He shifted his thick white leathery wings and slowly glided down to a remote peak near the southern part of the mountain range. Landing in a thick snow bank, Darrion-Quieness craned his head over the edge. He could see what appeared to be a small dwarven army. They were dressed in their plate armor and were marching down a thin path into a valley that was covered with a thick blanket of fog. So the halfling prince had a few dwarven friends also?

Darrion-Quieness gave a quick count to the bearded folk that were descending the rocky pass. He counted exactly three hundred. A sizeable force for dwarves. Darrion-Quieness had learned in the past how troublesome the bearded folk could be. They were remarkably more difficult to hit than humans and they were a lot sturdier. Darrion-Quieness enjoyed the fact they were seldom ever mages or sorcerers. That pleased him. He knew that if he crossed a powerful wizard he could find himself in a great deal of trouble. Wizards were another troublesome lot he made a point to stay clear of.

The great white launched himself from his peak and glided down the side of the mountain, following the dwarves into the fog-covered valley. He would teach these stupid dwarves to serve a foolish halfling prince.

Tharxton and his men marched down the narrow path that ran down the rocky slope. It was snow covered and the dwarves all wore large metal cleats that fastened to the bottom of their boots to help them get traction on the icy path. Tharxton smiled as he descended the rocky pass. His men were a sight to see. They were all dressed in full, dwarven, well-polished plate mail bearing the symbol of Clan Stoneheart on their chests. They each had a long white silk cape that danced and flapped in the mountain breeze and hung down from their shoulders to show they came in peace. Tharxton had brought some of the best warriors to represent his clan in case a battle ensued. They had a better chance of making it back up the rocky pass to Mountain Heart.

Once they pierced the fog veil and entered the lush green valley the air went from icy and bitter to cool and pleasant. They marched single file until they reached the end of the rocky trail, where they paused to remove their metal cleats. They placed the metallic footwear in their packs and marched three abreast down the valley to where the human army camped. When they reached the camp they were taken aback. Tharxton had known the numbers of the human army before he started down the mountain, but to see the endless wave of tents and men was astounding. How could his clan resist such a force? There were tents and men as far as the eye could see. They were well armed and appeared to be well organized, but worst of all, they were well supplied. Tharxton lost count of the number of supply wagons and carts. The dwarven king had hoped that he could outlast the Beyklans in a siege, but it became readily apparent that the human army was prepared to siege for at least a year. It was evident that he had little choice but to negotiate peace regardless of the price. Otherwise, his people would surely perish.

Tharxton looked past the tents as men scrambled to fetch their king to meet with him. He scanned ranks looking for this dragon that his scouts had reported seeing in the mountains. Tharxton doubted the king would be able to enlist the service of one of the beasts, but he was aware that the kingdom's mage guilds were some of the strongest in the realms. It was possible, but Tharxton couldn't see any sign of the great beast. His scouts had reported that it was a white dragon. Those reports did not go over well with him since whites were evil. Tharxton knew the Beyklans were power hungry, but he didn't think they would go as far as to enlist the aid of a white. The dwarven king figured that a young white had moved in and that he and the clan would have to move him out as soon as this treaty was complete.

Tharxton stood with his fingers entwined in front of him as the humans fetched their king. Tharxton had never met the king of Beykla, but he knew him to be ruthless. Perhaps Amerix wasn't all wrong in his approach to dealing with King Theobold. The young dwarf king let his gaze fall on his officers that had come down the trail with him. They looked fierce and determined in their polished plate armor, ready to battle at the drop of a feather. Tharxton hoped the talks would be just that that, talks. He prayed that the day wouldn't come to swordplay. His clan would surely be destroyed.

King Theobold sat in his lavish tent enjoying his breakfast. The mantle was ablaze with a warm fire that crackled and popped and he sipped warm cider from a crystal goblet. He wore a thick wool red and yellow robe that hung down to his bare feet, which he had propped up on a small velvet stool to warm by the fire. His servants stood closely by, polished his armor. Deep in thought, the king contemplated, *either the dwarves would come to speak with me by midday, or I am going to siege them out.* He was frustrated that he had not received word from the cavalrymen he had sent around the mountain pass. They were instructed to only go out from sunrise to sunset. If they did not find a pass by then, they were to turn around, making their trip no longer than two days. Yet here it was the morning of the third day, and no word. He would see the lieutenant personally stripped of rank when they returned.

General Bodrell entered the king's tent with a bow. He wore his fancy red lace tunic with a pair of bright yellow leather breeches. His long sword was strapped to his side and he removed his bright yellow silk gloves and tucked them into his pocket. The king sat up in his chair and finished his cider. After three long gulps, the king wiped his mouth and gestured for the general to sit. Bodrell bowed again curtly and took his seat on a small wooden stool. "Good morning, general. What news of the horsemen?"

General Bodrell shook his head from side to side slowly. "No word, Sire. Perhaps they met an ill fate?"

The king slammed his fist down on his eating tray. His fork rattled against his porcelain plate and bits of egg and crumbs of toast bounced in the air. He had been receiving such suggestions all day. The thought that his own officers could admit defeat of a seasoned cavalry unit of a thousand strong angered him. "*Ill fate?* They were a thousand strong! The damned dwarves could have sent the entire force that battled the Torrent Manor against them, and they would have failed. It is more like your foolish lieutenant decided to twist my orders and has stayed out longer than he was given permission to."

General Bodrell narrowed his eyes. He had personally trained the lieutenant himself. The man was no hero, that was for sure. But at first sign of any dwarves, he would have returned promptly to report, not try to earn any merits. "Perhaps they have hit a mountain storm?"

The king shook his head and stood up. "Excuses, general. You offer me excuses. General Stromson would not offer me excuses. He would offer me truths," the king taunted.

Bodrell rose, but made sure he waited a second after the king did. It was disrespectful to remain seated while the king stood, and he wanted every small victory he could get from the arrogant king. Bodrell had liked King Theobold prior to this excursion, but he didn't really know the king before. The more he was getting to know the man, the less he liked him. "Perhaps I shall return when I have answers," Bodrell offered as he removed his silk gloves from his pocket and placed them on his manicured hand.

The king shook his head and waved his hand in dismissal. "Don't bother, General. I am planning the invasion this afternoon."

General Bodrell felt his jaw drop. "This afternoon? Sire, I urge you to reconsider. Perhaps the horsemen where attacked by the beast that felled the scout party. Or..."

King Theobold cut the general off. "Must I remind you who is king, and who is the replaceable general?"

Bodrell cut himself off and shook his head. "No, Sire. I

only thought..."

"Do us both a favor, general, and don't think. I only want you to defeat the enemy I aim you at. Do not think of anything else. There is no beast that could kill a thousand horsemen, and if there was, it is surely severely wounded and we will finish it off. Now go and ready the men," King Theobold commanded.

General Bodrell bowed and started out of the king's pampered quarters when a messenger called out from outside. "Sire, the dwarven king has arrived. He awaits your audience at the north side of the camp."

Bodrell watched incredulously as the king visibly lowered his shoulders and looked disappointed. "Thank you, messenger. I shall meet with him shortly."

General Bodrell smiled. "This is good news, sire. Perhaps the war can be averted after all."

The king glared at the general. "Is it? I will determine the worth of reports. Now go and ready the men."

"But, Sire...," Bodrell pleaded.

"I grow tired of your constant comments, Bodrell. Ready the men!" the king commanded as he shook his finger in the general's face angrily.

It was the shouts and screams that came from the north of camp that put a smile on the Theobold's face. "Perhaps they wanted to fight after all, General," the king said as he turned to his attendant. "Fetch my armor. I have an enemy to defeat."

Bodrell rushed from the king's cosset tent and hurried to his own. The dwarves would be fools to attack an army of this size in the valley. They are outnumbered and the open space would surely work against them. Bodrell knew this Tharxton was no fool. He rushed to get his armor on. He doubted the dwarves attacked. Anything that would challenge an army of this size had to be much worse than the dwarves. Much, much worse.

Darrion-Quieness stretched his wide white leathery

wings wide and glided into the dense fog of the valley. He didn't want to fly full speed into the impenetrable mist for fear he might fly into a cliff face or a large boulder. Splitting his own skull before he could rein death onto the dwarves was not in his plan of battle. The great dragon landed gently on the soft green grass of the valley floor. His iron-hard black talons deftly probed the soft earth and he folded his powerful wings under themselves and tucked them back against his body. He was proud of his ability to land as quiet as a feather despite his immense size. The great white inhaled the wintry fog, trying to determine through smell where the dwarves had gone, but the wet air prevented him from narrowing it down. It seemed to the dragon that there were more horsemen in the haze, by scents he smelled, but he didn't see any horses among the dwarves.

The great white knew dwarves seldom rode anyway. Shaking his heavy scaled head, he closed his eyes and summoned the inner force that connected him with the ice and cold of the mountain. Darrion-Quieness called upon the frost. Great swirls of ice crystals began to form in the air around him. The ice crystals were so small; they drifted among the air like a frozen mist. Just as he had done against the horsemen north of the mountain, he sent frozen fog forward, mixing with the current miasma that blanketed the ceiling of the lush green valley. The warm air in the valley was miserable for the great white, but when the frozen fog began to rocket down the pass, he entered it and was refreshed by its icy chill. Darrion-Quieness charged down the lush green gorge hidden behind a wall of freezing fog.

Tharxton leaned on his great hammer. Its thick stone head sunk under the valley grass from the weight of the sturdy dwarven king. His heavy white cloak stirred in an artic breeze that seemed to flow from the valley behind him. The bitter air froze Tharxton's face and blew his red braided beard about. He turned and gazed in confusion as a wall of impenetrable fog seemed to rush down the valley toward him. His men murmured amongst themselves at the sight of the unnatural mist.

"What do ye make of this?" one of the dwarves called out.

"Some strange weather, huh?" another answered. Tharxton felt the hair on the back of his neck stand up. *Something was wrong. The fog was surely unnatural. What could create such an event? Did the humans have wizards among them? But what would the purpose be?* Tharxton and his men had come down from the mountains under the conditions of peace. Why would the human wizards cast against them and what would be the point of such a fog? It would hinder their army as much, if not more, than it would hinder his small gathering of dwarven leaders. Did the humans hope to kill his officers? Tharxton had expected that might be a possibility and had kept most of the higher command back at the stronghold.

The frozen blast that hit the dwarf king answered all of his queries. Thick ice crystals stung his face and formed in his thick red braided beard. The valley was too warm to support such a fog. Had the white wall been created by an avalanche, they would have heard the rumble from the pounding snow long ago. No, the only thing, save for the wizards the humans had, if they had any at all, was the white dragon his scouts had reported seeing. And only the largest and most powerful whites could summon such a fog. Terror tore through the dwarf king's heart as he and his men felt the tiny reverberations in the valley floor. There was no way the humans could have felt the vibrations. They were not akin to the mountain, but the dwarves were. They knew something big was rocketing toward them. Something deadly.

"Fall back to trail! Get to the east wall, and move yer arses!" Tharxton bellowed as he sprinted from the center of the valley toward the cliff face. The dwarves rushed toward the rock cliff as fast as their short thick legs would carry them, the sounds of their heavy plate armor sending out shrill rings. Tharxton reached the rocky cliff face and urged his men to duck down behind the large heavy boulders. He was standing on the edge of the rock face when he saw the form of the giant beast in the white wall of fog. It was the largest thing Tharxton had ever seen in his life. Its head was lost in the impenetrable fog, but its body was at least two hundred feet from chest to tail. Tharxton could make out the murky white form of the beast as it paused even with his dwarves. There were about fifteen to twenty of his dwarven brethren still rushing toward the rock wall when he felt the air being sucked in toward the hulking mass of scales and claws.

"Shields up!" Tharxton screamed as he tried to loosen his shield that was strapped to his back. He slid one strap off of the shoulder and the heavy dwarven shield slid into his hand. He started to lift the armor piece up when it hit him. There was a deafening roar that tore into his ears. His skin went numb immediately and a dull burn raged in his muscles. His sight turned to a blinding white and he felt his hair and beard harden. He tried to lift his shield, but he could not make his arms move. Suddenly, Tharxton felt his body being pulled behind one of the large boulders. He landed roughly on his back. He could hear the excited and terrified voices of his men, though he could not distinguish what they were saying. There was a constant ringing in his ears and he felt his skin go from numb, to a sharp burn like it was on fire. He tried to lift his head, but he was pushed back down. All he could make out was that his officers were holding him still and shushing him. Against his better judgment, he lay still as the searing burn of his skin began to test his ability not to scream from the horrific pain.

He lay on his back for a few minutes when he heard the men beginning to speak again. Tharxton tried to move but he could not. His muscles had gone numb, but his skin was on fire like he was on a spike. The dwarven king could make out the words of his men, but his ears still sounded a shrill ring.

"Is he alive?"

"Aye, but he is badly burned from the cold. I do not know if he will live."

"What of the others?"

Tharxton heard a short pause and as one of the men clambered from around the edge of the boulder. He tried to open his eyes, but all he saw was an eternity of pallor. He heard the dwarf that clambered around the edge of the boulder climb back. He sat down hard, but he didn't hear him speak.

"What of the others? Well?"

Tharxton strained to hear the response. Had the men gotten their shields up in time? The dwarf king heard another of his officers as he clambered around the boulder that had sheltered them. Why wasn't the first one answering? He thought it was Brogan, but he couldn't tell voices from the horrible ringing that echoed in his head.

"Leska have mercy," Tharxton heard the second dwarf say from around the boulder. He heard others clamber around the rocky shield while one sat near to him.

"They are frozen in solid ice..."

"Let us pray to Leska that she receive them and welcome them to Yahna..."

Tharxton could hear the dwarves as they gave a quick prayer to the Earth Mother and asked for her to receive the dwarves into Yahna. Then he heard the shrill screams from the south from the humans. He felt his officers grab him and hoist him up.

"Let's get back to Mountain Heart. It's obvious the dragon wasn't sent by the humans, since he is attacking them, too."

"You think their soldiers will be able to kill the beast?"

"Regardless, they will wound each other, making our job easier."

The dwarves chuckled lightly, though Tharxton could hear the pain in their voices as they mourned the loss of their comrades. He tried to speak, to order the men back down the path to battle the dragon alongside of the humans. He knew what the humans would presume. Although if the dragon defeated them, it was unlikely the king would send a second army into the pass. Yet Tharxton was aware of the powerful mage guild that the humans had in Dawson.

Tharxton felt himself being hauled along the rocky pass. He could see nothing more than the empty white that seemed to engulf him and his skin burned like fire. The king found himself having difficulty thinking and soon drifted off into unconsciousness.

Darrion-Quieness rushed down the valley, hidden behind the wall of freezing fog. He was making good time, but his keen ears caught the sound of armored figures to his left. It didn't sound like many but the dragon dared not let anyone behind him. He paused and inhaled deeply. He sucked in the cold mountain air, filling his powerful lungs as the scales on his chest expanded and separated, exposing his soft flesh. Darrion-Quieness rocketed his head down and forced his abyssal cold. His frigid breath roared from his mouth and smothered the several dwarves that were trying to make it to a large boulder. He finished exhaling and examined his handiwork. The dwarves were frozen solid to the earth, some embedded in an icy tomb. Darrion-Quieness moved toward the boulder to see if there were any more dwarves behind it when his keen ears caught a trumpet sounding down the valley. He whipped his massive head around. The long white whiskers that hung down from his chin dangled from the heavy frost that clung to them. His bright green eyes narrowed as they scanned the white murky fog, but he could not see anything. He tucked his wings under him and hurried down the valley toward the sound. As he approached, it seemed as if there were more dwarves than the three hundred he counted while he was in flight.

Darrion-Quieness was surprised to find that the wall of fog was being held back by some invisible force. But what surprised him more was that in the green valley before him was an army of humans, an army so vast that he could not see where their numbers ended and the horizon began. Hundreds of men standing around the fog fell to the ground in shocked horror.

The great white ignored them and gave a quick count of the soldiers. Twenty nine thousand, six hundred and seventy two...no, seventy three counting the wizard. *Wizard! That was how his fog had been blocked.* Darrion-Quieness fixed his gaze on the robed man that was a few hundred yards away. The man turned and ducked back into his tent. Darrion-Quieness knew the power of wizards. They could be deadly, but if he was to kill the robed man, he would have to plunge right into the middle of the camp. Darrion-Quieness glanced back toward the mountain peak. He could be long gone in moments. This army was no group of lost horsemen, or a few hundred dwarves. This was an army that only the great dragons could face. These are the kinds of armies that Renagargus the Great Red would face. Or Androdius the Great Black, or Yohr-Acht the Great Green.

Darrion-Quieness turned and extended his wings to fly away. He didn't bargain on facing such a force. *To hell with that halfling prince if he could command such an army,* he thought. *The chance for injury just wasn't worth the vengeance.* Darrion-Quieness had a huge lair with great treasures to entertain him. He didn't need to face such dangers. The great white extended his wings and flexed his powerful legs. Just as he started to jump he felt a sharp sting in his leg, then another. He looked down. The stupid tiny humans were attacking him. Him! Just who did they think they were? And as the foolish men hurled spear after spear and bounced arrow after arrow harmlessly off his thick scaled side, he could see hundreds more charging him.

How dare they attack him! He was Darrion-Quieness, the Great White! Yes, he was powerful. It was time the world trembled at his power and shuddered when his name was mentioned. Darrion-Quieness turned and inhaled deeply, his powerful lungs sucking in immense amounts of air. It was then that an arrow struck him between his chest scales. He ignored the small sting, but realized he couldn't use his breath weapon unless he was airborne without risking injury when his scales separated from the expanding of his chest. Turning and facing the massive army, Darrion-Quieness exhaled his colossal cone of cold. The abyssal air cracked and popped as it engulfed the first three hundred men that were standing next to him. He moved his head from side to side in a sweeping motion, covering the entire valley. Men were frozen in solid blocks of ice. Some were killed immediately and others writhed in misery, with half of their bodies trapped in the icy tombs.

Darrion-Quieness stepped forward in disbelief as the army continued to pour toward him. He had just killed three hundred of their numbers in a single breath, yet they still charged. He needed to kill that wizard soon. He was going to need the fog to hide him, or he might not survive the day.

Bodrell strapped on his armor and rushed toward the front ranks of men. One hundred yards in front of him he could see a large wall of fog being held back by Talwin, the apprentice mage. The mage was standing in his blue robe and had both arms raised, creating some kind of force field from the fog. Bodrell slowed to a walk as he contemplated the necessity of blocking the white blanket.

The general could not see the dwarves. They must have fled, or they were on the other side of the wall of fog. It was then that his heart nearly leapt from his chest. A great dragon erupted from the wall of fog and stood startled in front of them. The beast seemed to be a hundred feet tall and was as wide as a large building. The single black horn protruding from the center rear of its head arced back over its neck, which had a thick white sail that hung down. The beast's thick leathery wings were outstretched, touching the valley walls on each side with its tips. Bodrell stood in awe at the spectacle of the great beast. Had he not known the dragon was a white, an incredibly evil one, he might have been able to enjoy the sight of the majestic creature. But as it stood, the dragon represented death, the same death that probably killed the first scouting party and probably killed the legion of horsemen that were sent out to find a rear pass to the valley.

Whether or not the dragon was working with the dwarves had yet to be proven, but he guessed that the beast happened to be in the area. Bodrell knew Clan Stoneheart was not an evil clan by nature and that they were not likely to side with a white, especially one of this one's size. Dragons, especially ones named for their color, were sinister and power hungry. They served no one unless they had too, and they allied themselves as seldom as possible. They wanted to rule, not serve alongside.

The general watched as the beast acted as if he was going to turn and leave. Then the dragon inhaled and fired a blast of its breath that was so cold, Bodrell heard the air crack and pop as hundreds of men were killed. Some were frozen where they stood, others were lifted from their feet and hurled through the air by the wicked blast. General Bodrell knew that no one could have survived the breath attack. He immediately turned and ran back toward the king's quarters. Regardless of whom, if anyone, sent the dragon, this was going to be a deadly battle that they might not win. Bodrell ran as he tried to think of how General Erik Stromson would have handled this before he retired. The young general decided that Stromson would have been prepared for the event after the first few reports and would have overruled the king, or ignored his orders. Bodrell could not do such things. He hadn't been general long enough for the men to back him and Theobold would have surely replaced him had he made such a callous move. This was the beginning of a very bloody day.

Darrion-Quieness launched himself into the air with his powerful legs. He forced his large wings down as he craned his neck forward to get lift. The fog around him swirled into hundreds of tiny eddies, like water in a lake when stirred by an oar. Hundreds of arrows hit his thick scaled hide and bounced away without disruption. Soldiers under him grabbed their helmets and tried to hold them to their heads from the gale force wind created by the beating of his massive wings. The grass was bent flat from the force as men fell to the earth.

Darrion-Quieness launched forward, hurling his two hundred ton frame to the earth in front of the mass of tents where the wizard fled. The dragon landed on all fours among the mass of men. Scores of soldiers screamed before they were crushed under the weight of great dragon, but others scrambled and hurled spears and shot arrows. Darrion-Quieness slapped at the men with his front claws, sending bodies flying through the air. He roared in an anger that echoed through valley like the bellow of an avalanche. The great white hoisted his tail high in the air, lifting his hind quarters, and then he slammed it into the tents. His great scaled tail hit with such force that many men were knocked from their feet. Some dropped their swords and covered their ears from the deafening crash.

Darrion-Quieness ignored the stinging axes and swords that cut into the soft scales of his feet and legs, kicking out randomly, killing scores of soldiers with each strike, yet hundreds more swarmed to replace them. The dead littered the green valley, which was slowly turning red from the blood of thousands. The dragon's keen sight spotted the pitiful wizard fleeing further away from him further south. The great white kicked out again with his front legs, killing twenty soldiers with the wicked swipe, while he lifted his rear feet and brought them crashing down, killing twenty more.

Darrion-Quieness started toward the mage when he saw what the wizard was fleeing towards. Four large ballistae were pointed at his direction and were being drawn back to fire. Men prepared to launch the giant spear through the air by cranking the wooden wheel, slowly drawing the giant metal cable back. The great white knew a single shot from the giant crossbows mounted on a wooden cart could kill him. Many dragons in the past had been slain by such wicked inventions of men, but without his fog, he knew he had little chance of defeating this army. But he was Darrion-Quieness. He was the Great White. He would be victorious then all the greats would see what he had done and surely acknowledge his power.

The dragon leapt into the air a second time, his powerful wings beating down, knocking soldiers from their feet. He saw one of the ballistae lose its giant spear. The fifty foot shaft sailed just under his thick body as he ascended into the foggy ceiling of the valley. As Darrion-Quieness erupted from the top of the fog, the bright sun glinted off of his white scales making his enormous body shine like a polished diamond. Thousands of tiny wooden arrows erupted from the fog under him and ricocheted off of his steel-hard scales. A few of the arrows hit home on his feet and lower legs where the scales were weaker, but the great white hardly noticed. He extended his enormous wings wide and glided south, occasionally turning his head to hear the sounds and screams of men below him. When he heard the clicking of the great ballistae as they were reloaded, he tucked his wings under himself and plunged into the thick fog.

"Kill the beast!" Theobold screamed as he emerged from his tent. He was clad in his full plate armor and great helm. His brass-colored mail shone in the pale light of the valley. He wore a great helm that had a shimmering red plum that erupted from the top and cascaded down his back. The helm's visor was up and the warrior king was still getting his greaves fastened by his attendants. Theobold took a step and pulled his attendant down to the ground. He looked down and glared angrily at the man. "Hurry up, fool! Or I will put a sword in your hand and send you to the front line!"

The attendant finished fastening the greave and stepped away, allowing Theobold to hurry to his horse. The animal could sense the carnage that was unfolding further up the valley. Theobold made his way to the great ballistae. One had been fired and the others where cocked and ready. He trotted his horse to the large heavy siege engines. General Bodrell stood in his plate armor, his red silk cape flowing around him as he stared at the foggy ceiling of the valley.

"Where is this beast?" Theobold asked as he looked around from the saddle of his horse. Bodrell pointed up. "It flew away. We fired the number six ballista at it and it fled. We have suffered many casualties on the front lines."

"How many is many?" Theobold asked, lifting his chin as he tried to peer a few hundred yards north. He could see many forms lying on the ground motionless, others hobbling from leg injuries, and some holding lifeless arms at their sides.

"About two thousand, I suspect," Bodrell answered as he continued to scan the fog ceiling.

Theobold nearly choked. "Two thousand? Surely your estimations are off, General."

Bodrell shrugged. "Could be, Sire, but by the size of the creature...," Bodrell trailed off as he spotted the white demon as it shot from the fog veil and crushed about a hundred men and several tents. The ground shook, causing the king's horse to skitter under him. Theobold fought the animal under control as he stared in awe at the immense size of the dragon. Bodies were hurled through the air effortlessly as the beast swatted at the remaining tents in the area. The great ballistae launched its giant bolts. The fifty foot long spear-like shafts sliced through the air. All but one of the bolts missed, hitting the rocky east wall and shattering into hundreds of splinters. But one struck the dragon in the rear flank, piercing his hide. The beast roared in pain, arching its neck back and extending its wings. The dragon reached back with his clawed hand and tried to pull the barbed bolt free but he could not. The dragon roared in pain as crimson blood seeped from the grievous wound and ran down his rear leg. Blood pooled under the dragon's scales near its hindquarters. He turned his evil gaze to the ballistae as the men hurried to reload them. They hoisted the heavy wooden bolts to the firing groove and then started to turn the crank that slowly pulled the heavy cable back into place.

"Why is he not attacking us?" Theobold shouted, watching hundreds of his men get effortlessly slaughtered by the colossal serpent.

Bodrell turned his attention to the fog wall. It was no longer being held by the magical barrier that Talwin had erected. "He must have killed Talwin. Look at the fog."

Theobold watched as a massive wall of fog rushed down the valley. It enveloped his men and rolled toward him and his general like a permeable tidal wave of water vapor. Theobold glanced back at the dragon and lost sight of him as he became engulfed in the fog. The king turned back and lifted his shield to cover his face from the stinging ice crystals that pinged off of his metal armor. He felt a wet water vapor cover him and immediately turn to a thin layer of ice on his armor and over his sword. Theobold spurred his horse and charged in the direction of the great white. As he made his way through the fog, around dead twisted bodies of his soldiers, he heard screams and snapping timbers behind him. The king turned, frustrated at the beast's mobility despite its injury. He raised his sword and spurred his horse back the way he came.

When Theobold arrived at the ballistae he saw that they had been destroyed. There were bodies everywhere and the ice was thickening over the splintered pieces of wood. A few men crawled out from under the wrecked siege engines, including General Bodrell. He had a thick piece of splintered wood protruding from his thigh, and the blood from the wood was frozen under a layer of ice on the brass-colored plate armor of his leg. Theobold dismounted and helped the wounded man to his feet. They both turned their heads to the screams of men being ripped apart and crushed. Theobold growled as he imagined the cost to his army.

"Damn those bearded bastards!" Theobold screamed as he sheathed his frozen blade. The long sword smacked into the ice-covered scabbard.

Bodrell didn't respond. He just shook his head and grimaced, pulling the long piece of wood from his thigh. He grunted and tossed the bloody stake to the icy grass. There was no sense in arguing or even voicing a disagreement with the arrogant king. He was obviously seeking any reason to attack the dwarves. He now had it, but the general wasn't sure how much of his army would be left, if any at all, to siege the bearded folk.

Darrion-Quieness tried to ignore the horrendous pain in his right flank from the wicked ballista bolt. The shaft was embedded deep into his hide, and the heavy wooden bolt bounced with each move he made during his attacks. Darrion-Quieness had quickly crushed the siege engines after doing away with the pesky mage. His freezing fog had just about reached its duration and there seemed to be nothing left of the human's army, save for scattered units that would take him days to kill. The wounded dragon gave a final parting breath into a mass of soldiers and launched himself into the air for the last time. As he crested the fog veil of the valley, he looked back at the wound in his flank. The large bolt had worked itself loose during the fighting. Darrion-Quieness reached back and pulled the shaft free.

He circled the fog-covered valley once and hurled the fifty foot spear toward the ground, hoping to kill a few more of the cursed humans. As far as he was concerned, he had defeated them. He couldn't get an accurate count due to the fog, but of the twenty nine thousand he was sure there were little more than seven thousand left. Regardless, he needed to return to his lair in Nalir. The great white didn't plan on staying long as he figured the defeat of this army would prompt others to attack. He needed to gather his most prized treasures, like his diamond collection, and make a new lair. He had thought about the polar flats north of Kai-Harkia. The flats were delightfully arctic year-round and he needed a wonderfully chilly, snowy lair to be able to rest for a few years to heal the horrific wound in his flank. He was getting too old for this kind of thing.

"The lust for power is much like an addiction. Theobold had a lust for power. He wanted to leave his mark on his kingdom, a legacy so-to-speak. The kings before him had expanded the borders of their kingdom, making Beykla one the largest and strongest in the realms. Theobold felt that he needed to expand his kingdom's borders to show that he was as great as his father and his father's father. But any fool can conquer land. Any fool can kill and make others bend to their will out of fear. But who can keep a land together when it is so large and covers so many different views? Theobold sought to eliminate those who thought differently than he. He wanted to rule how he felt his fathers had, with an iron hammer. But ultimately he failed. The men of Southern Beykla longed to pull away from his kingdom. They disagreed with his treatment of the dwarves and how he kept the country in a perpetual war. Theobold was king to govern his people. But he believed that his people were there to be ruled. History is riddled with kings that were overthrown by those they ruled. Even a king of the gods was overthrown by those he ruled. Leaders exist to provide for those they lead. Those who are led are not there to provide for their leader. Strange how many so-called leaders fail to realize this."

-Lancalion Levendis Lampara-

The Breach of Crowns

The bright orange light of the portal popped into existence. The small ginger ball stretched and elongated until it was several feet wide. The sparkling line of magical energy then split into two and moved away from each other, one moving higher and the other lower. On one side was a fantastic chamber of angelic carvings and formations. Dicermadon, God of Magic, stood with his arms crossed. His skin was now a dull gray and his hair had shifted to bright white. The god's beard had lengthened and he seemed to be tired and fatigued but his eyes still held their impenetrable steel blue gaze.

He was clothed in a heavy white loin cloth, held by a thick golden belt, that hung down past his knees. He wore durable sandals with an open toe. There was a smile on his stern face as he stared into the opening portal. On the other side, a more sinister view was exposed. There were many dark twisted gray slate rocks that seemed to expand forever in all directions. The sky was filled with black noxious clouds of gas that had bright yellow sulfurous highlights at their edges swirling and shifting in a myriad of wind currents that blew about the desolate land. Strange beasts flew in among the dark clouds and tortured screams echoed in the background.

Standing before the horrific scene was Bykalicus, an archdemon, a king of the Abyss. His bright red skin was taught over an incredibly muscled body. His thick, canine-like maw dripped acid drool while his bright yellow eyes had an aura that shone out past his face. Flames danced and rolled across his massive body erratically. The archdemon stood confidently. His arms were also crossed and the demon wore an expression of annoyance on his powerful face. He showed no signs of weakness or fatigue and he stood with an air of arrogant confidence that was not emulated by the exhausted looking figure on the other side.

"Your artifact didn't work, Dicermadon," the archdemon said angrily as his acidic spit dripped from his mouth and crackled on the cold slate floor of the Abyss.

Dicermadon tensed his muscles and tightened his fists. "How dare you contact me here, you fool. I have a mind to..."

"To what?" Bykalicus interrupted. "You are nothing but a shell of your former power. I know of the severance, and I know of the banding by the elementals. You are no longer the God King. You are nothing, at least until you reestablish your link. By the looks of things, you are trapped in your own palace while the other gods lay siege to your ever-weakening barriers," Bykalicus taunted as he stretched his neck to look through the portal.

Dicermadon glared fiercely at the archdemon. Normally he would have the power to reach through the gate and lay waste to the demon, but now... Now, he was weak and vulnerable. The archdemon was correct in his assessment, but Dicermadon was adamant against surrender. He had been King of the Gods longer than most of the other gods had existed.

Bykalicus's keen serpent eyes caught a glimpse of a strange jewel hovering above a bright golden crown resting flat on the God King's chamber floor. Around the crown were hundreds of intricately carved runes that circled around the crown and the jewel that hovered over it. "What is that, old one?"

Dicermadon turned and gestured to the hovering jewel. It was an amazing crystal, shaped like an oversized egg. It twinkled and sparkled, giving off flickering beams of ever-growing light that danced about the room. "That is my solace, you dog of a demon," the God King said through clenched teeth.

Bykalicus chuckled. "You dare to flatter me? Your power is drained. You can barely sustain yourself and it seems you are growing weaker by the moment. I demand to know why the necklace didn't work before you wilt into nothingness."

Dicermadon smiled triumphantly and fell to his knees.

He grabbed at the shinning post of his mighty golden throne. "I am anything but defeated, you fool. I know not what the future holds for me, or how the transformation will affect me, but I will never be defeated. Who can defeat me? You? You are nothing but a lap dog for Rha-Cordan, the god that doesn't even see morality in the same light as you. What will the other gods use to take my crown? They wield the very power I am god over. I know how each of their powers function more than they do. It was by sheer chance that they managed to weaken me and sever the link with humanity. Yet, I am still not defeated, merely... slowed," the God King said as he fell to his hands and knees. He lifted his head and rocked back to the seating position, holding himself up with weak arms. The god's face became hollow and his eyes became more sunken with every passing second. "I used you for a means to an end, Bykalicus. You have limited prophetic powers. All of your kind do, something that I do not. Prophecy is not a way of magic, but the sight of it. I can bend and manipulate the true power, but prophets and creations such as you sometimes can see what will come of those manipulations."

Bykalicus frowned and stepped toward the portal, only to step back as he heard the pounding of immensely powerful spells hammering against the god king's chamber walls. "I never prophesied for you!" the archdemon bellowed in a rage, shaking his fist at the ever-weakening God King.

"Ah, but...," Dicermadon paused to catch his weakening breath, "...but you have. You have done much for me, dog. Even your precious Delania serves me now unwittingly. If you ever want to have her, you will continue to serve me, or she will share the fate of Ecnal."

Ecnal. There was the mention of the fool human the king of Nalir kept summoning him about. What was the key to this mortal scum, and why did the God of Gods concern himself with him? Rage tore through the arch demon. The succubus was his! He would have her, one way or another! The flames that danced across his massive body became excited and flickered rapidly. He wanted to rush through the portal, but he did not. Something was amiss with the gateway. He didn't smell the disgustingly sweet air that always seeped in when he opened such doorways. The archdemon did not rise to be as powerful as he was by being foolish. He would research what was different, his serpent eyes memorizing the complex weaves and flows of the portal to ponder on later. "Pray that they destroy you, fool. For I will come again."

Dicermadon chuckled as he lay down and propped his exhausted head up with his shoulder. "Who shall I pray to, dog? I am all there is. But why do you not come for me? Come for me now, coward."

Bykalicus felt a surge or pure hate that burned his soul like the furnace of the earth, yet he was a being of timelessness. He would survive until slain on his native plane, or in Merioulus.

Dicermadon smiled triumphantly when the archdemon hesitated. "I used a dimensional anchor on the gateway you created. If you came through it, you would not be able to leave until you identified my complex anchor weaves, which I doubt you ever could. But even if you had the ability, the gods would have broken down my barrier long before, and you would have been torn to small pieces. You would beg them to turn you into a gweit so that you could spend eternity crawling on your belly and hiding from the weakest demons, rather than face the endless torture they would impose on you."

Bykalicus paused and tried to identify the weaves among his own, but could not see them. He glanced at the jewel that was spinning rapidly now and was shedding bright beams of light across the room. The walls shuddered and great pieces of stone exploded and skipped across the chamber. Bykalicus watched as Flunt, the God of Fire, burst into the room cloaked in his robe of molten rock. He held aloft a flaming sword that cackled and popped like a roaring fire and the air around him was distorted from his immense heat. His eyes were fiery red and ablaze with a fury more fierce than the arch demon had ever seen.

The jewel immediately sent a beam of light that hit the God of Fire in the chest. The beam stayed fixed on him and grew brighter than all the other beams as they bounced around the chamber. One by one, each beam came into contact with the God of Fire until there was only one beam that went from his chest, directly into the jewel. Flunt dropped his sword and screamed in pain. Other gods tried to enter the chamber but were repelled by yet another barrier.

Dicermadon smiled and weakly lifted his head. "Flunt, my dear fool. Did you think it was your great power that battered down my shield? In your own arrogant fury, did you assume that your will allowed you to slip through my final barrier, the one your fellow gods hammer at with all of their might?"

The God of Fire fell to his knees as the beam of light pulsed and grew. He fought to keep in his screams and tried to stand against the power of the jewel, but could not. The other gods watched helplessly as the events unfolded before them. Dicermadon sat upright, using what little strength that remained within him. "You cannot fight the jewel, Flunt. Even as it drains your essence, it also drains mine. But you see, my fiery friend, I am the God of Magic. I can manipulate it all. I can take what I want of your power and discard the rest. You and the others were right about my inability to re-establish a link to the prime material plane because I have no home plane. I am the God of Gods. I am bound to Merioulus. Well, Flunt... I am bound...NO...LONGER! I relinquish the crown and in doing so, I shall destroy it! There will never be a God King to follow me! The pantheon's foolish laws have allowed the birth of a Breedikai! And worse, you fools allow him to walk the planes unchecked! Do you not know what he will become? The earth will break him! He will suffer such wrongs that his imperfect soul will become blacker than that of Rha-Cordan! He will hate you all, and he will destroy all of this!" Dicermadon said as he gestured weakly around him. "I have seen it foretold. I will not fall prey to your foolishness! I will defeat the blasphemous creation with the same hate he will use against me. I will create a place where hate burns hotter than the intensity of a thousand white hot suns. And I will rule this plane and fill it with legions of the damned. They will be tortured day and night by creations that only I can imagine. These souls will hate all that is good and they will hate all that is evil. They will have so much hate in them that they will serve me inequitably with the hope that one day I might release them to cause the most minuscule amount of pain on the simplest of creatures. I will rule this place with an iron hand and I shall call it... Hell!"

As the withered form of Dicermadon finished speaking, the jewel erupted in a blinding flash of light.

Bykalicus howled in pain and closed the portal clutching his eyes and rolling around on the stone floor of the Abyss. He knew he needed to rise quickly and try to regain his sight. Many demons would seek to kill him if they thought he was weakened. The archdemon managed to rub the blindness from his eyes, but his vision was spotty at best. He stretched his great red and black bat wings and launched himself into the sulfuric air of the Abyss. He needed to return to his lair to ponder the words of the departed god king.

The barrier collapsed as the jewel shattered and Leska rushed into the room followed by the other elemental gods. She dropped to her knees and lifted the bald head of Flunt. The fire that danced across his eyes was gone and the flaming hair that flickered on his head was no more. His molten cape had hardened into a smoldering rocky tomb that was one with the floor.

The Earth Mother held Flunt's lifeless body close to hers and wept. Surshy bowed her head as did Whisten. They held a moment of silence for the passing of the Breedikai. As Leska and Surshy consoled each other, the God of Air walked over and picked up the twisted and melted crown. The golden mantle of the God of Gods burned hot in his hands, even though it was destroyed. The magic in it was gone and each of the jewels that were set into the teeth of the crown, representing each domain of divine worship, were shattered. He tossed the crown down at Surshy's and Leska's feet. The melted gold mantle clanged as it bounced off of the marbled floor of the God King's chamber.

The God of Air glanced at the small smoking mound of ashes that lay where the body of Dicermadon had been.

Whisten pondered the remnants for a moment. The God of Magic had died as Flunt had, destroyed by the very enchantment of the crown. Or had he? Flunt's body had not been destroyed by the shattering of the jewel; neither had the crown. Whisten suspected that the God King had managed to take magic from the artifact and meld it with his own somehow just as he had boasted.

"The fool has taken the God of Fire, breaking the quad of elementals. He has destroyed the mantle of power, taking our ability to crown a king. Without a crown, there can be no king. With no king, no new Breedikai can be raised to be the fourth elemental. Without the fourth, the link can never be re-established," Whisten said gravely.

"Merioulus is doomed," Surshy whispered as she rose from the lifeless form of Flunt. Her long wet hair hung down over her deep blue skin as she held her head in sadness. Leska bowed her head as she cradled Flunt in her arms. "If Panoleen were among us, may she have mercy, for the crown has been breached, and we are all surely doomed."

The morning came early for the orc. His dreams were haunted by hordes of humans and dragons trying to kill the old dwarf, Amerix. No matter how many he killed to protect his friend, more seemed to pop up and take their place. As the dreams waged on, he found his arms moving too slowly to parry strikes. When he tried to run, he couldn't run very fast while his enemies laughed and taunted him. Vlargcar didn't realize how much he had come to care for his old grizzled companion over the last few months. He sat up from his warm bedroll and scratched his chin. It had been itching furiously over the last few days and now he felt a small growth of hair on it. The small patch of hair wasn't thick by any means, but it was surely enough to irritate him. Rising and tossing the wool blanket to the side, he scanned the camp site for Amerix but he did not see him. He felt a hard lump growing in his throat and fear mounting as he wondered if hordes of dragons really did come and take his friend.

The orc stood up and wiped the sleep from his eyes and moved to the edge of camp. He looked down the rocky slope that was at the foot of the plateau, straining his eyes for a glimpse of his friend. To his relief he saw Amerix running toward him. It was then he heard the baying of hounds. Vlargcar hated dogs. The humans used them when they raided an orc village. The animals were vicious and ruthless, able to run down most orcs and kill them by sheer numbers.

Vlargcar ran back, slipped his chain armor over his head and secured his short sword with his thick leather belt. He hastily fastened the long sword to his shoulder and stepped back to the edge of camp. He drew both of his swords and rushed toward the dwarf while the sounds of the baying hounds drew nearer.

Amerix ran as fast as his short stubby little legs could carry him. His right leg stung from the crossbow bolt protruding from the back of it. He had been careless when hunting in the morning, hoping to kill a deer or anything other than the damned squirrels the orc always seemed to find. He had grown quite sick of the brown furry little morsels. He had been tracking a large doe when he stumbled right into three war dogs that had been tied to a tree. He was unable to escape the first one's reach in time, and had been forced to kill the animal. That alerted about a score of humans, who promptly fired a few crossbows at him. He fled back to the camp to alert the orc, when he took a bolt to the back of his right leg. The wound slowed him little and it hurt terribly. Amerix had suffered many wounds in his time. Pain was an old friend of his that made the most unwanted visits. He was almost at the camp and the dwarf suspected the men chased him with the hounds on leashes. That was the only explanation why the animals had not caught up with him yet.

As Amerix started up the hill he saw Vlargcar rushing down the hill with his swords in his hand. The orc was truly a chilling sight. He held both steady as his powerful legs churned, rocketing him down the hill. He leapt over small rocks and fallen trees wearing a visage of sheer anger and determination. It reminded Amerix of his younger days, when he would have turned and fought, rather than ran, but Vlargcar was not skilled enough with his swords to fight an experienced swordsman. Had he not been with the orc, the Amerix would have turned and fought, but he had more to think about than himself. "Turn back, ye green-skinned fool!" Amerix shouted between labored breaths.

Vlargcar slowed and frowned in confusion. He held his swords out and shrugged his shoulders. Amerix didn't slow as he approached he orc. "We have to scale the cliff face!"

Vlargcar waited for Amerix to run by before he turned and ran toward the camp. The orc didn't understand why they just didn't turn and fight. *How skilled could the humans be?* His tribe had killed hundreds since he was a boy. Humans were generally weak and if you ate a few of them, the rest would run. Amerix ran over and snatched up his leather pack without stopping his run up the rocky slope to the cliff face and tossed it over his shoulder as he followed the old dwarf. He had kept most of his belongings securely inside in case they were forced to flee.

The baying of the hounds drew nearer as the pair rushed over the rocky slope. As they neared the top, the trees became sparser and the terrain turned from average sized boulders to great ones. Often they had to squeeze between a small crevice and climb atop the boulders that littered the base of the cliff face. Amerix ignored the pain in his leg as he climbed, leaving an obvious trail of bright blood on the dark brown rocks. The orc was faring better at climbing and seemed to be a natural at it. He scaled the large boulders easily, often pausing to haul the dwarf up. When they reached the highest point of the rocky slope, they paused. The hound's baying changed into frustrated whelps and whines when they could not climb the rocks to follow the pair. Relief washed over Amerix when he heard the frustrated hounds, but the grizzled old dwarf knew they had little time. If the hounds were at the base of the large rocks, so were the humans.

The old dwarf slid his pack down from his shoulder and pulled out the brown waxed rope. The rope wasn't thick, but Amerix figured it to hold him and the orc. He had waxed it at while at his stay with the smith, knowing a waxed rope was stronger. The coat of wax kept out water and dirt that would break down the rope's fibers. Amerix handed the rope to Vlargcar. "Ye think ye can toss this thing up the wall a bit?" Amerix whispered through pain-clenched teeth.

Vlargcar frowned as he stooped low with the old dwarf. "Why would I do that? Let's cut the scum down," the orc suggested, as he flexed his ever-growing muscular arms and shook his long sword.

Amerix grabbed the orc's sword and lowered it. "There be a time fer fighting and a time fer running. This be the time fer running," Amerix said as he ripped the bolt from the back of his thigh. Tears welled up in his eyes from the stinging pain, but the old dwarf ignored it, as he had countless times before.

Vlargcar frowned and glanced past the kneeling dwarf and down into the rocky slopes below them. It didn't seem right to run. There couldn't be that many of them, but he trusted Amerix. "I still think we should be fighting, but if you say run, run it is."

Amerix nodded and gestured to the orc with the rope a second time. Vlargcar took the rope in his hands and glanced up the cliff. It was surely too far to throw the rope to the top, and there was not enough length to it anyway. Vlargcar looked back at the old dwarf. "There isn't enough rope to make the throw."

"No kidding, ye dumb lummox," Amerix growled through clenched teeth. "Just throw the thing as high as you can and hope it hooks on a rock so we can climb out of here."

Vlargcar frowned and scooted down to the edge of the large brown boulder. He set himself low and twirled the rope with a small metal grappling hook on the end. He adjusted the spin until his tight twirling circle rotated vertically, and then he let it fly. The small metal hook soared high into the air, landing on a small ledge. Vlargcar pulled gently, fearing the hook would tumble over and come crashing down on his head, but to his surprise the hook managed to wedge itself in a small crevice. Vlargcar turned and motioned to Amerix who was lying on his belly glancing over the edge of the rock toward the location where the men were. The old dwarf stayed low and skittered over to the rope. "They heard the rope hit and are coming this way. We need to hurry, ye goes first."

Vlargcar started to protest but the stern look the dwarf gave him urged him on. He grabbed the rope in his large hands and began to climb. Vlargcar quickly discovered that it was almost as easy for him to climb without the rope as it was with. The cliff was covered in hundreds of handholds and small crevices to place his feet. He hurried up the rope as he heard shouts from the men down below. He didn't know what they were saying – he didn't understand common – but the shouts were obviously anything but friendly. When he reached the top, he reached over the ledge and felt a long wide crack where he could get a nice handhold. He flexed his powerful arms and pulled himself up. After getting all the way onto the rocky perch, he noticed that it had cracked from its own weight. Water must have drained into the fracture, freezing in the winter and forcing the ledge further away from the wall until it fell like the other large boulders shattered at the foot of the cliff face. Vlargcar glanced down from the ledge and saw Amerix scampering up the rope. He did a fair job of the climbing but his wounded leg was hampering his efforts considerably. The orc stood atop the rocky shelf and scanned the edge of the trees but did not see the humans. He looked back down at the dwarf when a crossbow bolt whizzed by his head and shattered on the rocks behind him. He flinched and ducked down. "Hurry Amerix, they are shooting at us."

"No kidding, ye green-skinned baboon! Why do ye think I am climbing so fast?" Amerix bellowed sarcastically as he scampered up the rope.

Vlargcar didn't know what a baboon was, but if it had green skin, he figured it couldn't be that bad. Of course trolls had green skin, and he hated those beasts. At least the warriors of his clan did. He had never fought one. In truth, he didn't see what the big deal was. If they would have chopped them long enough, they would surely die.

Vlargcar slowly poked his head over the edge only to stare into the fiery gaze of Amerix's deep blue eyes. "Get out of me way! I have had one arrow in me behind today, I don't want another one!" the dwarf screamed as he shoved Vlarg-car to the side.

Vlargcar grabbed the dwarf by his backpack and helped him up the ledge, despite the dwarf's insistent demands to do it alone. More crossbow bolts hit the rocks around them, showering them in splinters of wood and small rock chips. Amerix rolled onto his back and sighed. "Those scum are relentless."

"What's a baboon?" Vlargcar asked as he sat with his legs crossed back against the rock wall of the ledge.

Amerix eyed the orc suspiciously. "We sit on a rock ledge some hundred or so feet off the ground while humans with crossbows shoot a barrage of bolts all around us and ye want to know about a blasted baboon?" the dwarf asked, ducking another bolt that shattered on the rock wall above him.

Vlargcar shrugged. "I don't think they can hit us from here and you called me a green-skinned baboon. I was wondering what a baboon was."

Amerix dusted himself off and scooted to the far area of the ledge next to the rock wall as he hoisted up the waxed rope. "A baboon is a stupid animal that worries about stupid things when he should be worried about his own ass," the dwarf said with obvious disgust.

Vlargcar nodded as if he understood but he did not. "What makes a green-skinned baboon different than other skin colored baboons?"

Amerix paused and regarded the orc. For an orc that was so smart, the blasted idiot sure lacked common sense. "Green-skinned baboons are annoying idiots and they are usually named Vlargcar," Amerix said angrily, then turned and stared at the cliff. "Here, toss this up again when it gets dark. We won't climb until nightfall. The human scum won't be able see to hit us in the dark."

Vlargcar stood up and pondered what the dwarf said. He knew he didn't understand something. Amerix spoke in riddles like that sometimes, but perhaps that was where his mother got his name. It didn't matter. He quickly pushed the painfully memory of his mother away as quickly as it rose from the dark recesses of his mind and neatly prepared the rope and grappling hook to throw once nightfall came. The orc sat back down, lounging on the ledge. Placing his hands behind his head, he leaned back against the rock wall. He took off his pack and rummaged around inside until he found a brown fur-covered animal that he had killed the day before. "Squirrel?" he said, offering the dead thing to Amerix. The animal's limp tail dangled from Vlargcar's green fist as he held it in front of the dwarf's face. The old dwarf shook his head from side to side slowly and groaned. Vlargcar shrugged his shoulders and bit off the squirrel's head. "Suit yourself," he said as he crunched the fur-covered squirrel skull. Amerix merely groaned again and closed his eyes.

Nightfall came quickly for the orc, but it seemed like an eternity for Amerix. The humans seemed to think they had them trapped on the ledge and it was merely a waiting game. Amerix lay on his belly overlooking the edge of the cliff, and spied down below at the large camp fire. He spotted about ten men, all of whom carried themselves with a sense of confidence. The men wore chain armor with long swords and crossbows. They seemed little concerned with him and Vlargcar. They didn't wear any kind of uniform among them and their clothing was rough and dirty at best. They certainly were not soldiers but they seemed to act together and complement each other like soldiers did. Amerix figured that if they were not soldiers, the men had surely worked with one another a long time. Amerix watched for about an hour, trying to identify a leader, but he could not. They all joked around one another, and displayed no salutes or gestures that would indicate a superior. He didn't see one tent that was greater than the others and none carried any weapons that stood out. The men drank and sang songs, none of which the old dwarf understood, but they were surely songs of victory and rich fantasies.

Amerix watched for a while longer when he noticed that one of the men didn't walk like the others. The man had been seated for most of the night and when he rose he was not surefooted and seemed awkward in his armor. Amerix compared the man's walk with the other men, thinking perhaps it was merely a drunken stupor, but even the drunken men moved more fluid than this one did. Amerix watched with growing interest for a time. The man drank from his flagon with his right hand, yet his sword was on his left side. Every good warrior keeps their weapon at a cross draw, and they would not drink with their weapon hand in case they needed to jump into battle. All the other men drank with their left hands, the same hand as their sword side. Either the man was an inexperienced warrior, which Amerix doubted since this was a hard seasoned crew, or he was something else.

"Vlargcar, come here," Amerix whispered as he turned and looked behind him, but he didn't see the orc anywhere on the rocky shelf. He quickly rolled onto his back. Did the fool orc start climbing already? Amerix gazed up as far as his vision would allow, yet not only didn't he see any sign of the orc, he didn't see any sign on the rocks above him, where Vlargcar could have climbed up. If the orc hadn't climbed up, then he had to have climbed down. Amerix felt a twinge of panic. He rushed back over to the edge of the rocky shelf and peered back down. He scanned the edges of the camp. He strained his old eyes, trying to detect the slightest hint of movement. He saw nothing. Amerix scooted away from the edge and moved back to the north side of the shelf as quietly as he could. He examined the rocks and saw that a dusty hand had been smeared on this side. The old dwarf glanced back to the south side, the side they had climbed up during the day. The old dwarf fought fear and anger. The fool orc had climbed down. And for what, he wasn't sure. Hunting maybe? The orc showed remarkable signs of intelligence, and just when Amerix thought the orc was smart, the damned green-skinned fool would show that he had the wisdom of a three year old babe. It wasn't until he heard steel ringing on steel and the scream of a man as he died that Amerix knew why the green-skinned whelp had climbed down.

Amerix rushed to the orc's pack and picked up the rope. He wedged one of the grappling hook's teeth into the wide crack of the ledge and tossed the rope over the side, hoping he could get there in time.

The old dwarf grabbed Songsinger from the scabbard

near his pack and slipped the sheathed sword on his back. The weapon seemed to call out to him to help the orc. The rope fell into darkness, bouncing off the rock wall and dangling into the shadows. Amerix shuffled to the edge of the rocky shelf and lowered himself over carefully. The old dwarf knew he needed to get to the orc quickly before the fool whelp got himself killed, but he was not a skilled climber. Amerix knew he could not help Vlargcar at all if he slipped from the shelf and fell to his death.

Amerix hastily lowered himself down the waxed rope while his ears captured every ring of steel on steel and each cry as a human died. The old dwarf cringed with each sound, expecting to hear the orc's moan of death next.

Then as abruptly as it started, the battle ended. Amerix dropped to the rocky floor and grunted under his weight as he landed on his wounded leg. The wound was sore, making his leg stiff and awkward. Amerix drew Songsinger and made his way down the rocky slopes and into the dark forest. As he entered the bright campfire, he heard one of the men call out. He couldn't understand what the man was saying, but he figured the orc was already dead. Anger tore through Amerix like a tidal wave down a deep valley. He felt all the hate from his past welling up inside of him. The thought of losing the orc was like that of losing his wife and son. Once again the blasted humans had taken something from him that he cared about. And once again they would feel the sting of his blade as he cut them down. The hate he had discarded after emerging from the plunge into the Dawson River filled him anew. He drew Songsinger and held it aloft. "It's you and me, sword," he whispered as he stared at the glint of the blade in the pale moonlight. A shrill hum echoed in his mind as he started into the camp. The sword had been broken for months, and now it started to work again. The old dwarf didn't have time to ponder the manifestation of the strange weapon. He had enemies to kill, enemies that did not know the true demon they hunted. Enemies that Amerix longed to educate.

"Arrogance. It is known by men to be a foolish state of mind, yet still many more fall prey to from it. Champions are defeated, thrones are stolen, and kingdoms are crushed all by the simple yet profound little word. King Theobold was arrogant in his belief that he had the dwarves cowed. The commander of the Torrent was arrogant in his belief that his keep was unsackable and even Tharxton Stoneheart himself was arrogant in how he believed he unequivocally ruled his own clan. And because of this, all three suffered.

Some say Amerix was arrogant, but I say nay, he was confident. He did not have a steadfast belief in his men, or his ability to lead them. He merely knew what was needed to achieve victory and he exploited this knowledge. Arrogance and confidence; these are two more words with profoundly different meanings that can easily become lost into one."

-Lancalion Levendis Lampara-

The Snare of Meirgan

Meirgan made camp at the base of the rocky slope to ensure that he and his men had a clear shot of the dwarf on the ledge. Normally they would be out of range with the bow, but the crafty bounty hunter had equipped his men with heavy crossbows and the mage, Tallnok, had used some kind of spell on his arrows to help them fly further. Meirgan knew little of magic and quickly grew annoyed when the mage tried to explain to him how it worked. He angrily said that he was not paying him to educate, but rather to perform. Meirgan was fine as long as the blasted spell worked. And as far as the bounty hunter was concerned, the spell worked well. His men were almost doubling their normal range with the heavy bolts.

Meirgan had received a tip from one of his contacts on the royal guard that the renegade dwarven general, Amerix Stormhammer, had been seen in the southern hamlet of Portia. The bounty hunter felt he should hire a party of men when he learned that Oswald Thorrin was being dispatched in a few days to investigate the claim. Meirgan immediately hired a crew and set out to the south. He had hired Tallnok at the Hentridge Farm, south of Central City. Meirgan frequently visited the farm as he was friends with Master Hentridge. The bounty hunter had first learned his way with a sword at the orc hunting guild disguised as a farm. He had learned the ways the kingdom used the farm to not only hunt reports of orcs in the region, but how to downplay the reports to keep the citizens from thinking that there was as big of an orc problem as there really was.

Meirgan had made many contacts and information wells while he worked for the king-sponsored farm. Normally Meirgan didn't work with mages. He didn't trust the lot, and they were relatively a secretive bunch, but when he stopped by the farm, David Hentridge had recommended the wily wizard. The bounty hunter hashed over the idea, finally agreeing to take the mage on when David spoke of how deadly the dwarf was that they would be hunting. Regardless, Meirgan made sure the wizard had the ability to make the dwarf look like Amerix if it turned out to be a different one. Meirgan didn't plan on hiring such an expensive crew, only to find he had caught the wrong dwarf.

Once on the trail, the bounty hunter was impressed by the dwarf's ability to make unexpected maneuvers when he and his crew had made time on them. The ranger he hired, Ickten Norris, had come with indisputable references, yet Meirgan thought him mad when he first said the dwarf was traveling with an orc. He had gotten into many arguments thereafter with the ranger, and debated on taking a side bet with the man, save for he knew nothing of tracking so he had little to go on. Meirgan, however, did know much about dwarves. He knew they hated few other creatures as much as they hated orcs. He figured only elves hated the green-skinned monsters more. Meirgan figured the dwarf was trailing an orc, but if that were true, it was the orc that was anticipating his movements and adjusting the flight path. He doubted that the orc was smart enough to do that. The bounty hunter was even more surprised when they caught up with the old silver-streaked bearded dwarf, only to discover he was in fact running with an orc. Fortunately for the ranger, he never mentioned the fact he was right and Meirgan was wrong. The cruel bounty hunter would have made sure the arrogant fool never woke from his sleep.

He and his men had managed to pin the unlikely pair atop a rocky shelf about a hundred or so feet off the ground. One of his men claimed to have shot the dwarf in the back of the leg, and they found smeared blood on leaves and underbrush to collaborate the man's story. So now he had a wounded old dwarf that should have died from natural causes at least fifty years ago and an orc pinned down on a rock ledge. Meirgan had decided to make camp and in the morning they would lay siege to the rock ledge and force them either to their deaths or to surrender. It mattered to him little. The bounty hunter was concerned with the fact that they might climb to the top of the plateau, but when he thought about the sheer height of the cliff, he dismissed the idea. Short of flying, nothing was going to get to the top of it.

Meirgan had settled in for the night. They had built a large fire to attract the attention of the pair and his other group of men he had sent farther south in case the dwarf took an unexpected route again. Hoping to crush the dwarf's and the orc's morale, the fire acted as a constant reminder in the long night that they were waiting for them. He had stationed a sentry near the rock ledge who was to alert them by a sounding horn if the dwarf tried to make a break for it and climb down in the night. He knew dwarves could see in the dark. He would be sending out the sentry's relief soon and he was getting tired from the relentless pace the dwarf had set since leaving Portia.

Tallnok wandered around the camp, wearing the heavy chain armor and the long sword. His short trimmed hair was in stark contrast to the other men's long disheveled looks, and regardless of how many times he told the fool not to drink, eat, or pick anything up with his right hand, the dope mage would do it anyway. He hoped the dwarf wasn't watching the camp too closely, or he might see through the mage's disguise. In the scheme of things it mattered little because Tallnok would expose himself soon enough, but Meirgan knew the old dwarf was crafty and battle wise. If he could see a mage, he would surely target him first. Without the wizard in battle, it would surely be more difficult to capture the bearded renegade.

Meirgan was not concerned with the orc at all. The mage would deal with him easily. Orcs had low intelligence and were more than susceptible to mind influencing spells. The only real concern Meirgan had was if the mage was forced to cast before he could change from the armor. Tallnok expressed much distaste for the heavy metal garb and argued that it might hinder his spell-casting abilities.

Meirgan sat on a thick log that his men had drug to use as firewood sipping a flagon of warm honeyed ale. He sat around the blazing campfire and pondered the encounter and the different strategies that he might use in the final battle. He wore his thick chain armor that bore hundreds of scars from battles past and his enchanted short sword lay next to him. The green blade had been owned by a renowned thief-assassin from the wererat guild in Central City. Meirgan had accepted the sword as payment for helping the thief escape the city with his life, when he crossed his fat guild leader, Pav-co. Meirgan had worked with the chubby guild leader on several occasions and he even offered the bounty hunter a fair price for the thief's head. But when Meirgan caught up with the thief, the silver-tongued cut purse had enticed him with an enchanted blade that paralyzed its victims. Meirgan had used the blade for several years and it had served him well. The pommel of the blade was made of silver in the shape of a snake head that had two finely cut emeralds set for eyes. The hilt was also made of silver and was shaped like two serpent heads facing away from the blade that also had finely cut emeralds set for eyes. The blade itself was made of a silver alloy that could injure the lycanthropes of the Central City thieves' guild. Grascon had explained that was why he carried it, to protect himself from the backstabbing Pav-co, but Meirgan suspected Grascon was the back stabber. Regardless, it mattered little to the bounty hunter. He worked for the highest bidder. The thief won out with the sword that Meirgan had used with success many times over the years.

It was the gurgling sound of blood pooling in a man's airway that roused the bounty hunter from his memories. He reached down and grabbed the silver blade and moved to the other side of the fire. From there he heard his men shouting and the ring of steel on steel. To his amazement he witnessed the most incredible thing. The orc that was running with the dwarf had ambushed them, but not in the normal orc sense. Orcs usually waited until you were close enough to charge, then the stupid method less fools screamed as they charged, getting half of their numbers cut down before they reached the battle because they insisted on using a battle cry. But, this one had killed the sentry on the north side of camp and had most likely killed the one under the base of the rocky shelf.

The orc didn't scream a battle cry, he merely fought quietly as he parried the deft strikes of his men. What astonished the bounty hunter even further was that the orc was not fighting with the normal heavy cumbersome orc weapons. He fought with two swords in a double bladed technique, much like the rare rangers and the elven legionnaires.

Meirgan watched in awe as the orc ducked, parried and lashed out, slowly cutting the numbers of his men. "Tallnok! Subdue that beast," he commanded, then changed his mind as Ickten Norris approached. "Hold that, Tallnok, but ready your spell." The mage nodded as he quickly unfastened the straps that held his chain armor in place, slipping the heavy chain shirt over his head and tossing it on the ground.

The orc had slain four of his men and stood challenging the ranger as he approached. Ickten held his long sword aloft and he kept his other low and in front of him. The orc studied the ranger, shifting his hold on his short sword so the blade was back against his forearm and the long sword was stretched out in front. Meirgan was amazed. He could clearly see the intelligence in the orc's stance. He measured his enemy and didn't rush in. Not only that, he doubted the orc was much older than eleven. Orcs didn't mature until they were about fourteen and this one was almost six foot tall! Meirgan had learned about the green-skinned beasts while he worked with the Hentridge Farm, and the orc whelp that stood before his ranger betrayed everything he had been taught. "Do not kill the whelp," Meirgan commanded.

The ranger shot the bounty hunter a doubting look. To both the ranger's and Meirgan's surprise, the orc lunged forward. Ickten reacted with lightning speed, easily deflecting the strike with his short sword. He ducked and slashed in with his long sword when the orc brought up his offhand and laid a deep slice across the ranger's forearm.

Ickten cursed aloud and immediately went on the defensive as the orc launch a vicious barrage of attacks. Meirgan clasped his hands in delight as he turned to Tallnok. "Did you see that thrust? It was a feint. He wanted Ickten to parry it with his short sword, that way he would be able to match his speed with his offhand, against the slower long sword of the ranger! Amazing, don't you think?"

The wizard shrugged his shoulders and he awkwardly kicked his leg out of the chain greaves that seemed to cling to his foot. Tallnok had no skill in swordplay and understood little of the finer points of battle. "Meirgan, all I see is a man and an orc each with a two swords in hand, swinging them at each other."

Meirgan made a face as he scoffed at the wizard and turned his attention back to battle at hand to enjoy the weapons display. Ickten regained his composer and ignored the sting of the deep cut the orc had laid in his right forearm. It was not a crippling move, but it could have been had the orc known to slice the inside of the arm – where the rope ways of the arm were – instead of the outside. Severing them would render the sword arm useless. The orc was learned in the ways of fighting with two blades, but he was no master by far. Ickten recovered from the orc's flurry of attacks and turned the flow of the battle and launched a barrage of his own. The orc was not overly quick, but his incredible strength seemed to make the weapons move in his arms as if they were light as feathers. Ickten kept pressing the battle. He knew eventually the orc's muscles would fail and his skill and prowess would win the day. And just as the ranger predicted, the orc began to slow. His dark green skin shone from perspiration and he inhaled large gulps of air. Ickten laid a neat slice across the orc's chest with his long sword and stabbed his short sword into the beast's shoulder. To his surprise the orc, didn't cry out in pain, but his strength renewed a bit as he fought off the ranger's blows and added another offensive.

Meirgan clasped his hands together a second time and punched the mage in the shoulder. "Do you see that, wizard? That orc has the heart of a champion. I can sell him for some serious money."

The wizard rubbed his shoulder painfully and stepped out of the bounty hunter's reach. "Sell him where? Who would buy an orc?"

Meirgan chuckled as he turned back to the splendid display of swordsmanship. "Why, the gladiator arena of course."

The battle raged on for minutes, with the orc suffering nicks here and there. His dark green skin was covered in superficial wounds and the puncture in his shoulder from the ranger's short sword weakened his arm, which carried the larger and heavier long sword. To the surprise of both Ickten and Meirgan, the orc tossed the heavy weapon down and began to parry each strike with his short sword. Meirgan began to get worried. "He cannot be overly offensive with only one blade, Ickten. I think he plans to flee!"

The ranger merely nodded and pressed his attacks to the orc's left side, forcing him to circle back toward the camp. Meirgan smiled as his skilled ranger easily forced the orc to where he wished. "Tallnok, be ready to subdue the beast," the bounty hunter commanded as he watched the battle unfold. It had been a long time since Ickten had met a swordsman skilled enough to make him bleed.

The orc lunged forward with the short sword accepting a heavy strike from the long sword on his left shoulder, but he rammed his weapon deep into the ranger's thigh. Ickten screamed in pain, hitting the orc on top of the head with the pommel of his short sword. The orc staggered to the ground, dazed as Ickten dropped his swords and clutched the pommel of the orc's blade that protruded from his thigh. "Meirgan, capture the damned thing! I cannot continue to fight it without killing it. It is too well-trained," the ranger commanded through his pain.

Meirgan nodded to Tallnok. The wizard moved his arms out in front of himself, grasping at the magical energy that floated around him, and sent them out at the orc. Bright flows of magical energy erupted from his fingers and wrapped the orc, pinning his arms to his side.

Ickten cursed as he managed to pull the blade free and tossed it to the ground. "I think the damned thing pierced my leg bone," the ranger said as he limped over to the bounty hunter.

Meirgan ignored the ranger and brushed by him as he walked over to the short sword that the orc had used. He kneeled down and examined the weapon. It was covered in bright red blood from Ickten's leg, but what struck the bounty hunter as odd was the fact it was a Central City militia sword. Meirgan rose and walked over to the long sword and examined it. That weapon too was a Central City militia sword. The bounty hunter tossed the swords down next to each other and looked at the grimacing face of the wounded ranger.

"Just let me kill it," Ickten said through pain clenched teeth. "You can take what you owe me in pay out of what you think you will get for it."

Meirgan chuckled. "I am not paying you that much, ranger. This orc should fetch me a platinum crown at least."

"A platinum? Have you gone mad, bounty hunter? Sure, he has skill, but he is just an orc. Orcs do not become gladiator heroes. They fight and die for the crowd's amusement. They are used against lions and other monsters or during the Freedom Festival in the summer. No one is going to pay more than five silver for the stupid animal," Ickten said as he hobbled over to the log that Meirgan had sat on earlier. He pulled a pack around from behind the stump and pulled out a thick bandage and began to dress his wound. "Besides, he has saved you four gold, five if the sentry at the rock wall is dead also."

Meirgan nodded. It was true the orc had saved him some money by killing his hired men, but Meirgan didn't come here to capture a sword savvy orc. He came to capture the renegade dwarven general. "Be on your toes," Meirgan said to the other men as he walked to the edge of camp. "The dwarf is out there somewhere and we have his whelp. He obviously taught the orc how to fight. That means that, for whatever reason, he likes the stupid thing," Meirgan paused as he scanned the black impenetrable forest line. "He isn't going to run. He is probably at the forest's edge watching us right now. Stay vigilant men. Triple pay for the man that brings me his head."

Tallnok readied another spell as he stood by the fire. "When are the others due back?"

Meirgan frowned as he thought. "They should be back in a few hours. I was unsure if the dwarf planned to hide on the rocky slopes or make his way south. They should see our blazing campfire and return when they can't find any tracks. Hopefully they will get here before the fool dwarf wades into us with his sword a blazing. I understand he fights like a demon and has never lost a battle," Meirgan said before he chuckled at the worried faces of his remaining men. "Fear not, my men," Meirgan said. "So he has never lost a battle. He only needs to lose one."

The dwarf quickly made his way through the dark forest, crouching as he ran. The chrome-bladed sword glinted as an occasional moonbeam made its way through the forest canopy. He hopped over mossy logs and his frosty breath shot out from his mouth in rapid explosions that vanished in the cold night air.

As he made his way to the edge of the camp, Songsinger's shrill ring was even louder. The old dwarf was worried the noise would alert the men in the camp, but they seemed oblivious to the enchanted blade's song. The sound that had always annoyed the dwarf was somehow comforting to him.

Amerix slowed and was careful not to make any noise as he moved to the tree line. He stepped lightly, rolling the blade of his foot to the ball, minimizing the surface area of his step and making him as silent as a cat. The old dwarf had survived many years in the under mountain where sound traveled long distances, alerting some of the most vicious predators in the realms. To move quietly was synonymous with survival.

Amerix's bright beaming smile was hidden in the veil of darkness. He was pleased with the four dead men, five counting the dead sentry at the bottom of the cliff. Another was lame from a vicious stab wound in his leg and the man had a deep gash on his forearm. The orc was growing into a skilled swordsman. There were four other men in the camp that seemed to be seasoned warriors and one that wore no armor. The orc was lying on the ground conscious, but he seemed as if he couldn't move. His thick muscular arms were pinned to his side and he lay face down on the ground.

The veins in his neck bulged as he strained against the invisible bond that seemed to hold him. Magic. The word left a bitter taste in the old dwarf's mouth. Amerix's gaze immediately shot to the man wearing no armor. The old dwarf recognized him as the awkward soldier from earlier. It all fell into place. It was no wonder the man did not move well in the heavy chain and that he ate and drank with the wrong hand. He was no swordsman at all. He was some kind of damned wizard.

Amerix then turned his gaze to the larger man. He had brown hair and was a little over six foot tall. He wore heavy chain armor and carried a short sword at his side which seemed out of place for his large frame. The man moved with a warrior's grace and had an air of intelligence and arrogance about him. Amerix cared little. The man would be dead soon, as would the rest of them. The renegade general figured to kill the wizard first, and then make his way to the lesser men, until he finally killed the larger man who seemed to be in charge. The fool would pay for messing with Amerix Alistair Stormhammer – the same mistake thousands of enemies, long since dead, had made.

Just as the dwarf flexed his leg muscles to spring into the camp, he paused when a second group of men walked into the clearing. They were garbed as the others –heavy chain mail shirt and leggings, good riding boots and they held four large war dogs in thin chain leashes. The dogs seemed tired, and the dwarf was upwind of them so they didn't detect him. The old dwarf cared little. He would charge in sooner than later. His rescue suddenly became a lot more difficult, but he had battled greater odds in his life.

Amerix fumbled around on the ground until he found a rock the size of his fist. The dark gray fragment was not completely round, but he figured it would fly fairly straight. The old dwarf took a deep breath and charged into the camp. As soon as he cleared the trees he set his legs and twisted his hips, firing the sharp rock at the mage. The odd shape sent the rock a few inches high, but it still caught the unsuspecting wizard in the top of the head. The rock made a sickening thud as it bounced off the wizard's skull. Blood poured from the wound and ran down his head as he fell to the ground writhing in pain. The other men shouted in alarm and drew their swords. Amerix met the charge of the first man. He ducked the overhead strike and sent Songsinger rocketing forward. The keen chrome blade slashed through the man's heavy chain as if it were soft leather. Blood poured from the fresh wound as he was knocked to the ground by the charging dwarf. The man screamed in pain, clutching his chest as dark red blood bubbled and frothed from the horrific slice.

The men surrounded Amerix in hopes to contain him as they timed their attacks. They were an experienced group and the old general recognized their cohesiveness, so he pressed his assault. One by one the bearded demon cut the men down. They screamed in terror as they tried in vain to parry Amerix's masterful strikes and feints. Soon there were three – the wounded man, the unconscious mage, and the large leader with the little sword.

Amerix squared off and growled. He held Songsinger out in front of him as bright crimson blood dripped like thick syrup from its chrome blade. His face and armor were covered in splattered gore from his enemies and the renegade general stood with a gaze of death on his face. He was committed to killing these men.

The wounded warrior that wielded two swords stepped forward. He said some things the dwarf didn't understand. He figured it to be some sort of arrogant speech or some kind of taunting, so he didn't wait for the longwinded fool to finish before he launched his flurry of attacks. The man was caught off guard and immediately went to the defensive. He met the dwarf's speed and ferocity with skill and finesse. Amerix enjoyed fighting the man. He was a fine swordsman, but Amerix knew the game he was playing. The human undoubtedly knew he couldn't match his power, so he would have to remain on the defensive until he tired. Amerix had faced many opponents that had become comfortable with this fighting style. He simply feigned weakness after a long strenuous battle. When the fool launched his offensive, thinking the dwarf was spent, Amerix would cut him down. Not to mention he would exploit the man's wounded leg.

Anything less and the swordsman would suspect the dwarf feigning ineptness.

Amerix watched the larger man out of the corner of his eye. He smiled confidently as he watched the battle unfold. Amerix was sure he was aware of the game the swordsman played. He was sure that was how he defeated the orc. What he didn't understand was that Amerix had spent more time swinging his sword than these fools had been alive. The renegade general pushed the battle forward. Songsinger glinted in the moonlight like a deadly beacon, steadily slowing his attacks and slightly sending him off balance. Amerix grudgingly accepted a few minor slices from the swordsman's blade to complete his facade. The swordsman became overconfident, just as Amerix expected, and his strikes became lazy and exaggerated. He focused more on the offensive than the defensive.

The old dwarf turned his attacks to complete parries, barely deflecting the precision strikes from the ranger. The over-confident human lunged in for a crippling blow. Amerix was confused by the strike. He intentionally left a killing blow open, but the ranger went for a crippling attack. The dwarven general launched Songsinger with unexpected quickness, knocking the sword from the ranger's hand. The long sword skittered across the hard frozen ground and came to rest near the fire. The stunned ranger, immediately began backpedaling, fending off the dwarves lightning quick strikes. Amerix could see the fear in the man's eyes and it made him smile. Songsinger whistled through the air slicing the ranger's face, and then the dwarf reversed the flow of the attack and stabbed the long sword through the man's wrist. The ranger screamed and fell to the ground, holding the spurting wound with his other hand. His short sword lay at his feet, but the dying man ignored the weapon as he tried to keep his lifeblood from spilling all over the ground. As Amerix raised the sword for the killing blow, he found he could not move his arms. He dropped Songsinger to the hard frozen earth as his arms were forced to his sides by an invisible barrier. *That damned mage*, he thought. He should have made sure the wizard was dead.

The larger human walked forward clapping his hands in triumph, while the ranger shouted something in a pleading tone as he tried to stifle his blood loss. With his short sword, the large human pulled a thin cloth from his belt pouch and tossed it at the feet of the bleeding ranger, who quickly lashed the cloth around his wrist to stop the bleeding.

Amerix saw the mage standing next to him holding his bloody head. The large man said something else that the old dwarf didn't understand, as he picked up a stout wooden club. He brought the club down toward Amerix's head and all went black.

Meirgan stood over the unconscious body of the orc and the dwarf. He had lost all of his men, save for the wizard and the ranger, and he wasn't sure if the ranger would live or not. He had lost a lot of blood. But alas, he had the dwarf! What a hellion he had been. Never in his day had he seen such swordsmanship. He was confident the dwarf would have easily killed the ranger and turned his attention onto him. Meirgan wasn't sure he would have fared much better against the tireless bearded demon. Had it not been for the wizard, he could have died this night.

The bounty hunter clasped the bloody mage on the shoulder. The mage had a large knot on the side of his head, three shades of purple, and a long split in the skin that still dripped blood. He was surprised the wizard was able to cast at all, but he was not about to doubt his luck. "Wrap them in the shackles and the chains. We will have a time transporting them to back to the road."

Ickten felt dizzy from the blood loss and struggled to his feet. "I hope you plan on transporting them by horseback until you get to the road. It seems we have an abundance of extra horses," the ranger said, falling roughly against a tree.

Meirgan nodded as he started rounding up the horses and untying the dogs. He was pleased at how well trained they were. They didn't bother barking during the fight since they were not trained to bark unless commanded. If he could only find men like that to hire, he would be able to keep a good crew together; instead of having them all killed every few hunts.

"Yea, we will ride back to the road and then head north, until we can hail a merchant wagon. I will pay him to take us back north."

The wizard was kneeling beside the dwarf placing the heavy iron manacles on his stocky wrists when he looked up. "What if the wagon doesn't want to turn around?" the wizard asked.

Meirgan shrugged as he picked up Songsinger and examined the masterfully crafted blade under the pale moonlight. "Then we kill him," the bounty hunter said nonchalantly.

Meirgan found everything about the chrome blade fascinating, especially the annoying, shrill hum it made when he held it. He fastened the sword and scabbard to the girth ring on the front of his saddle and started to pick up camp. Ickten was getting some color back to his face, giving Meirgan hope that he might live after all, and the mage was just finishing putting the manacles and shackles on the orc.

Meirgan expected to fetch a fair price for the remarkable long sword, but he had little time to ponder it. They had a long trek ahead of them and a lot of work to do until then. The bounty hunter shook his head a second time as he thought about how lucky he was the wizard managed to subdue the dwarf. *The battle could have easily turned out differently,* he told himself. *But ah... it didn't.*

Men crawled across the soft green grass of the valley floor. Moans of the injured and dying echoed across the canyon walls like a morbid orchestra of demise. Soldiers with shattered bones from the incredible tail sweeps of the dragon were piled up at the cliff faces on each side of the valley. Thousands were frozen under thick layers of ice in a macabre garden of crystalline statues. The stench of death and the coppery smell of blood from the pulverized bodies hung in the foggy air. Some bodies were so badly disfigured it was impossible to determine the cause of death, let alone their identity.

General Bodrell covered his mouth with a silk rag as surgeons and doctors scrambled among the dead and dying, trying to triage who they could save and who they could not. Never before had he seen such carnage on this scale, and never before had he witnessed the power of a great dragon. He had ordered most of the men to ignore the dead and dying, unless they had been a close friend. He wanted to keep morale as high as it could be. The grisly scene, if witnessed in its entirety, could drive the hardest soldier to desert the troops.

Bodrell had asked for two hundred volunteers to aid the surgeons and the few clerics they had with them, to help gather up the sick and injured. After the volunteers mustered, he explained they could lead a regiment of wounded home for their efforts. Bodrell expected them to be crushed after witnessing the horror they faced. Yet to his surprise, only seven men agreed to lead the wounded home. The first was one of Bodrell's favorite sergeants, Sargoth. He was a skilled swordsman and braver than most of the men in the army, but Bodrell knew why he volunteered first. It was not to go home, or to avoid the upcoming battle with the dwarves. It was to encourage the other volunteers to leave with him. Sargoth knew of the horrors they would endure. He knew how it would break a man, yet still only six others agreed to the assignment. The rest asked to be summarily reassigned to other units. Sargoth faced ridicule to save a few of his men – a wise and noble act. The general had already put in the paperwork for the man's promotion with the king when they returned home. Yet even as the seven men finished piling up the dead, the rumors of Sargoth the Cowardly were circulating around the camp. There would be many rumors of such. Bodrell was no fool. He would have a few hundred deserters also. Beyklan law demanded that they be hunted down after the battle and executed – another unpopular task to do after a war. The young general just wanted to go home and relax. He had enough of war already, and the battle was yet to begin.

General Bodrell ran his fingers through his damp hair, pulled down on his tight collared red and gold laced tunic and stretched his neck. He was not surprised by the king's command to reassemble at once and push into the valley, though Bodrell considered it suicide. The dwarves no doubt had great fortifications to resist siege and the dragon, if in their employ, was severely wounded but surely not dead. By every estimation, Bodrell figured he had only fifteen of the original thirty thousand men. They had one operating ballista and no functioning catapults. They were leaving most of their provisions here, in the valley, using the carts and oxen to haul back the dead. Bodrell suggested making a mass grave here in the valley; returning so many dead to the city would hurt his standing with the nobles. Yet the king refused, arguing that he was king, and needed no particular standing with anyone. Theobold was as arrogant as he was foolish.

It took most of the day to place the dead on the long wooden provision carts. The bodies were stacked sometimes six deep, some carts holding as many as fifty dead. The large carts were covered with canvas tops from tents and the men were ordered to bunk with three to a tent as opposed to the normal two. To Bodrell's surprise, the men complained little. They were eager to kill the dwarves who they believed had set the horrible white hellion upon them. Many men with shattered arms had to be forced onto the wounded carts, as they wanted to continue to fight.

Never had the general heard men so eager to spill an enemy's blood since the vicious orc wars some fifty years ago. And even then, the soldiers were either deadly afraid, or foolishly brave. It was late in the evening when Bodrell gave the command to march north into the valley. He had two men tracking the dwarves, instead a larger cavalry unit. He had only about five hundred cavalry men left, and he doubted they would be able to make their way into the mountains, let alone participate in the battle.

They marched up the rocky pass most of the night that was more of a trail at best. It was only about fifteen feet wide and covered with dirt and half-buried rocks with sharp protruding edges. The had army climbed high enough that they entered the foggy veil that covered the valley, and the men tripped and fell, tumbling into one another. When they broke the foggy veil the conditions went from bad to worse. The trail became ice-laden and covered with snow in many places. The men were not equipped to climb steep surfaces and the journey was slow and arduous. When they finally reached the summit, it was late in the night. The general could see a large stone structure that was carved out of the side of the mountain. The structure appeared as the frame of a giant wooden door. The stonework of the outside was incredible. It was covered with hundreds of designs – sculptures of dwarves and dwarven runes. In the center of the structure was a thick wooden door that was covered in shining steel plates that held the enormous portal together. The door seemed to be as impenetrable as the mountain itself. Had he been there for any other reason, Bodrell figured he would have found some beauty to the carving. But, as it was, he was here for war.

General Bodrell ordered camp immediately and fortifications created in case the dwarves charged from their large door. He doubted they would, since their strengths were inside their dwelling. The general held his thick, red, fur-covered cloak tight against his body to keep out the cold driving wind. He watched as the men immediately erected the tent for the king, who was bringing up the rear of the army as it marched up the slippery path. The flamboyant domicile made the general want to wretch. There was no place on the battlefield for such luxuries. The fool king slept in a multi-roomed tent made of thick fur-lined canvas walls that housed rich furniture and warm meals, while his men ate dried meat and cold vegetables, and slept three to a tent. The general made his rounds around the camp, encouraging the men as they tried in vain to dig trenches in the rock hard frozen earth, until finally he had them make mounds of snow. His men seemed alert and eager, something he never expected after such a crushing blow by the great white. He hoped the siege didn't take long. If the front door of the dwarven stronghold was any indicator of how the siege was going to go, it would be long and bloody.

The dwarven sentries manned their stations in the morning at the command of King Stoneheart. Tharxton was amazed at the size of the army that was still growing as it reached the summit of the valley. He recognized that the army was about half the size as it had been, but was still a force to be reckoned with. What pleased the dwarf king was that he saw only enough parts to assemble a single ballista. Where the great white had come from and why it attacked the humans was beyond him, but the dwarf king considered it a sign from Leska that the mountain people would not be enslaved. Tharxton imagined that if Amerix had been there, he would have called it a sign from Durion and charged out into the mass of humans by himself and cut them all down. Tharxton missed the old general at times like this. The black-bearded traitor was clearly wicked, but in war wickedness was often a great ally.

"They are massing outside the mouth," the dwarven sentry said as he peered out of a small peephole that had been carved into the mountain to allow air to flow in and out.

"Do they look angry?" asked a second dwarf standing behind the first, trying to peer over the sentry's shoulder to catch a glance at his enemy.

The first dwarf shrugged his shoulders, but kept his dark eyes fixed on the ever-growing army camped outside of the front door to his beloved city. "Beats me. But I bet they aren't. King Tharxton said they were attacked by a white dragon. Probably a great white he said, by the size of it."

The second whistled through his teeth. "A great white! Really? And they are still alive. They must be powerful indeed!"

"Don't give them too much credit, Gillmak. I don't see any wounded with them. I reckon they figure us seeing their wounded will make us think they are weak," the sentry said with his eyes glued to the campsite.

The young dwarf known as Gillmak didn't respond for

a few seconds. His visions were filled with the fantastic battle that surely took place between the humans and the great white. "Do you think they killed it? The great white, I mean?"

The sentry shrugged his shoulders. "Beats me, but I don't see it anywhere. They either killed it, or made it run away. It was only a white, you know."

Gillmak nodded slowly and scratched his short brown beard. "Yea. Whites aren't that tough, but it still was a great! Even a great brown could kill lots of folks."

The sentry nodded again slowly, and then whipped his head around. "A what? A great brown? There is no such thing. Browns aren't really dragons, you rock head. Browns don't even have wings."

Gillmak put his hands on his hips and scowled at the sentry. "They are too dragons."

"Then where are their wings? All dragons have wings."

"If all dragons had wings, then browns would have them," Gillmak said.

The sentry took a deep breath. "You are impossible, Gillmak. Trust me. Browns are not really dragons. If your orc-sized brain thinks they are, go asked Targavian. He knows about dragons."

Gillmak huffed. "Fine. I will. And I'll be back and you will have to eat dirt."

The sentry chuckled as Gillmak stormed down the corridor. His soft leather boots padded down the hard stone floor. He turned his attention to the humans outside and nearly choked as they were assembling the large ballista. "Gillmak wait!" he shouted as he ran from the small peephole. Gillmak stopped and turned, wearing an angry scowl. "Never mind the browns. They are putting the ballista together! Quick, go and tell Targavian!" Gillmak turned and ran down the narrow stone corridor as fast as his short stubby little legs would carry him.

The sentry turned back and watched as the men began strapping on their armor and tightening the heavy bolts on the ballista. Heavy foot-falls landed around him as three hundred dwarven crossbow men ran down the narrow stone corridor to the stone stairs that were on either side of the great door. The crossbowmen were heavily armored in plate mail. They wore thick open-faced helms for shooting and had three quivers full of bolts strapped to their backs. They kept a razor sharp battle axe hanging from their belts in case they were forced to engage in melee. The sentry turned back and looked one last time at the horde of humans that waited outside to kill him, before turning and running down the corridor.

He passed Tharxton as the king marched toward the mouth of Mountain Heart. He had one thousand dwarves in full plate armor marching behind him. Their heavy armored boots pounded the stone floor in unison like a thousand drums of war. The dwarf king's red beard was braided into a single braid that was capped with a bright golden ring that hung stiffly from his chin. His thick plate armor had the Stoneheart crest on the chest and he wore a thick blue cape that fastened to the shoulder plates of his armor. Atop his head, he wore a great helm with a bright blue plume that hung down to one side. His soldiers stopped about fifty paces from the open area behind the door. He marched up the set of stairs on the right side that expanded about forty feet up and then went west about twenty feet to a large stone walkway. The walkway was still embedded in the side of the mountain with only a narrow horizontal slit that spanned the hundred yard battlement.

Tharxton made his way to the center of the battlement and faced the human horde that was massed before him. The dwarf king estimated the human army to be about fifteen thousand men, almost half of what it was prior to the dragon attack. There was a great ballista aimed at the mouth of the dwarven city and a great chain that was attached to the end of it. Standing in the center of the flat were three men. The first was dressed in brass-colored full plate armor. He wore a red silk cape that hung down over his horse and a helmet that was shaped like a crown.

To his left was a man also garbed in brass-colored plate armor but he wore a much thinner helm and no cape. To the king's right was a man wearing that same brass-colored plate armor, but his bore a holy symbol on the chest. Tharxton recognized the emblem immediately as the goddess of water, Surshy. Tharxton ground his teeth and called out to the king. "Who dares to march an army upon the doorstep of Mountain Heart without first sending a banner of peace?"

The king's horse shifted under him and the he tightened the reins as he spoke. "A banner of peace?"

Theobold scoffed. "You have unleashed your evil pet onto my men, and we have vanquished the foe. To insult us further, you send a white dragon, to mock the white banner of peace. I do not come in such a fashion."

There was some murmuring among the dwarves on the battlement at what the human king said. Tharxton figured the humans would figure he sent the dragon, if not merely use that as an excuse to go ahead with the war in the first place. No one marches thirty thousand men to the far reaches of a kingdom, into a hostile mountain climate, to discuss peace.

The human king cleared his throat. "As I said, I do not come in peace, foul dwarf. I come for your head. *And I will not be denied,*" Theobold growled as he drew his sword from its sheath.

"Then come and get it, dog! I will be waiting for you around a shroud of your men!" Tharxton spat. As soon as the spittle hit the dry stone floor of the chamber, the dwarves loosed their bolts. The rain of death shot down into the ranks of the humans. The thick bolts from the dwarven crossbows hit the men, piercing their armor and embedding themselves to the fletching. The bolts hit with such force, they knocked the men from their feet. A bolt struck the king's horse in the head, killing the animal instantly. Another rooted itself into the king's thigh. He cried out in pain and clutched the protruding shaft as his horse fell.

One of the shafts struck Bodrell in the chest, knocking him from his horse. The cleric managed to avoid the first volley. He leapt from his horse and retreated behind the mass of soldiers. The Beyklans returned fire with their bowman. The arrows hit the rock wall and shattered in a shower of wood splinters. A few arrows managed to make it into the slender slits on the rock battlement. A few dwarves died from the arrows, but the others continued to fire their heavy bolts, killing scores of human.

Tharxton stumbled down the stairs of the battlement. He had suffered frostbite on his fingers and toes from the dragon's blast, making it difficult for him to walk. He staggered his way back to his men that were waiting in the corridor.

"The battle has begun, my brethren. We will fight to the man and I shall stand among you as we face our darkest hour. Fear not...."

The dwarven king's speech was interrupted by a deafening crash as the huge ballista bolt's steel spearhead erupted from the door. Large pieces of wood bounced down the corridor. The bolt then was hauled backwards until the great barbs of the spearhead dug into the door. He could hear the screams of human soldiers being shot by his crossbowmen as they tried to pull the ballista bolt back, ripping the doors from the hinges. Tharxton started again, ignoring the several foot long ballista bolt sticking through the gates behind him. "Fear not. Leska is with us and the human dogs will rue the day they tried to invade Mountain Heart. No enemy has breached these walls since the beginning of time. And no enemy ever will!"

The battle raged for hours. Thousands of Beyklan soldiers lay dead around the outside of the wooden doors. The dwarven archers eventually ran out of bolts for their crossbows and immediately abandoned their posts. They ran in an orderly fashion from the stone battlements. Tharxton and his foot soldiers waited patiently in the corridor. They quickly moved to the side as the archers hurried past into Mountain Heart. The lightly armored dwarves had to don heavier plate and weapons to aid Tharxton and the footmen when the humans managed to breach the thick double doors.

With the dwarves no longer raining down the bolts of death, the humans began to succeed at pulling the barbed ballista bolt, tearing the thick wooden door from the entrance of the dwarven keep.

Tharxton and his men gripped their weapons. The hall was silent, save for the muffled cries and shouts from the other side of the door. The dwarven king wiped the sweat from his brow with his dark, frost-bitten hand. He had difficulty gripping his heavy hammer and he wondered how he would fair using it in battle.

Suddenly the door creaked as the huge ballista bolt pulled against it. Large cracks appeared and pieces of wood splintered and fell to the floor just before the door flexed and split. The boom from the shattered wood echoed down the corridor as the hall was lit up with brilliant rays of the setting sun. The dwarves raised their hands to their faces to shield their sensitive eyes.

The Beyklans poured into the corridor in a deafening roar. They ran with weapons raised, screaming their battle cry. The Beyklan soldiers bounded over the remnants of the door like an army of two-legged ants.

"Hold steady!" Tharxton yelled over the deafening charge. The humans charged forward as they filled narrow hall.

"On my command!" Tharxton yelled, his bright red beard bouncing about his chest as the charging humans were a few dozen feet away.

"Now!"

The dwarves rushed forward as one force and met the charge of men. Steel rang against steel. Men screamed as they were cut down and dwarves gurgled on their own blood as they were killed. Tharxton brought his heavy hammer down in a vicious overhand strike that hit a man in the head. The soldier's helmet prevented the blow from injuring his head, but the force of the hammer snapped his neck. The man instantly fell dead and another rose up and took his place.

The soldiers on both sides could hardly attack as the weight of those behind them pushed forward. The dwarves quickly dropped their weapons to the ground and drew small narrow daggers that were more suited for fighting in close quarters. The dwarves had defended this hall in the past, and had sound tactics for its defense. The bearded folk stabbed and cut into the near helpless soldiers at the front lines. Four humans died for every dwarf as the bearded folk were slowly pushed back by the sheer force of the thousands of men that pressed into the tunnel.

The fighting was fierce and deadly. Tharxton bore several wounds in his arms and one deep stab wound on his shoulder, but he continued to fight. Many of the humans were still wearing their hard-soled walking boots and slipped in the wet blood that covered the corridor floors, only to be trampled to death by their charging comrades.

Tharxton remained at the front of his men, slaying more than twenty Beyklans as they were slowly pushed back into the deep corridor. Tharxton knew it would be only a matter of time before he would hit the staircase that ascended into the larger mushroom garden. The young red bearded king almost smiled as he imagined what he had in store for the humans when they reached the garden. Mountain Heart may fall, but when the humans reflected back on this bloody day, their children's children would have nightmares.

Theobold removed the bolt from his leg and made his way into the mouth of the keep. He had managed to get a line formed where the troops funneled in and around, like a river, shifting fresh troops from the back to the front and vice versa. He was forced to sacrifice some of his army's momentum, but even in his arrogance of military superiority, he knew keeping fresh troops at the front line was important. The reports were that the dwarves were not rotating, enabling them to stand their ground longer, but the men at the front would tire sooner. Word had traveled that the dwarven king, Tharxton, was at the front line fighting. Theobold thought it admirable that he would stand before his men and his enemy, but the king knew it was also foolish. If he were killed, it would surely weaken dwarven morale. Sometimes a leader's place is in back of the fighting, regardless of how much he doesn't want to be there.

Theobold smiled as he regarded the interior of the keep.

It was difficult to see, even with the torch bearers holding the lanterns and torches high into the air, affixed to strong wooden poles. He decided to push for a few more hours, and then command a slow retreat to see if the dwarves would press the fight. He was unsure if the foul bearded folk would use that time to prepare defenses, or if they hoped to tire the men by fighting. He had lost about three thousand men outside of the entrance to this fortress and another thousand inside the walls. There were reports that indicated that the dwarves had lost a mere four hundred or so.

As the sun set in the west, the waning light sent a warning to Theobold that his time was running out. The king's brass-colored armor was covered in bright, splattered blood from his vanquished foes. He was exhausted from battle and his wounded leg screamed with pain, even though the thick wooden bolt no longer protruded from thigh. Fresh blood streamed down from the wound and mixed with the dried blood of his fallen enemies. Theobold was angry and confused why the cleric's spell didn't protect him from the dwarves' crossbowmen, but he also did not understand why the dwarves had not used any of their clerics in battle. Exceptionally powerful clerics could call down jets of flames from the heavens, or give warriors incredible strength. Theobold had seen many wonders from the clerics of many different gods. He had hoped to use his cleric's ability to light the tunnels so that he could continue the battle, but to his dismay, all of the clerics he brought reported that they could not wield any divine magic.

The wise king kept this fact from his men, knowing that if they believed the gods were against them, the already weak morale would surely break. His men had endured a tremendous battle against a great white dragon. They defeated the beast and pushed forward. It was his obligation to the men to drive the foul dwarves deep into the mountain. He could not afford to withdraw back onto the summit. The dwarves would re-fortify, but he saw little choice. Fighting in the dark tunnels of this underground keep would be slaughter.

Theobold watched the battle as it raged on. Steel rang against steel. Dwarves and men alike roared cries of battle and cries of death. His army had pushed the dwarves back down the narrow corridor for over a hundred yards. Each inch the dwarves fell back came at the cost of scores of his men. It would be a bloody affair to make the push again tomorrow, but the king knew he had more soldiers than the fetid dwarves had.

Theobold sighed and grabbed at the sword that hung down from a tiny chain that was affixed to his metal gauntlets. His tired fingers ached as he closed them around the hilt of the weapon, raising it high above his head. "Fall back, men! We have killed enough today!"

A few of the soldiers around Theobold heard the command and started repeating it. Soon, hundreds of soldiers slowly started falling back toward the mouth of the underground keep. The dwarves roared in a victorious cry and pushed harder, fighting all the way to the two staircases, just inside of the downed wooden door at the mouth of the keep. Theobold's soldiers backed to the snow outside of the mouth of the keep. The cold mountain wind hit the tired king like an icy punch. The nostrils of his nose stuck together as he inhaled, and the frigid air made his lungs burn. The king's already tired arms and legs suddenly became stiff from the cold.

The dwarves roared as they stood just inside of the cave. The bearded folk raised weapons and shields as they laughed and shouted cries of victory. Theobold struggled to raise his weary arm for a final command of the day. "Archers ready!"

The men standing just outside of the keep's mouth were bloody and tired. Many had wounds that would have rendered them useless in other battles but when they felt weak or wanted to lie down and succumbed to their bearded enemies, someone would shout, "Remember the Torrent!"

The simple mantra always seemed to revitalize the men and allowed them to fight on when they should have fell. Now these weary and wounded men stepped to the side, allowing their archers to step between their numbers. The lightly armored bowmen raised polished longbows to their cheeks. The bent bows gleamed from the bright red setting sun as taught bowstrings creaked under the strain of being drawn in the cold mountain air.

The dwarves immediately recognized the danger of the bows and began to scramble back into the mouth of the keep.

"Fire!" Theobold shouted as he lowered his sword arm.

Half of the archers fired their arrows into the mass of fleeing dwarves. The bearded folk screamed as the thin shafts pierced their necks and other exposed areas. Many of the dwarves simply raised their shields and backed down the corridor as the thin flight arrows shattered against their sturdy mail. After the first group launched their volley, they immediately began to draw another arrow from their quivers. As if on command, the second group fired their arrows, cutting down the dwarves as they fled down the passage. Theobold smiled for the first time since the beginning of the battle. He allowed the archers to fire three volleys before calling for a halt. It didn't take long for the dwarves to disappear into the dark corners of the keep and the king did not want to waste any precious arrows shooting at shadows that could not be discerned as enemies.

The wounded king wandered through his camp. Everywhere soldiers flocked to the surgeon tents. The once white fluffy snow of the summit was now an icy slush of frozen blood mixed with mud. Soldiers had difficulty keeping their tent stakes in the ground, and the howling wind blew any loose tents to the ground. Fires were scarce in order to conserve what little wood the army had and men huddled together for warmth while sitting on the wet corners of their tents to keep them from being blown away. Men were being escorted down the mountain by the hundreds and the dead were piled up on the southern edge of the summit and covered with snow.

"Sire," said a voice from behind the bone-weary king. He turned slowly and faced one of his many useless clerics. His tired face bore an apathy so striking, that the cleric gulped and took a step backwards. "Sire, I urge you to come to the surgeon tents. The general has taken a bolt in the chest and is doing poorly. They managed to remove the foul thing, but he lost a lot of blood and might not survive the night," the cleric said as he struggled to keep his dark cloak from blowing around.

Theobold stared the young cleric in the eye, but his thoughts were elsewhere. He pondered how to make the attack tomorrow. Would the archers at the gates be sufficient to hold off a nighttime dwarven attack? If they did manage to push the dwarves back past the flight of stairs at the end of the corridor, what lay in store for them there? Was it an ambush? Or was it a wide open street of their lair, like a human city. How deep did the keep go? Would they need light sources regardless of the time of day? Probably. If the dwarves would burrow hundreds of miles to sack the Torrent, they surely have enough tunnels that it would be impossible to root them out completely.

The cleric gathered his cloak around him as his teeth chattered from the frigid wind. "Sire?"

Theobold turned and limped through the snow toward his tent. "I'll be in my tent. Tell the head surgeon I have many men dying. I do not have time to single any of them out."

The cleric nodded in disgust. Certainly a true statement, but his clerics liked Bodrell. "Yes, Sire, I shall deliver your message," said the cold cleric, who doubted the king even heard him as he made his way to his lavish, and no doubt, heated tent. Hopping up and down for warmth until the king had left sight, the cleric hurried back to the surgeon's tent. There was a lot of work to be done before tomorrow, which would surely bring more wounded and dead. And many tomorrows from now would bring victory.

DARRION-QUIEDESS

Glossary

Aboe- (a-bow) Kingdom on the southernmost peninsula of Terrigan. The kingdom has little or no army, but does not fear being conquered due to the great mountain reaches that surround its borders. Kingdom is wealthy and home of merchants and pirate alike. Of all the kingdoms in Terrigan, it is the most racially diverse with humans, dwarves, and elves holding political offices.

Adoria- (A-door-ee-ah) Kingdom just west of Beykla. It waged a bloody civil war against its western half, Andoria.

Alexis Alexandria Overmoon- (a-lex-us / al-ecks-zan-dree-uh / Over moon) Daughter heir of King Christopher Calamon Overmoon. High Lord of the Minok Vale. She travels with Apollisian Bargoe, a paladin of justice, trying to learn the ways of justice to aid her when she becomes queen.

Amerix Alistair Stormhammer- (am-er-icks / ali-stair / storm ham-er) Dwarven general of Clan Stoneheart, formerly of Clan Stormhammer. His clan was wiped out before him, when he was a young man, by dark dwarves and a white dragon. He fled with a few survivors and was welcomed into Clan Stoneheart where he excelled in the art of war.

Androdius- (an-drode-ee-us) Evil black dragon of immense power that lives in the swamp west of Aquabar.

Apollisian Bargoe- (A-paul-issi-in / bar-go) Paladin of justice that was sent from his order in Westvon keep to oversee the negotiations between the humans and the dwarves from Clan Stoneheart, in attempt to derail a conflict, when he was caught in the middle of the war.

Andoria- (an-door-ee-ah) Formally western Adoria, this kingdom's brief history came when it declared its independence from Adoria. It waged an eight month long war with Adoria, but was eventually re-conquered.

Aquabar- (awk-wuh-bar) Capitol of Aten, which lies

near the great swamp and the Mountains of Meara.

Arluda- (are-loo-duh) Blue mistress and friend of Delania.

Artamanake- (art-man-uh-key) Dark dwarven general.

Aten- (A-ten) Queendom to the far west that is ran solely by women. Males of any race are considered inferior and are immediately made into slaves, or killed at birth. Only a choice few males are kept alive for reproduction purposes only. The women of Aten are adept sorceresses and keep a rigid society of backstabbing and political maneuvering.

Ayden- (A-den) Powerful salomin that used Therrig to gain control of a large clan of Dark Dwarves.

Barbetin- (bar-bet-in) Also known as the lake of the damned. It is the lake in the Abyss that damned souls are thrown into to be tortured for eternity by the demons that swim among it.

Beovi- (bee-o-vi) Subterranean fish that live in the deepest freshwater caverns of the underworld. They are a delicacy to dwarves, dark dwarves, dark elves and other subterranean races. These fish can grow to unlimited size, depending on the lake or river in which they live.

Beykla- (bay-kla) Human kingdom on the northeastern corner of Terrigan. The kingdom is well-to-do, militantly powerful, and well patrolled. It has never, in its long history, been conquered.

Blue Dragon Inn- Inn in Central City that is closest to the Dawson River and the Dawson River bridge, where Lance, Kaisha, Ryshander, and Apollisian battled the dwarven horde, until the king arrived with re-enforcements.

Borkin- (bore-kin) Small wooden device that is inserted into the mouth that keeps the wearer from closing their jaws.

Bureland- (bur-land) small hamlet, in the southern part of Beykla, where Lance spent most of his childhood and early adult life with his adoptive father, Davohn.

Brohe-tah- (Bro-tah) Orc word equivalent to comrade.

The orcs use in reference to another that he or she likes as a friend. Though the orcish language does not have a single word for friend, it has over a dozen for enemy.

Breedikai- (bree-da-kii) Original gods, or gods that were created. They have no soul and most dwell in Merioulus.

Bykalicus- (Bye-kal-eh-kus) Powerful archdemon that controls much of the Abyss.

Cadacka- (ka-doc-uh) Black ceremonial robe worn by elves when they have lost a loved one and are mourning. Most elves never remove the cloak once it is donned.

Calours- (ka-loo-ers) Non sedimentary rocks found in the underworld. Subterranean races, mostly species of dwarves, use them to cook meat on.

Calito, battle of- (kuh-lee-toe) Battle that took place in Adoria near the town of Dalzan Adorian knights fought against an evil necromancer named Randolph Forlinger who commanded over a thousand undead soldiers.

Carcarass- (kar-kar-us) Training school that raises and trains Aten-born pureblood males to be slaves as they age.

Central City- City just south of the Dawson Stronghold that is in the center of the Beyklan nation.

Christopher Calamon Overmoon- (Kris-toe-fur / Kal-a-mon / O-ver-moon) High King of the Minok Vale.

Clan Cutstone- Clan that makes its home under the Lalin Plateau in Southern Beykla.

Colonel Mortan Ganover- First lieutenant of Duke Dolin Blackhawk, and acting mayor when the Duke is gone. He is considered responsible for the slaughter at Central City by the dwarves due to his inability to act on the paladin Apollisian's recommendations.

Commander Fehzban Algor Stoneheart- (fez-ben / al-gore) Commander and loyal follower of general Amerix Stormhammer. He was tried and convicted of treason after the Torrent Manor and the Central City campaigns.

Copel Nin- (cope-ul) Fat keeper of the gladiator slaves in the arena in Central City. Copel was once a gladiator champion but in the fight he earned his freedom he was severely injured, ending his career as a fighter. He was hired by the Duke to be the keeper of the slaves. Copel always worked hard at the job but as he aged, his injury and time took its toll on him, preventing his ability to stay in shape. He soon became fat, but he enjoyed his job at the arena as he longed for the days to hear the roar of the crowd once more.

Council of Wise- Consists of ten elders that sit on the governing seat at Monk Vale, though not all ten are usually present at meeting, There has to be at least six to hold a vote.

Cranetium- (krane-tee-um) Official title given to an elven high mage. The title means little to other elves, save for the wizards and sorcerers of their Vales.

Dadramedion- (day-drom-uh-dee-in) Powerful archdemon and enemy to Bykalicus.

Dall-kal-Mour- (doll-kal-moo-ur) Title given to bloodborn men from Aten. They are the only males that are allowed to reproduce. They are expensive slaves and only the highest ranking or wealthy own them. It is a status symbol for Mothers or heads of septs to own more than one, since they will never give birth.

Dalzon- (dal-zohn) Small city in the northwestern side of Adoria.

Darayal Legion- (dar-ray-all) One hundred of the finest elite elven rangers that patrol the Minok Vale in pairs. They are skilled swordsmen who wield a weapon in each hand during battle. They are as feared as they are awed.

Darious Theobold- (dare-ee-us / They-bold) Eleven year old son of King Theobold.

Dark Dwarves- Dwarves that live solely in the underworld. They have pupil less eyes that have adapted over time to see in the dark by detecting heat patterns. They hate bright light as it is painful for them, and have turned to wicked and evil ways as a society.

Dargruden - (dar-grude-in) Dall-Kal-Mour that runs the gearian.

Darren Brightson, Duke- (Dare-in / bright-sun) Duke of the Adorian lands just to the east of the northeastern border of Aten. Governs over the small hamlet of Lostom.

Darrion-Quieness- (dare-ee-on / kwee-eh-ness) Great white dragon. Oldest of all white dragons and most powerful. His lair is in the mountains of Nalir, but he roams all over the realms. He often leads lesser races against their enemies, and takes the majority of the treasure after the victory. His last major campaign was in aide of the dark dwarves against the dwarven Clan Stormhammer.

Davohn Ecnal- (da-von) Adoptive father of Lance. He is a woodcutter that made his home in Bureland and found Lance when Lance was only six years old. He raised him as his son until Lance left when he was seventeen.

Dawson River- Largest river that runs in Terrigan. It stretches from the Sea of Balfour, north of Beykla, all the way through the southern kingdom of Aboe.

Dawson Stronghold- Capital of Beykla, this port city is the largest hub in the Bay of Balfour.

Delania- (duh-lane-ee-uh) Beautiful succubus that dwells in the Abyss.

Dicermadon- (die-sir-ma-don) God of Gods, Dicermadon plots with demons to kill the son of a goddess, drawing the wrath of the gods that he governs.

Diltz Quest- (Dilts) Ceremony in which Dall-Kal-Mours, Aten full-blooded males, compete in a gladiator competition to be selected as a mate for the queen.

Dolgo seeds- (dole-go) A tasty mountain nut found on the steepest slopes of the highest mountain. Considered a delicacy by all dwarves and mountain people.

Dome of the Rock- Ancient dwarven temple that was supposedly built by Durion, the dwarven mountain god. The temple is rumored to be atop the Lalin Plateau.

Donk- Aten word for the male reproductive organ. It is an insulting word in their culture and is associated with mental weakness and stupidity.

Doogan Raymer- (doo-gun / ray-muhr) Northern noble from Dawson. Doogan is a conniving tactician who has made his estates through double dealing and backstabbing. He shows his family tree as being distantly related to the king, and hopes to one day return his house the throne.

Dorcastig- (door-cast-ig) Tall muscled priest of Rha-Cordan. Follows under Resin Darkhand. One of the priests that participated in the DeNaucght.

Durion- (doog-a thee-in) Dwarven Mountain God.

Dregan City- (dree-gan) Home of the Clan Stormhammer before it was wiped out by the dark dwarves and a white dragon.

Drunda- (drun-duh) The god the orcs follow. It is not known if he actually exists, or even if he is male.

Dweamor- (Dwee-mer) Another name for a spell.

Earth Oath- Oath an elf makes that they will give their lives trying to uphold.

Ecnal- (eck-null) Surname given to all orphans of Beykla before they were killed by unknown assassins.

Elder Bartoke- (bar-toke) Elder of the Minok Vale, member of the council of the wise, and Keeper of the sealed passings.

Elder Darmond- (dar-mond) Elder of the Minok Vale, member of the council of the wise, and Keeper of the sealed passings.

Elder Humas- (hue-mass) Elder of the Minok Vale, member of the council of the wise, and Keeper of the sealed passings.

Elder Varmintan- (Var-mint-ton) Elder of the Minok Vale, member of the council of wise, and Keeper of the sealed passings.

Erik Stromson- (stahm-son) General of the Beyklan Western army and hero of the orc wars.

Eucladower Strongbow- Oldest Elder of the Minok council of wise and Keeper of the passings.

Famen's Tree- (fay-mens) Large tree three miles east of the Dawson River bridge. The tree was named after Jeddis Famen, a Central City militia leader that held off an orc attack. After the battle he led a group of militiamen after the fleeing orcs, and managed to slay one of the orc leaders as they fled. He nailed the orc's head on a spike to the tree as a message to any other orcs. That was the last orc battle against Central City during the orc wars. The people believed the orcs were afraid of him, but in truth they were massing to finish the elves at the Minok Vale.

Flunt- God of Fire, and one of the four elemental gods.

Freedom Festival- Holiday celebrated in Beykla to commemorate the end of the twenty-year-long orc wars.

Garlibane- (gar-lee-bane) High Mage and Elder of the council of wise in Minok.

Gearian- (Gear-ee-in) Collection of incorrigible sudas that exist for the sole purpose of raping and killing women in Aten who have been convicted of the most serious crimes. The women are stripped of their power and thrown into the pit for spectators to watch as they are raped repeatedly over many days until they are killed or die.

General Laricin West- (lair-iss-in) Late general for the northern Beyklan army that was responsible for scattering the orc horde, in the battle that was later referred to as The Quigen. General Laricin and his men fought to the last man, keeping the orc horde from wiping out what was left of the elven resistance.

Gorsan- (gore-sahn) Dwarven brew master and distant relative to Fehzban. Gorsan lives in Dalzan and sells dwarven ales to the locals.

Gregory Herwain- (her-wane) Southern noble who is chairmen of affairs in southern Beykla. He is leader of House

Herwain that is well-known for saying much and doing little. He hosts the monthly meetings of the southern nobles in the city of Motivas at the house of affairs.

Gweits- (ga-weets) Tiny insect-like demons that dwell on the rocky floor of the Abyss. They feed on flesh, and burrow under skin with their horrific claws and hooks.

Heart of the Rock- A gemstone mounted on a gold ring that is said to have magical properties that can prevent the wearer from being harmed by dragon's breath.

Hector De Scoran- (heck-tor / day-skore-an) Evil warrior wizard that is king of Nalir. He believes that Lance was prophesized to destroy his kingdom, and will stop at nothing until the boy is dead.

Henrious- (Hen-ree-us) Ex-Diltz Quest gladiator and Dall-Kal-Mour that helps Tonya of the white and the freedom movement.

Hiramem- (her-uh-mem) Old female sorceress that lives in Aten. She often works for Ramasiel in the red tower and has a limited ability at foretelling. She often uses old chicken bones, stones and other small objects that she tosses about on a board with elven skin stretched over it. She is from Beykla originally. She grew up in Sineuvia.

Hourid Thigguard- (hor-id / thig-guard) Master of arms and father of Mylaneia.

Ian Silverman- (E-uhn) Human knight under Duke Darren Brightstar. Fought in the Battle of Calito. Has two sons, Ian Silverman II and Myer Silverman. Both are adventurers and Ian does not agree with their lifestyles.

Ickten Norris- (ick-ton) Ranger that works for the Hentridge farm south of Central City. He is an expert tracker and skilled swordsman. His favored enemies are orcs.

Illilander tree- (ill-lee-land-er) Largest trees in the realms. Over five hundred feet tall.

Jordan Gersian- (jor-dun / Ger-see-in) Southern Nobleman that is leading the plot to pull southern Beykla away from the north.

Jude- (Jewd) Mercenary swordsman from Bureland. He sold his sword to fight brigands, polecats and other minor enemies of Bureland. He is also Lance's best friend.

Kai-Harkia- (Kay-hark-ee-uh) Mountain kingdom northwest of Beykla. Its people are dark-skinned, dark-haired, heavy-chested, nomad swordsmen. They seldom form static villages, though some do exist.

Kalen Al-Kalidius- (kay-lin / al-kal-id-ee-us) Grey elf ex-stepson of King Overmoon of the Minok Vale. Kalen has turned to the shadow and hungers for power, hoping to take over the throne of Nalir when Hector dies.

Kalistirsts- (kal-eh-stirsts) Underground mole people with no eyes that live in the underworld.

Kalliman Theobold- (kall-eh-man) King of Beykla.

Kalliman Castle- (kall-eh-man) Castle and home of King Kalliman Theobold.

Kareeg Hut- (kuh-reeg) Nobleman that owned more land than any other noble in all of Beykla. His lands were in the north that extended from just south of the Torrent Manor all that way west to the border of Beykla and all the way east to the Dawson River right up Dawson itself. His brother was a Captain that was stationed at the Torrent Manor when it fell. He hates the dwarves more than any other Beyklan.

Kellacun- (kell-eh-kun) Wererat assassin that worked for the guild in Central City before it was destroyed. Now she works for Kalen in attempt to kill Lance.

Kingsford City- Largest city in Terrigan. Capitol of Ladathon.

Kornicus- (corn-uh-cus) Demon imp servant of Delania.

Ladathon- (lad-uh-thon) Southern country, south of Tyrine, where mysterious animals live in thick jungle. Kingsford City, the largest city in the world, is its capitol.

Lancalion Levendis Lampara- (lance-uh-lion / lev-undis / lamb-par-uh) Birth name given to Lance Ecnal.

Lalin Platue- (lay-lin) large plateau that is the middle of Southern Beykla. It is covered by a thick lush forest and is nearly impossible to scale its thousand-foot-high sheer rock walls. Stories tell of ancient ruins at the top, but few have climbed to its summit to validate the claims. What makes the plateau so unique is that the Dawson River runs through the inside of it in a great river cave.

Lance Ecnal- Adopted son of Davohn Ecnal. Lance's birth name is Lancalion Levendis Lampara. His natural mother was Panoleen, the Goddess of Mercy. Lance is prophesized to bring plague and death on the world, though he sees himself as nothing more than an orphan trying to discover his past.

Leska- (les-kuh) The Earth Mother goddess. She reins over all living things while they are alive, including plants and animals. She is one of the four elemental gods.

Lostom- (lose-tom) Small Hamlet on the border of Aten and Adoria.

Lostos- (low-stoes) Name for the underground complex of the severed heart guild of wererats in Central City.

Lukerey- (lou-kear-ee) God of Luck and mischief.

Lunarian- (lou-nar-ee-in) Enchanted wells that priestly elves or other good forest creatures bless by the powers of Leska to rejuvenate and to heal one another.

Lyndall- (lin-doll) Gladiator champion in Central City. A skilled swordsman that had fought over two hundred forty fights. He is only four fights away from earning his freedom.

Malwinar- (Mal-win-are) Elf wizard assistant to Garlibane.

Markus- (Mark-us) Suda in Ramasiel's tower who is secret lover with Reena.

Marlana- (Mar-lane-uh) Backstabbing mistress of the blue sept that conspired with Ramasiel to overthrow the mother of the blue sept in order for her to control a second vote in the senate.

Marzahna- (marr-zohn-uh) Mother of the yellow sept that was banished for wanting to marry. She built a smaller tower on the border of Aten in the hamlet of Lostom.

Mary of the Yellow Robe- Mistress of the banished yellow mother, Marzahna.

Master David Hentridge- (hint-ridge) Leader of small mercenary guild that is disguised as a farm, just south of Central City. King Theobold uses them to hunt and kill orcs that he does not want the public to know exists, keeping their awareness of the actual amount of the green-skinned beasts that still live in his kingdom.

Meirgan- (Mare-gun) Ruthless bounty hunter from Beykla.

Merioulus- (mare-ee-oh-you-lus) City of the gods. Set on a form of the Astral plane.

Mersaat- (mare-sat) Great Blue Dragon that lives in the Desert of Tyrine. A scroll was stolen from his lair by a hapless thief. The scroll was sold several times until it ended up at the great library in Kingsford City where Ladathon scholars identified the text as draconian. What made the scroll unique was that it was written in humanoid size. Few humans know draconic. It gave credibility that there is a secret sept of priests that worship the great serpents, but it led others to believe that once the beasts fully mature, they gain the ability to transform into a man-like creature. All of these theories are yet to be proven.

Mershul- (mur-shul) God of Serpents, some believe the god does not exist and is only worshipped by a cult following known as the sept of serpents. Mershul is also the term referred to for men who go into berserker rage in battle. The rage is so intense the men do not feel pain, can continue to battle long after their body has died, and have a hard time differing friend from foe on the battlefield. Mershuls are as feared as they are respected as warriors, though they never fight with comrades as a Mershul often claims the lives of those around him while he is in his rage, unable to determine friend from foe.

Midagord Milence Stormhammer- (mid-uh-gord / my-lence) Amerix Stormhammer's deceased father.

Minok Vale- (my-nock) Name of the elven sovereignty that is set in Beykla.

Motivas- (moe-ta-vis) Southernmost city in Beykla. City is built on a large brick foundation that is rumored to be ruins of an ancient civilization.

Mountain Heart- Home city of Clan Stoneheart, located in the Pyberian Mountains.

Mount Steeple- The largest mountain on Terrigan. The mountain is rumored to hold the roadway to Merioulus as its peak cannot be seen as it ascends into a permanent veil of clouds.

Mowaka- (moe-walk-uh) camouflage cloak-like blanket that elven archers, and sometimes rangers, use to spy on their enemies.

Myer Silverman- (my-er) Son of Ian Silverman of Lostom.

Mylaneia Thigguard- (my-lane-ya / thig-guard) Young daughter of Hourid Thigguard, and courtier of Tharxton Stoneheart.

Nalir- (nall-er) Evil southern empire made primarily of swamps and quagmires. A militantly powerful nation that worships most of the evil gods.

Necromidus- (neck-rom-eh-dus) A collection of the first four tiers of necromancy spells.

Oswald Thorrin- (oz-wald / Thor-in) Captain of the royal Beyklan guard and bounty hunter, though he only collects on lawful bounties set by the magistrates.

Panoleen- (pan-oh-leen) Goddess of Mercy that was banished from the heavens.

Pav-co- (pahv-coe) Fat wererat guild leader in Central City.

Pyberian Mountains- (pie-beer-ee-an) Mountain range in the northwest corner of Beykla, near Adoria.

Quadry Proudarrow- (Quad-ree) Darayal Legionnaire of the Minok Vale.

Quigen- (kwi-jin) Elven word for sacrifice. Most widely known as the name of the great battlefield where General Laricin West scattered the orcish horde by fighting until every man in his army fell in the Serrin plains.

Ramasiel- (ram-uh-zeal) One of the three mothers of the red order in Aten. She is a powerful sorceress and a political power in Aquabar.

Randolph Forlinger- (ran-doff / four-ling-er) Powerful necromancer that was defeated and slain at the Battle of Calito.

Reagle, The- A fancy clothing store in Aquabar that makes dresses and other articles of women's clothing. It does not make any article of clothing that could be used in an intimate way to make the women more attractive. Atenians believe that men have no right to be attracted to women, that the act should be gratifying to the woman only.

Reena- (ree-nuh) Third sorceress, also called third sister, of the red sept in Aten. Second only to Ramasiel herself.

Rha-Cordan- (rah-kor-don) God of Death and Dying. Not inherently evil, he reins over the placement of souls when they enter the afterlife, though he has been known to be incredibly vengeful to those who prolong their lives through magical means.

Salomin- (sal-low-men) Subterranean humanoid species with powerful mind-controlling abilities. Also known as mind eaters.

Serrin Plains- (sare-in) Dangerous expansive grassland just south of Minok Vale where most of the evil races that live in Beykla dwell.

Sha-Shor'Nai- (sha-shore-nigh) God of the Sun and Light.

Silas Proudarrow- (sigh-less) Darayal Legionnaire of

the Minok Vale.

Stephanis- (stuh-fawn-is) God of Justice.

Stieny Gittledorf- (stie-knee / get-tull-dorf) Halfling thief who became mixed up with the dragon Darrion-Quieness.

Stormghast- The great stone doors that seals Mountain Heart from the dark uncharted reaches of the under mountain.

Suda- (sue-duh) Title given to all non-eunuch slaves in Aten. A suda is looked at as a lower form of a man by the tuda, or eunuch.

Surelda Al-Kalidius- (sir-el-da / al-kuh-lid-ee-us) Ex-wife of King Overmoon and mother of Kalen, Ultsa, and Ulma Al-Kalidius.

Surshy- (sir-she) Goddess of Water. One of the four elemental gods.

Takash- (Tah-kosh) Place in an Aten tower where the sudas are brainwashed.

Tallnok- (tal-knock) Young wizard that works for the Hentridge Farm south of Central City. Occasionally hires himself out for specific jobs.

Talwin- (tall-win) Young apprentice war wizard that joined the Western Beyklan army instead of staying with the mage guild in Dawson.

Targavian Hollen Stoneheart - (tar-gave-ee-in / hall-in) New general promoted by Tharxton after the betrayal of Amerix and his officers.

Terrigan- (ter-eh-gun) Name of the continent that all known civilizations exists.

Tharxton Stoneheart- (tharx-ton) Young king of Clan Stoneheart and political rival with Amerix Alistair Stormhammer.

Therrig Alistair Delastan- (ther-ig / al-eh-stair / del-eh-stan) One of the few surviving members of Clan Stormhammer.

Thomas Smith (Arwar)- (are-wahr) Blacksmith that worked at the Torrent Manor before Amerix attacked. He was head of the ambassador's liaison between the two peoples and he learned dwarven from his many dwarven friends at Mountain Heart before he retired and moved back to Poria.

Tonya- Former mother of the white tower, who staged her death so that she could anonymously lead the freedom movement of Aten.

Torrent Manor- small keep northwest of Central City that was built specifically for enforcing the trade embargo on the dwarves that dwelled in the Pyberian Mountains, and the Adorians in the civil war.

Trinidy- (trin-eh-dee) Dead paladin of Dicermadon that was raised from the dead by evil priests of Rha-Cordan, creating the first death knight.

Tuda- (too-duh) Title given to all eunuch slaves in Aten.

Tyrine- (tie-reen) Kingdom south west of Beykla.

Valley of Mist - Lush green valley just below the entrance to Mountain Heart in the Pyberian Mountains.

Vendaigehn- (vin-day-gun) Type of horse from the plains of Vendaiga. The steeds are marked with white spots on their flanks, and are taller than most horses with longer, thinner legs. Legend says that Vendaigehn steeds are the offspring of a Pegasus and a unicorn, though that has never been proven.

Victor DeVulge- (day-vul-juh) Slain squire of Apollisian Bargoe.

Vlargcar- (va-larg-car) Orc whelp saved by Amerix when he and his mother was ordered killed by their tribe.

Vrescan Alistair Delastan- Therrig's father who was killed fighting side by side with Midagord Stormhammer in defense of Dregan City.

Walter Thigpen - Middle-aged royal guard crossbowman and longtime friend of Captain Oswald Thorrin.

Westvon Keep- (west-van) Large keep and hamlet to the far east in Beykla on the banks of the Dawson River.

Whisten- (wiss-ton) God of Air, and one of the four elemental gods.

Yahna- (ya-nuh) City in the heavens where mortal souls, blessed by their gods, dwell.

Yohr-Acht- (your-awk-tuh) Great green dragon that makes his lair atop the Lalin Plateau.

About the Author

Shane Moore grew up on a farm in rural Illinois. An only child that was six miles from his nearest peer, Shane often created wild tales of heroes and villains during his many trips into the deep woods that surrounded his rural home.

Shane was accelerated in his class and started his senior year of high school at age sixteen. After graduating and getting a waiver for his age, Shane joined the United States Navy to pay for college. He participated in campaigns; "Provide Hope" and "Secure Democracy" during the Yugoslavian civil war. Shane received several naval awards and citations and was one of the highest trained members of his ship.

After getting out of the service, Shane began college. He was soon hired by the Carlinville Police Department, beginning his multiple venue police career. Shane retired as a detective for the Gillespie Police Department after serving twelve years. His police career was quite notable with awards for bravery and with one life saving medal. He was named Officer of the Year in 2005.

A lesser known truth about Shane is that he played eight years of semi pro football with the Central Illinois Cougars. Shane is the team's all-time tackle leader and holds the record for most special teams tackles in a season and the most tackles in a game. Shane received many awards including Defensive Player of the Year in 2005.

January 14th, 2008. Shane retires from his police career to be a professional novelist.

Mr. Moore resides in Central Illinois with his son, Dakota.

SHADE MOORE

www.ingramcontent.com/pod-product-compliance
Lightning Source LLC
Chambersburg PA
CBHW060406260626
47160CB00006B/2454